# Forsaken – Book 1 i Shadows Series

**This novel is entirely a work of fiction**

The names, characters and incidents portrayed in it are the work of the author's imagination and any resemblance to actual persons, living or dead, events or localities is entirely coincidental.

Written by: Christopher Savage

Edited by: Jon C Dixon

Front cover designed by: David Pye

**17/05/2020**

## Dedication

To my wife and family who patiently weathered the storm of my passion to write, and to those who have given me the inspiration.

# Forsaken

Prelude

Moscow, Russia. 15th June 1993.

Anastasia Kaplinski watched proudly as her daughter stood in-line with her peers performing the first through fifth basic positions that are fundamental to modern ballet. The moment took Anastasia back to her own childhood, when she performed those same standard foot placements in front of her mother and now history was repeating itself. It was Ava's fifth birthday, and Anastasia was amazed at how alike her she had grown. Other than that Ava had red hair and Anastasia blonde, they would have been identical at that age. Anastasia had gone on to achieve prima ballerina and wondered whether little Ava might do the same one day.

Life and times had been hard in Russia for Anastasia, and it was dance that had made the difference. Anastasia dearly wanted Ava to enjoy that same privilege, so the ballet lessons would be part of her daughter's life now. Ava looked beautiful in her little white tutu with her flame of red hair tied up in a high ponytail. She beamed proudly at her mother, sat amongst the others who had come to support their children. The performance ended and the teacher dismissed her class, sending the children eagerly off to their proudly waiting parents.

"Did you see me Mummy? Was I as good as the other girls?"

Ava's questions came thick and fast, hardly allowing Anastasia time to reply.

"You were wonderful Ava, and I am so proud of you. Your poise and shapes were just perfect. Now go and get changed quickly darling, I have a birthday surprise for you."

Anastasia felt a pang of guilt as her daughter ran off eagerly with the others. She had planned to spend the rest of the day at the

Moscow zoo with her, but now she would have to cut it short. Ava's absent father had called out of the blue that morning wanting to meet. It had nothing to do with Ava's birthday though, it would simply be for sex and she knew that. Anastasia was addicted to this bad man though, and could neither disappoint nor refuse him. He had a power over her that out-ranked all else and was completely indifferent to Ava, to the point of ignoring her very existence. Anastasia took meagre comfort in that she would have another three hours with her daughter, before having to farm her out to her sister Alisa. The whole thing was made worse though, by the fact that Ava didn't like him. Not in the slightest. There was no father-daughter bond between them, he hadn't allowed it; nor did Ava want it or even know who he was. Ava simply saw him as a man that treated her mother badly and who took her away from her.

---

Those three hours at the zoo went by too quickly. Anastasia revelled in her daughter's wonderment as little Ava saw the creatures for the first time that she had only previously read about in her books. Anastasia enjoyed her daughter's infectious excitement as she peeked at the scary lions and tigers from the safety of her skirts and again as she marvelled at the giants, that were the elephants and rhinos of the zoo. There were so many new experiences for her to behold. Afterwards, they sat in the park eating cakes and drinking Coca Colas. It was something that was a rare treat for Ava.

Ballerinas don't do that apparently, Ava had been told.

They checked into the Metropol where the fun and games continued until Ava fell asleep at last, safe and secure in her mother's loving arms. She could never have known that it was to be the last time in her short life.

To this day, Ava had almost no clear memories of what happened after that. She did remember playing up when that horrible man had arrived at the hotel with her mother, spoiling her birthday, and that he had sent her to bed. Then she recalled waking up to the frantic screams of her mother, and that there was a dark haired man in her bedroom with his hands around her throat. Ava's next clear memory was being in another room with small windows and several desks covered with papers. There were three men and a woman in the room, asking her lots of questions but not listening to her answers. They said that her mother had killed herself, but Ava knew that it wasn't true. None of them believed her though and said that she was making it up. Ava felt that she had betrayed her mother by not stopping the man from hurting her, and again for not being able to make anybody believe her.

That was the end of Ava's perfect little world and the beginning of her nightmare.

--------------------------------------------------------------------------------

Chapter 1

September 2014. Moscow, Russia. Twenty-one years later.

The long Moscow summer of 2014 had been particularly hot and humid. The capacity crowd, some three thousand in all, had left the air conditioned Bolshoi Theatre and visibly wilted as the oppressive night air enfolded them. They had come to witness Tchaikovsky's Swan Lake, performed by a most gifted prima ballerina, recreating the double-roles of Odette and Odile, not performed on stage since Pierina Legnani, the legendary Italian ballerina. Legnani had raised the bar and introduced the thirty-two *fouettés en tournant,* which were fast whipping consecutive turns on one foot, a legacy that became a curse to all aspiring ballerinas that followed her.

Ava Kaplinski was currently the incumbent prima ballerina at the Bolshoi, renowned for her flawless performances of this highly emotional and technically difficult dance. Tonight's ballet had been danced with such grace and discipline that the crowd could still be heard murmuring their accolades long after the theatre had cleared. As was customary, the elite of the audience consisting of royalty, oligarchs and socialites, were invited for drinks at the bar and entitled to the company of the ballerinas. In recent years, top ballerinas had quit the Bolshoi making accusations of being pressurised to offer sexual favours to those select clients. This of course was vehemently refuted by the management, but accepted as common practice amongst the ballerinas and the privileged.

The enforced socialising was the part of being a famous ballerina that Ava detested, but it was a condition of her employment. Her elevation to prima ballerina had only served to heighten her desirability and compound the problem. Ava shuddered as she entered the plush theatre bar. Immediately all eyes turned to her and there was a ripple of applause. She composed herself and smiled politely, before making her way towards the bar, trying not to catch anybody's eye. Ava was taller than usual for a ballerina, in her late twenties, slim and elegant with the sublime deportment that was typical of her art. Her full length, figure-hugging black dress was cut radically from her shoulders to her waist and from her thigh to the floor. Ava smiled politely, tipping her head slightly towards the guests in appreciation of their acknowledgement. It was a graceful act that accentuated the length of her neck and femininity. Ava had piled her long auburn hair high on her head, further enhancing her height and slenderness.

Ava desperately hoped she could make it alone to the barstool, but a clammy hand gripped her upper arm. She turned to face the over-weight and balding man, forcing his attention upon her. Ava recognised the man immediately as the one she had hoped to avoid; Sergei Bortnik, a royal pain in the arse.

"You appear to be ignoring me tonight my lovely."

Bortnik's grip tightened as he spoke, his vodka breath making Ava gag. He steered her rudely towards the bar without concern for what others might think. Such is the power of wealth.

"My name is Ava as you well know and I am not *your lovely!* Go away; I can buy my own drink thank you."

He had been to the last four performances and wasn't taking no for an answer this time. Worse, each time Bortnik had arrived, he was considerably more intoxicated and abusive.

"Ava there you are!" Katarina, one of the other ballerinas, had seen her plight. "I have some friends who are just dying to meet you."

She was a pretty brunette of delicate build, almost childlike, with the face of a cherub. Her lively brown eyes danced mischievously as if she was hatching a plot.

Ava was by far the most popular of the dancers, whether that was the men or women of the troupe. Even her ascension to prima ballerina, had not brought about the usual female jealousy. Katarina took Ava's free hand to lead her away, but the pudgy man shoved her rudely against the bar, knocking the wind out of her. Yuri, the barman, raised a protest but the look that he got back from Bortnik cut him down immediately and he reluctantly backed off.

"Send a couple of bottles of Bollinger up to my room with three glasses. I have guests!"

The Bolshoi Theatre had rooms for those favoured by the management, and Bortnik was one of them. The Russian oligarch leered menacingly at Ava.

"Now listen and pay attention young lady. I can make your position here very difficult." Bortnik paused thoughtfully. "No, I will re-phrase that. I can make your *life* very difficult and that of your trollop friend here, clumping along on her two left feet."

Bortnik took a pinch of Katarina's cheek between his fat thumb and forefinger, squeezing it and forcing it to bruise. Katarina screamed out.

"On the other hand I can be most generous," he added releasing Katarina's cheek.

He used that free hand to cup his genitals and grinned lewdly at the two women.

"There's plenty in here for the both of you," he boasted.

The despicable man's lascivious smile was short-lived. To Bortnik's absolute astonishment and horror, his grip inexplicably tightened, crushing his genitals. The arrogant smirk immediately turned into a grimace. He screamed out in pain and began to vomit, but his eyes never left Ava's. It felt to Bortnik as if she was commanding him, forcing him to damage himself. Finally the fat man lost consciousness and collapsed in an untidy heap on the lounge floor. Even in Bortnik's unconscious state, none of the men there could free his vice-like grip, nor understand why he hurting himself.

At last Ava looked away and the fat man's hand relaxed. The ability to take control of someone's mind was something that she could thank her mother for. Apparently telepathy, mind control and telekinesis were just some of the skills that had run through their ancestry, as did a muscular strength that far surpassed normal expectations.

The problem was that Ava had little and mostly no control over her given talents. It was a dark power that only showed itself in moments of rage such as this, but never in times of joy. Consequently, Ava was deeply afraid of her abilities and wondered if she was evil or perhaps possessed. At night, she was troubled by restless spirits who manifested themselves to her, demanding something, but Ava never knew what it was. She used to deny them and chase them away, but they would return with a vengeance. She somehow knew that they came to her because of her sadness and lack of fulfilment, feeding on her emptiness. Ava knew that they would do so forever, unless she found completeness. Ava needed help, but dared not ask for fear of being declared mad, and then locked up with her demons. Her thoughts turned back to Katarina.

"Come with me Kat. I'll fix that with a little concealer."

Tears still flowed down Katarina's face and her cheek looked like a bee had stung it.

As they left for the powder room, Ava felt sickened that a man could harm such a fragile and beautiful woman. Ava draped her arm protectively around Katarina's shoulder and murmured her thanks for her bravery. When Katarina looked in the mirror she spat out her disdain.

"That fat bastard. Look what he's done!" She turned to face Ava with a look of anger and consternation on her face. "Why on Earth did he do *that* to himself?"

"Just a little drunk I guess Kat and perhaps a little crazy on cocaine. Whatever, I don't think he'll be using that *thing* of his again for a long time!"

The women erupted into tears of laughter, releasing the tension that had built up inside them. Katarina decided that it would be prudent to not display her injury in the bar, and left Ava with cuddles and declarations of her life-long love and friendship. Ava returned to the bar for a much needed Dirty Martini. This time, she managed to get to her seat unnoticed, as the guests and artists were still distracted by the bizarre event that had taken place. Yuri placed the Martini in front of Ava and made an attempt to excuse himself for not having come to Katarina's rescue. She took his hand reassuringly.

"Relax dear Yuri. There was nothing you could have done that wouldn't have cost you your job. Katarina wouldn't have expected you to take that risk on her behalf," she smiled affectionately.

Ava stirred her Dirty Martini thoughtfully, then reached across and pecked Yuri on the cheek. He coloured up immediately. Yuri was besotted with Ava, but then who wasn't?

Ava finished her third drink, raised her glass and tipped it towards Yuri for another. He went to work on it eagerly, like a faithful puppy. Yuri was Mr. Average in Ava's eyes. Average height, average build and average looks. He was too nondescript for her to notice the goodness in his heart and the humour in his conversation. She picked up his thoughts though, as she always could when she chose to, and was shocked to find that they were all about her. His thoughts dallied to become more of a carnal nature. Not in a million years! Ava thought, somewhat shocked, but somehow she had unintentionally transmitted that thought. Yuri turned to face her with a look of devastation and guilt on his face.

"Shit!" Ava muttered under her breath, turning away. "I didn't mean to do that."

Ava felt sullied by the evening's events and her heartlessness. She absentmindedly caught sight of her own image in the mirror at the back of the bar. The reflection showed a beautiful young woman, slim with a pretty face, good bone structure and small features. She had bright blue eyes with unusual brown flecks that twinkled like stars beneath long groomed eyelashes. Her auburn hair shone almost red in the bar lighting, and her lips were full, red and promising. To any other, the reflection was of a rare beauty indeed, but all that Ava could see was the ugliness in her soul. It was that part of her that she couldn't control, that dark beast that constantly lurked there in the shadows. She looked hatefully at her own image for several seconds. The brown flecks in her blue eyes gathered and darkened, as her rage grew until at last the mirror shattered. Ava immediately looked away and the blueness returned to her eyes.

"Are you alright Ava; what happened?"

Yuri had recovered from Ava's rebuke and was now afraid for her and clearly startled by the sound of breaking glass.

"I don't know Yuri; the mirror was probably screwed on too tightly. That often happens," she said dismissively. "I'll have that Dirty Martini now, if you don't mind."

Ava became curiously aware of a man sat at the other end of the bar. He was of indeterminate age. Late forties, early fifties maybe, tanned and dangerously handsome, for sure. His dark, almost black hair was flecked with grey, giving him a deliciously mature look. He was expensively dressed in a designer suit, white shirt and bow tie. Extremely well groomed and suave would describe him; Bond-like in fact, with amazing presence. He was clean shaven which accentuated his strong chin. Ava's eyes were drawn to follow the line of his jaw to where it met his well-formed ear. Inexplicably she imagined running her tongue around the edge. The thought immediately sent a rush of blood to her groin, the impact of which disorientating her. Ava had to divert her thoughts quickly. These were classic symptoms, early warnings if you like, of her about to make a fool of herself. Making a fool of herself was something that Ava had done too many times with too many perfect strangers.

She questioned what it was that made men of a certain age so hot? Her question needed no answer. Ava already knew. To her it was their experience, their power and their wealth. Most of all the delicious danger of the challenge!

Ava continued her examination and tried to be pragmatic, even though her sudden rush of blood was becoming distracting to her. He was athletic in build with good shoulders and she guessed that he would be around six foot two when he stood. Dangerously handsome too, she concluded.

Ava blushed involuntarily over what she was thinking and smiled openly at him. To her annoyance, he didn't look up. There was something intriguing about this dark and dangerous man, Ava thought and her mind continued to wander. The drinks were doing their trick and Ava began to relax after her distressing ordeal with Bortnik. Her intrigue over this stranger was fast becoming a physical thing that she needed to explore further; *much* further. Despite some fairly obvious affectations to get his attention, like letting her long auburn hair down and shaking it, allowing her skirt to fall strategically open to expose her leg right up to her lingerie and dropping her purse to the floor with a rather exaggerated sigh, the dark stranger remained aloof and seemingly unaware of her.

Ava had already embarked on the road to her own physical satisfaction and was in far too deep to give up. She decided to do the one thing that *always* gets a man's attention, the public and provocative application of red lipstick. Ava waited until she had eye contact and then gave him the full performance. This time he didn't look away, he just held her gaze throughout until she finished.

Yes! The word screamed out inside her. Ava instantly felt her whole-body flush once again with anticipation, becoming painfully aware of her nipples that had hardened and were testing the elasticity of her slinky dress. She wondered if the man had noticed, and smiled mischievously as she let her purse fall to the floor again. This time the ridiculously handsome man stood, drained his glass and walked towards her. He swept the purse from the floor and smiled knowingly as he handed it to her. Ava felt triumphant and was about to engage when, without so much of a backward glance, the man walked on towards the door and left the theatre. Ava's chin dropped leaving her open-mouthed in astonishment. Men just didn't do this to her.

"You bastard!" she cursed.

That was all Ava could find to say to avenge her brutal rejection. She called Yuri to recharge her glass. The night was going to be another to regret, she realised fatalistically.

-----------------------------------------------------------------------------

Chapter 2

Ava woke with the mother of all hangovers. After the stranger had left her in disarray, she had taken to drinking herself into oblivion. Ava would have preferred oblivion through physically exhausting herself on the stranger, but that was not to be. The binge drinking was partly to purge her mind from the memory of the damage she had inflicted on the fat, lecherous Russian, but mostly it was to try and get the handsome stranger out of her mind. Ava had failed on both counts and her dreams had haunted her throughout the night. She raised her head to look at the bedside clock; it was after midday. A shard of blinding light glared through a chink in the curtains and fell unkindly on her face. Ava winced as the pain drilled into her brain. She dragged a pillow over her face, giving her instant relief, the acute pain dulling to a sickly ache. Ava reflected on the previous night at the Bolshoi, but her mind was still confused. She struggled to recount the evening. Finally clarity came to her with a shock.

"Oh my God no! How could I have?" Ava groaned.

The embarrassing memories came flooding back. Ava drew her knees up to her chest to the foetal position and pulled them to her at the shame of what she had done the previous night, wondering how she could have behaved so wantonly.

The image of the strong, dark and extremely desirable stranger was still vivid in Ava's mind. She could remember every detail of his face, the line of his chin and the seductive slant of his eyes, even the clothes he wore. Worse still, the fantasy she had of running her tongue around the edge of his ear, brought the same impact now as it did then. Ava immediately felt her excitement mount at the thought of having him. It was only the memory of that arrogant look on his face when he refused her that momentarily curbed her passion. Even that rejection was a powerful aphrodisiac though. Rejection was alien to Ava. Men *always* wanted her for sex and she *always* had the upper hand. Ava was totally outside of her comfort zone now, which made her even more desperate to have the mysterious man.

She dragged the pillow from her face into a defensive cuddle, rolling from side to side in embarrassment, chastising herself.

"Oh Ava you sad bitch!" she cried out.

Despite her efforts, Ava couldn't force the stranger's image from her mind, becoming more and more excited by her own carnal thoughts. Without intention, Ava's hands naturally began to caress her neck and explore her body, lost in her erotic thoughts of having this man. Her fingers began to take her to that place she desperately wanted to be. Finally Ava found release, her back arching with the sheer enormity of her climax. She was left drenched and wasted, breathless in some place between Heaven and Hell.

"Get a grip girl!" she shouted out. "What the fuck do you think you're doing? He's just a jerk for God's sake!"

Ava threw off the covers, swivelled her hips and left the bed as if it was on fire. She threw her pillow petulantly across the room and walked naked into the shower. Ava was furious with herself. The cold water brought her thoughts back under control and at last she could push the man's image out of her mind. All Ava could feel now was the invigorating caress of the cool water as it ran in rivulets down her lean body, cleansing her and purging her soul. At last the throbbing inside her abated.

Twenty minutes later, Ava sat herself in front of her computer with a mug of black coffee. Her capacity for rejuvenation was little short of miraculous. It was another gift that Ava had inherited from her mother. She was already searching the internet for the 'hot topics' of world news. Expanding her mind was part of Ava's strict daily routine and had been since she was five years old. Improving her intellect was an absolute condition laid down by her sponsor.

Ava's gaze fell on the framed picture on the table beside her. The image squeezed her heart. It was of another prima ballerina, blonde and not too dissimilar in looks to Ava. The photograph was signed 'Anastasia Kaplinski', Ava's mother, and dated 1993.

The photograph was taken in the same year that her mother had died, leaving Ava effectively orphaned at just five years old. Nobody knew of, or had ever seen her father. Since the death of her mother, Ava had received the protection of a mysterious sponsor and benefactor, who had remained anonymous over the ensuing years. Even the Bolshoi, who had been commissioned to educate and train Ava in her mother's art, had no idea as to her sponsor's identity.

After twenty-three years, Ava's memories of her mother hadn't faded. She could still remember how she moved, every laughter line on her face, her voice and even how she smelt. Most of all, she remembered how it had felt to be loved, truly loved; unconditionally loved. Unfortunately, she could also remember every minute detail of how she was murdered. Her killing had happened right before her, but no-one had believed her.

*'It was a clear case of suicide'*, the authorities had quickly decided.

Ava pushed her laptop away. Yet again the detail of those devastating memories invaded her mind. She covered her face with her hands and sobbed her heart out. It was something that she had done countless times since her mother was murdered, and always would.

Ava remembered being so outrageously happy that day. It was her fifth birthday and she had spent the morning with her mother at the recently renovated Moscow Zoo. Ava remembered the impressive rock castle entrance that gave way to a wonderland of adventure. There were aviaries with birds of every colour and song, an aquarium with creatures that were simply from another world and an exhibition of *Creatures of the Night* that had enthralled Ava, leaving her excited and a little frightened.

Ava recalled that they had cakes and Coca-Cola for lunch there, a rare treat indeed, and something that her mother seldom permitted.

"Cakes and Coca-Cola are not conducive to being a ballerina." Ava remembered her mother's conspiratorial words.

Since then, Ava had spent a lifetime passionately and hopelessly attracted to food. She rated it as equally desirable to good sex, which was quite a statement from a woman with an appetite like Ava's. Afterwards, they had checked into a suite at the Metropol Hotel, opposite the Bolshoi theatre. It was an impressive Art Nouveau hotel, built at the turn of the nineteenth century. In the past, the Bolshoi had been frequented by famous names such as George Bernard Shaw, John F Kennedy and Michael Jackson. Ava allowed herself a smile as she remembered how she and her mother had jumped up and down on the huge, well-sprung bed, giggling like school children. The fun lasted until Ava had fallen asleep, exhausted in her mother's arms, feeling safe and secure. Ava didn't know it at the time, but that was to be the last time that she would ever feel that way.

Ava's mother had to leave in the middle afternoon to meet someone at the Bolshoi, having previously arranged for her Aunt Alisa to look after her.

"It will only be for an hour or two," her Mother had said at the time.

Ava remembered that she was suddenly and inexplicably filled with dread in that moment. It was the first time that she had experienced a premonition, something that would later become common to her. She recalled begging her mother to stay.

"Don't go Mummy please! Something's wrong. Something dreadful is going to happen to us. Please!"

Ava's pleas went unheeded though. Her mother was insistent and left Ava with Alisa. When her mother finally returned, she was with a man, laughing and touching him fondly. Ava remembered feeling side-lined and jealous, playing up until she was inevitably sent to her room, where she had cried herself to sleep. It was sometime later when Ava woke to the frenzied screams of her mother in the next room. When Ava burst into their room, the man had his hands around her naked mother's throat, choking the life out of her. Ava had jumped on him desperately yelling for him to stop.

"Leave my Mummy alone!"

Ava had screamed, but the man simply released one hand and struck her viciously across her face, knocking out three baby teeth with the power of the blow. Ava was sent spinning, half conscious across the room where she remained and watched as her mother's frantic thrashing slowed until she became still. The man stood up and dragged her mother's naked and limp body to the centre of the room. He crossed to the window, pulled down the curtain sash-cord and threw it over the heavy chandelier. Moments later her mother was hoisted by her neck to the ceiling. The last thing he did was to kick the bedside table into the middle of the room, then left without even a backward glance at Ava with her blooded face, cowering in the corner of the room. When Ava raised the alarm, nobody had believed her story about the man.

'She imagined it', they had all insisted.

Although Ava could remember every detail of what had happened, somehow she couldn't remember the man's face except for his strong jawline. It was bizarre. The harrowing memory seemed to have been completely erased from her mind. Later she was dismissed as suffering from post-traumatic stress disorder.

Now, Ava's enduring emotion was guilt. She had failed to save her mother when she desperately needed her, despite having this dark and dreadful power within her; a power which Ava believed should have manifested itself in her rage. The fact that it didn't, left Ava feeling that she hadn't loved her mother enough to bring out that passion. Ava had never again known peace or love since that terrifying night.

The only close family Ava had was her Aunt Alisa; also a dancer and single mother, struggling to make ends meet. When the letter arrived from an anonymous benefactor, undertaking to enrol Ava and educate her at the Bolshoi, she remembered that her aunt had broken down in tears of relief at the news. Two weeks later, Ava was enrolled at the Bolshoi on her sponsored scholarship. It was the very same day that the first mysterious package arrived for her. Ava remembered taking it to her room, wondering who could have sent it. When she opened the parcel, there was a bundle of books and a brief letter written in masculine script. The content was perfunctory:

*'Ava,*

*In return for your education and upkeep, you will study and learn all that I ask of you without question and it will be to the very highest of standards. You will write to me monthly, in your own hand, with a full report on your progress. Based solely on your report, I will assess your achievements and send you your next month's objectives.*

*I will not tolerate tardiness or lack of application. Should you not come up to the standard expected, then your enrolment at the Bolshoi will be terminated and you will be cast out. I trust that our business arrangement is clear.*

*Faithfully,*

*Your sponsor'*

The letter meant little to Ava then, but now at the age of twenty-eight, its meaning was crystal clear.

She was being groomed for something, but had no idea what. At first Ava thought that it might be for her artistic talents, but her enforced studies were mostly languages, science, politics and history. Later, her studies changed to embrace organic chemistry and biology, including the destructive powers off both. More recently it was nuclear physics, particle theory and quantum mechanics. Again, the slant was towards the destructive nature of them. Ava somehow knew that her debt was soon to be called in, and it filled her with the deepest dread.

---

There was no ballet performance scheduled that evening, so Ava had arranged to go out with the girls for drinks and dinner at eight. She checked the time. It was a little after one o'clock in the afternoon, leaving her another six hours to devote to her studies. Along with telepathy, mind control and telekinesis, Ava's mother had blessed Ava with other talents; one of those was perfect retention. It was more than a photographic memory. Ava swiftly developed an empirical understanding of all subjects that she studied. She could achieve a university degree level in any subject in less than six months of intensive study. In a year, she could lecture in it. Ava put all thoughts of her childhood behind her and immersed herself in her studies. It was seven o'clock before she knew it.

"Shit, is that really the time?" Ava gasped.

She was going to be late *again* and could already imagine the scolding she was going to get from the girls. Ava closed the laptop with a sigh and rubbed her tired eyes. She could feel a migraine coming on. Ava always got a migraine when she burned the candle at both ends, and when her stress levels were high. She left the dressing table that served as her desk, and looked in the mirror. Ava's eyes were like windows into her soul. They had dulled, and her pupils were like pinpricks. Ava knew that if she took her pain killers immediately and darkened the room then, just maybe, she could sleep the migraine off. The last thing she did before drifting into a drug induced sleep, was to text Katarina.

*'Sorry Kat migraine. Talk tomorrow x'*

It was nearly midnight when Ava woke. The pain had gone and she felt both reenergised and famished. She hadn't planned to eat in, so there was nothing in her fridge. A contingency plan quickly formed in her head. The bar at the Bolshoi didn't close until three in the morning. She could get a sandwich there and meet the girls for a last drink, she decided. Ava threw on a pair of jeans and a top, then put on eye-liner and some lippy. As Ava applied the red lipstick, she had a flash-back to the night before at the bar and smiled at herself in the mirror.

"You hussy, how could you have been such a tart?" Ava asked her reflection innocently.

With any luck the handsome stranger would be there tonight she thought, licking her freshly applied lipstick in anticipation of the encounter.

--------------------------------------------------------------------------------

When Ava took her usual seat at the bar she looked visibly deflated. The stranger wasn't there. She was about to be sensible and order an orange juice, when Yuri placed a Dirty Martini and a club sandwich in front of her. He looked so pleased with himself for his insight that Ava couldn't refuse.

"Hey-ho," she acknowledged. "What the hell?"

Yuri was quick to engage her in conversation, his enthusiasm evident. Ava was preoccupied with her own thoughts though and hadn't taken in a word. Completely out of context, she asked him a question pointing at an empty barstool.

"Has the stranger who sat there last night been in this evening?"

Yuri shook his head sadly, crest-fallen. His crush on Ava was massive but she was as far out of his reach as the Moon. He turned away so that she wouldn't read him and busied himself behind the bar.

Oblivious to Yuri's feelings, Ava stirred her cocktail and reflected on the previous evening. She had made a dangerous enemy.

20

Sergei Bortnik was one of the richest and most deadly men on the planet. He wasn't going to let a chance to bed her go by without a fight.

Ava's ability to read and control minds brought with it a sinister revelation. She had discovered that all men were not equal. There were at least three different species, similar in appearance but dissimilar in their natures. Bortnik was from the dark side; they called themselves *Shadows*. His race was the least prevalent but they generally held positions of power. Shadows were always ruthless and domineering, but not usually as cruel and dangerous as Bortnik. Another idiosyncrasy was that they always had brown eyes. At the other extreme were a more benevolent people. They were much easier for her to detect as they seemed to transmit a feeling of well-being, and always had vivid blue or green eyes. These were referred to by the Shadows as *Angels*; although Ava was certain that there was no religious foundation to either of these names.

It was clear to Ava that these two races conflicted with each other, but she had never been able to probe deep enough into their minds to find out why. Between these two opposites was the multitude, the indigenous species. There appeared to be a fourth species though and it so far numbered only one on the planet; just her. Ava didn't conform to any of these gene pools and wondered what kind of freak she was. The stranger definitely came from the dark side though, he was a Shadow. Ava had a fatal attraction for bad boys and that attraction had already cost her dearly. She hadn't learned her lesson though and probably never would. Ava was drawn to them like a moth to a flame.

Ava finished her sandwich and drained her glass. She gave Yuri a cheeky smile and an appreciative wink, and then left the bar to find the girls and hopefully, trouble!

-------------------------------------------------------------------------

Chapter 3

It was another morning hangover for Ava. She opened her eyes in trepidation, anxious about what she might see and was relieved when she recognised the room. It wasn't hers, although it was fragrant and feminine in décor. The girl asleep in her arms was Katarina. They were entwined in an intimate embrace, Ava's hand naturally cupping Katarina's left breast. Flashbacks of the cocaine fuelled party the night before, came crashing into her consciousness. Eight of them had gone clubbing at the famous Soho Rooms, one of Moscow's most notorious venues. It was a club frequented by the elite, and enjoyed a certain amount of anonymity. Politicians, dubious businessmen and the police, went there for its atmosphere, drugs and the inevitable sex. Ava's nasal passages were still burning from cocaine abuse, which triggered the image in her mind of Rudi's leering face above her.

Rudi was a product of Moscow's working class, struggling to meet western expectations. He had graduated from car thief to pimp and then drug dealer. He was strongly built, not through his genes though, but rather from working out and street fighting. He was in his late twenties, a little short of six foot tall, bald and as rotten as a pear. Ava hated him and everything that he stood for, but that wasn't enough to stop her being turned on by him. It was Ava that had invited him to the club to supply the cocaine, Ava that had enticed him up to the private rooms above the Disco Room and Ava who had given herself to him.

They were both wired on cocaine and whiskey, and things had gone too far. The sex had been hard and brutal and Ava had loved every minute, right up until Rudi had lost control. It was only by luck that Katarina had come to find Ava when she did. Hearing Ava's screams, Katarina burst into the room, catching them in the act. Rudi's hands were around Ava's throat, strangling her to heighten their climax. Katarina could see that Rudi was out of his mind on drugs and was not going to stop. She picked up a half full whiskey bottle and smashed it in Rudi's face, otherwise Ava would have died there and then.

After tending to Ava, Katarina checked Rudi and screamed out in terror. He was staring sightlessly into space. Both immediately knew that he was dead. Katarina had quickly helped Ava to dress, and got her out through the back door. They could only hope that the Soho Rooms could not afford the scandal of a low-life drug dealer like Rudi being found dead there, and would ensure that the problem disappeared. If the police were to investigate thoroughly, there was enough DNA on the bed sheets alone to secure a life sentence for Ava.

When they got back to Katarina's apartment, Ava needed caring for and gentle and meaningful sex. For this she always turned to Katarina; her love making was all about giving and Katarina could give in abundance.

Ava was suddenly aware that she was touching herself at the erotic thought of her near-death experience. No boy too bad, it would seem. She lost herself in her own body and the sheer danger of her encounter at the Soho Rooms.

When Ava was finally exorcised of this bad boy, her hands began to explore the sleeping girl next to her. Katarina roused slowly to Ava's gentle demands and offered her mouth for Ava's kiss as she did so. Ava skilfully touched and caressed her until Katarina cried out in ecstasy. It was at times like this that Ava felt herself to be one hundred percent woman. Afterwards, they showered together and exchanged vows of eternal love. Ava departed feeling more alive than she had in months. The only problem was that despite the events of the night at the Soho Rooms, Ava still couldn't get the dark and dangerous stranger from the Bolshoi out of her mind.

-------------------------------------------------------------------------

For everybody else it was a national holiday, but for Ava it was just another day of study. She had resisted opening the parcel from her sponsor until after her night out. It would simply have filled her with guilt otherwise. Ava removed the stiff brown paper wrapping exposing various in-house publications on cyber-warfare, banking and world infrastructure. A memory stick and the usual hand-written note in manly script were its only other contents:


'Ava,

*First, I would like to compliment you on your clear and fundamental understanding of quantum mechanics.'*

A rare compliment, Ava noted.

*'The challenges you have made to current thinking has been escalated to the very highest level and raised great interest there. I will write to you in due course with their response.*

*Your next challenge is to gain a full understanding of world Information Technology infrastructure and its interdependencies. I need you to understand its strengths and weaknesses, particularly its weaknesses. This will include world banking, national security, defence and communications.*

*As an aside, I want you to put together a directory of all the key players in each of the subject areas.*

*You will complete this study in nine months from today.*

*Faithfully,*

*Your sponsor'*


Ava folded the letter up thoughtfully and put it back in the envelope. She wondered how things had got so fucked up. She had no control of her working life at the Bolshoi, no control of her private life and clearly no control at all of her sex life. Men ruled her in all these things. More insidiously, this anonymous benefactor owned her life. Another man, she assumed.

That was the common denominator; men. Her dilemma started with her absent father whom she had never known. After having his fun, he had left her mother with a baby and no support. It was a man who had used her mother for sex and then brutally killed her, then a series of men who had abused her Aunt Alisa, the woman who had adopted Ava after her mother's death. The stress of having another child to look after with no support had turned her Aunt to drink, and the string of rubbish boyfriends who followed. Later, in her young teens, when Ava came home for weekends and holidays, those same men lusted after her instead of her beautiful aunt, and abused her.

The first time that Ava fully experienced the dreadful power within her, was when one of her aunt's tacky boyfriends molested and raped her. He was a man in his early sixties with dark curly hair, glasses and a stale odour of tobacco and ale about him. She was barely fourteen. He had arrived at the house supposedly to see her Aunt Alisa, but he knew full well that she would be out and that Ava would be at home alone. Ava had felt uncomfortable letting him in, but then she was compromised by not wanting to appear rude. She remembered that he kept looking nervously at his watch. With hindsight, she realised that he was gauging how much time he had before Alisa arrived. He came and sat inappropriately close to her on the sofa, placing his hand paternally on her thigh, as if about to give some fatherly advice. Ava had pulled her dressing gown tightly around herself and then froze, hoping that he would pick up on her rejection. He didn't.

"Aunt Alisa will be home shortly," Ava had said but the predator knew that she wouldn't.

The touch became a stroke and he slipped his hands between her legs searching urgently.

"No! Don't! Please don't," Ava's voice trembled. She was petrified, with no experience on how to deal with the situation.

The big man had rolled off the sofa onto his knees pressing her legs open until they were either side of him. She vividly remembered the horror of the moment when he pulled her forwards to meet his pelvis. Then it all happened so quickly. He forced himself into her and all she could do was cry pitifully. The injustice and humiliation of her rape was unbearable.

A black rage mounted inside Ava until it became an almost physical manifestation. She recalled looking up into the man's bloated face as he violated her. Bizarrely, she had watched the vein in his neck throbbing like a blacksmith's bellows at the intensity of his rape. What happened next was without precedence in Ava's life. Her rage had brought something else with it, something inexplicably powerful and evil. The golden flecks in Ava's vivid blue eyes somehow darkened, merging into the darkest brown and her look became steely. She no longer accepted being the passive victim and instead drove him on relentlessly.

Ava had taken control of her rapist's mind and would not let him stop, or even slow the punishing physical exertion of his assault. Despite his efforts to pull out, the old man simply could not. He was locked into a rhythm that his body could simply not sustain. His face began to purple and twist with the strain, as if he was suffering a stroke. Still Ava had forced him on. When full cardiac arrest came, the man's eyes bulged and his breath left his flabby body like a snorting bull. The despicable man collapsed over Ava in grotesque death.

Ava shoved the man's corpse contemptuously to the floor, feeling no remorse. Instead, she felt empowered. The killing of this vile man had the strangest effect on her. It had woken a dormant and dreadful power inside her; something malevolent; something to be deeply afraid of.

Ever since that disgusting and traumatic experience, Ava had been a living paradox. To most of those who knew her, she was a sweet, tender and caring woman; a loyal and good friend with an enormous capacity for love in its purest form. The truth was that she displayed classic signs of schizophrenia, and the catalysts for her transformation to the dark side of her nature were alcohol, bad men, rough sex and black rage. Ava dreaded that one day the man and the scenario might come together at the same time.

With all those stimulants in play, God only knew what she might be capable of, or more likely than God, Satan!

As Ava grew older and had freedom of choice, she chose the same kind of rubbish men as her aunt and her mother. They just helped themselves to her body and trashed her cars. Ava had always thought that, if she nurtured these men enough, she could turn them around. She never did of course. They just abused her kindness, took more and gave less. Even now, Ava still naively believed that leopards could change their spots and continued to waste her life on them. Ava was damaged, her innocence taken from her by that repulsive man, and all of the men who had subsequently followed.

Ava broke down and sobbed her heart out at the hopelessness of her situation all and wondered just how much longer she could continue this nothing life. All she ever really wanted was a man to love her unconditionally, and to protect her from herself before she finally pressed the self-destruct button. It was a pipe-dream though. No such men existed, Ava conceded, and knew she was a tragedy in the making.

Ava sighed at the inevitability of her decline, inserted the memory stick into her computer and began to scroll through the files. It was going to be another long and hard day of studies.

---------------------------------------------------------------------------

Chapter 4

March 1955. Princeton, New Jersey. America.

It was early spring in Princeton, New Jersey and the morning chill was still in the air. Albert jammed his cold hands in his pockets as he walked his dog in the grounds of Fuld Hall, home of the Institute for Advanced Study. The winter of 1954 had been particularly severe. Even now, in March, the daytime temperature had seldom risen above five degrees.

Walking his dog was part of Albert's daily routine. Even in sickness, he had never been known to miss exercising his beloved Cocker Spaniel, Lucy. He had just celebrated his seventy-sixth birthday, and wasn't to know that this spring was to be his last.

Albert enjoyed the surroundings of academia. Princeton was a Mecca for physicists from around the world. The environment enabled him to think and reflect on his lifetime achievements, not less all he had left undone, undiscovered. It takes more than one man's diligence, he mused. That is the reason why the young are born; to continue our good work, to right our wrongs and to correct our misunderstandings.

Albert Einstein had taken to philosophising in his later years and to walking with a cane. He looked rather *Chaplinesque* in the institute grounds with his shock of unruly grey hair and full moustache. Somehow the old Spaniel had grown to look and walk like him, as happens with long standing and close friends. Albert often wondered whether that popular theory was actually the other way around.

The old man conceded that Lucy was struggling and needed to rest a while. An onlooker might have read the signs differently, that the dog had recognised her master's struggle, and had allowed him to stop and rest without giving him cause for guilt. Either way, they stopped. Albert sat on the bench and rested just as he had done on countless occasions before. Lucy laid herself across her master's feet to keep the chill air off them, just as she too had done on the same countless occasions.

A man was already sat on the bench, reading the *Daily Princetonian*, a university publication. The headline read, "Einstein. Genius or madman?"

"Good question," Albert muttered to himself.

A wry smile crossed his face. To his surprise the stranger dropped his newspaper so that he was looking directly at him. His wasn't a face that Albert recalled. The man was in the middle of his age, with the darkest of eyes that shone from a tanned face. Black stubble darkened a strong chin and he had the physique of a man who worked out. Most would describe the man as ruggedly handsome, and yet there was an air of something dangerous about him too. Lucy picked up on this sense of danger and growled, baring her teeth.

"Lucy! Now then," Albert gently chastised her. He felt a little embarrassed and went on to excuse her. "She's a bit possessive don't you see?"

"And so she should be Mr Einstein," the stranger confirmed. "No offence taken."

"And none implied." Albert raised one of his bushy eyebrows. "Do we know each other? Only I could write from memory the most complex mathematical formula, but faces and names seem to escape me these days. Age you see," he conceded.

"Well I don't think that $E=mc2$ is so hard to remember, but only one of the sharpest minds of all time could have come up with the e formula in the first place!"

"You are too kind... Mr?"

"Demitri Papandreou. And no, we have never met. However, I have admired your work for over ninety years."

What appeared to be a glib comment had an immediate effect on the old man sat next to Demitri and he bristled with contempt.

"Are you mocking me *young* man? A crass newspaper headline does not give you the latitude to ridicule my work, something that you are hardly likely to even begin to understand!"

Einstein was furious and disdainful. Lucy responded by barking and her hackles were raised.

"I am not mocking you Mr Einstein, far from it. You are a man amongst much lesser men. Your knowledge transcends the universe and your mind is open to possibility." Demitri's manner was non-confrontational but assertive. "May I ask you what it is that limits man's ability the most?"

Albert recognised that this dark stranger was not an *ordinary* man and that their encounter had not altogether been an accidental one.

"His experience and prejudices are his limiting factor," Albert confirmed. "I myself have been guilty of that same prejudice. Quantum mechanics did not entirely support my theories and I wasted many years trying to refute the theory."

"Indeed!" Demitri held Einstein's eyes. "Are you open to the possibility that I am some thousands of years older than you and that I am not from your time, not even from your planet? Can you accept also that your theories concerning time-travel and *wormholes* in the universe that provide shortcuts in space-time, do exist?"

By way of proof Demitri handed Einstein his mobile phone.

"What you are holding in the palm of your hands has a sixty-four billion-byte processor. It is a computer, a telephone, a camera and a music centre. In fact, it's almost anything that you want it to be, and it's pretty much standard issue for people living in the second decade of the 21st century."

Albert's mouth opened in astonishment. The futuristic device in his hand and its heritage was irrefutable. It could not have come from his time.

"So, I was right, not just theories. I was actually right." A tear squeezed from the corner of his eye and Albert brushed it away.

Demitri sensed that the time was already right.

"You will die within the month Albert. Would you like the opportunity to come with me and prove your theories, experience the fourth dimension and travel in time?"

Albert was old now and looked forlornly at his dog, Lucy.

"And what will become of her?"

"Don't worry old friend, I will make it my personal pledge to you that she is cared for."

Albert Einstein had aged visibly in those few moments, but it wasn't for fear of death. He had seen and done enough. It was that he now knew that he would fail to see out the life of his faithful friend. He reached down and picked Lucy up pressing his face into her neck, breathing her in.

"What is it you would have me do Demitri? Everything comes at a price." Even at great age, Albert was nobody's fool.

"I would ask you to choose a select group of scientists from across all time and work together to deliver me the fifth dimension."

Demitri's statement was unequivocal and its bluntness unsettled Albert.

"Have you any idea what the fifth dimension is, or might be?" Albert tested.

"Not really," Demitri confessed dismissively. "But I am sure that you do."

"Perhaps, but only perhaps," Albert conceded. "You are moving into the territory that exists somewhere between Man and God, and you should be careful of what you seek."

The old man's eyes came sharply into focus, as he considered the stranger's proposition.

"What makes you think that I would even attempt to do this for you?" Albert challenged.

"Because you have no choice Albert. You couldn't refuse me even if you wanted to. Your curiosity would not permit it." Demitri was sure of his man. "Imagine if the greatest intellects in all of history were in the same room at the same time expounding and challenging their ideas. Imagine too, if those same men were in my time, with our technology. Imagine the possibilities Albert Einstein. What a legacy to give to mankind!"

"It would simply become another war-machine," Albert lamented. "Everything becomes a war-machine."

Albert looked sad and reflective. As a persecuted Jew, he had left Germany when Adolf Hitler came to power in 1933, to continue his studies on particle theory and nuclear fission. On the eve of World War Two, he had endorsed a letter to President Franklin D Roosevelt warning him of the potential development of *extremely powerful bombs of a new type*, and recommended that America begin similar research. Later, he had publicly denounced the use of nuclear fission as a weapon. Now he could see it happening over again but infinitely worse.

"You are right," Albert announced at last. "I have no choice. It is deep within my psyche, but if I have only a month left to live, then you are asking too much of me."

"History books will record that you died on 18th April 1955 and you will. If you come with me, then you will live outside of your time for as long as it takes. When your journey is done, I will return you to this very time and place for you to fulfil your destiny."

"Do I die peacefully?"

The old man was already philosophical about his own passing. It is how you are when you have had enough of life.

"Peacefully and with dignity old friend," Demitri assured.

---------------------------------------------------------------------------

# Chapter 5

June 2015. Thessaloniki, Greece.

Nine months had passed since Ava had been given the assignment by her sponsor relating to the study of world Information Technology infrastructure, banking and national security.

It was eight o'clock in the morning and the rays of the Grecian sunshine were already pleasingly warming. Demitri Papandreou sat on the balcony of his luxury town house in Thessaloniki, breakfasting in his white silk robe as was custom. The five million Euro house looked out southwards across the foothills, which grew into the peaks which finally formed Mount Olympus itself. That view had hardly changed since he had moved there over five hundred years ago, although the town had renewed itself several times over since then. The sun was still low in the south-eastern skies, bathing him in a warm orange light. Vassos, his *aide-de-camp*, poured the hot sweet Turkish coffee and passed him the morning paper, along with his mail. Demitri took the post from Vassos' slim, well-manicured hand without looking up.

"The parcel you have been waiting for from the Bolshoi has arrived *Kyrie*," Vassos' voice was gentle, somewhat effeminate.

He looked to his master for some sign of gratitude. As usual, none was forthcoming.

"There is no need to state the obvious. Do you think that I am a fool Vassos?" Demitri's voice was harsh. He exuded power, corrupt power, and his aide was humbled in his presence.

"No *Kyrie* I meant nothing by it, I just..." Vassos was close to tears. Demitri cut him off coldly.

"That will be all!" Demitri waved him away without even glancing at his crest-fallen manservant.

Vassos looked helplessly at his master, left him to breakfast and open the mail alone. The young aide had to hide the huge crush he had on his master. It wasn't only women who found him irresistible. Demitri was a ruthless killer, unscrupulous businessman, and a danger to all women. They came to him helplessly, like lambs to the slaughter. His countless conquests all despised themselves for it afterwards but remarkably, never despised him.

Demitri discarded all but the brown parcel that was neatly wrapped and tied with coarse string. He flipped it over and smiled as he read the sender's address:

*'Ava Kaplinski*

*Bolshoi Theatre,*

*Teatralnaya Square 1,*

*125009 Moscow,*

*Russia.'*

It was nine months, almost to the day, since he had tasked his ward to gain a full understanding of his chosen topics. Demitri knew that he wasn't going to be disappointed with Ava's synopsis and dissertation. He flicked impatiently to the back of the dossier and found what he was particularly interested in. He had told her to gain a detailed understanding of the infrastructure's strengths and weaknesses, particularly around world banking, national security, defence and communications. Her brief was also to include key players, financial and technical.

"Good girl!" he said out loud, with great personal satisfaction.

Demitri saw his name amongst the top financiers on the list. He would have been disappointed in Ava had she failed to uncover his involvement. Apart from Demitri's global banking interests, he was a major player in pharmaceuticals, oil, technical research laboratories and an underwriter for Lloyds. The Papandreou family, one way or another, had some control or at least inroads into most of the global organisations.

Over the next three hours, Demitri read and assimilated Ava's summation of the high-level mechanics and interdependencies of global infrastructure. It was an excellent dossier, succinct and totally in line with her brief. She was almost ready now, Demitri decided. Once radicalised and adequately bedded, she would become his puppet and the most dangerous spy and assassin since Mata Hari; another woman he had groomed and placed in the world of espionage. Hari was an exotic dancer, famous for her *honey trap* technique, and was ultimately responsible for the death of over fifty thousand allied soldiers. She was finally tried and executed by firing squad on 15th October 1917, at the age of forty-one. It had always been assumed that she worked for the Germans, but she was in fact a Shadow agent. When push came to shove, she was expendable, just as Ava Kaplinski ultimately would be.

Six months in the madrassas and terrorist training camps of Pakistan would complete her, Demitri concluded. As for bedding her, well that was already a foregone conclusion. Demitri recalled with sadistic pleasure, how Ava was literally begging for it that night at the Bolshoi. It was just as her mother had done nearly thirty years earlier, before he strangled and hung her from the chandelier in the hotel bedroom.

Demitri had another card to play in the absolute control of Ava Kaplinski. It was he who had dealt with the body of Rudi after his murder on that night at the Soho Rooms in Moscow. The room was cleansed but not before photographing the crime scene and then bagging all of the evidence. The theft of the CCTV video security tapes was the final piece of evidence that put both Ava and Katarina in the room on that night. Ava's DNA would do the rest.

He smiled to himself with satisfaction. Ava was now his to do with as he pleased. Demitri had a plan for how to make her isolation complete, to make that a certainty.

Chapter 6

Once again Ava woke up to the mother of all hangovers. Today was to be her day off so at least she took some comfort in that. It felt like *Groundhog Day* though. Hazy memories of the night before, banging head, burning nose, sick stomach, sore breasts and she felt like she had been kicked in the crotch. Ava touched herself for reassurance and, to her relief, it had felt worse.

The last thing Ava remembered was the ride in the taxi back from the club with two Russian soldiers. She had let them share with her to save cost but that was just a façade, a ploy to ensnare them. Ava had met them at the Soho Rooms. They were both athletic in build and fired up with alcohol, bravado and testosterone. It was a heady mix and something that she wanted. Ava had danced with them lewdly in the Disco Room and they had both recognised a dead cert when they saw it.

Ava cringed as she remembered rubbing herself against the taller one. He was lean, blond almost Scandinavian looking, with perfect teeth and a cheeky smile. To her it was just a bonus that he had a decent looking mate and she was already fantasising about what they would do to her later.

Ava vaguely remembered that even as they piled into the taxi, the *Scandinavian* one who was probably not much into his twenties, had her breasts cupped in his hands teasing her nipples roughly with his fingers. It was delicious. If the journey hadn't been so short, they would have already had her on the back seat. While the one was roughly taking pleasure from her breasts, the other was fixing lines of coke for them. She remembered snorting it but little else afterwards. The boys had diverted the taxi to their barracks and the rest of her memories were just a confusion of sexual acts that had no particular order about them. That and being thrown around the room like a rag-doll!

Ava collected herself and opened a reluctant eye. She was in trepidation of what she might see. The room was a mess and she felt deeply ashamed as she always did, after these losses of control. Clothes were everywhere, furniture tumbled and one of the curtains had been dragged from its track. Two empty bottles of whiskey were evidence that the night had not just been a cocaine fest. She rolled over and winced at the pain. The carpet burns on her knees, elbows and spine had stuck to the bed sheets during the night.

Ava glanced and noted the roughness of the cheap carpet on the floor, prompting flash-backs of her being taken energetically from behind by the Scandinavian's friend. He was a bull of a lad who was slightly too well endowed for comfort. She remembered how her face had been forced into the skirting board in several places around the room as her small body had given ground to each and every one of his powerful thrusts, almost walking her about the room as he took his pleasure.

Ava remembered that it had started with him on top of her on the bed, fucking her enthusiastically until he had driven her off it and onto the floor. She had landed on her back with him still on top. The stud didn't even lose his powerful rhythm; he just kept pounding away, driving her along the carpet on her back. The erotic feeling of him inside her had distracted Ava from the pain as the carpet stripped the skin off her prominent spine. All that Ava could remember now, were her multiple orgasms.

Ava sat up and re-appraised the naked Scandinavian asleep, facedown beside her. He was undeniably an Adonis with the most perfectly shaped and muscular bum she had ever seen. Ava could see the bruises her fingers had made in his sides, as she had encouraged him to drive deeper and harder into her. She leaned over the bed to see his friend also naked and uncovered on his back.

"God," she mumbled. "He is still hard, even in his sleep."

Ava wasn't sure if she could take any more delicious abuse. She left the bed silently, slid her dress over her head, gathered her possessions and left without waking them.

-------------------------------------------------------------------------------

Quite naturally Ava's next port of call was Katarina's apartment. She knew that Katarina would be worrying about her, as she always did when she went clubbing alone. Katarina was the only constant in Ava's life and she loved her more than she loved life itself. It was only Katarina's unconditional love for her, which had stopped Ava's total decline into the dark side of her nature. They both knew the inevitability of her eventually succumbing to it one day, and that she was indeed a tragedy in the making. All that Katarina could do was to postpone that day for as long as she could.

When Ava arrived, she let herself in as was common practice. She found Katarina asleep in a lover's embrace with a pretty and petite blonde girl. Ava was not in the slightest bit jealous and smiled to herself at the thought of Katarina's contentment. She closed the door on them and went on to the kitchen. Ava was ravenous! Twenty minutes later, she had poached eggs on toast and a steaming mug of strong coffee in front of her. There was no elegance at all in the way Ava cleared her plate; she was on a mission. Sated, Ava tidied the plates and refreshed her coffee.

She was already over the drug and alcohol abuse. Ava had inhuman powers of recuperation; but then she knew that she wasn't human. Even the soreness and heavy bruising from the previous night had abated and the carpet burns were no longer wet and angry. Regeneration was another of those abilities that Ava had inherited from her late mother and was perhaps the only one that she enjoyed as a blessing and not a curse. Katarina entered the kitchen in a slinky pale blue slip and embraced her. They kissed.

"What have you done precious?"

Katarina cupped Ava's face in her small elegant hands as she searched those troubled blue eyes of hers that so openly gave her away. A single tear welled up in the corner of Ava's eye and escaped, running silently down her cheek. It betrayed Ava's despair of herself and was enough to open the flood gates. Moments later, she was sobbing at the shame of what she had done.

"I'm a whore Kat, nothing but a disgusting whore. Just trash, worthless trash," Ava's words came out in bursts amongst her sobs.

"Shush now. Let me bathe you little one, then you will feel better about yourself."

Ava found it strange that such a petite girl as Katarina could call her *little one,* but then the endearment perfectly described her. It was not in terms of stature; Ava was by far the bigger of the two in that respect, it was that Ava had grown up with low self-esteem and expectations, such that her decision making was almost childlike and at best flawed.

When you don't value yourself, being abused comes naturally. This was the case with Ava. She behaved promiscuously, not solely for the want of sexual gratification, but because she had never been truly loved by a man for the intelligent and loving woman she was. Her lack of self-esteem was the result of being unwanted and abandoned by her father as a child. Ava just wanted to be loved and reached out desperately to men to find that love. Unfortunately Ava always reached for the wrong ones, attracting takers like nectar does bees.

The bathroom was from another era. It had a large white enamel tub on four bronze legs set in the middle of the room, with a bronze tap sculpted as a lion's mouth. The floor was scrubbed wooden floorboards, with a large window that commanded the far wall, looking out on the spires of a cathedral. Katarina had feminised the room with drapes, candles and the paraphernalia that girls collect along the way.

Katarina ran the bath and added the oils she assured Ava would have a healing and spiritual cleansing effect. Katarina believed that to be true, and Ava was in need enough not to challenge it. Having left the soldiers in their barracks so suddenly, all that Ava had to remove was her crumpled dress which she did and stood there naked before her friend. Katarina checked her over intimately. Even though Ava's regeneration had already repaired half of the damage Katarina gasped out loud.

"Jesus Ava! What have they done to you?"

"All that I asked for and less than I deserved," Ava replied ashamedly.

Katarina gently kissed each of the little bruises and sores, tutting at the unfairness of the damage as she did so. With that done, she took Ava's hands and steadied her as she stepped into the bath, immersing herself in the soothing waters. Katarina sponged her and made little cooing noises as if she was talking to a baby, sending Ava into a state of total peace until at last she fell into a much-needed sleep. Ava slept like the dead for almost two hours in the bath while Katarina took jugs of water out and replaced them with hot throughout. When Ava awoke, Katarina was still by her side.

"Thank you, Kat. I feel amazing now," Ava said with the most loving look in her eyes. Katarina really was the most precious thing to her. Then, after some reflection she added. "Is your friend still here?"

"No, she left."

"I'm sorry, that was selfish of me. Is she the one?"

Katarina glanced away, unable to hold Ava's gaze.

"No you are," she said shyly.

It was Kat's turn to cry. She loved Ava with all her heart, but knew that she couldn't give her all the things that she needed. Ava craved bad men for rough sex and any other punishment they chose to dish out; such was her hatred of herself. Katarina could never have known that her self-hatred stemmed from Ava's guilt for not protecting her mother when she needed her. That and her underlying hatred of men for what they had done to them both.

Ava *looked* into Katarina's mind as was her given talent. She could see the giddy heights of her love and the profound depth of her despair. Ava reached for the bathrobe and stepped gracefully out of the bath, knotting the bathrobe. She knelt by Katarina's side.

"Kat, I treasure your love and I will always love you." Ava used her sleeve to dab away the tears. "The men are for sex and you are for love. They cannot compare."

"They can, you just choose badly. You need a man Ava; you really do, but not a man who just takes, you need one who gives in abundance; a man who can love you unconditionally and cherish you and bed you; your own knight in shining armour. That man is out there Ava and he will find you. He will make you shine so brightly but..." Katarina couldn't finish her sentence.

"But what Kat?"

Ava had already read Katarina's thoughts but asked her anyway. It was with the greatest of difficulty and personal anguish that Katarina replied.

"He will come and he will win you Ava, and you will shine as bright as any star. You will feel so right in his company and so happy and free, but you will push him away and your demons will come flooding back to fill that empty place in your soul."

"Why would I do a stupid thing like that Kat?" Ava already knew what she would say.

"Because you don't love yourself enough to have him," Katarina replied thinly.

The answer was simple and they both knew that it was true.

---------------------------------------------------------------------------

It was late in the afternoon when Ava finally got back to her apartment and checked her mailbox. More than a month had passed since she had sent her sponsor her dissertation. In over twenty-three years, this was the longest that she had ever waited for the parcel that would contain her next assignment. The long wait had troubled Ava such that she feared she might have come to the end of her sponsorship. In truth it would be a blessing, Ava thought, because she knew that *payback* time was surely coming.

There was a single envelope in the mailbox. She checked the handwriting and it was in the hand of her sponsor. In all the years she had never received a letter from him; it was always a parcel. So this was indeed a milestone. Her hands began to tremble, sensing that the content of the letter was going to be monumental. Her courage finally deserted her and she placed it unopened on her desk. Ava needed to steady herself. She reached for the vodka bottle and a glass, something that was becoming too much of a habit lately. Ava was about to pour, when she had a moment of reflection. At least part of Katarina's lecture had stayed in her head. She walked to the sink and emptied the contents of the bottle into it.

"New page in my life!" she declared.

Ava set the light under the coffee pot with a wry smile on her face. Minutes later, she was sat at her desk with the mysterious envelope in front of her. Ava sipped thoughtfully from the steaming mug as she steeled herself for the moment.

"Here goes everything," she muttered apprehensively.

Ava split the envelope with her paper knife. There was a brief note in his unmistakable handwriting and a one-way airline ticket to Islamabad, Pakistan. The note read:


*'Ava,*

*I trust that this letter finds you in good health.*

*You will already have seen the ticket from Moscow to Islamabad, flying out on Qatar Airways leaving this Friday. I judge that by the time you read this that you will have two days to finalise your affairs and make any necessary purchases.*

*I have already terminated your employment at the Bolshoi.*

*You will be met at the airport at Islamabad by the Mullah Ismael Alansari and your objectives will be made clear to you there.*

*Faithfully,*

*Your sponsor.'*


"Christ, what does he want of me?" she said out loud.

Ava wondered what influence her sponsor might have that *he* could terminate her employment. Her thoughts immediately turned to Katarina. Telling her she was leaving the Bolshoi for an indeterminable period of time, was going to break her heart. Ava reached for her mobile and made the call before her fear of making it could get the better of her. Katarina answered sleepily after the fourth ring.

"Hello darling, you're not already in trouble again are you?"

It was said in humour, but there was a noticeable inflection in Katarina's tone that gave away her concern. Ava was more than capable of screwing up, even after being left alone for just a few hours.

"No not in trouble honey. I don't think so anyway, but then I can never be totally certain."

"God Ava, your life is such a car-crash. What is it now?"

Ava tried ironic.

"Good news and bad news I suppose. Good news is I've kicked the booze."

That was at least partly true. She had poured the vodka down the sink and wasn't likely to get a drink in a Muslim country.

"And the bad news?" Katarina prompted, with her heart in her mouth.

"The bad news is that I'm leaving the Bolshoi destined for Pakistan this Friday. For how long, I just don't know."

There was a sound like Katarina had dropped her phone. It was some moments before she could reply.

"But you can't. You can't leave me. Besides, the Bolshoi will hold you to your contract," Katarina sounded desperate. "Who will look after you and protect you from yourself if not me?" Katarina broke down in tears, truly heartbroken.

"Take me with you!" she blurted in desperation.

"Sweet thing I cannot. The choice is not mine, it's my sponsor's and I owe him everything. You know that. Something will work out for us. You will see." Not even Ava herself believed that.

Ava spent the next hour trying to reassure her desolated friend. Finally, Katarina was resigned to the fact that Ava was leaving and that there was nothing she could do about it. The conversation became more positive.

"We must give you a big send-off Ava, one that you will always remember. Tomorrow is your last night, so I'll arrange something and maybe invite the others?" Then she added coyly. "Perhaps just you and me could start with a few drinks at the Bolshoi so I can have you to myself for a while?"

Ava could sense how much it meant to her to maximise their time together. She also read between the lines that Katarina was absolutely convinced that she would never see her again and that the thought was crushing her. Ava conceded to Katarina's wishes.

"Yes. You can come to mine first and we can glam up together over a bottle of wine," Ava suggested.

"So much for *kicking the booze* then Ava," Katarina said sardonically.

"Leopards and spots Kat, leopards and spots…"

---

There were so many things that Ava had to do in the single day left before her leaving party. Strangely, none of them had anything to do with her work though. No handover to another ballerina, no mentoring, no last performance; nothing. It was like her name and memory had been scrubbed from the billboard. She had become nobody to the Bolshoi overnight, which said something about the power of her sponsor, she realised. Ava felt physically sick about what her future had in store for her.

She spent the daylight hours shopping for the essentials that she could only *imagine* that she might need in Pakistan. Ironically, she had focussed on the needs of a celebrity lifestyle, all of which would prove useless to her. That done, Ava went about settling her bills, packing her house up and quitting her rental agreement. She was now free and unencumbered. The only two people in Ava's life that knew her well enough to care where she had gone, were Katarina and her aunt Alisa; otherwise she would be invisible and totally isolated. This fact was not overlooked by Demitri, her sponsor.

By the time Ava had finished her tasks and packed her bags, it was past seven o'clock in the evening. The flight was scheduled for four o'clock the following afternoon, for which Ava was thankful. An early morning departure really would have been a challenge, even for her. With Ava's literally superhuman powers of recovery, she was confident that no matter how much alcohol she consumed at the party, she would still make an afternoon flight. Ava had just finished when Katarina let herself in.

"It's only me!" Katarina called out from the hallway.

She bundled her overnight bag and neatly pressed dress through the door. The dress slid off its hanger and Katarina tangled her feet in it, nearly falling over.

"Shit!" she swore as she scooped the dress up, kicking the door shut. Ava met her in the passage way.

"Let me take your dress Kat; I'll give it press it for you. Sounds like you need a drink?"

"Sorry about the language. It's been a hectic day getting all of your friends sorted for tonight, and I needed to go out and buy a new dress for the occasion, didn't I?"

"Kat you have more dresses than a princess. You just like buying clothes. And since when have you needed an excuse?" They laughed at the absolute truth of Ava's statement.

Ava had a couple of bottles of Dom Pérignon on ice, and opened one. The cork popped violently from the neck of the bottle, cascading froth everywhere, before Ava captured the sparkling wine in two long stemmed glasses.

They sipped as they chatted and listened to music while Ava ironed Katarina's strapless, backless dress. Music was very intimate to them, and it invariably stirred their emotions. The track playing was one of their favourites and they kissed to it.

"You do something to me Kat," Ava whispered in her mouth.

They were both lost in the rhythm, the lyrics and their kiss, which lasted the full length of the track. Katarina instinctively knew it would be the last time they would ever listen to it together and it saddened her deeply. When at last they pulled apart, Katarina's face was expectant.

"Make love to me Ava," she demanded breathlessly. "I want to remember the moment forever."

They stumbled into the bedroom and fell on the bed, locked in a loving kiss that was swiftly becoming all consuming. The kiss rapidly lost its softness as their desperation to make love consumed them. Ava fumbled with the confounding buckle of Katarina's belt, cursing as it refused to oblige. At last it did, allowing Ava to press Katarina's jeans down to her hips. Katarina smirked knowingly back at Ava as she raised her pelvis to let her pull her tight jeans free. Still smirking, Katarina opened her legs invitingly smiling coyly at her lover, willing her to touch her there. Ava did. She felt the exciting warmth of Katarina's femininity through the sheer fabric of her black lace panties as she gently stroked her. Ava gasped as the erotic act sent

48

shockwaves to her brain and groin, and she flushed with the glorious anticipation of what was to come.

Ava knelt beside her petite friend and unbuttoned her shirt, kissing her shoulders as it dropped to her waist. Katarina reached behind her back and unclipped her black lace bra, letting it fall off her shoulders exposing her small pert breasts. Ava's mouth naturally went to them and she wondered at the hardness of Katarina's nipples and how she shuddered in ecstasy with every caress of her tongue.

Ava was naked beneath her own robe. She pulled the cord and shrugged it off, proudly displaying her nudity. Knelt there, Ava's breasts were only inches from Katarina's face. Ava used her free hand to gently pull her lover's head to her breasts and slipped her fingers under the elastic of Katarina's delicate panties. She gasped at the sweet invasion. Both were lost in each other's touch and their passion soared, taking them inexorably to their release.

-----------------------------------------------------------------------

Afterwards, they lay there at peace in each other's arms, talking for some time. It was getting late but neither wanted the precious moment to end. Both wished they hadn't arranged the party and could just stay there as lovers all night. The reality of Ava leaving was crushing for both of them. Ava needed to distract herself, lest the tears that were welling in her eyes let her down. She had to be strong for Katarina's sake, and desperately needed to divert their thoughts back to the party.

"I'd better finish your dress Kat, or we won't have any time together at the bar at the Bolshoi, before we meet the others."

Ava jumped purposefully out of bed and went back to the ironing.

"Jesus Kat, there's nothing here to iron. You might as well go to the party naked!" Ava cocked a knowing eye at her gorgeous dark haired friend. "Who were you trying to impress anyway?"

"Only you Ava. It has only ever been you." Katarina brushed a tear from her cheek with the back of her hand. "Can I come back here after the party and stay with you? Only I know that when you leave for the airport, I will never see you again. I just know it."

Ava's heart felt like it was going to burst. She could read Katarina's mind and therefore knew she really believed it would be so.

"Sweet thing; there is nobody on this Earth I would rather sleep with tonight, and I absolutely promise that it will *not* be the last time. I swear it on my life."

Katarina managed a thin smile. She knew that there was nothing more fragile than Ava's life expectancy.

--------------------------------------------------------------------------

It was after ten o'clock in the evening when they finally arrived at the Bolshoi. Both were done up to the nines and *stunning* hardly described these beautiful women. Ava had chosen a white dress to contrast with Katarina's choice of black. The dress was low-cut and figure hugging, with long tight sleeves and a high hemline that drew attention to her long smooth legs. It was a *young* dress so she had chosen to complete the look by wearing her auburn hair in a high ponytail. Her red gloss lipstick was the finishing touch that accentuated her even white teeth and alluring smile.

They sat at the bar on the high stools and Yuri served Dirty Martinis. Anyone could see that he was visibly hurting and his eyes seldom left Ava's face. The girl of his dreams was leaving. He had only worked at the Bolshoi to see Ava and watch over her. Yuri had decided to quit at the end of the week and Ava sensed his turmoil.

"Yuri, don't leave because of me. You need the work and I will be back, I promise," Ava assured him.

The transformation in Yuri was immediate and it showed in his devoted smile. Ava could see Yuri's puzzlement as he pondered how she could have known that he was leaving his employment in the first place. He hadn't told anyone.

Ava looked at Yuri or 'Mr Average' as she had always thought of him. It suddenly dawned on her that he was not average at all, far from it. She had just never taken the trouble to look more closely at him. Yes, maybe not particularly tall, but then not short either. It was his muscularity that surprised her. He was powerfully set with great arms and shoulders. Perhaps it was this *squareness* about Yuri that made him not seem so tall. His fair hair was cut short in the Russian way, presenting a strong brow and alert, blue eyes beneath. Yuri had a square chin, which he held high, Ava observed, showing that he was a proud man, even though his manner was understated.

Yes, she thought, I have got you so wrong Yuri. You really are quite a hunk.

Ava's curiosity was roused and she found her body turning on to him. She couldn't help herself and looked into his mind. Ava was shocked by what she found there.

God Yuri, you are an *Angel*! She had only ever met a few but he was definitely one of them.

Yuri *felt* the invasion of his mind and spun around. Although just a thought transfer, he heard it as if she had shouted from the rooftops. He trapped her in his gaze, which was bordering on a smirk. She felt him enter her mind and blushed uncontrollably; something here-to unheard of. Yuri had accessed her mind at the very moment she was having carnal thoughts of him. She looked like a rabbit caught in the headlights.

"Shit he can read me," Ava mumbled, turning away to face Katarina.

Ava didn't know that Angels could do that. It was the first time someone had read her thoughts and it came as quite a shock and not least, embarrassing.

"What is it? Who can read you?" Katarina asked with real concern, she had never seen Ava in a full blush before.

51

"Oh, it's nothing really Kat. I think I just made a fool of myself in front of Yuri. Forget it."

Ava didn't see the look of pure elation on Yuri's face as he flamboyantly spun a bottle, de-capped it and poured it for the next customer. She was however dreading the embarrassment of calling him over for their next drink, and was both relieved and impressed when he refreshed them discretely without being asked, or even looking at her. It was approaching eleven o'clock when Ava ordered their last Dirty Martinis. By then she was way over her embarrassment and had begun to openly flirt with Yuri.

"Remember your promise Ava," Katarina gently rebuked.

She was feeling a little jealous over the attention that Ava was paying to Yuri.

"Sorry Kat; leopards and spots again." A mischievous glint came into Ava's eyes and those brown flecks darkened and merged just for a moment. "You are my date tonight, come with me to the powder room and I will prove that to you."

Ava took Katarina's hand, helped her down from her bar stool and led her away. They were both drunk and giggling like schoolgirls. Neither had noticed the two dark suited men sat in the comfortable seats behind them.

As soon the girls were out of sight, one of the men got up and crossed to the bar, placing himself between the two empty stools and ordered vodkas. He was a dark haired thick set man, and too muscular for his suit which made him look apish. The scar that split his forehead and eyebrow was further evidence that he wasn't a business man, or one to mess with. When Yuri's back was turned, the suited man emptied the contents of a small phial into the Dirty Martinis and gave them a quick swirl. He pocketed the empty vessel, paid for the vodkas and returned to his comrade. Twenty minutes later, the girls returned to their bar stools still giggling and looking flushed from their liaison. They stirred their drinks and sipped at them nonchalantly, deep in conspiratorial conversation. Both were too drunk and too much in love to taste the Rohypnol mixed into their Martinis.

---

The black windowed stretch limousine pulled up outside the Bolshoi. Two dark suited men sat in the front and a third sat alone in the spacious back lounge area. He was fat to the point of obesity, balding and drunk. Bortnik slid open the privacy window that separated the front seats and leered through it.

"Go and get the bitches. I'm feeling horny, so don't be long about it."

Bortnik had waited months for his revenge on the *two white whores* as he had called them. He would never forget, nor forgive, the humiliation of that night at the Bolshoi, which had earned the two ballerinas a death sentence. The two bodyguards left the car and crossed the road to the grand entrance of the Bolshoi. Less than five minutes later, they were sat in the comfortable chairs in the lounge drinking their vodkas. It wasn't hard to recognise the two girls at the bar from Bortnik's description.

"That's them," the dark haired, thick set man said inclining his scarred face discretely in the girls' direction. "The boss will want the redhead to himself but we might get a shot at the other."

He looked lasciviously at Katarina who was too deep in conversation to notice.

"She's hot enough for both of us. That skimpy dress will come off in one tug. You can go second of course." He winked conspiratorially at his colleague.

The men laughed cruelly as they planned on how she was going to *get it*. They were biding their time, waiting for the right moment. Girls always go to the bathroom together so they knew it was only a matter of when. The second bodyguard had a military bearing about him, taller, athletic and ramrod straight. Fair cropped hair, thin lips and eyes that forever scanned the horizon demonstrated that he was a predator, a man used to being in dangerous situations. He was assessing which of the clients in the bar might be brave enough to come to the girls' rescue. There were none, he decided.

Their opportunity finally arrived. Ava and Katarina left their drinks at the bar and headed for the powder rooms, holding hands and giggling as girls do. The man with the scar stood up and went over to the bar. He called the waiter and ordered drinks. As the barman turned away he administered the Rohypnol to the girls' Martinis. Moments later he was back in his chair with the vodkas. They clashed glasses and downed them in one.

Twenty long minutes passed and still the girls hadn't returned, causing the men to fear that they might have already left via the back door of the Bolshoi. The one with the scar was just about to go and check, when to his relief, they came back arm in arm, still giggling.

Their lovemaking had left the girls sated and thirsty and so they downed their Martini's swiftly, oblivious to the fact they had been tampered with. Ava decided it was to be their last and called Yuri over to arrange a taxi. Just minutes later the Rohypnol began to take its insidious effect. The girls quickly became confused, rocking precariously on their barstools, at which point that the two men decided to make their move.

"Girls!"

The man with the scar called out, before putting his arm around Ava's shoulder to steady her. His tall and lean associate did the same to Katarina.

"You seem to have had a few too many drinks tonight. It looks like you could both use some fresh air."

"No, it's OK. I just feel a little woozy and..." Ava stopped mid-sentence, unable to get her mouth around the rest of her words.

Katarina, being smaller and not sharing Ava's unique powers, had already fully succumbed to the drug, and was unaware of what was going on around her. The men removed them from the establishment in as discrete a manner as was possible. They both gave excuses to the concerned guests as they passed by.

"Going away party apparently, and they've got a bit carried away with the drinks."

It was all the onlookers needed to appease their concerns.

Once outside and out of sight, the men were no longer concerned with appearances. They dragged the women, with their feet trailing along the rough road surface. The delicate leather of their stilettos shredded until the road finally dragged them from their feet.

Bortnik threw the door of the limousine open and the men dumped the girls unceremoniously on the floor in front of him. After checking the street for witnesses, they climbed in and dragged the slack bodies of the girls onto the sofa style seats. They were now sat opposite and facing each other. Both girls were conscious but confused; Katarina more so. The drug had affected both girls' motor skills such that neither could coordinate an effort to resist. The two bodyguards sat themselves either side of Katarina, with Bortnik opposite alongside Ava. He placed a pudgy hand under Ava's skirt, high up the inside of her thigh and twisted her head to face him with the other.

"Do you recognise me bitch?" Bortnik's eyes were as cold and emotionless as a shark's. "You are going to watch these men fuck your little slut friend from every direction, and then you're going to watch them choke the life out of her. Pay attention whore and know that when they are through with her, you are going to get the same from me!"

Bortnik nodded to his men to begin, twisting Ava's face so she was looking directly at Katarina.

The scarred man took hold of both sides of Katarina's low-cut dress in his fists and wrenched them apart. Her flimsy dress split in half exposing her small round breasts with only her black lace panties protecting her modesty. Katarina's face remained expressionless but her eyes showed the enormity of her terror. She began to mumble something incoherently; it sounded like a nursery rhyme to Ava.

"See Ava, the bitch is singing to us. She likes it!" Bortnik guffawed.

He slid his pudgy hand up over Ava's mound, feeling her sex through her sheer lace panties. The feel of her clearly arousing him as he urged his men on.

"Take off her pants and open the bitch so I can see what she's been hiding from me."

Bortnik's men needed no encouragement. They grabbed the delicate waistband of her panties and ripped them off, leaving her naked and vulnerable. Katarina offered no resistance as they spread her. She couldn't, she just carried on mumbling the nursery rhyme, staring imploringly into Ava's eyes with tears rolling down her face.

Just looking at Katarina in that vulnerable position was not enough for Bortnik, he urgently needed to violate her and make her suffer and let go of Ava to focus solely on her petite friend. Without his support, Ava slumped over onto her shoulder, watching helplessly as the sick rape of her dearest friend began to unfold in front of her, dreading the murder that would surely follow. Bortnik knelt between Katarina's legs dropping his trousers and briefs. He was fully aroused and about to press himself into Katarina, when he felt the cold barrel of a pistol pressed into the back of his neck.

Ava's relief was monumental. Her saviour had his back to her so she couldn't see his face, but the line of his jaw and his well-formed ear were familiar. Thank God we're saved, was Ava's last thought, before she lost consciousness.

-------------------------------------------------------------------------

"Put that in her and I'll blow your fucking head off!"

Bortnik recognised the gunman's voice immediately, putting his hands on his head without turning to face him. The gunman was Demitri Papandreou, a fellow Shadow and one of the Senate, powerful above all others, except for *the Hydra* herself, the Supreme Senator. Bortnik desperately tried the comrade approach.

"Demitri my old friend, I mean you no harm. These are just whores we are having some fun with. That is all," Bortnik pleaded, only to receive a pistol whipping from Demitri.

He held the back of his head, cowering at the force of the double strike. Bortnik waited for the gunshot that would end his life.

"I choose my friends Bortnik and you don't qualify," Demitri's disdain was evident in his tone. "I have invested years and a small fortune in this redhead. You will pay for stealing from me with your life, worthless as it is."

Demitri increased the pressure on the trigger.

"Don't Demitri please!" Bortnik begged. "I'll do anything for you, anything. Just spare my life."

Demitri paused for a moment, considering his options. Bortnik's life was in the balance. At last, it tipped his way and Demitri released the trigger, holstering his gun.

"In exchange for your worthless life Bortnik, you will kill this one's Aunt." He pointed at Ava. "Her name is Alisa Pashkov. You will find her in the Moscow directory. I want no trail that leads back to me on pain of your death. Do you understand?"

Demitri's glare reinforced the message and Bortnik nodded thankfully.

"And what of this one?"

Bortnik jerked his head towards Katarina. She had found the strength to tuck her arms protectively around her knees, still mumbling the nursery rhyme and staring into oblivion.

"Do what you will with her and then kill her."

Demitri's voice was cold and devoid of any mercy. He left the limousine with a sadistic smile that said everything. By morning Ava would be totally isolated without a friend in the world.

---------------------------------------------------------------------------

Ava was lost in that space that exists somewhere between madness and reality. In her dreams, she was walking along a cliff top with Katarina looking out to sea. They were laughing and holding hands, content with each other. Ava declared her undying troth to her best friend and lover.

"I will look after you forever Katarina and you will always be safe with me. I will never let you down, never. That I promise to you with all of my heart."

Their love was an almost tangible thing and Ava felt buoyed by the power of that emotion. She gazed into Katarina's soft brown eyes, seeing her love and trust reflected in them. Ava felt happier in that moment than ever before in her life, but that was before the shadows of fear passed like clouds across Katarina's gaze. Her beautiful face contorting as terror gripped her. She began to mumble a nursery rhyme as she regressed into some inner sanctuary, trying to find escape and solace.

"What is it Kat? You're scaring me. Please stop it." Ava was confused and desperate.

Somehow they were much closer to the cliff edge now, slipping ever closer. Ava tried to find some traction under her feet to pull Katarina away from the drop that seemed to beckon them. The harder she tried, the closer they got.

"Help me Ava, please help me! Don't let me die. You said you would look after me forever. You promised me Ava, you promised!"

Katarina was terrified as she teetered on the very edge of the cliff. The ground began to crumble beneath her feet and her terror mounted.

"Ava!" Katarina screamed, as she dropped over the edge.

Ava gripped Katarina's hand for all she was worth, her grip tremulously preserving their future and their love. The sudden weight dragged Ava down though, and she fell heavily on her chest. Katarina was left dangling above the rocks below clinging desperately to Ava's hand.

"Save me Ava, save me! You promised."

Ava could feel Katarina's hand slipping through hers and screamed out.

"I'm trying Kat, God I'm trying. I love you so much!"

With that, their hands parted. Katarina plummeted to the craggy rocks below, screaming out her last words.

"You promised me Ava!"

Ava could never have known that Katarina's fall happened at the precise moment that Bortnik's big pudgy hands choked the last breath out of her dearest friend.

The shock and terror of the dream brought Ava momentarily back to a state of semi consciousness. She was lying on her back in her bedroom. A man's face was above hers, dripping sweat on her as he pounded into her. His face was angled up so that all she could see was the line of his jaw and a well-formed ear. He was familiar. She knew for sure that she had seen this man in some other bedroom in some other time. Before Ava could piece it all together, she slipped back into her drug and shock induced nightmare, oblivious to the man, still relentlessly taking his pleasure from her body.

----------------------------------------------------------------------------

The black limousine came to a stop outside the high-rise apartment block on the outskirts of Moscow. The building was one of those poorly built post-war constructions that had not aged well. In consequence, it had attracted a mixed society of some of Russia's more seedy citizens. It was a dangerous neighbourhood, but all that Alisa Pashkov could afford. She lived on the ninth of fifteen floors where the lifts seldom worked, either through age or vandalism.

Bortnik cursed as he passed the seventh floor with two still to climb. He was dressed in a dark, ill-fitting suit and was sweating profusely. The perspiration from his bald pate ran into his eyes, stinging them and worsening his mood. He continued plodding up the stairs until he arrived outside the door of number 911, the name on the bell-push confirming that it was the right address. Bortnik waited a full five minutes until he had recovered enough to enjoy the act that was soon to follow. He checked his watch. It was now nearly two o'clock in the morning and likely that Alisa would be sound asleep. He gave the bell a long press, hearing the clangour through the thin prefabricated walls. He kept pressing.

----------------------------------------------------------------------------

Alisa woke to the bedlam of a bell being pressed for far too long. It added to her disorientation and panicked her, as she dragged herself from deep sleep. Alisa was in her late forties, pretty, slim and elegant. She left the bed and pulled on her white silk gown to cover her nakedness. Knowing instinctively that something was wrong, she picked up the heavy candlestick as she passed through the hallway to the door. To do so was a sad indictment of the neighbourhood that she now lived in.

"Who is it? What do you want at this ungodly hour?" Alisa tried to stop the fear from sounding in her voice.

"Something has happened to Ava. She needs you right away Alisa. I have a car waiting outside to take you straight to the hospital."

"The hospital! Oh my God what's happened to her?"

Alisa was fooled, opening the door at the mention of Ava's plight. Bortnik burst into her apartment, kicked the door closed behind him and took Alisa by the throat. She dropped the candlestick to free her hands, desperately trying to claw his grip from her neck. The man was in and there was nothing she could do about it.

Bortnik drove Alisa backwards through the house, towards the lounge where her screams would be less likely to be heard. Committing violent acts against women aroused Bortnik intensely. He shoved Alisa towards the sofa where she collapsed into a sitting position as the backs of her legs struck the edge of the seat. Alisa wanted to scream out for help, but his grip on her throat was choking her. She felt him tugging at the cord of her gown and pressed her knees together in futile defence.

"Struggle and I will kill you bitch," Bortnik hissed. "Go along with it and I'll be out of you and out of here in no time."

He slightly relaxed his grip on Alisa's throat to encourage her to obey. The tie now free, Bortnik opened her gown, his cold eyes feasting on his petrified victim. Alisa had small but pert breasts and the body of a dancer. Her legs were long and slim, with good muscle tone. Alisa's knees were still tightly pressed together though, which angered Bortnik. He slipped his big hand between her inner thighs and gave her a rat bite there, crushing her delicate skin in his big hand. Alisa screamed out in pain and opened her legs.

"Remember that I will kill you if you resist, but if you please me, I will let you go," Bortnik lied, releasing his grip on Alisa's flesh.

His pudgy hand now free, he began to probe her, noting with some satisfaction that she was dry.

Bortnik liked his women *dry*. He always thought that the wetness was for their comfort and satisfaction, not his. Foreplay was never part of Bortnik's sex, only self-gratification. He buried his face in Alisa's breasts, the stubble on his chin like sandpaper against her sensitive white skin. Bortnik began to lick them lasciviously while he fumbled with his belt to free himself.

Alisa was in a state of shock, gagging as the vulgar reality of what was about to happen fully dawned on her. The pressure of Bortnik's hand on her throat stopped the bile rising, and so the acidic fluid just burned there in her throat. She grimaced at the pain as Bortnik forced his way into her, silent tears of rage and shame flowing like rivers down her face. It didn't take Bortnik long. It never did. As he got closer and closer to his climax his hand tightened on Alisa's throat. She looked back at him in horror and disbelief. Above all else Bortnik was a liar. Her life ended in the same seconds that Bortnik found release.

"I lied," he said simply, confirming Alisa's last thought.

Bortnik stood up and fastened his trousers as he looked down at his victim disdainfully. There was something extremely sexy about naked and dead women to him. He reached into his pocket taking out his mobile. The picture he took of Alisa, violated in death, would go well in his collection, alongside the one of Katarina, he thought. Bortnik turned, leaving Alisa to be found by some other in that pitiful and undignified position.

--------------------------------------------------------------------------

It was well after midday when Ava woke with a start and a dreadful feeling of foreboding. Something was wrong, terribly wrong and she *felt* it. She was at home but didn't have a clue how she had got there. Ava reached for the bedside phone and called Katarina's number. Her heart was in her mouth, dreading that Katarina might not answer. The telephone rang endlessly, and Ava's despair for her dearest friend mounted unbearably.

Ava became aware of soreness in her groin and breasts. She felt herself and realised the worst. Her sheets were still wet with the aftermath of sex, further proof of what she feared. There was an acrid smell of a sweaty man still pervaded the air and made her gag. The image of a man above her, flashed through Ava's mind, he was faceless though. All she could remember was the strong line of his jaw and that shapely ear. She had been raped and the realisation of it disgusted her.

She tried Katarina's number again, but the call went unanswered. Her brain felt like a wet sponge inside her throbbing head, such that she couldn't think clearly. Tears of anger and humiliation ran down her face as she recalled the two men at the Bolshoi. She realised that they must have spiked their drinks and felt sure that Katarina would be waking up to the same humiliation.

Ava checked the time. It was already nearly one o'clock in the afternoon and her flight left at four. Allowing for travel and check in, she had less than thirty minutes to get ready and go. She tried Katarina's number yet again, but still there was no response. Ava needed to get a message to her and called her Aunt Alisa, but her phone remained unanswered too.

"Shit!" she cursed out loud.

Ava dragged her aching and bruised body out of bed, desperately needing to shower and get the stench of this man off her. She ran the water cold to shock her brain into action and stepped in, scrubbing her body brutally as if it would also cleanse her soul, and purge her of the disgusting ordeal. It was inevitable that something like this would happen to her one day and she hated herself for getting into these situations, more so that she had put Katarina in danger too. Ava knew she had to change her life and perhaps going away to a Muslim country might make the difference, she thought. Out of nowhere came the most dreadful realisation.

"Bortnik!" she cried out.

The memories of what happened in the limousine, suppressed by the drug, came crashing back to her in graphic detail.

"Oh my God Katarina!" she screamed out.

Ava went into a state of panic. Katarina was in the hands of this murderous monster and she felt sick with the worry and guilt of having placed her in that predicament. She quickly wound the events of the night back in her mind. The man she briefly saw on top of her in her narcosis was not Bortnik, wrong jawline for sure. That meant that he was probably the man with the gun that had rescued them. The fact that Ava was violated but safe showed that he was a pervert, not a killer. Also, he had chosen to rape her, not Katarina. She concluded that, in all likelihood, Katarina was sleeping off a drug induced hangover somewhere. Ava tried her number, but still no reply. She decided to call her again from the airport, now feeling a little easier.

Ava picked up her bags, shuddered at the memory of her last night at the Bolshoi, and left in haste for the airport.

-------------------------------------------------------------------------------

Chapter 7

It was eleven o'clock in the evening local time when Ava landed at Islamabad International Airport. The five-hour flight had been murder for her, not knowing if Katarina was safe or not. She felt guilty too about leaving her, but knew that her sponsor would not have endorsed a delay, nor permitted it. He had always said there was absolutely no margin to disobey him. Ava had already set her mobile to roaming and selected Katarina's number. Again the call failed to connect. She tried Alisa's number with the same result. The time would have been nine o'clock in Moscow and both should have been available. One mobile could be faulty but two was unlikely. Ava was desperate. The only other person she could reasonably rely on was Yuri, but she didn't have his number. There was a slim chance that he would be working at the Bolshoi at that hour. She rang and her called was put through to the bar. Yuri answered.

"Yuri! I can't tell you how relieved I am that you are there. I've been so scared." Ava started to cry with pure relief.

"Hey Ava, what's the matter? Where are you?" Yuri's concern for the girl he loved was evident.

"I've just arrived in Pakistan but I've left behind such a mess. Last night Katarina and me were at the bar, do you remember?"

"Yes of course I remember."

Yuri was a little disappointed that Ava even felt the need to ask. He knew where this was going and was already agonising about how he would tell her the terrible news.

"Well there were two men there in suits I remember. One had a scarred face and the other was taller and mean-looking. They must have put something in our drinks when we went to the bathroom. Bortnik was outside in his car, waiting to rape and kill us." Ava was going at a hundred miles an hour.

"Take a breath Ava and slow down." Yuri needed her calm for what he had to tell her.

65

"Yes, sorry. Only I don't know what happened to her. A man came into the car with a gun and he must have saved us from Bortnik. But afterwards he…" Ava couldn't say the words.

"Afterwards he did what Ava?" Yuri was firm but calm.

"Afterwards he raped me in my apartment, but Katarina wasn't there," Ava blurted.

She was half hoping that, if she said the words quickly enough, Yuri wouldn't hear. But he did and a dark rage was immediately upon him.

"The filthy scumbag! That wouldn't have happened if Bortnik hadn't abducted you in the first place. I swear to God I will find the bastard and kill him, and his two *suits*!"

Ava could tell that Yuri meant every word and shuddered at the thought.

"What did the rapist look like? I'll kill him too!"

Ava winced at the hard reality of his statement.

"I don't know. If it was the man with the gun, then he was dark and powerful with a strong chin, but that's all I saw or can remember."

"Maybe Bortnik knows him. If he does, he will tell me before he dies. You can take that as Gospel," Yuri's voice was as cold as ice.

"No Yuri, you aren't equipped to fight these men. They'll kill you and besides I'm OK, just a little soiled is all."

"Ava, you know nothing about me. To you I am just *Mr Average* but I have skills they would be wise to fear."

Yuri's words came as a shock to Ava, realising that he must have been reading her all along. She wondered who he might be. She knew that Yuri was an Angel but didn't actually know what that meant.

"You say that you will get over the abuse Ava and maybe you will, but there is something I have to tell you that will be very much harder." Yuri took a deep breath to settle himself. "There were two women murdered last night and one of them was Katarina."

Suddenly, there was no air in the building and the ceiling seemed to hit the floor. A full half minute passed before Ava could reply. When she did, her response was cold and measured.

"Swear to me that you won't kill Bortnik Yuri. He is mine. Swear it on your life!" Ava's hate for this despicable man was equal to her grief and she wanted revenge. "Who was the other?"

"I swear it," Yuri conceded. "The other murder last night was a woman called Alisa Pashkov, not associated with the Bolshoi."

That was the knock-out blow. Ava collapsed, her mobile phone shattering as it hit the marble flooring, spewing its casing and SIM card across the corridor. Ava's last means of contacting the outside world was lost. She was now truly alone.

--------------------------------------------------------------------------

When Ava regained consciousness in the back of an ambulance, she was being attended by a medic, a giant of a man in a rumpled, ill-fitting uniform. Another was sat on the bench seat, dressed in a traditional *shalwar kameez*. His baggy pants were white with a three quarter length white shirt buttoned high in the neck. A long and dense grey beard adorned most of his face and he wore open sandals. The man looked old but resilient, with a rangy frame and not an ounce of fat on him. It was as if this arid land had dried him out and fossilised him. He smiled back at Ava through gapped teeth, but there was nothing spontaneous about his smile. His was a smile without a soul.

"I am the Mullah Ismael Alansari, blessed with the pleasure of being your mentor for the next six months. Your sponsor has deemed that it be so."

Ava had expected his voice to be feeble but it was vibrant, almost vitriolic. His tone unnerved her.

"I'm sorry but I have to leave on the next plane only something terrible has happened at home and I must..."

The Mullah cut her short.

"There is no question of you returning woman," his tone was derisive. "*Allah* has chosen you to do his holy work. You *will* obey and give your life in exchange for martyrdom, if *Allah* deems that gift necessary."

There was coldness in the man's eyes that went way past icy. The snakes of fear began to coil in Ava's stomach.

"*Allah* is not my God!" she countered petulantly, sitting up with clear intent to leave.

"Blasphemy!" the Mullah shrieked as he struck Ava across the face with the back of his hand. "You will pay for that with lashes, until you declare *Allah* to be your one and only God."

The Mullah turned to the medic.

"Tie her up and sedate her. The disbeliever will soon learn both the wrath and forgiveness of the one true God!"

Ava tried to resist and focus her anger to summon up her inner destructive powers, but once again they let her down. She was helpless. The injection stung like a bee and then there was peace.

--------------------------------------------------------------------------

When Ava woke, she was naked in a gloomy room with a single barred window set high up. A shard of light slashed through the room falling on a whitewashed wall on the far side. Its reflection only partially illuminating the room, otherwise the room was almost completely dark. Her first reaction to her nakedness was to check herself. She sighed in relief, as she confirmed that she hadn't been violated.

As Ava's eyes became more accustomed to the sombre light, she surveyed her quarter. She got up shakily and walked across to the rough wooden door. There was some kind of service hatch set at head level but both door and hatch were locked. It wasn't a room she concluded, it was a cell. Ava had always been afraid of being locked away with her demons and now she was. There was an iron bunk with a dirty mattress and a single blanket, set against the windowed wall. Opposite, was an open-holed latrine with an old enamel basin and a single leaky tap set to one side. The stench from the latrine was overpowering and Ava dreaded ever having to use it, vowing unreasonably that she would kill herself first.

The only other furniture in the cell was a table and a single chair set in the middle of the room. Placed on the table was a book, a candle and a black garment of some kind. Ava picked up the book.

"The *Quran*," she read out loud. "Great that's just what I need."

Ava put the book down and picked up the neatly folded garment. She shook it until the folds fell out and was horrified as she realised that it was a burka.

"What the fuck?" she gasped.

Ava buckled at the knees. The fear of what lay ahead hit her like a kick in the stomach and she felt faint. Ava grabbed the table for support until the giddiness passed, then sat down on the chair with her head in her hands.

"Oh Katarina, what have I done?" she wailed.

Ava had never felt so totally alone and scared. Not even after her mother had been murdered. She cried until there were no more tears to be shed. After that, she swore an oath out loud so that all who cared could hear.

"I will survive this and have my revenge!" Ava needed something to focus her hatred on and thought of Bortnik. "You will die a thousand deaths when I find you Bortnik, and I *will* find you, I swear it on Katarina's grave!"

Ava suddenly became aware of the cold, having been too numb with shock to notice before. Now, shivering violently, she reluctantly slipped the rough cotton burka over her head, letting it envelop her body, until it reached the floor around her feet. All that showed of her former identity were her eyes, but they were no longer blue. The brown flecks in her eyes had gathered and condensed until they were almost black. There was a storm brewing inside Ava, something she vaguely recognised from before. It filled her with fear and dread. If only she could harness that force and release it on command, then God help them! They would learn to fear who, or what she really was, which was something close to an ungodly monster.

"I will show them fire and brimstone on a biblical scale," Ava muttered venomously. "They will all rue the day they ever met Ava Kaplinski!"

She smiled for the first time since she and Katarina were at the bar in the Bolshoi. That smile was empty though; as empty as her life.

---------------------------------------------------------------------------

Ava hardly slept through the night through fear, cold and hunger. She couldn't believe that Pakistan could be this cold at night in late July, and concluded that she must be in a basement underground. That would explain the window being so unusually high up the wall. A dungeon no less, she surmised.

Ava had no idea of the time or indeed how long she had been there. It couldn't be more than twenty-four hours she deduced; otherwise she would have been absolutely starving and dehydrated. Ava recalled the tanned Arab in the ambulance, with his craggy face, grey beard and gapped teeth. She decided that the Mullah was not only religious, but a zealot. He had talked of a lashing for her blasphemy and didn't look the type to make idle threats.

They will not break me, Ava pledged. I will take what they give and feed my hatred with it until this dark force inside me emerges. Ava had an inner strength in line with her physical strength, something else that her mother's genes had blessed her with. She could place herself outside of her body for short periods and disassociate herself from pain.

"I will take that beating," Ava declared, "and use your cesspool of a toilet. When I come through this, and I will, revenge will be sweet!"

Ava glared defiantly at the locked cell door, her jaw purposely set; reinforcing the words she had just spoken. At last Ava fell into a deep sleep and found solace in oblivion.

-----------------------------------------------------------------------------

Ava stirred from her slumber to the sound of jangling keys and the heavy door latch opening. Two men entered dressed in their traditional white *shalwar kameez's* and round *Sindhi* caps. They were both lean and bearded and spoke in Urdu, the national language of Pakistan. It was one of the many languages her sponsor had instructed her to learn, which now appeared to be no coincidence. He would be another man that she would find and kill, she decided.

"Get up infidel!" the taller of the two cried out in disdain.

Ava glared back at them in defiance. The force of the blow she received for that pathetic show of resistance bloodied her nose and loosed three teeth. Ava swallowed her pride and capitulated, knowing that this wasn't the time to rebel, needing to first learn and prepare. The blow did however reinforce Ava's hatred of her captors. She was determined to draw strength from that emotion and use it to reinforce her resolve. Ava needed to endure to avenge Katarina and Alisa.

The guards took an arm each and forced them up behind Ava's back. Now unable to resist, they frog-marched her out of the cell and up the stone steps that led to a small courtyard. When Ava stepped outside into the brilliant sunshine, it took a few moments for her eyes to become accustomed to the glare. When they did, she saw two men in traditional dress standing by a wooden structure. That structure looked very much like gallows to Ava, even to the rope dangling from it. Her blood ran cold.

One of the men swished a dark brown leather whip menacingly, and the other was the Mullah. The two guards marched her roughly to the gallows.

"Strip the whore that she may better feel the whip on her back and repent her sins!" the Mullah's voice was shrill and fanatical. "Not until you accept *Allah* as your one true God and beg his mercy, will the beating stop. Praise be to the prophet Mohammed, defender of the faith!"

They reversed Ava's arms and lashed them roughly above her head so that she was strung from the gallows on her tiptoes. The coarse rope burnt like fire on her slim wrists but Ava looked back defiantly at the men with her chin held high.

"Fuck you, fuck your prophets and fuck *Allah*!" Ava spat out the words in pure hatred.

"Let the thrashing begin!" the Mullah screamed. "The whore will beg forgiveness for her blasphemy, or die by the whip."

His subordinate uncoiled the thick leather whip like a snake. Ava stared back at the Mullah with eyes blazing.

"Fuck you!" she yelled again in defiance.

The whip slashed through the air and cracked like the snapping of a dried branch, wrapping around Ava's back. The thick cord of the whip immediately brought up a red welt as thick as a man's finger.

The pain was excruciating but Ava didn't flinch. Instead she used it to focus on disassociating her mind from her body to free her spirit. By the time the fifth lash came Ava was already in that *out of body* state, her hatred mounting with each crack of the man's whip, building the dark forces within her.

The Mullah came over to Ava until they were face to face.

"Repent woman!" he ordered.

The normally implacable Mullah was becoming unnerved at Ava's resilience; caught between losing face, or suffering the wrath of Demitri should this unholy creature die in his hands.

"Fuck you!" she spat the words mixed with saliva in his face.

Ava never took her eyes off the Mullah. They were pitch black now and burned like coals with her hatred. She grinned back at him in defiance. By the time the twentieth blow landed, the two men who had brought her up from the cell were already looking away. Even they were uncomfortable with the brutal torture inflicted on such a delicate looking woman.

"He will kill her," one muttered.

"It is in *Allah's* hands," replied the other.

As Ava's tormentor raised the whip for the twenty-fifth time, Ava jerked her gaze away from the Mullah, casting those murderous black eyes on her assailant, almost freezing him in time.

The blood-soaked, plaited leather thong that had torn away Ava's flesh seemed to have taken on a life of its own. The whip inexplicably coiled around the man's neck like a snake until his eye balls bulged and his face purpled. Ava's stare bored into the man's soul as the rope tightened, choking the life out of him, forcing him to his knees, his squat tongue protruding from pursed lips as he desperately tried to claw the whip from his throat. When death came, the man toppled forwards, his bulging eyes still staring sightlessly at his executioner. He would never have seen Ava's eyes changing back to blue with those golden brown flecks, as she slipped into unconsciousness. Despite her dreadful ordeal, there was a peaceful smile on Ava's face. At last she had found some control over the dark powers that lay within her, powers that she needed to nurture and hone to wreak the revenge they all deserved.

The Mullah had to quickly re-think the situation. He had not been warned. This woman was not human nor of his breed. She was an anomaly, an abomination of nature; something to be feared. He considered she might be an Angel, but ruled that possibility out on the grounds that they would never resort to the needless killing of others, as this woman had done. For now though, the Mullah had to make sure she didn't take an infection and die under his control. That would make a dangerous enemy of Demitri and probably cost his life.

"Take the demon woman and bathe her!" the Mullah demanded. "Coat her wounds in antiseptic and wrap them with clean cotton. From now on you will only go to her cell armed and in twos. If she dies then so will you."

Neither guard had any doubt that it would not be so.

--------------------------------------------------------------------------

Ava lay on her bunk staring up into the darkness. The out of body experience and her supercharge of adrenaline, had deserted her, leaving her depleted and in agony. Her first conscious breath expanded her rib cage, stretching the flayed skin on her back. The pain was excruciating and Ava cried out. She gingerly pulled up her burka to inspect the damage and was relieved to see that they had tended to her. Ava knew that her natural powers of regeneration would do the rest within days. Until then, all she could do was to bear the pain and be patient.

Ava considered what had happened to her, what she had done and why they had troubled to treat her wounds. Clearly, they hadn't wanted to kill her, or they would not have bandaged her, conceding that she must be of some value to them. Ava was puzzled though. The beating had made no sense. She doubted that the accusation of blasphemy would have warranted such brutality. So why then; why had they whipped her? It was control by fear, she concluded.

Ava had shown none though. She realised that fact alone, would place her in even more danger. They would be afraid of her now; that was for sure. Ava resigned herself to the fact that she might have to cooperate with her captors in order to survive, for now at least. Something positive had come out of the beating though, for the first time, Ava had been able to focus her anger and control it. Until then, her telekinetic powers had been destructive but random. She naturally thought of how she had failed to focus that rage and save her mother and Katarina, when they desperately needed her. The pain of those failures hurt even more than the brutal flogging. Ava felt no remorse for the man that she had killed though, making her feel even more inhuman than she already was.

"He deserved to die," Ava whispered, by means of justification. "And he won't be the last!" she vowed.

Ava pondered that if *they* were interested in her before showing those destructive powers, then they would be even more so now. The key to everything was her sponsor. Ava was sure of that. Somehow, she had to find him, and the Mullah would lead her there. Ava was sure of that too. She decided to go along with whatever they wanted, endure and feed her hatred.

Was the man her benefactor or betrayer? She wondered. Only time would tell. For now though, what Ava really needed was sleep and hate; lots of hate. To that end she thought of Bortnik, the Mullah and revenge. There was no space right now for grief and self-pity. She would only allow herself that later, when her ordeal was all over.

------------------------------------------------------------------------

Chapter 8

24th November 2015. London Heathrow.

Callum Knight disembarked from the Boeing VC-25 at London Heathrow airport, in-bound from Moscow. He had travelled nearly two thousand miles but not exchanged the weather, as it was still raining and bitter cold. The summit meeting he had attended was essentially a sub-set of the United Nations National Security Council, which had solved nothing nor revealed any surprises. The usual inertia, international politics and posturing had denied any tangible benefits arising from the five days of talks. Of course there would be the usual spin put on the outcome to convince the people that their governments had at least a clue, or even cared about what was going on in the world. Moscow had essentially been chosen as the venue to encourage the engagement of the Russians, who were currently obstructing any kind of cohesive international approach to terrorism.

Callum was in his early fifties, with a good head of fair, sun streaked hair, swept back exposing a broad forehead above a strong nose and clear blue lively eyes. His bronzed face was etched with the character lines of his age, but otherwise, in attitude and deportment, he appeared to be in his early forties. He was an approachable man who exuded confidence and credibility. Callum, a retired Major in the Parachute Regiment, had attended the conference as strategic and tactical advisor to the Prime Minister, consulted in all matters pertaining to terrorism and arms escalation. On this occasion, Callum was there particularly to assist the Prime Minister in the understanding of the political posturing of the increasingly dangerous countries that made up the United Nations.

Most of what he dealt with was off the public agenda. Three burning issues were the imminent threats of a dirty bomb, biological attack and cyber-warfare, all three coming out of a destabilised Middle East. The *Arab Spring* had isolated Russia and brought with it the greatly increased risk of all these occurrences. Current intelligence had raised the threat level for international terrorism in the UK from 'severe' to 'critical', meaning that an attack was imminent.

Fortunately, Britain and the USA had their own handshakes in place. Callum was *en-route* to meet the British Prime Minister and the President of the United States at Number 10 Downing Street. Information already received, confirmed that a small radioactive explosive device, otherwise known as a dirty bomb, had already been designed and ready for deployment. The bomb was rumoured to be a strategic product of the Iranian government, comprised of a network of unelected institutions controlled by the all-powerful conservative Supreme Leader. The bomb's existence was known only to a select few, but its impact would have been felt politically around the world.

Strategic placement of this device could easily de-stabilise the already precariously balanced world peace initiative, and plunge those countries with nuclear capability into confusion. This scenario had been discussed behind closed doors at the summit and was rigorously denied by the Iranian government. It was the general and informed consensus of them all, that the Iranian government was in fact aware of the existence of the dirty bomb, but unable to control the situation.

The initiative was almost certainly planned by the *Shadow organisation.* Iran was powerless against them and would simply pick up the blame, conveniently giving the Americans just cause to intercede and dismantle their nuclear capability. Such intervention would then unite the warring factions of the Arab Nations to fight as one against the *infidels* in a holy war. This would fulfil one of the Islamic end-of-time prophecies, further destabilising the Middle East and therefore the world. It was manipulation such as this that enhanced the successful outcome of the Shadow organisation's plans for expansion.

The very existence of that organisation was itself a matter of the highest security. Outside of secret departments within America, Britain and Israel, nobody knew of their official existence. That ignorance included both incumbents, the Prime Minister and the President.

Callum followed behind the Prime Minister's limousine in one of the security outriders that formed the cavalcade heading for Downing Street. He was sharing the car and a glass of Bollinger with his American counterpart, Bud Lewinski. Bud was a product of the American military, a Green Beret, tough talker, strategist, drinker and a worthy adversary. Both had worked in covert operations over the last thirty years and had a deep respect for each other. They also shared the same genes, *Angel* genes.

"It's time to come clean at the highest level," Callum began, tabling the possibility.

He had the measure of his long-standing ally and had judged his moment well.

"Indeed," the burly American conceded. "Desperate times call for desperate measures. And it don't get more desperate than this Callum. Armageddon is staring us right in the goddamn face."

-------------------------------------------------------------------------

Callum Knight and Bud Lewinski sat informally in the Prime Minister's lounge in the company of the two world leaders. Their personal secretaries and stenographer had been asked to leave. What was going to be said now had to remain behind closed doors, as the consequences of a security breach were unthinkable. The President, a tall imposing man in his early fifties, with a good head of brown hair and piercing blue eyes was first to broach the subject. He turned to their two tactical advisors in nothing less than an accusing manner.

"So perhaps you two cowboys can tell us what the hell is going on out there?"

Callum exchanged glances with his counterpart and there was an unspoken accord between them. Callum would be the more eloquent in this situation.

"Mr President, Prime Minister. There has been a potentially catastrophic shift in the axis of power globally. We are not talking between nation and nation; we are talking about something

78

between races. Let me advise you that the information you are about to hear may make you subsequently un-electable by your own people."

The Prime Minister, a rotund man in his sixties, balding but alert, turned to Callum, his advisor, and put it to him frankly.

"Do we reasonably have any choice Callum?"

"No Sir," he began. "What we have to say will happen in the period of both of your offices' unless we stop it. If what we fear does happen, then you will not escape your responsibilities. To make it perfectly clear gentlemen, this problem is imminent and will not transcend elections."

Callum was one of those unique men that naturally commanded the attention of his subordinates, peers and superiors. He was a man who could walk through worlds.

The Prime Minister and President had clearly come to an agreement during their journey back from Moscow on board Air Force One, the Presidential aircraft. The President spoke for both.

"We are ready to hear what you have to say; all of it and God help us."

Callum continued in his easy manner.

"What we have to say will challenge all that you currently accept as fact and probably your religion too. All your extra-terrestrial fears of what Area 51 in the Nevada desert could be, well they simply are."

There was a visible and reluctant acceptance by two of the most powerful men on Earth, about what they were about to hear.

"To understand the present, you need to understand the past." Callum handed over two folders tied in red ribbon marked 'Top Secret'. "All you need to know is in this document but I will *précis* it for you now."

Callum knew that what he was about to tell the leaders, was going to blow them away.

"It is now a known fact that our planet has been under observation by an alien nation across the millennia. Over five thousand years ago, that nation sent a manned expedition to colonise this planet. There were two humanoid life forms on board the craft originating from two different worlds in the Andromeda Galaxy, both subsequently lost to planet-killing asteroids. They numbered three hundred and fifty of which three hundred were from the planet, *Angelos*. These people we now know as *Angels*. There is no religious connotation here gentlemen; it is simply about their origin. They were a highly evolved and compassionate race, genetically compatible with us. They chose to integrate, and their bloodline is now as ingrained in our people as that of any other culture. You would not recognise them apart, and indeed you work alongside some of them daily."

The Prime Minister and President exchanged disbelieving looks.

"Working alongside aliens? You've gotta be shitting me!"

The words from the President were of surprise, not challenge. No one would dare to feed him disinformation.

"Indeed not," Callum continued. "The influence of the Angels on our society has been positive. Our science and medicine have advanced significantly more than they might have otherwise. More importantly, and despite appearances, the Angels have brought more peace, harmony and freedom than we would otherwise have enjoyed. Their high level of evolution brought some amazing skills such as telepathy, mind control, telekinesis, longevity and rejuvenation. Unfortunately, these skills have mostly diminished with the mixing of bloods over the millennia. Now only few Angels have them to any significant degree."

Callum paused; the world changing information was a lot for his audience to take in.

"That is the good news gentlemen. The other fifty colonials were from the planet *Shados*. We know them as *Shadows*. It is their organisation that is now responsible for the destabilisation of the Middle East, including the current threat of the deployment of a dirty bomb."

"And what did the Shadows bring with them?" the Prime Minister asked.

He was pretty sure that he wasn't going to like the response.

"Most of the confusion that exists today is the simple answer Prime Minister," Callum continued. "The Shadows did not integrate and consequently did not dilute their abilities, although they were lesser than the Angels' in the first place. These powers include mind control, great physical strength and a longevity that allows them to live for some thousands of years. Because they maintained a pure bloodline, the balance of power has tipped their way. They have become the ruling power in today's global society consisting of the oligarchs, corrupt politicians, religious leaders, zealots and terrorists. Most wars and even the Spanish Inquisition, which cost the lives of millions, were instigated by this Shadow organisation. The latter was a covert way of orchestrating the genocide of the entire Angel race, which was the only obstacle that stood, and still stands, in the Shadows' way to total global control."

"So, we're talking here about a war between the Illuminati and Guardian Angels then?" offered the President.

In the President's mind, there had to be a connection between the Shadows and an organisation as globally powerful as the Illuminati.

"If you like," Callum conceded, "but not in a religious way, as I have already said."

"Why the hell, after thousands of years of secrecy, are you telling us now?" the President pressed.

"Because things have recently gotten out of hand," Bud interjected.

He had taken the opportunity to step in and expand on Callum's brief.

"As Major Knight has explained; the Angel race has been losing their genetic skills and supremacy over time through human couplings. Their decision to integrate started the clock ticking. Now they no longer hold sway over the Shadows, whose network of power is becoming unstoppable. The Shadow organisation has recently escalated their plans to destabilise the world and gain control, not only through the strategic detonation of the dirty bomb that we have talked of, but through parallel campaigns. Our latest intelligence suggests that the bomb will be followed immediately by some kind of a biological attack and cyber-warfare."

"And what exactly is the mechanism that will give them ultimate global control?" The Prime Minister was already considering his options.

"First, you've got to understand that the Shadows already have huge international financial control through legitimate business, including communications, shipping, oil, gas, electricity, research laboratories and world banking. They have infiltrated religions and governments, enabling them to exercise their control through false prophets and corrupt politicians. It goes on…"

Bud let that sink in before continuing.

"If you add to this perfect storm, the panic that ensues from radioactive fallout and a biological release; then cripple the world banking organisation through some kind of cyber-attack, so there isn't any money. Well you know where that takes us. We'd be held to ransom by our own people, and there wouldn't be a goddamn thing we could do about it but give up and pay up."

It was a sobering thought. The Prime Minister nodded to his American ally. They were in agreement.

"You can leave us now while we read these documents and consider our individual positions. Remain available. We will reconvene later this evening. Thank you gentlemen, that will be all for now."

-----------------------------------------------------------------------

Three long hours later, Callum and Bud were recalled to continue with their brief. The Prime Minister and President were sat in comfortable chairs by the open fire, papers strewn on the low table, and both drinking Jack Daniels with ice.

"Pour yourselves a drink and join us boys, I think we're all going need one."

The President's casual manner confirmed that the meeting was still informal. They poured themselves whiskey and sat down in the two chairs set for them. Bud paid particular attention to his drink, swilling the ice around and savouring the classic light liquorice aroma of the Jack Daniels.

"We've both read and considered your report," the President began. "What it contains changes all we currently understand about world organisation, its players and its politics. It is apparent that we must now consider two new super-powers; one a friend and ally and the other a deadly foe. Am I right?"

The President fixed them with an inquisitive look but the question was rhetorical. He continued, not waiting for a reply.

"First, tell us more about our allies; this Principal Matriarch, their leader *Maelströminha*. What's her story?"

Callum fielded the question.

"She's the older of two sisters that are the only remaining Angels of true blood. They were chosen to secure their bloodline, breeding stock to put it bluntly. Maelströminha or *May*, as she is known and her sister *Crystalita*, are both over five thousand years old. In appearance though, you would place them in their mid-twenties. Maelströminha, I'm sorry May, is currently with child. That offspring will be the first birthing of a near pure Angel in millennia and that child will have near full Angel ability. The birth will signal the start of the rejuvenation of their race. This is what has caused the Shadows to take radical action now, while they still can."

"These Angel powers interest me." The President looked openly intrigued. "I mean how devastating are they?"

Callum was expecting the President to home in on the power aspect and was already prepared.

"That depends on the individual's ancestry. The number of times that their ancestors married into the Angel bloodline is the defining factor. They can attain great age, but again that is dependent on the quality and integrity of their genes. Physically they can be significantly stronger. Their bone density is generally greater than ours and they have denser muscle tissue, which greatly increases their power making them phenomenal athletes. But that is the least of their abilities."

Callum could sense the two leaders' astonishment. They were willing him on.

"You have to understand that the Angel race is many millions of years older and more advanced than ours. The *powers* that they have are only where we will finally evolve to, where we will be in tens of millions of years' time. That is if we don't destroy our civilisation first," Callum added ironically.

"Their brains have evolved to use almost all of their potential, whereas we have yet to unleash even a fraction of ours. As said, their skills include telepathy, mind control, self-healing, regeneration and telekinesis, which is their most impressive ability. That ability depends on how pure the bloodline is and can be hugely destructive. Again, this is in varying degrees from almost nothing to May's full skill-set."

"And that is?" the President prompted.

"All of those I have mentioned, but May and her full-blooded sister have a destructive power over nature on a biblical scale; fire and brimstone if you like. They can influence physical systems; cause lightning to strike, the earth to quake and the elements to change their state. It is not beyond them to cause an eternal winter."

This was testing the bounds of credibility for the President.

"You can't keep powers like that secret over thousands of years. It's not possible, preposterous even. Someone would have to have known and spilled the beans."

"No, they are smarter than that," Callum assured. "A lot of the early and significant manifestations of Angel power has been manipulated and found its way into myth and folk law. The Angels created the myth of the ancient Gods as a way to educate the world and to give us a code of conduct to follow. Even the Ten Commandments were an Angel initiative. They have exercised gentle control over us for thousands of years, guiding us towards the better side of our nature, helping us to make the right choices."

"This beggars belief!" The Prime Minister was incredulous.

He stood and walked to the widow, looking out onto the street below. It was almost as if to confirm that the *real* world still existed somewhere out there.

Callum sipped on his Jack Daniels as he considered how much of the facts he needed to impart at this stage. There was a real danger of telling these powerful men too much. If word got out, the world's super powers would compete to gain control of the Angel's gifts. They would try and use them in war. He decided not to tell them about the existence of the *portals*. The idea of being able to access other times and travel through space would be an unmissable opportunity. There would be an all-out race to gain control of what would be the ultimate war machine. He decided to allude to their possibility only at this stage.

"Angel and indeed even Shadow technology, is infinitely more advanced than ours. We have intelligence that suggests that the Shadows are well advanced in the possibility of four dimensional and maybe even five dimensional travel. We believe they have recruited some of the world's most prominent scientists to explore this possibility."

His statement was part of the truth at least. The fact was that the Shadows already had control of ten of the fifty portals that came with the mother ship over five thousand years ago. They were already well versed in time travel. Research into the possibility of fifth dimensional travel was the new threat which surpassed any other form of warfare. The shock of what Callum had imparted was patently evident on the faces of the two leaders. It was the Prime Minister who recovered his power of speech first.

"The fourth dimension is time, isn't it? What on Earth is the fifth?"

Bud swilled the ice around his glass and downed the drink in one copious mouthful before taking over from Callum.

"Right on the button Mr. Prime Minister, the fourth *is* time. If you could travel backward, then you could change the order of things and control the outcome. Then again if you could travel forward in time, you could see the result of your actions and change them accordingly. It would be an infinitely more powerful weapon than the atomic bomb."

Bud paused to refresh his glass.

"Mind if I fix myself another?"

The Prime Minister signalled his consent with a dismissive wave of his hand. Bud continued as he poured.

"Now as for the fifth dimension, well we're not entirely sure. We believe that it's our consciousness, spiritual maybe. It might be imagination, infinite possibility if you like. All we can be sure of is that it's no *physical* place. You are not going to travel there other than in your dreams."

"Are you talking about a fantasy world?" the Prime Minister asked.

He stood up again and began to pace up and down the lounge, trying to make sense or this madness.

"In part Prime Minister," Bud continued. "But the implications of a fifth dimension are boundless. The world is only what we perceive it to be with our given senses. If you've gotten control of the fifth dimension, well you could rewrite the whole goddamn book."

"Armageddon," the Prime Minister conceded. "So that's why you have chosen to confide in us? You want us to meet with this *Maelströminha*, or May as you call her, and join her in war against the Shadows."

This was going to be the tough bit. Bud strategically dipped out to let Callum answer the tricky question.

"Well no, not exactly Prime Minister. May is apolitical and would not agree to meet with you. Nor would you wish her to do so. Your minds would be an open book to her. You wouldn't be able to hide your thoughts and innermost desires. She already knows that you would be unable to stop yourselves from plotting on how you might take control and use her powers to your own ends."

The Prime Minister and the President exchanged glances. They knew that she was right. It would be irresistible. The President spoke for the both.

"What is that you would have us do?"

------------------------------------------------------------------------

After their meeting, Callum and Bud left Number 10 on foot for the Savoy Hotel in London's Strand. It was a cold, dark and wet November night and they needed the fresh air to clear their heads. Besides, it was only a fifteen-minute brisk walk. They chose the scenic route, taking them down to Victoria Embankment following the Thames to the Savoy Pier before cutting north to the Strand. The walk gave them the opportunity to reflect on their meeting.

"Well the cat's well and truly out of the bag now," Bud initiated the exchange.

"Indeed it is. But *if* we can sort this mess out favourably, then Maelströminha will erase all memories of the occurrence later. After all she's done that on numerous occasions before."

"Quite Callum; but that little word *if* scares the shit outta me."

"Let's count the positives Bud. We have now secured whatever American and British resources we need without any questions being asked, plus unlimited funding. On top of that, we have secured the support of the Israelis. Not bad for a day's work, I would say!"

"Not bad at all," Bud agreed, nodding his head thoughtfully. "Setting up our HQ on the British Sovereign Base at *Ágios Nikólaos* in Cyprus does it for me. Those boys from the Joint Service Signal Organisation, or JSSO, can listen right into the heart of Russia and the Middle East. The intel we can gather there will make finding that dirty bomb pretty much a walk in the park."

Lewinski's summation was perhaps an over simplification. But under the employ of the British Secret Intelligence Service, more commonly known as MI6, this listening station was tracking every media broadcast and targeted phone call in this troubled and volatile region.

"We need to set up a core team of professionals. Any names come to mind Callum?"

"Well Ralph Robinson, Mike Jackson and Red Jake, for starters. They all have impeccable records and Middle East experience in covert operations. They will of course have their own teams to bring into play. Then there's Craig Jamieson for his medical skills. He has saved my life on more than one occasion and Sean

O'Malley is a must. Best helicopter pilot you'll ever find on both sides of the Atlantic." Callum paused for thought.

"Oh, and you can add to that Ben and Elizabeth Robinson. They might appear young, but they were trained and developed by May herself. Working together they're a formidable force, having virtually the same powers as the Matriarch."

It was much the list that Bud had expected, but he had the drop on Callum, having just received the latest update from the Matriarch.

"Sorry Callum but no-can-do on the Robinsons. News just in from Maelströminha is that she and Elizabeth are too close to popping babies. Ben's powers without his sister to reinforce them are not sufficient to take the risk of losing him. Ralph has his hands full with all of them, so we got to do this outside of their gene pool; bigger fish to fry and all that."

Bud took just a little too much pleasure from being one step ahead of Callum, who let it go gracefully and put the matter down to friendly rivalry.

"OK I'll think on it. Who have you got?"

"I can add Bart Jeffries for his logistical talents, and Larry Madison for his nuclear experience. Then we've got to have some eye candy, that'll be Kayla Lovell."

Bud was perfectly aware that Callum already knew Kayla and there was a mischievous twinkle in his eye. It was common knowledge that Callum and Kayla had history; a torrid love affair that had ended acrimoniously. Callum was the kind of man to put a ring on a girl's finger. Kayla, on the other hand, was a collector of rings. She had issues with fidelity.

Callum had to concede to her selection though. There was no sharper mind, linguist, innovator and strategist than Major General Kayla Lovell. She alone could make the difference.

"Yeah, I'll go with that," was all that Callum could say under the circumstances.

-----------------------------------------------------------------------------

## Chapter 9

Demitri Papandreou stood on his balcony looking out across the foothills towards Mount Olympus. The air was humid and heavy and the skies dark and threatening. It was early December and today the Grecian sun was not shining on the port city of Thessaloniki. A stiff north-easterly breeze agitated the Aegean Sea, raising white horses as it was drawn in to feed the thunderheads forming like anvils above the mythical mountain of Olympus. As was custom, Demitri wore his white silk robe that he favoured at breakfast time.

"A storm is brewing on the mountain Hydie," Demitri said thoughtfully.

He turned to face the slim, beautiful and elegant woman sat with him at the breakfast table. She appeared to be in her early forties but *the Hydra*, Supreme Senator of all Shadows, had been on this Earth for nearly five thousand years. She was named after the serpent in Greek mythology, who was the guardian of the gates to the Underworld. Like the mythical Hydra, Hydie Papandreou was guardian of the Shadow Empire. Just as the fabled serpent grew two heads for each cut off, this Hydra managed to grow twice as strong after each attempt on overthrowing her government. Despite her beauty and elegance, the Hydra was a ruthless dictator and killer. Her word was obeyed to the letter, even by her husband, Demitri.

"It won't be the first storm to have brewed there, will it *agápe mou*?"

The dark-haired beauty raised a perfectly groomed eyebrow teasingly. Demitri understood her innuendo. She was referring to when they had conceived their son *Anaxis* on that very mountain.

"But that was over a thousand years ago, Hydie. There have been many *storms* since then." Demitri was referring to their tempestuous relationship.

"Perhaps Demitri, but none that can compare; none that left me with the creation of life in my womb afterwards."

The softness in Hydie's eyes suddenly evaporated like clouds and they became hard and steely.

She remembered how the Principal Matriarch of the Angels, Maelströminha, had taken Anaxis's life in the mother of all battles between their races. Even the passing of a thousand years had not dulled the pain. Demitri came over to comfort her.

"We still have time *agápe mou*. You are still fertile and will be for some hundreds of years yet. We must be patient."

"Patient!" the Hydra was fuming. "Don't patronise me Demitri. It didn't take you long to impregnate that dancing whore's mother! Only weeks, wasn't it? You have always saved your best for someone else."

Demitri was on dangerous ground now. The subject of his organised affair with Anastasia Kaplinski often came up in times of rage, particularly when she was reminded of their son Anaxis.

"Hydie, I know that it still pains you as it pains me, but it was not an affair of the heart with Anastasia, it was a means to an end as well you know. Besides, I killed her when she was of no further use to us, did I not?"

It was the same conversation they'd had for almost three decades. Somehow to talk of their loss was cathartic for the Hydra and so Demitri tolerated her rebukes.

"We now have a weapon that we can use against the Angels, one that is all powerful. Soon we will have the control of one who can walk undetected amongst them. There is enough Angel in Ava Kaplinski from her mother, that she will pass all scrutiny. Ultimately, we will place her beside the Matriarch and she will avenge our son. This will happen for us Hydie, I swear it."

The Hydra's manner mellowed. She knew that Demitri had seduced Anastasia for her and the greater good of all Shadows. Hydie was a woman though, a woman with pride. Months had passed since they were together and there was much to catch up on.

"Tell me of this half-breed daughter of yours Demitri, and of the fifth dimension project. I am intrigued."

Demitri had weathered the storm and welcomed the change of topic.

"The girl is in Islamabad as we speak. She is with our friend and ally, the Mullah Ismael Alansari. They are camped in one of the madrassas there, where she is isolated and alone. I had Bortnik kill her one true friend and lover, and her aunt. She is now invisible and will be un-missed."

The Hydra nodded her approval. It was everything that she wanted to hear. Demitri continued.

"Ava is being radicalised even now, partly through her uptake of religious dogma and Islamic fundamentalism, the cornerstones to becoming a jihadist, but mainly through the acts of isolating, defiling and dehumanising her."

Demitri had little faith in someone of Ava's intellect becoming brainwashed solely by religion. That was only one of the many tools at his disposal. Dehumanising was his way. When you are made to feel worthless, then you have nothing to lose and everything to gain.

"As I have said Hydie, she is totally isolated. For the last five months, her only contact has been with the Mullah and her mentor, the old Imam. She fought against their indoctrination at first, but now she is broken and devoid of spirit."

To Demitri's relief, the Hydra looked placated. He continued, tangibly relieved.

"Ava has been wearing a burka to take away her identity. There are no mirrors to reassure her of who she was. Her daily routine of labour and scriptures has been worse than punishing. She is only allowed four hours of sleep in each twenty-four, with three meagre meals a day. In short, Ava is disorientated, lonely, confused, tired and hungry; without an ally in the world. When the time is right, I will befriend her and rescue her from the hell that I have created for her. She will then be indebted to me forever."

Demitri sensed the Hydra's approval, but he realised that she might not be so enamoured about the rest of Ava's preparation. He continued cautiously.

"Ava is an extremely sexual woman Hydie, and will be finding celibacy extremely difficult. She has already seen me at the Bolshoi and made her interest in me plain. The fact that I refused her will not sit well. Once I have freed her and bedded her adequately, she will become my puppet."

The Hydra's eyes flared but she controlled her jealousy, this was as agreed.

It would have been foolish though, for Demitri to have confessed that he had already taken advantage of Ava's body, when she was in drug induced unconsciousness. The Hydra may well have killed him for that.

"And how will you place your *daughter* with the Angels?"

The Hydra's inflexion of the word *daughter* clearly portrayed her disdain and jealousy. Demitri swiftly moved on, so as not to be drawn in by her jibe.

"We have already placed some information in the hands of the Angels, Hydie. They believe that we are in an advanced stage in the manufacture of a nuclear device, which indeed we are, and ready to deploy. Also, that we have a planned cyber-attack on world banking and infrastructure. This is only a half-truth. In reality, we are still a year away from that. We have given the Angels good reason to believe that we have biotechnology and Nanotech war capability, and that a controlled release in a major city is an immediate threat. Then for good measure, we have begun a series of terrorist attacks on tourism through our comrades in the Islamic State to further destabilise the Arab States."

Demitri allowed himself a wry smile. He knew that he had a winning hand; one that would gain the Hydra's favour.

"The seeds of disinformation have already borne fruit my love. The President of the United States and his lap dog the British Prime Minister, have called another emergency summit meeting of the United Nations National Security Council. The summit will be held in Moscow next month, from the 6th to the 10<sup>th</sup> of January. Not coincidentally, that will be the month following the completion of Ava Kaplinski's radicalisation."

"You are spoon feeding me again Demitri. Get to the point!"

This was no more than her sources had already told her.

"The point *agápe mou*, is that the President and Prime Minister have already put a task force together headed by Callum Knight and Bud Lewinski. Both are Angels, which you are well aware of. Both have cost our cause dearly, through their numerous campaigns against us. The Kaplinski girl has been highly educated in all the necessary scientific fields, which along with her language skills would make her extremely valuable to this task force."

Demitri was back in his comfort zone and exuded confidence, an attribute that Hydie Papandreou found infinitely sexy.

Knight is a lady's man Hydie, and as such fatally flawed. Making a *honey trap* by placing the Kaplinski girl alongside him would be simple. Once the information dries up she simply kills him and moves on to the other Angel generals. The bigger picture is of course to expose Maelströminha and her sister; then kill them, something that would be a natural progression as the Angel hierarchy depletes and Ava Kaplinski becomes established."

The Hydra clapped her hands at the deadly thrill of Demitri's plan, the thought of revenge against the Matriarch of the Angels and justice at last, arousing her sexuality.

"*Agápe mou* you are so sexy when you talk of violence and death. Bed me then talk of the fifth dimension and those mad scientists you have brought back from the past. I am intrigued on that front too."

She imagined Demitri making love to her in his usual dominant manner, and was already lost in the delicious thought of the sex that would naturally follow.

--------------------------------------------------------------------------

Chapter 10

6th December 2015. Islamabad, Pakistan.

Ava was now into her sixth month of captivity and could no longer be sure of the day of the week, each feeling much the same as the next. She had meticulously etched the record of her incarceration on the wall above her bunk, which somehow helped to orientate her. Her captors had not physically abused her since the thrashing that she had received on the first day. They were clearly afraid of who or what she was. The regime of mental cruelty however was relentless and fatiguing. Beaten down and degraded, Ava had reluctantly succumbed to their demands. Any will to resist was waning rapidly. She was broken; subservient. Now, Ava could no longer see the truth. Nothing mattered to her anymore, not even revenge.

Ava was woken before dawn every morning by the sound of a fist banging on the door. One of the guards would open the hatch and pass her a fresh burka, a cup of sour milk and something resembling porridge. If Ava failed to get to the door in ten seconds, the hatch would be slammed shut and she would go hungry. That only happened twice. Ava knew that she needed all the nourishment she could get to survive this ordeal, and would lick her plate clean. She would then have fifteen minutes to do her ablutions, using the foul latrine, and be ready to leave her cell to go to morning prayers.

The guards would take her to another whitewashed room above ground, light and airy. It was such a refreshing contrast to the cold and gloomy cell that Ava actually looked forward to going there for prayers and to read the scriptures. With her exceptional talent for retention, Ava had almost committed the *Quran* and *Hadith*, books of the Prophet Muhammad's deeds and teachings, to memory and could quote freely from them.

Her mentor was an old Imam, a small delicately built man with a white beard and dark bushy eyebrows that he used expressively. He always wore a black robe and a neat black turban. The Imam was much kinder by nature than the Mullah, but strict and demanding, with an amazing brain. He was probably one of the most intelligent men that Ava had ever met. She had come to enjoy debating the meaning of the scriptures with him. Despite his apparent kindness, the Imam was a hard lined fanatic and believed in Jihadism and the fulfilment of the Islamic end-of-time prophecies, where the *Mahdi* would unite all Muslims in a single army and bring victory over all those who opposed the *sharia.*

"It has already begun!" the Imam cried out vitriolically. "Islamic State have captured and killed the first American infidels in the town of Dabiq in Syria, where the *Hadith* tells us the holy war will take place. This and other acts of provocation will insight the *dog of Rome*, Obama, to invoke a ground war against us, uniting all Muslims in holy war!"

Ava remembered how fanatical his eyes were as he expounded the prophecy.

"When the battle begins, one-third of the Muslim jihadists will flee and feel the wrath of *Allah* as they burn in Hell. Another third will die honourably as martyrs to the cause. *Allah* will grant them seventy virgin wives and everlasting happiness. The remaining jihadists will win the battle and go on to conquer all infidels. The world will then unite under *Allah*; the one true God!"

The Imam's rhetoric was inspiring and, without the dilution of any other distractions, became all-consuming and totally believable. His preaching had become the truth to Ava and she found it hard to consider or question the injustice of her incarceration. These prayers, readings from the scriptures and the debating of them, would last until the sun was at its zenith. At this time, Ava was allowed to walk alone in the searing heat of the courtyard for only ten minutes, anonymous in her heavy black burka. She was not however allowed to mix or even talk with others camped at the madrassa.

Every day, Ava would take the opportunity to focus her mind on the gallows in the middle of the yard and force herself to remember how it all began. She would visit those painful memories of her aunt and Katarina and swear vengeance for them through the killing of Bortnik. As the months passed though, her objectives were becoming less clear. The brainwashing was having its effect by degree. Now, it was only the death of Bortnik that mattered to her.

After her stroll, Ava would be given fresh fruit and water, barely enough to assuage her hunger pains, but enough to sustain life. She would have ten minutes to eat this before going down to the laundry rooms, where she would singlehandedly wash and iron the burkas and robes of everybody there at the madrassa. This task would take her through to sunset, when she would eat a handful of rough bread with a cup of sour milk, before meeting the Imam in the prayer room to study until after midnight. The only diversion from this routine, was that once every week the Mullah would replace the Imam. Ava guessed that it was to monitor her progress, but even that was losing its relevance.

There was however a completely different slant to his teachings. He used the *Quran* and *Hadith* as a framework to expound the war of the Shadows.

*Allah's* servants, as he called them were the Shadows, pitted against the Angels who were the oppressors and infidels.

*Allah* appeared to have another lesser known, even secret prophet who still lived to this day. That prophet was a woman known as *the Hydra* who all must obey. She had placed a *fatwa* on all Angels, that they may be expunged from the Earth. The Mullah expounded that the Hydra had chosen Ava to carry out God's will and join the holy war to assist in this ethnic cleansing. In turn, this would assure Ava her place in *Jannah*, the Muslim Paradise, where she would once again be united with her loved ones. Ava wanted to believe this and, in her desperation, imagined meeting her mother, Katarina and her aunt Alisa once more. She had already lost her perception of reality and found solace in this belief, which soon became her principal driver.

Occasionally, Ava had more lucid moments where it was still clear to her that she was indeed being radicalised. Her ability to fight against indoctrination though, had become weak and seemingly pointless. The only thing that truly endured was her rage. Each night before she drifted into a death-like sleep, she would focus on her hatred of Bortnik and what he had done. Ava had become able to harness that hatred and use it to summon up and control her telekinesis. She practiced moving objects around her cell and, after some thousand failed attempts, managed to make the water from her leaky tap drip upwards. Ava was even able to stir the air in her cell and create a breeze on humid nights to give her restful sleep.

Ava no longer had the will to escape though, becoming fatalistic about what they had planned for her. She made a game of using her will to slide open the mortise lock on her cell door at night. In the mornings, the puzzled guard questioned his sanity when he regularly found it open. Sometimes he would lock and unlock the door several times before he felt safe enough to leave, returning an hour later to check and find the door open. Ava's ability to read thoughts made this game even more fun, as she witnessed the guard descending into insanity. A new skill that Ava discovered was that once she had penetrated the guard's conscious state, she could follow him out into the courtyard and see the world as if through his eyes. This enabled Ava to hear and see the truth about what the madrassa actually was, and how they were manipulating young minds to do *God's will*. This had nothing to do with God and Ava knew it, but somehow the punishing regime and indoctrination made the use of sound logic totally irrelevant.

Life was all about pleasing your tormentor and survival. Nothing more. Ava had long since realised that reality was only as you perceived it and that there was nothing remotely *real* about it at all. You are given a scenario, and given rules. You obey rules and kill if you must or be killed. Glory is only achieved through death, and truth is simply another lie. Life had become simple to Ava Kaplinski.

Demitri Papandreou left the air-conditioned comfort of his private Lear Jet and boarded the Mercedes shuttle taxi to take him to arrivals. It was December in Islamabad and the temperature still in the early twenties; higher than normal for that time of year. The Benazir Bhutto International Airport in the province of Punjab is the third-largest in Pakistan, serving the capital and its twin city, Rawalpindi. Unfortunately, the airport was also famous for its long delays at check-in and arrivals. Demitri was met by a tanned, well presented woman in a pressed blue uniform and white blouse who fast tracked him through VIP customs, out to the limousine idling in the parking bay. The Mullah was already waiting in the car, dressed in his traditional white attire.

"*Salaam* Demitri. I trust that you have journeyed well?" The Mullah smiled his gapped smile through his dense grey beard.

"Indeed, I have old friend. I retired the captain for the day to get a few flying hours in."

This was common practice. Demitri had a love for flying and his Lear Jet was the largest, fastest and most capable private jet ever built; such were the trappings of wealth.

They exchanged niceties, as was the Arab tradition, and then went straight down to business.

"So, Mullah Ismael, tell me of the woman. I need her to be ready, is she?" Demitri was a dangerous man to disappoint.

"As ready as the sun is to rise at dawn," was the Mullah's confident reply.

Demitri rewarded him with a smile, a rare gift from such a man as he.

"Tell me more," Demitri prompted.

"The woman is different from all others," the Mullah began. "She is neither of us nor the Angels and there is a rage inside her deeper and darker than I have ever seen. It is a rage fuelled by pain and hatred. The woman is one to be truly afraid of my friend."

"She is a hybrid, an abomination of nature," Demitri's voice was devoid of all feeling. "I sired her and she was born of her Angel mother who is no more. She can walk between worlds Ismael, undetected by Angel or Shadow. She will be both our spy and our assassin."

"You are aware that she has *certain powers*, are you not?" The Mullah stroked his tangled beard pensively.

"I am counting on that," Demitri returned. "What have you identified so far?"

"The woman has strong telekinetic ability and an eager capacity to kill with it. She can both mind read and mind control. Regrettably, we had to punish her the first day for her insolence. Her back was flayed to the bone but she regenerated in but a few days. She can control pain by taking herself outside of her body, but she is yet a novice in her skills and there will be more to come. Her abilities are more akin to Angel than Shadow, which places her as a danger to us. If we lose control of her, she could become almost as dangerous as the Matriarch Maelströminha herself."

"Have no fear of her allegiance old friend. I will be her liberator today and show her kindness and hope. Ava has an equally high capacity for love as she does for hate but there is nobody left in her life to love. I will fill that need within her and she will gladly give me her sex which will give me ultimate control of her."

The fact that Ava was his daughter was of no concern to Demitri Papandreou.

-------------------------------------------------------------------------

Ava was in the laundry room doing her chores when two guards entered with a woman dressed in a blue burka. She kept her eyes diverted, not meeting Ava's gaze. All inmates of the madrassa had strict instructions not to make any contact whatsoever with Ava, not even a glance, at pain of receiving a flogging. She immediately busied herself with the washing and never looked up. The guards escorted Ava back to her cell, instructing her to bathe and to be ready in fifteen minutes. This was unprecedented in six months of daily routine, so unsurprisingly Ava was deeply concerned, expecting another thrashing. She mentally prepared herself for the worst.

The guards returned precisely on the minute. Ava walked between them up the steps into the sunlit courtyard. As they walked towards the gallows, Ava's blood ran cold, her knees buckling at the thought of another beating. To her relief, they walked past the wooden structure, on towards the Mullah's billet on the far side.

A flight of eight hand scrubbed stone steps led up to an ornately carved wooden door, framed by two armed guards, dressed in their dun coloured military fatigues. They beckoned her forward and opened the grand door so she might enter. Ava's legs felt leaden as a feeling of dread came over her. Those eight small steps felt like a mountain for her to climb, but somehow she made it. The two soldiers watched disdainfully as Ava teetered on the top step. Seeing she was close to collapse, they grabbed her and steered her through the doorway, into a large hallway with tapestries covering the walls on both sides. At the end of the hallway was another door, half open. She could hear the distinctive tone of the Mullah's voice in conversation with another whose accent was middle European. His wasn't a voice that she could place, but somehow it echoed through her mind like a distant memory or from a dream. She shuddered involuntarily at the feeling of *déjà vu*.

Ava's guards left her just inside and closed the heavy door behind her. The room was lit by two small windows, a big paddle fan stirring the stale air above them. Mullah Ismael Alansari was sat facing her at an old oak table, cluttered with papers. The other man there, dressed in a well cut European suit, sat in a chair angled towards the Mullah. Ava could only see part of his profile but he was dark and tanned with a strong angular jawline that seemed familiar to her.

"Ah Ava! I would like you to meet a friend of mine, Demitri Papandreou."

The Mullah bowed slightly in respect and raised his right hand, palm upwards with his fingers close to his forehead in the typical Muslim salute. The guest stood and turned to face Ava.

"You!" Ava gasped in astonishment.

It was the elusive handsome stranger she had met that night at the Bolshoi. Ava once again went weak at the knees; this time however, for a completely different reason.

Ava was disorientated and needed to either sit or fall down, wondering why him of all people? Demitri could read her thoughts as Shadows can.

"I've been searching for you ever since you disappeared so suddenly from the Bolshoi Miss Kaplinski," he lied. "The police have been searching too. Apparently, you are wanted for the double murder of your aunt Alisa and a dancer called Katarina Romanov."

Ava was shocked at his lie, increasing her confusion.

"But I didn't! I mean we were both drugged by Bortnik. It was him. I only left because my sponsor sent me here and I didn't know it then. I swear…"

Ava was truly panicked. All the two men could see of her desolation however, was the haunted look in her tearful eyes through the slash in her burka. Demitri had Ava mortally wounded and was about to go in for the kill.

"The police are looking at this as a follow-up killing to that of one of Moscow's low-life drug dealers, Rudi Kopov. He was found above the Soho Rooms with his face smashed in and your DNA all over the bed sheets."

It was another lie. Demitri had removed the majority of the incriminating evidence linking Ava to the murder, but Ava was not to know that.

"Oh, my God." Ava put her head in her hands and sobbed her heart out.

Five minutes passed before she could speak.

"Have you come to arrest me then?" her voice feeble with shock, fear and inevitability.

Ava looked at the handsome stranger's implacable face. She was a beaten woman with no fight left in her. They could all do with her as they pleased. Life no longer mattered.

"I have come to save you Ava, nothing more." Demitri flashed his perfect smile.

Ava's eyes were drawn to that powerful chin line of his that ended in the softness of his perfect ear. The image triggered a multitude of confused memories in her, but none that she could place.

"It took me some time to trace you to this place," Demitri continued. "It would seem that your sponsor had plans for you as do I, but my way is not to incarcerate you and make you a slave."

"What is *your way* then Mr Papandreou?"

Ava was far from naive. She knew that everything in life had a price and that price more often than not involved sex.

"Mine is to give you freedom of choice Ava. You simply have to compare a lifetime of control by your sponsor, culminating in the misery of these last six cruel months, with working for me of your own free will. What will it be Miss Kaplinski?"

"And what will my duties be?" Ava asked, cautiously.

She was certain he hadn't followed a murderess around the world just for some private dancing.

"You will be collecting certain information for me," he replied cryptically, "and on occasion, you will eradicate those whom I decide are worthy of death."

"I have already told you that I am no killer Mr. Papandreou. You ask too much of me!" Anger coursed through Ava's body.

"I assure you the people I select will be those you will enjoy killing," he smirked, "just as you enjoyed killing the man who thrashed you in the courtyard when you arrived here."

Ava squirmed at his cutting and factual comment. The aftermath of his killing had resulted in the only orgasm she had experienced since Moscow.

"We are not so different Ava Kaplinski. I think you will find that our causes and reasons match perfectly."

Demitri knew that Ava's radicalisation would do the rest, well that and the sex of course. He picked up a parcel from the desk, stood and walked across to her.

"I believe that these will be in your size Miss Kaplinski. Will you do me the honour of trying them on please?"

Ava looked for somewhere to undress discretely, but Demitri stopped her abruptly.

"That won't be necessary," he directed. "You are far from a modest woman, and besides I need to see how much damage we have to repair to make you presentable and desirable again."

His words were a horrible slight on her womanhood but Ava obeyed. She pulled the heavy burka off over her head and stood there naked before them, painfully aware that her nipples had immediately hardened and silently loathed the occurrence. It drew the men's eyes to her pitifully depleted breasts. In her eyes,

Ava looked like something out of the concentration camps of World War Two. Her mound was an unruly chaos of red curls and she dropped a hand to protect her modesty.

Demitri circled his finger instructing Ava to turn around and she was thankful to turn her emaciated body away from them. The months of toil and starvation had taken their toll and there was nothing left of the ballerina. Her buttocks were wasted and her legs no longer lean and muscular, just shapeless and thin, accentuating that gap that so many men found sexy, but at too high a price. Ava had spent so many months in celibacy and the privacy of her burka, that she felt uncomfortable to have their eyes on her. Worse still, for the first time in her life Ava was ashamed of her body.

"Dress yourself please Miss Kaplinski," Demitri ordered, pointing at the parcel.

He watched Ava closely and critically as she untied the parcel and unpacked its contents. Clearly the sight and touch of expensive and feminine western clothing was too much for her. Ava became completely unaware of her audience and lost herself in the pleasure of the experience.

The clothes were clearly chosen by a man who appreciated his women and the labels were *haute couture* proclaiming the best of Paris. Ava picked up the sheer black panties first and held them to her face. She unashamedly brushed the delicate fabric against her skin, delighting in its touch, before stepping into them and drawing the waistband over her now prominent hip bones. Gradually Ava began once more to feel like a woman. She reached for the matching bra, holding it in front of her by the shoulder straps to appreciate the cut. Demitri had chosen a little padding to give her more confidence and Ava subconsciously raised a brow in appreciation. She slipped it on, cupping each breast in turn, sliding them into the smooth fabric support. Ava was completely oblivious to everything except her newly found comfort.

Demitri's choice of dress was a simple black 'A' line number, intelligently purchased to fall from the shoulder straps and not require too much in the way of fitting. The dress was short, as would be chosen by a man who appreciated a woman's legs. High heeled shoes and a handbag gave the finishing touch. Ava looked into the bag. Her liberator had thought of everything; hairbrush, bands, lipstick red of course, a mirror and mascara. He had even considered her womanly needs. Ava brushed her long auburn hair and used the band to put it in a high ponytail, applied the lipstick and mascara then looked more confidently back at the two men.

Ava was unaware of the Mullah, but she felt Demitri's eyes on her and sensed his arousal, the biggest compliment she had felt in months, and Ava's body responded with a mild frisson, a distant memory of her previous sexual exploits. She could not meet Demitri's eyes. Memories of that night at the Bolshoi began to trickle back into her mind, her wanton attraction and desire for this stranger. Now that stranger was her salvation, her shining knight.

"A few good meals and you will do just fine Miss Kaplinski. Mullah Ismael; have her ready to leave within the hour." Demitri waved his hand dismissively.

Ava walked to the door and let herself out, shaking every bit as much on the way out as she was on the way in. The only difference was that she had exchanged fear for something infinitely more potent, the increasing desire that her knight transform from rescuer to seducer.

---

The Lear Jet taxied to the north end of the runway to take off into the stiff night breeze blowing in from the south east. Demitri was sat opposite Ava in the luxurious club style cabin. Two pretty hostesses were strapped into their seats next to the galley and both looked disapprovingly at Ava. Demitri hadn't simply chosen them for their in-flight skills and both were harbouring their annoyance at having to share the flight back with this skinny red-headed wench. Demitri was famous for his sexual athleticism and stamina and these girls had been looking forward to receiving some of his attention. They just sat there and seethed.

The pilot gunned the powerful twin engines sending the jet hurtling down the runway and up into the southern skies. At an altitude of five thousand feet, he banked the Lear Jet to starboard taking a north-westerly course to Moscow. The pilot eased off the throttle and let the jet climb on upwards through local turbulence to a cruising height of thirty thousand feet. When the roar of the engines eventually subsided in the cabin, the hostesses left their seats to prepare drinks. Ava and Demitri had only exchanged pleasantries up to that point and there was much that Ava wanted to know.

"Where are you taking me Mr Papandreou?" Ava held his eyes confidently.

For the first time in her life she was in control of that monster that lived within her and felt able to defend herself. That, coupled with no longer caring if she lived or died, had given Ava a feeling of immortality. Her eyes were blue and there was sereneness about her.

"First, you can drop the *Mister*. I am Demitri to my friends and I will be that to you."

"Call me Ava then, and I'm pleased to meet you Demitri. Well at least I hope that I will be."

Ava offered her hand to shake and her smile was genuine. Demitri accepted, but leant forward and kissed it instead.

"*Enchanté*," he returned.

Smooth. Very smooth, Ava thought and her expression showed that she liked the gesture.

"The answer to your question is Moscow."

"Moscow!" Ava was horrified. "But I am a wanted woman there."

"But fortunately for you young lady, not wanted by the police as much as you are by me."

Ava pulled her hand away as if she had been burned.

"Don't play with me Demitri, I am nobody's fool."

Ava was suddenly enraged; the brown flecks in her eyes gathering like storm clouds in the sky.

"Easy Ava, I am not playing. What I say is true. I have been studying you for all of your lifetime."

"Since you were about fifteen then," Ava's tone was dismissive.

"You are nobody's fool Ava and you will have already noticed that I am not of this world and neither are you. You will just have to accept that my life on this Earth crosses millennia, not just decades. You have been of great scientific interest to me."

Ava had indeed recognised that he was a Shadow when she first saw him at the Bolshoi. She had felt his aurora of power and danger then and it was a heady mixture that excited her base instincts. Ava was physically drawn to this man; it was as if her womb craved his genes.

"Your *scientific interest*, so what am I then?"

Ava had long since known that she didn't belong to any of the gene pools that she knew of.

"You are a half-breed," Demitri answered, almost disdainfully, "neither fish nor fowl. Your mother was of the Angel race and your father, who is also your *sponsor*, is of the Shadow race."

Ava was open-mouthed with astonishment.

"You know my sponsor, I mean my father?" Ava gasped.

The fact that her sponsor was also her absent father was monumental news to Ava, such that she couldn't catch her breath.

"No, I only know of him and that he is rich, powerful and ruthless."

Well it was at least partly true. Demitri was all those things.

Ava was unbalanced by this life changing revelation and needed a few moments to collect her thoughts.

"And what have you learnt about me that makes me so interesting?" Ava challenged.

"Mostly, I have followed your education through university records and your CV is most impressive."

Demitri rolled off some of Ava's academic achievements to date.

"Honours in several languages: physics, chemistry, biology, information technology, mathematics, the list goes on. Your studies have taken you into the specialist areas of nuclear fission, nanotechnology, biological warfare, world banking and infrastructure. If you were my *protégé* Ava Kaplinski, I would also have given you these studies. You are the finished product and your intellect will be your passport to wherever I need to place you."

One of the hostesses had set flutes of Champagne in front of them. Demitri raised his glass and looked appraisingly at Ava over the rim.

"To our union, Ava."

The look in his Demitri's eye was proof that it was an intended *double entendre*.

Ava reddened at the innuendo and the thoughts that his words evoked. She chinked her glass against his, desperately trying to read his mind but Demitri was guarded against her invasion, a closed book to her, something that she wasn't used to. Ava found his aloofness sexy though, heightening her desire for this unfathomable man to the point of pain. Ava felt so totally aroused, that she needed to divert herself, less she threw herself at him. To compound her confusion, Demitri's knowing smile said it all, but he was gentleman enough to throw her a lifeline. He reached into his travel bag and passed Ava a small package.

"You will need to change your appearance before you land. I have a passport for you in the name of Ava Thompson, an American scientist working at one of my research laboratories in Moscow. You will travel the world more freely as an American and your accent is perfect. I think you will find the work there interesting, alongside some renowned scientists who will be familiar to you. Your research will be in fifth dimensional theory."

Ava's mouth dropped in disbelief. The scenario was beyond unlikely and she wasn't expecting anything like it.

"The fifth dimension?" Ava questioned. "I don't even know what the fifth dimension is."

"Nobody does Ava, but when you meet the scientists you will see that I have chosen well. Your task is not to deliver the project but to be my knowledgeable eyes and ears and evaluate whether these men have the remotest possibility of a successful outcome."

"And this?" Ava pointed at the parcel.

"Black hair dye. As I said, you need to change your appearance; the police will be looking for you."

"I don't need the dye." Ava shook her main of red curls. To Demitri's astonishment they turned silky black in front of his eyes. "Or do you prefer blondes, most men do?" She shook them again and they fell in platinum blonde locks.

Demitri grinned; it was a skill that he hadn't expected.

"Collar and cuffs?" he challenged.

"That's for me to know and you to find out!" Ava teased.

"Quite a skill, I bet you have lots of tricks," Demitri countered, his meaning not going unnoticed by Ava.

"It's just an illusion Demitri. My hair is still red. All I did was to change your perception of me," Ava admitted. "Is that skill Angel or Shadow?"

"Definitely Angel, as are most of your other skills Ava. Shadows were cursed with a lesser skill-set but blessed with a better capacity to employ them. It is the weakness of the Angels that has caused so much of the world to be at war. Their weakness to not enforce strict regimes has caused those wars, famine, disease and poverty. Sometimes you must sacrifice the few for the many. Pandering to an individual's civil rights leads to anarchy and anarchy leads to rebellion. Then rebellion leads to war, famine, disease and poverty. You get my point?" Demitri didn't wait for a reply.

"The masses would have a better life under Shadow rule Ava and this will be our quest. Like a dog obeys and respects a strong master, the masses need a strong and just ruler. Your Angel skills will be of immense use to our cause. Through you, we will be able to shape the world and make it a better place for the masses, not just for the elite few."

Demitri's rhetoric was worthy of the Mullah, Ava mused but he turned it off suddenly like a tap, as if it was said for the moment to impress her. That insincerity made the statement seem disingenuous and left Ava a little cautious as to his intentions. Demitri called the hostess, almost as an announcement that their discussion was over.

"I want you to feed this woman until she can eat no more. When you have succeeded in that, I want you to feed her again. Is that clear?" he demanded.

The hostess smiled falsely at Ava and departed to do as she was bid. Demitri turned back to Ava.

"And you young lady, have five days to put on eight kilos and tone up. Don't fail me, understood?"

Without waiting for an answer, Demitri stood abruptly and left to fly the plane. Ava just sat there dumbfounded at the rudeness of his demand, while the two hostesses simply looked back at Ava triumphantly. One went to the galley to do as she had been asked, and the other followed Demitri towards the flight deck. She glanced conspiratorially back at her friend as the pilot exited, closing the cabin door behind her. The other stewardess crossed to Ava and gave her the most plastic of smiles.

"More Champagne Miss?"

------------------------------------------------------------------------

Chapter 11

11th December 2015. Moscow, Russia.

Ava Thompson paid the driver and stepped out of the taxi outside the main gates of the 'Papandreou Research Laboratories, Moscow Plc'. It was Ava's fifth day of freedom and she had put on the eight kilos demanded of her, now looking toned, healthy, vital and attractive again.

Ava had not seen or heard from Demitri since he had disappeared into the pilot's cabin on the flight back from Pakistan, other than to impart an address and date. She was still seething at the memory of the hostesses entering and leaving the cabin in turns, each time looking more flushed and more radiant with each passing episode. Ava remembered their cruel smirks as they served her and their *girlie* chat that was deliberately loud enough and graphic enough for her to overhear.

Ava was already hurting enough from being rejected by Demitri for the second time, without this display of girl bitchiness. It had all become too much for Ava on the flight and she had resorted to a dirty tricks campaign, unworthy of her, but the bitchy stewardesses had it coming. That said, Ava couldn't help but enjoy the shocked expressions on the girl's faces as they both simultaneously flooded with a gush of menstrual blood, soaking their legs and uniforms. Both had clutched themselves in desperation and hurried knock-kneed to the bathroom. Ava felt avenged, which was justification enough.

Demitri had turned out to be a disappointment too, giving her the address of the laboratories by email without even taking the trouble to brief or reassure her; just the address. He was a solid gold bastard, but then what girl doesn't find that attractive in a man and a challenge? Ava wondered, agreeing with the sentiment that girls having a bad time either enjoyed it or deserved it.

That sentiment was true if only for Ava, and she knew it. She had low self-esteem, low expectations and thrived on guilt, fear, pity, prescription drugs and alcohol; all of which made her the perfect victim. Ava was the perfect *Lucy Jordan*, on the road to her own self-made disaster. Katarina had warned her that she was a tragedy in the making, but Ava was beyond salvation. Not even the worthiest of knights could ever win her and deliver her from her demons. Ava's only chance of salvation was to wake up and value herself, but there was little chance of that without hitting rock bottom first. The question was how much further could she fall?

It was a bitter cold morning, the north-easterly wind from Siberia having blown relentlessly for two weeks, sending the daytime temperatures to ten degrees below zero. Ava headed into the icy breeze, thankful for the protection of her long sheepskin coat and traditional *ushanka* fur hat with upturned peak and floppy ears. She was stopped at the gatehouse to check her identity and then sent through to reception. A plump fresh faced woman with short brown cropped hair was sat behind the desk.

"Ava Thompson isn't it?" she beamed a friendly smile. "We have been expecting you." Ava was thankful for that and greatly reassured.

"You will be working in one of our top security laboratories, using retinal recognition security for access, so I will need to scan your eyes. It won't hurt I promise. You have been assigned to the '5D' section in the Computer Science and Artificial Intelligence section and expected to live in there until your secondment is over, but I don't see a bag?"

"Well no, I wasn't told," Ava floundered.

"Mr Papandreou wasn't it?" the question was rhetorical. "He is a busy man and often forgets the minor detail," she excused.

The woman scanned Ava's eyes, then busied herself preparing Ava's pass. When that was done she engaged Ava again.

"Prepare me a list of all you need and I will make the necessary arrangements. Oh and by the way, in Mr Papandreou speak, *expected* means that you *will*. I hope that is clear?"

The woman didn't look embarrassed in the slightest for making her point so succinctly.

"Crystal," Ava confirmed. Her smile said nothing about her disdain.

She cheered herself up with the thought that at least she was back in Moscow. The Soho Rooms were already calling her. Ava needed a thorough sexual episode and needed it soon. There was a certain barman at the Bolshoi whom she had seriously underestimated that needed rewarding.

Twenty minutes later, a guard collected Ava and took her down through several shiny steel corridors that led to the 5D sector. At last they arrived at yet another steel door, flush fitted in the steel walls, such that it was almost invisible. The only evidence that it was indeed a door was the retinal scanner mounted upon it. Ava's guard showed her how to use the eye recognition and the door slid open with a pneumatic hiss. Ava took a deep breath and walked in alone, the door closed automatically behind her, effectively sealing her in. Ava momentarily panicked, having flashbacks to her locked cell at the madrassah. She had to prove that the door would open several times, before feeling comfortable about being shut in.

Ava appeared to be in an office with a studio style bedroom to the side and a full-length glass wall that looked into a modern, sterile-looking laboratory. Two men in white coats sat at a table deep in conversation, while a third appeared to be examining an old ornate mirror which was almost the size of a door. The old fashioned appearance of the mirror looked incongruous in the modern environment of the laboratory, and Ava wondered why it might be there. She returned her attention to the office. The desk was clear, other than a computer and a brown envelope with her name written in typeface. Her desk, she assumed and sat down opening the envelope, hoping that it was a letter from Demitri. To her great disappointment, it wasn't, just the logon details for the computer and a web address. A few minutes later, Ava was through Internet security and the 'Welcome' screen popped up. She entered the web address provided into the browser, which took her to a file called 'Tutorial', with a pre-recorded video link. Ava selected it and smiled fondly as Demitri's image appeared.

'Good morning Ava and welcome to Papandreou Research Laboratories. You will soon meet three of the most prominent scientists to have ever graced academia. Their names are Albert, Isaac and Galileo. They together with, should I say less dated technical scientists, will be working on theories to bound and access the fifth dimension.

You will only be concerned with these three men that I have named, as their skills are in their ability to have pure thought and pragmatism. The others in the team will work remotely until these three have completed the conceptual phase of the project. By that I mean defining the fifth dimension and how one might gain access to it.

Prepare yourself Ava, this will challenge your current understanding of what the world was, is and will be. It will change your views on humanity and religion; you will even question whether you actually exist or are just a figment of some greater power's imagination. If we succeed, then all things will become possible and we will ascend to the level of the Gods.

Your stay here will be brief because all I want is your pragmatic assessment of the feasibility of the project. Your intellect is comparable to these great minds, although in much more diversity. Once the concept is proven, we have our own scientists that will take the project to completion.

To afford you a head start, I have attached the three scientists' profiles to give you some background of their achievements to date. You have ten days, taking you to 20th December. At that point I will have another mission for you. By way of preparation, I want you to find out all you can about Callum Knight and how you might get close to him. He is the strategic and tactical advisor to the British Prime Minister and as such his personal file enjoys the status of 'Top Secret'. I doubt

118

*whether this presents much of an obstacle to a woman of your resourcefulness though Ava. I am counting on you succeeding on both missions and failure is not tolerated.*

*You can leave messages in this mailbox and I will check daily for an update.'*

The screen went black and that was it. Ava pushed her chair back to let her instructions sink in.

"Not even a kiss my arse," she muttered disappointedly, wondering if she had just got out of the frying pan and into the fire.

The thought briefly crossed Ava's mind that Demitri gave written instruction in much the same manner and tone as her sponsor used to, but she was quickly distracted by carnal thoughts of him before she questioned that thought. In truth, she was frustrated that there wasn't going to be any one to one time in this business arrangement. Six months of celibacy did not go well with a woman of Ava's promiscuity. She was as horny as hell and to make matters worse, she had been confined to barracks. Ava almost felt sorry for the first man to attempt to satisfy her lust, hoping that it might be Yuri. He wouldn't forget her in a hurry, she mused.

Yuri's puppy-dog eyes came to her mind. Then she reflected on the muscles that went with them, quickly deciding that her employers were not going to keep her locked up tonight under any circumstances! Ava needed the distraction of work to take her mind off sex and opened the file with the scientists' profiles. She skim-read the headlines.

"Oh my God, it can't be so!" she gasped.

Ava had thought that the names Demitri had given her were code names, but the profiles in front of her were indeed those of Albert Einstein, Sir Isaac Newton and Galileo Galilei; three of the finest brains in the last five hundred years or, in all probability, ever.

These men's successes were only limited by the scientific instruments available to them in their time. As far as having an empirical understanding of the universe, the physics that bind it and innovative thought, there were none to compare or probably ever would be.

"But this can't be possible," Ava said out loud and crossed the room to the window that looked into the laboratory.

She studied the three men more closely. The man stood in front of the ornate mirror was old with a shock of white hair and a full moustache. He shuffled rather than walked and was *Chaplinesque* in appearance. Ava had already studied this man as part of one of her dissertations in physics. He was of German birth and instrumental in developing modern physics as we know it. There was no doubting that he was indeed Albert Einstein, but how? She remembered that he had died in 1955 at the age of seventy-six.

The two in conference sat at the table also featured in her studies as they would have for any scholar of physics. The familiar long face of Sir Isaac Newton, an Englishman with his mane of long curly locks and prominent nose, made him a dead ringer for King James II. He was one of the most influential scientists of all time and his view of the physical universe dominated science for three hundred years after his death. He was in animated conversation with a smaller man in his seventies with a generous full grey beard and receding grey hair. This man was the Italian scientist Galileo Galilei, known as 'the father of modern physics'.

"Impossible," Ava gasped, "this just cannot be true."

Ava sat down again wondering what on Earth she was going to say to them. Hello, my name is Ava; I'm from the future... No, that wouldn't do at all. Hello my name is Ava; you must be from the past... That was equally as absurd.

Ava laughed uncontrollably at the nonsense of her dilemma. But it wasn't nonsense. They were there, here and now! Ava wondered at what power this dark handsome stranger, Demitri

Papandreou, had. Who was he? She needed to know much more about him. One thing was certain though; Ava wasn't going to just research Callum Knight's background tonight, Demitri was fascinating her!

------------------------------------------------------------------------

Ava had at last recovered her wits and now believed the unbelievable. She put on the neatly pressed white lab coat that had clearly been left for her, picked up her notebook and walked into the lab, startling the men. The observation glass to the office was one-way and the scientists hadn't seen her until then. She looked both stunning and the consummate professional with her thick black hair piled high and notebook to hand. As old as, and as engrossed in their science as the scientists were, Ava had their utmost attention from the outset.

"Good morning gentlemen. My name is Ava and I have come to assist you with your research into the fifth dimension," Ava's voice and manner was entirely confident.

Galileo was the first to find his tongue. As an Italian, charming females was second nature to him.

"How refreshing to have the company of a young lady to brighten the drear of old men's conversation," he charmed.

Galileo had a gorgeous accent and a twinkle in his eye, Ava noticed.

"I do hope that you learned men are going to take me seriously," Ava demurred, "only I take no prisoners and you will get as good as you give. I might even put you under house arrest again Galileo."

Ava was referring to the Roman Inquisition in 1615 when Galileo was charged with heresy for his views that didn't support *heliocentrism*. That theory expounded that the Earth was the centre of the universe and that the other planets and stars simply spun around it. He spent the rest of his life under house arrest for his blasphemy. Galileo guffawed at Ava's playful insolence and fell in love with her immediately, as Italians are reputedly famous for.

"And who is the beautiful Ava and why have we been honoured with such a quick mind?"

They now surrounded, Ava shaking her hand and welcoming her. Any fears that Ava had about meeting these highly intellectual men evaporated as she realised they were just ordinary men with extraordinary minds.

"Well," Ava began, "I am simply here to listen and understand and to debate your theories. Then to assist if I can, but most of all to evaluate if the project to define and deliver the fifth dimension is feasible."

Her summary was honest and to the point. That honesty was clearly respected by the three of them. Albert spoke for them all.

"Young lady, why do you think that three old sages such as ourselves would travel across time to unite in such a quest?"

Ava could tell that Albert's question was not meant to test her, and that it was rhetorical. She let him continue.

"If I was able to say that it was for the good of mankind, then I could die in peace. But nothing good can come of this. The project will become a war machine, as powerful things do, used to kill and control. So I ask you again young Ava. Why are we here? Sadly, the answer is curiosity and vanity, nothing more." Albert looked tired. "But we cannot help ourselves. Knowledge is everything for people like us and together we will riddle this. God help us and forgive us for we know not what we do." His sadness was palpable.

"So Albert, tell me what you have found. Do you know what the fifth dimension is yet? Can we travel there and will it be the greatest discovery of all time?"

Ava had always had a hunger for knowledge and already knew that she was about to share a moment in history.

Albert gestured towards the table that they might sit and left to prepare tea in the galley. When he returned, the atmosphere was jovial and innocently flirtatious.

"We will always be boys in our hearts," he chuckled at the truth of his statement.

Isaac, a highly educated and eloquent product of academia, naturally took on the role of presenter. He was the archetypical Englishman; with such a quaint old English accent that Ava hung on every word he spoke.

"Interestingly, we all arrived here with totally different conceptions of what the fifth dimension might be," he began. "Then, after some debate, we realised that the reason was because of the *baggage* that we all carry, defending our own hypotheses. All of us were too precious about our work to see the bigger picture."

"Guilty as charged." Albert raised his hand in capitulation.

He had wasted years defending his theories against the claims of quantum mechanics, only to have to ultimately concede.

"And you are far from unique my dear friend," Galileo responded supportively.

Ava, being a woman, didn't want this to start from the beginning of time with the *Big Bang* theory, 'And then the Earth was formed, cooled and first life crawled out of the primordial pond...' she wanted the full gossip and she wanted it now. Ava was sensitive enough to make light of the situation though.

"Listen I am a woman! You will kill me if you don't get to the point. What do you know?"

Isaac puffed like an old steam engine, totally de-railed, not used to being barracked and told to get on with it by a woman. Albert took over.

"We are as certain as we reasonably can be, at the conceptual phase of this project, that the fifth dimension is infinite possibility. The first three dimensions take us through space and the fourth, time."

Albert paused to gather his thoughts.

"If you consider that anything could happen at any discrete point in time and space, then you have infinite possibility. If you have infinite possibility, then you have infinite different outcomes. If you have infinite different outcomes, then you move into the space of thought. If your thoughts can control the outcome, then you move into the space of God." Albert raised a bushy grey eyebrow. "And if you move into the space of God, then you rule Heaven and Earth."

There was no comment from the other scientists. They had already come to terms with the magnitude of what was being implied, but this knocked all sensibility out of Ava. The outcome of this project was either salvation or Armageddon, depending on whose hands the fifth dimension fell into.

They talked at length about the detail that supported their hypothesis and to Ava, with her scientific bent, it all seemed entirely plausible. Ava recalled an old TV series, *The Twilight Zone*, from the late fifties that was repeated when she was a child. The programme used to terrify her. She recalled that each episode began with these words,

*'There is a fifth dimension beyond that which is known to man. It is a dimension as vast as space and as timeless as infinity. It is the middle ground between light and shadow, between science and superstition, and it lies between man's fears and the summit of his knowledge. This is the dimension of imagination.'*

As a frightened child, Ava could never have known how prophetic those words would turn out to be and they sent a cold chill down her spine. The memory prompted Ava's first contribution to the project.

"If, as you say, the fifth dimension is infinite possibility and that our thoughts can control the outcome, then surely the gateway to the fifth dimension must be through our imagination? If you accept that concept then all you need to find is a conduit for our imagination, there would be no *physical* aspect to the journey, yes?"

The three old scientists simply looked back at her open-mouthed in disbelief. Ava felt totally stupid about her clearly crass hypothesis and wished the Earth would just swallow her up.

"I'm sorry, that's nonsense. I should know when to listen and when to shut up. I do apologise," Ava looked totally ashamed.

Albert took her firmly by the elbows and his eyes burned with excitement.

"No not nonsense at all Ava! Sometimes we get too close to see the obvious, when it is staring us in the face."

"What do you mean?" Ava was unaware of the importance of her statement.

"Humour me for a minute and come over to this old mirror," Albert asked.

He took Ava's hand and walked with her the few steps to the old ornate mirror while Isaac and Galileo looked on.

"What do you see Ava?" Albert cocked one of his unruly eyebrows inquisitively at her.

"I see a very large and beautiful antique mirror," she replied.

"What more?" Albert challenged. "Inspect the mirror more closely."

"Well of course I see us, or a reflection of us." Ava ran her fingers around the ornate frame. "There is a magnificent frieze of cherubs, with their bows and harps, carved around the frame. It is beautifully painted in gilt and has clearly been cherished for hundreds of years because of its condition."

"Perhaps too perfect?" Albert suggested. "Touch the glass please and tell me what you think?" Ava obliged.

"It's vibrating and humming!" Ava instinctively took her hand away. "And it stops when I remove my hand."

Ava noted, now looking more closely at the mirror. She breathed on it, and then replaced her hand tentatively. The mirror began to vibrate again.

"The mirror doesn't mist or smear either, and the glass isn't cold to touch. In which case, it is definitely not made of glass," Ava deduced.

The magnitude of the vibration increased the longer Ava left her hand on the mirror, until the phenomenon eventually scared her. She removed her hand, immediately covering her mouth with it in awe.

"All good scientific observations Ava," Albert confirmed. "No, indeed what we are looking at is not a mirror, although it does reflect. It is the portal we came to your time through, a gateway through time and space."

"Oh, my God it's a *wormhole*!" Ava blurted; "just as your theory of general relativity alluded to in the 1930's Albert." Ava was totally blown away by the magnitude of his statement.

"Strange, don't you think, that I should experience my own discovery sixty years after my death?" he mused. "But I digress. What is clear is that the mirror is a passage through the time-space continuum. How the portal does that however, is not. It somehow links to our thoughts, our *imagination* as you so clearly deduced Ava, and takes us there. You can either view the happening that you are imagining, or simply step through the portal and be there. Have you a particular childhood memory you would like to visit?"

126

"Yes!" Ava enthused.

Her response was instant. Ava's last happy memory was on her fifth birthday, when she spent the day at the Moscow Zoo with her mother.

"Put your hand back on the mirror Ava. Imagine the time and the place that you want to go to, but you have to focus to the exclusion of all else."

Ava lost herself in her memories. Her coordinates in time and space were precise. She was entirely confident of the place, the year and almost the very hour. At last their reflections in the mirror began to recede, replaced by another image. It was that of an impressive rock castle entrance leading into the Moscow Zoo. The crowd spilled in through it and the faces of the children were expectant. Ava spotted her mother immediately, a slim and elegant woman in her late twenties, with long blonde hair. She was holding a child's hand who was beaming excitedly back at her.

"Mum, I'm here!" Ava shouted, as if she might hear her.

Ava was oblivious of her audience, tears of love and regret flowed freely like rivers down her cheeks.

The child with her mother was a happy five-year old, with a mane of red hair. Anastasia cupped the infant's face in her hands and said something that made the little girl jump up and down with excitement.

"That's me!" Ava shouted to the scientists and returned her attention to the mirror.

The little girl kissed her mother excitedly then ran ahead towards the *creatures of the night* exhibition. Ava recalled that this had both enthralled and frightened her that day. She looked on lovingly at her mother, the woman who had been stolen from her. That memory made Ava think of the last time that she had seen her mother alive. It was in the bedroom of the hotel.

The image in the mirror changed in that instant reflecting Ava's next thought, replaced by that of a dark-haired man. All she could see of his face was his strong jawline, as he choked the life out of her mother. A child's voice suddenly cried out.

"Leave my Mummy alone!"

The little girl bravely tried to stop the man, but he lashed out at her, striking her in the face, bloodying her mouth and sending her spinning across the room...

"Stop it! I don't want to see anymore," Ava yelled in deep distress.

She turned her back on the mirror and held her head in her hands, covering her ears. The image receded until there was only her reflection and that of Albert. Ava broke down in inconsolable tears of agony. Albert took her in a fatherly embrace and shushed her. It was only after some considerable time that Ava regained control. His apologies were heartfelt and profound.

"I cannot tell you how sorry I am that my demonstration wounded you so. We all have memories that we would rather not visit. I should have thought more about the dangers. As wise as a man gets, he can still be just an obtuse old fool sometimes."

"You meant no harm Albert, and you were not to know. I will be alright now," Ava lied. "Please go on with what you were telling me about the fifth dimension and imagination being the key."

The men were thankful that Ava had pulled herself together. None of them, as academics in a man's world, had much experience in dealing with a woman in tears.

"Yes well," Albert began, clearing his throat with a nervous cough, "you accessed another time and another place through the science behind this mirror and your own thoughts, *imagination* if you like. You imagined the scene and your thoughts took you there. So we know that this portal can access the four dimensions of time and space simply by interacting with your imagination through thought. It works because we have a clear understanding of the concept of time and space and can visualise our destination. I am sure that you have already deduced this Ava."

The statement needed no response. Albert was simply setting the scenario as a springboard for the theories that he was about to expound.

"Up until your opening summation Ava, we had been foolishly looking at this mirror simply as a conduit between time and space. The chains of our logical thought processes limited us to that, stopping us from thinking outside of the box if you like. In short, we have been trying too hard to understand the *science* behind the mirror instead of understanding the mechanics of our imaginations. I now suspect that the mirror, this portal, can span *all* dimensions. We just need to visualise our destination in the same way that you visualised your past."

Albert paused to collect his thoughts. Decision made, he raised a bushy eyebrow and continued.

"I see now that it matters not that we do not understand the interactions of the mirror, we just have to accept that as a given, which is difficult for us scientists. The portal simply does what it does. I think that the first step into the fifth dimension is to make the mirror reflect an abstract thought, as opposed to a happening in time and space; something that has only existed in *dream-space*. If we can create that abstract world, then just maybe we can step into it, if not physically then mentally, as you inferred Ava. It would be a world of unlimited imagination."

"Then that abstract thought should be love," Ava decided.

"Love?" Galileo interjected. "Why love?"

"Because love is the purest of emotions and it is love that captures our spirit and brings us closer to God, if there is one. Just as importantly, if your experiment doesn't go to plan, then I for one would rather spend eternity in an imaginative world of love than anywhere else."

Ava's logic was sound. Galileo nodded his accord and expanded on the idea.

"It seems to me that the creation of a powerful abstract thought, such as love, which might be communicated to the portal, would need to be to a high degree of completeness, before it might reflect and become a reality. I somehow doubt whether this ability exists within the skill-set of us as pragmatic scientists. Such a thought and concept would be more conducive to the mind-set of a poet or bard, or indeed of an artist."

"Leonardo da Vinci!" Ava exclaimed. "We need Leonardo da Vinci! Apart from him being a renowned scientist, he had an imagination far beyond his time. Amongst many other inventions his sketches depicted flying machines, helicopters, scuba gear and even robots, all of which have since been realised over time. But for us, much more importantly, he was a prolific sculptor, painter, writer, musician and poet."

Ava was truly excited.

"Leonardo epitomised the Renaissance humanist ideal. You could not find a man with better credentials to interact with the mirror. He had a fertile imagination, abstract thought and demonstrated that he embraced possibility through his prophetic sketches of machines outside of his world."

"Eureka!" Albert proclaimed, usurping that of the ancient Archimedes. "You have found just the man. He pre-dates us all but he was the most diversely talented person to have ever lived. If there ever was a man that could visualise and flesh out a thought, it would be he. And if we can flesh out a thought, then we have the key that could open up the fifth dimension!"

All three scientists new of Leonardo da Vinci's unsurpassed accomplishments, as he even predated Galileo. Albert looked reflectively at Ava for several seconds then nodded at his own conclusion.

"You are not of us are you Ava? Nor are you of Demitri's kind I would wager. Your intellect is apparent but you don't have that same coldness of spirit that blights Demitri's soul. I would feel safe if the conduit to the fifth dimension was in your hands but not with him." Albert shook his head despairingly.

"Then why do you continue dear friend?" Ava felt his grief.

"We are trapped by our quest for knowledge and curiosity. Knowledge is everything to scientists like us you see. It is simply our reason to be and Demitri has tempted us by exploiting our own vanity," Albert lamented.

"You are right Albert. I am not of your kind and I don't even know what *kind* I am."

Ava had not fully recovered from the vision of her mother's murder and was still feeling morose.

"And you would be wrong to entrust me with the fifth dimension. There is an evil in me that brings death to all those that I grow to love. I am the Angel of Death."

Ava was close to tears again and Albert sensed that another fatherly hug was in order.

"Don't give up on yourself Ava. I see goodness in your heart and a will to prove it. Despite being a scientist and a pragmatist, I do believe that fate has a role to play in our lives. Perhaps fate brought you to this project for some divine purpose. Time will tell Ava. Time reveals all things."

The look Albert gave Ava in that moment was as if he already knew the outcome. That look of inevitability sent a cold chill of premonition down Ava's spine. It was the same feeling of dread that she had experienced when she begged her mother not to go to meet the man that subsequently killed her in that hotel room.

------------------------------------------------------------------------

Their animated discussions continued through the morning and into the middle afternoon, before they finally had a structured approach as to how they might access the fifth dimension. The plan hinged around a number of key assumptions:

- That Demitri could convince Leonardo da Vinci to join the project
- That the mirror, or portal, could indeed access all dimensions with no need for the understanding of how (This had to be a *given* as the science behind the mirror was of an order of magnitude way beyond man's evolution)
- That imagination and infinite possibility was indeed the fifth dimension
- That da Vinci had sufficient intellect to integrate with the portal

On the latter point, all hoped by that da Vinci could at the very least achieve rudimentary interaction with the mirror and thus achieve *proof of science*. Ava strongly suspected that, once proven, Demitri would already have a candidate in mind for full integration. That person would become the most powerful being on Earth, and in Ava's opinion, could only be the Hydra. It seemed a natural conclusion to her, after all she had been indoctrinated by the Mullah to worship the Hydra alongside *Allah* and the prophet Mohammed.

Ava's regime of prayer that became her life at the madrassa was something that she had continued to practice faithfully five times a day, as is demanded by the second of the *Five Pillars of Islam*. The slant of Ava's radicalisation had been towards fidelity with the Hydra and the Shadow nation, rather than to the established Muslim doctrine. Her indoctrination had removed Ava's ability to recognise, or even question, that she was worshipping a false prophet. Ava had never considered that the Hydra's hands could possibly be unsafe.

She checked her watch. Sunset and s*alat al-maghrib* would be in another half an hour. This was time that Ava set aside for prayer. Since leaving the Madrassa, Ava hadn't failed in her regime of worship and supplication. It was as if her very soul depended on the reassertion of her faith through prayer. *Allah* and his wishes meant everything to Ava now. She had just sufficient time to write her daily report to Demitri first. Her *précis* of the day's events and findings was succinct and ended:

*'And so if you can augment this team with da Vinci and his humanistic skills, then I believe that you are indeed in with a reasonable chance of successfully delivering your project.'*

Ava selected 'send' and closed the program. She still had fifteen minutes left, enough for a quick internet search on Callum Knight and Demitri Papandreou. She would look in more detail later, but for now she just needed to satisfy her curiosity as women must.

Her search confirmed that Callum Knight was indeed the strategic and tactical advisor to the Prime Minister, a position he had held across the last two governments. She found a cover story about him in the GQ magazine, concentrating mostly on his social, sporting and private life, rather than his political profile and covert accomplishments. Ava would find out more about that later through some of her more dubious friends who were mercenary hackers. As such, they had no loyalties or conscience, just a love for their illicit work and money.

Knight's photograph commanded the front cover. He was sat astride his fluorescent green Kawasaki Ninja ZX motorcycle in his leathers, cradling his crash helmet in his arm. The picture captured him running his fingers back through sun streaked brown hair, smiling openly and naturally to someone outside of the frame. Ava judged that he was in his late forties with handsome features, a good jaw and prominent character lines, etched in his bronzed face. His eyes were blue, set below a strong brow. Ava imagined that the person he was smiling at outside of the picture was probably a woman, judging by the flirtatiousness of his expression.

"A lady's man for sure," she said out loud. "I can't wait to meet you!"

Ava read on to find that he was formerly a Major in the Parachute Regiment, a bachelor, never married and romantically linked to a string of beauties. They were mostly *it girls* or work colleagues. Apparently Callum Knight had not generally fared well at their hands, his heart having been broken on numerous occasions. The common denominators seemed to be that he gave too much, too soon. It appeared that Callum's work was all consuming, giving his lovers too much latitude to dally. His loves were dangerous sports and, as he himself publically confessed, dangerous women. None more dangerous than me, Ava mused and began her search for Demitri.

She recalled Demitri's name cropping up when she searched for key players in world infrastructure and finance, for a submission to her sponsor. Ava found his name linked to most global organisations. He was a Greek oligarch, ruthless businessman, politician and womaniser. Strangely, he had no connections with the Greek Mafia, which meant one of two things; he either lived in fear of them or owned them. Ava was pretty sure that he wasn't afraid of them.

Ava romanticised that he and Callum would make a hell of a threesome! Her body quickly responded to her carnal thoughts, which she quickly diverted to thoughts of Yuri. Ava didn't want fantasy right now, she needed reality. She needed a man, preferably Yuri.

Ava shut down her computer and went to her quarter, adjacent. The apartment was sparse but adequate, with a kitchenette, shower room and a generous sized double bed. It wasn't hard for Ava to imagine that Demitri had probably *initiated* many of his employees there and couldn't help but wonder if she was to get lucky.

It was after seven o'clock by the time Ava had prayed, bathed and dressed appropriately for a night out at the Bolshoi. She called a taxi, put on her sheepskin coat and ushanka, then crossed to the retinal scanner.

"Access denied," the security unit declared.

Really? Ava mused, concentrating on the door mechanism. Moments later there was the hum of an electric motor and the door slid open on its track. Ava was out of the building and on her quest to get well and truly laid.

-------------------------------------------------------------------------

Chapter 12

It felt strange walking into the Bolshoi for the first time in over six months. The only thing that had changed was her. Ava was far from the drugged and naive girl that was frog-marched out of the premises on that last fateful night. Ava shuddered at the very thought as she handed her hat and coat to the cloakroom assistant. The girl didn't appear to recognise her as one of the Bolshoi's past ballerina's, but then Ava had maintained her illusion of black hair and altered her makeup, giving her a different look. That, along with some gentle controlling of other's mental perception of her, appeared to be working.

The Bolshoi was frequented by numerous high-ranking officers from the Russian *politsiya* and others of the Ministry of Internal Affairs. None could have failed to pay attention as she walked into the bar, because to simply call her *striking*, would have been an understatement. Ava wore her hair up and had chosen a full-length figure hugging dress with high heels that accentuated her height and slimness. The V-necked, rushed bodice presented her bust tantalisingly, and a large teardrop ruby set in her cleavage assured that any admirer would likely focus there. But tonight wasn't about just *any* admirer; it was Yuri that Ava wanted.

Ava entered the bar with her heart in her mouth, desperately hoping that Yuri would be there. She didn't have long to wait for the answer.

"Ava!" Yuri's voice was positively joyous.

Ava had deliberately not hidden her appearance to him. She was still the sassy redhead that he had always known and loved. Yuri stepped out from behind the bar and they embraced earnestly. Ava had to fight back her tears of relief. She had been lonely and isolated for so long, that it was like having family again. Yuri called across to his colleague and asked for a little time out, then sat with Ava at the bar, calming her.

"Hey, it's OK little one," he reassured.

Ava buried her head in Yuri's shoulder, hiding her emotions. Even in that intensively emotional moment, Ava wondered that yet another who knew her, called her *little one*. Those words triggered memories of Katarina and more regrets. Ava felt safe there with Yuri and was in no hurry to break her hold on him. His strength buoyed her up and his manly smell was both comforting and intoxicating. Just for a moment, Ava forgot that he was an Angel and could *read* her. She quickly reined her thoughts back from the sensual place they were taking her. If she had indeed lapsed and given her emotions away, then Yuri was too much of a gentleman to let her know, or feel compromised by them.

"I have missed you Ava," he began. "You never rang me after I told you the bad news. I thought perhaps you held me responsible for your pain. The police linked the two murders, through DNA, to the same killer and to you as a common acquaintance. They want to talk to you."

That wasn't quite how Demitri had put it, Ava thought, but let it go. Yuri continued.

"I wondered whether the killer had followed you to Pakistan and found you. It was hard to believe that you wouldn't have called me after so many months. In fact I had almost given up hope that you were still alive."

Yuri was close to tears himself, but they were genuine tears of relief and his love for this woman.

"Oh Yuri, I have so much to tell you. When you told me that Katarina and Alisa were dead, the shock caused me to drop my phone. I remember it shattering on the marble floor of the airport and then I must have passed out."

Ava was so desperate to tell her story and share her misery that she was almost babbling.

"When I regained consciousness, I was in an ambulance. There was a man inside that they call the Mullah. He hit me and drugged me. It wasn't a work opportunity at all. I was abducted and imprisoned by my sponsor. They beat me and starved me and taught me about *Allah*, the one true God and his prophets. That was the only good thing that came out of my ordeal. Now that I have found *Allah*, I need to devote myself to him and beg his forgiveness for killing a man at the madrassa. God help me."

Ava was now indeed babbling as if she was purging her soul by doing so.

"And then I met Demitri, the stranger I met here at the Bolshoi and asked you about. Do you remember?" Ava didn't wait for an answer. "He liberated me and now I work for him and he's amazing."

Yuri held Ava's hand and listened for almost an hour, only breaking his attention momentarily to order yet another Dirty Martini for her. When Ava finished, she felt like the world had come off her shoulders.

"Tell me more about this man Demitri, the man who liberated you from your sponsor and the Mullah."

Yuri was deeply concerned about this new-found allegiance. It was too coincidental. He could see that Ava's mind had been manipulated and that she couldn't separate fact from lies. He was even more concerned about her total and unquestioning conversion to the Muslim faith, after only a few months in Pakistan, and then as a captive. The change was insidious and so out of character for Ava.

"Apparently Demitri has had a watchful eye on me for years." Ava was still fixed on the positives. "That's why he was here, checking on me, shortly before I left for Pakistan."

Ava omitted to say that she remembered the encounter so clearly because she was so physically attracted to the man.

"So what does this *Demitri* want of you that made him travel half way around the world searching for you?"

Ava picked up the slant of Yuri's question, and immediately went on the defensive.

"Just my mind and *not* my body as you are thinking," her answer was curt.

More's the pity, was what she really thought. Yuri's pupils contract momentarily. Ava realised that he had picked up on her sexual thought. There were no words to put the indiscretion right, and so she blustered on instead, now more careful of hiding her emotions.

"I'm working at one of his research laboratories here in Moscow. I can't tell you exactly what on, as I'm sworn to secrecy. But it's of a scientific nature and world-changing if the research comes off."

"But what could a dancer possibly bring to the party Ava? That wasn't meant to be an innuendo," he hastened to add, "It's just an observation."

Yuri felt awkward and they both laughed at his clumsiness. It did however relieve the tension that had been rapidly building between them.

"I'm just concerned for you Ava," he continued. "Don't read any harm into what I say. I just want you to be safe, that's all."

Yuri's smile was honest and showed his deep concern.

"I am safe at last Yuri. It was my sponsor who was grooming me, although I never recognised the fact, or the evil in him. As for 'what can I bring to the party'? Well you don't know me Yuri, not really. I was blessed, or cursed, with perfect retention. My sponsor has controlled my education from the day I came to the Bolshoi as a five year old. I have degrees in almost every subject you can think of and have researched far beyond that. Demitri recognised that talent from the beginning and has been waiting for me to develop, I guess."

"And so, your sponsor spends a king's ransom on you, abducts you to indoctrinate you and then gives up at the first hurdle? I don't think so Ava."

Yuri's statement derailed Ava. She hadn't considered that as a possibility. But then she wasn't aware of her radicalisation either, as it was done in such a subliminal way. Ava tried to defend her impossible position and turned to petulance.

"You don't understand Yuri! You say *indoctrinated* but I wasn't. I was just shown a new way, a new religion. I made all my own choices!"

Ava clearly believed her own propaganda. Such was the thoroughness of her conditioning, her radicalisation.

"And as for my sponsor returning, Demitri is one of the most powerful men on Earth! My protector! He will *never* allow any harm to come to me."

Yuri let the matter go. They were getting nowhere. He just needed to keep an eye on her from now on and changed the subject.

"So then Ava, why have you come here tonight, is it nostalgia?" Yuri's smile was warm, genuine, and loving.

"Only to see you Yuri," Ave demurred. "I have thought about you so much and I have such regrets."

Ava had to glance away out of shyness, which was an unusual experience for her and she liked it.

"Regrets? Why do you have regrets?"

"Because you have always been there for me, only I never saw it that way. I never saw past you as a barman. I never saw the *man* behind the bar. I like him Yuri, I really do."

This time Ava's neck and face flushed, but she held Yuri's eyes, even though it was painfully difficult for her to do so. Yuri rescued her.

"Then I suppose I should find the courage to ask you out at last." His smile was easy.

There was a confidence in Yuri, something else that Ava had failed to notice. In fact, he was nothing like *Mr Average* at all. He continued with that confidence.

"I finish tonight at ten and would love you to be my date for the night. Perhaps we could go to the Soho Rooms?"

"I would be honoured," Ava replied graciously, screaming a silent *yes*!

"I had better get back to work." Yuri kissed her affectionately on the forehead and parted with a cheeky wink and a million dollar smile.

The Dirty Martinis were doing their trick, as they always did when Ava drank enough of them and fast losing her inhibitions. Ava watched Yuri closely as he worked. His intelligent blue eyes sparkled below his broad brow and his fair, almost blonde cropped hair shone like a halo under the spotlights.

Yes, you really are an Angel, Ava thought. She watched Yuri's powerful biceps bunch in manly fashion as he flexed them to open a bottle or lift a crate. She noticed for the first time that he had a strong back with great muscular definition that filled his fitted shirt. She imagined him above her, digging her fingernails into those muscles and deliberately let him pick up her thoughts. The look she got in return, and the thought that he sent with it, made her feel unashamedly wanton, drenching her immediately. Ava needed little by way of physical stimulation, her own thoughts were often enough to take her over the edge. She was in glorious confusion and in danger of having a moment right there at the bar. Worse still she knew that Yuri knew it too!

Ava had to escape before the inevitable happened. She picked up her clutch bag and hurried to the cloakrooms leaving Yuri smiling knowingly. He was enjoying the massive physical affect that he just had on her.

"Are you alright?" someone called out, banging on the door. "Are you OK?" the woman repeated with more urgency.

"Um yes, I just felt a little sick. Too many Martinis I guess," Ava replied guiltily, which was only half the truth.

Ava waited until she was sure that the room was empty before stepping out. She just couldn't have faced that woman. Ava checked herself over in the mirror and noticed that her eyes were clear blue, which was always a sign that she was content. Ava was about to put on some red lipstick, then decided it would be much more seductive if Yuri watched her whilst listening in on her thoughts. She walked back to the bar as if on a mission, which she most definitely was.

Ava was halted by what she saw. There, sat at the bar just where she had seen him that first time, was Demitri Papandreou talking casually on his mobile phone, but looking directly back at her through black accusing eyes.

"Shit!" Ava cursed.

He had caught her and would be angry. Flustered and disorientated, she returned to her barstool and began talking to Yuri, although she hadn't a clue what she was saying. She just needed a minute to compose herself and put some kind of an excuse together. Yuri picked up on the change in her immediately.

"What is it Ava, what's happened?" he didn't need a reply, he *read* it in her. "That's him isn't it, Demitri?"

"Damn it yes, and he will kill me now." Ava looked petrified.

"I thought he was your *protector*. If he hurts you then he's a dead man. That I swear to you Ava. You made me swear not to kill Bortnik but I won't do that twice, not even for you." Ava knew that Yuri meant what he said and moderated her statement.

"I didn't mean *kill* literally Yuri. It's just that I wasn't supposed to have left work tonight, first day at the office and all that. He will be cross with me. That is all," Ava gave Yuri a hollow smile. "I must go to him."

Ava stood and pulled her clinging dress down to straighten it. Taking a deep breath, she walked nervously over to the now particularly dangerous looking stranger who just cut his call.

---

Bortnik sat in the dressing chair at his suite at the Metropol, his white silk gown open, with nothing beneath. He looked down over his copious belly at the young black girl whose head was buried in his lap. The girl was fifteen at best, but that was to Bortnik's preference. His mobile phone rang. Bortnik ignored it, cursing the distraction. It was set on answerphone and loudspeaker, nothing was more important to Bortnik than his own pleasure, or so he thought. The call connected.

"Pick the goddamn phone up you fat bastard or I will kill you!"

It was Demitri's voice and it put the fear of God into Bortnik. He wrenched himself free of the girl and grabbed the phone. His manhood now limp through sudden fright.

"Demitri, I was in the shower…"

"Shut up and listen. There's a man who works the bar at the Bolshoi that I seem to have overlooked. His name is Yuri Alexandrov. I want him dead and I want him dead tonight. Understood?"

"Yes but…" Bortnik tried to buy time to gather his wits.

"But nothing Bortnik. I want him killed. I want it to be slow and I want him mutilated and found. Don't fail me Bortnik."

Demitri cut the call just as Ava appeared from the cloakrooms. Bortnik was left open mouthed and looking ridiculous.

---

Only ten steps separated them, but it felt like a mile to Ava as she walked on, trembling with fear. Demitri disconnected the call and tossed the phone disdainfully onto the bar. His eyes never left hers, not even to blink.

"Sit!" he ordered.

Ava obeyed without question. Demitri simply glared back at her fuming for a full half minute before he spoke again.

"You owe me an explanation and an apology Ava Thompson. Don't make the mistake of thinking that I don't own you right now."

His black eyes drilled into hers. They were cold and implacable. Ava felt like a naughty girl in the sheer power of his presence, her voice penitent and manner, petrified.

"I'm so desperately sorry Demitri. What I did was stupid and ungrateful of me. Please forgive me; it won't happen again I promise."

Ava was desolated. Her complete subservience was all Demitri needed to hear. He needed Ava to acknowledge him as her master and to feel obliged and indebted to him. Her indoctrination, finely honed at the madrassa, just needed re-activating. She would be his puppet now, he was sure of that. Demitri switched to 'Mr. Nice Guy'. Conditioning is as much about rewarding the subject for good behaviour as punishing bad. Total subservience was good behaviour.

"Ava. Do you not see that I love you, that I have always loved you? Why do you think I searched for you when you were taken?"

Demitri seemed entirely earnest to Ava. She believed him because she wanted to, and because she had been conditioned to obey.

"It was just fortunate that the Mullah owed me a favour and that your sponsor chose him as your captor," Demitri continued. "The Mullah now lives in fear of his life for betraying him, but he will enjoy my protection as do all who are loyal and trust in me."

His was a great performance and Ava bought it all. Demitri smiled at her naivety. Ava mistook that smile for love and kindness and tears of relief squeezed from the corners of her eyes.

"Is he bothering you Ava?" Yuri interrupted.

Yuri seemed to have grown in both height and stature, as he glowered over Demitri, sat on the barstool. Ava noticed the tendons in Yuri's muscular neck were as taught as wire mast stays and that his eyes were murderous. He had already told her that he had *certain skills*. Now, she didn't doubt it. Ava needed to stop this confrontation and stop it quickly. If these two men fought for her, it would be to the death, of that she was certain.

"It's OK Yuri, Demitri is a friend and means well. The tears are just my foolishness. Please leave us and don't cause a scene. I'm fine. Really I am." Ava's smile was paper thin.

Yuri jutted his chin out in defiance, levelling his eyes accusingly at Demitri.

"I will be watching out for her," he warned.

Demitri's black eyes locked on Yuri's with equal hatred and disdain. They were two alpha males locked in combat, about to fight for their prize.

"Please Yuri!" Ava reached forward and touched his arm.

With monumental effort, Yuri let the moment go.

"I will do it for you Ava, but just this once." He looked threateningly at Demitri and ground out his words. "Be warned!"

Again Yuri's stare was met with equal defiance.

"Can we leave?" Ava asked Demitri anxiously, desperate to get out of the Bolshoi.

She needed to separate the men before this turned into the cock fight of the century. Demitri nodded and gestured for her to go ahead. As they walked out Ava caught Yuri's eye. Their minds linked and the exchange was without words.

I'm so sorry Yuri, please forgive me.

145

Ava couldn't quite fathom the look on his face and his feelings were guarded so that she couldn't read him. At the very least his expression was murderous and it chilled her to the bone.

Watch him and take care of yourself, was Yuri's measured response.

------------------------------------------------------------------------

It was just a twenty minute drive back to the research laboratories, but the journey there felt like an eternity to Ava. Demitri's brief spell of caring and cordiality had passed. Now she was getting the silent treatment. Ava tried to read his thoughts but he was a closed book to her, impregnable. She had only met a few people with that ability and it was always a sign of great intelligence. The good thing, was that Ava was pretty sure that Demitri couldn't access her mind either, which was fortuitous, as her emotions were a mixture of lust and hate. Given Ava's fatal attraction for absolute bastards, she already knew which primordial emotion would win.

Demitri waved his way through security, parking the Mercedes in the Managing Director's slot. When they exited, Demitri led the way with Ava obediently following behind. The act was another intentional demonstration of his male supremacy. Although Ava followed dutifully, she was secretly seething inside, more through her own spinelessness though, rather than his chauvinism. Ava hated herself for her weakness. The retinal scanner recognised Demitri and they walked in. He tossed his coat on the desk and turned to face Ava. His expression was feral and Ava's even more so. Ava, finished with being given the silent treatment was the first to speak.

"What are we going to do, ignore each other all night or fuck?"

"Fuck!" Demitri grunted.

Ava crossed purposefully to him, putting both hands behind the back of his neck; she pulled hard, forcing his lips on hers whilst at the same time, thrusting her pelvis into his. Her eyes opened wide in a mixture of astonishment and glee, as she realised that

Demitri's manhood was more than ready for her. That realisation set off a storm within Ava, one that would take much to calm. She had waited more than six months for this moment and every second without him inside her was agony and a second wasted. Ava drove Demitri backwards into the bedroom with her face locked to his, until the back of his knees buckled as they hit the bed. Within seconds, she was tearing at his shirt, pulling it off his back and unbuckling his belt. Ava needed him naked and at last he was.

She heard her expensive dress rip as it came apart in Demitri's powerful hands, leaving her exposed in her sheer black underwear. Demitri clearly wasn't into fasteners and tore them from her too. Ava was naked in seconds, her want beyond rational. It was as if madness had come upon her. She needed the brutish man inside her; she needed to be cruelly and brutally dealt with. Sex for Ava had always been about men more powerful than her taking all that they wanted. All she expected in return was equal animal release. Ava had never known love from a man, nor expected any. Their role was to provide the spike and hers to ride it into oblivion. Tonight Ava desperately needed that oblivion.

The moment Demitri had freed Ava of her underwear, she was upon him; wet and wanting, guiding him into her. She groaned at the pain of taking him, his size and hardness was beyond Ava's experience. She thrust her hips down on him, screaming out at the delicious agony of accepting him. It felt like riding an iron bar to Ava, as she slammed herself relentlessly on him, driving herself closer and closer to the oblivion she so desperately sought after months of denial. Ava's breathing became ragged. Colours started to explode in her head. She was close to climax and desperate for the release she had waited so long for. Just as she teetered on the very edge of ecstasy, Ava felt Demitri's powerful arms under her ribs as he threw her upwards and off him like a rag doll, landing her face down on the bed. The act was beyond cruel. Ava was furious, the moment having gone.

"You bastard, you absolute bastard!" she screamed in a hissy fit, hammering the pillow with her fists in temper.

Without Ava realising, Demitri was now behind her, lifting her pelvis off the bed until she was on her knees. His penetration was brutal; a single thrust that drove her into the mattress, and then began his relentless and angry rhythm, which had no semblance of love or respect. Ava tried to cry out to make him stop, but Demitri had his hands on her back pressing her face into the pillow, suffocating her. His pounding was merciless, and Ava almost at the point of unconsciousness. The image of Rudi's face randomly appeared in her mind as she recalled his expression when he was choking the life out of her at the Soho Rooms. That image triggered Ava's survival instincts. She put all her strength into forcing her face out of the pillow, turning it sideways to gulp in precious air. Demitri was oblivious to Ava's predicament, as he brutally took his pleasure.

Despite Ava's brutal and undignified treatment, he colours once again began to explode in her head, harbingers of her rapidly approaching orgasm. The rhythmical sound of his pelvis slamming into her buttocks and the pain of each powerful thrust, only served to drive Ava ever onwards. Accustomed to the pain now, Ava began to love every agonising second and wondered if it was normal for a girl to want to be fucked so hard and for so long? There had to be something deeply wrong with her, she had to concede.

"Don't stop, please don't stop. Fuck me!" Ava begged and this time he didn't.

Somehow, impossibly, he upped the tempo. Demitri's hands were now on Ava's hips dragging her onto him, forcing himself ever harder and deeper into her. There was no love in this, just animal fucking, but Ava no longer cared. Then it happened.

"Oh, my God. Oh, my God!"

The vivid and pulsating colours in Ava's head exploded into a blinding white light that filled her consciousness, seemingly driving her mind outside of her body to somewhere in paradise. On cloud nine, out on another plane. Her muscles went into spasm, locking him into her. Ava's base instinct of procreation ascended, she wanted his seed. Her sex went into rhythmical contractions, trying to milk him. Years of ballet had given Ava amazing flexibility. She managed to swing her leg high and rotate around him until she was on her back with him on top of her, without losing her grip on his manhood. Demitri grimaced at the pain, which only spurred him on to punish Ava more.

It was Ava's turn to take her man by the hips and encouraged him until he released himself deep inside her. Ava screamed out at the sheer satisfaction of the act, her eyes searching his face for some emotion. At last she saw it and was elated. He cared! A smile had lifted the corners of Demitri's mouth and his eyes showed some other emotion. Deep thought perhaps, love maybe. It was enough for Ava though. He was her man now. Almost at once her body relaxed, sated and she looked up lovingly at him. Ava's eyes followed the line of his jaw up to the softness of his perfect ear and she desperately wanted to kiss him there. Somehow, she had a feeling of *déjà* vu. That jawline seemed familiar, as if she had always known this man. At that moment, all Ava knew for certain, was that she would do anything for the man that was now deep inside her. Anything!

---

"What are we going to do, ignore each other all night or fuck?" Ava was finished with being given the silent treatment.

"Fuck!" Demitri grunted. It had gone exactly to plan. This girl was the perfect victim. She responded to abuse with a willingness to please and at the same time earn favour. The worse she was treated, the harder she would try for him. How well he bedded her in the next few hours would be the cement that would bind her to him for a lifetime. Demitri knew that. After all it had worked on that whore mother of hers, Demitri recalled with great satisfaction.

The urgency of Ava's charge, driving him into the bedroom amused Demitri. She was just like her mother, desperate for sex. It was a particular pleasure for him to deny Ava the climax that she so desperately craved. Demitri had almost laughed out loud at her fury at that denial. It was also a matter of principal to Demitri, and a part of Ava's conditioning, that he did not allow her the pleasure and satisfaction of fulfilling him, rather that he stayed in total control. *Girl on top empowered* was not an option that he would ever let her have again. Taking her roughly from behind like a bitch on heat was all that she deserved. She loved it that way though, and he knew she would still be feeling the damage of his abuse days later. For Demitri sex with Ava would only ever be about possession and control.

Demitri had allowed himself to come just this once, well twice if you count when she was comatose on Rohypnol. He vowed that he would never let her have the satisfaction of pleasing him again. He was simply *marking his territory* and controlling her. Ava thrived on guilt and he would use her inability to please him again and again.

Pathetic, he thought when she had gazed into his eyes desperately seeking the emotion of reciprocated love. Demitri could tell she thought she had found it when he smiled. But how was she to know that the smile was simply because he was thinking that Bortnik would be in the act of killing Yuri at that exact moment?

Demitri knew only too we'll how important total control over Ava would be. She had powers within her that she had yet to explore. Once she had found them and honed them, it would be he who would be at *her* mercy. Yuri was an Angel and in time, would have become a dangerous ally to Ava. The smile that Ava had mistaken for love, was simply him enjoying the thought of how desolated she would be in the morning when news broke of Yuri's death and mutilation. She would be alone on this Earth, without anyone to turn to and all he ever wanted her to be, right from her conception; his obedient servant and trophy, a chattel to adorn his arm and a weapon of war, no more, no less.

---

It had turned ten when Yuri handed the bar over to the late-night barman. Normally, he would have stayed for a single drink and share the news of the day with his colleague, but tonight Yuri's head was consumed with thoughts of Ava. He needed to get word back to Callum that she had turned up again and that she was with one of the most dangerous men on the planet.

Several months ago, Callum had placed Yuri close to Ava to keep a watchful eye on her, giving her the best possible chance of completing her destiny. The mirrors had shown that she was to play a pivotal part in the salvation of mankind. Maelströminha had glimpsed the future in them. The only alternative future, that didn't end in Armageddon, was the one where Ava survived Demitri.

Yuri had been told that Ava's chance of success was at best remote, but it was that minute possibility, that was the world's hope. Ava was always going to need guidance and support from Yuri, but now that the Shadows had brainwashed her, his support would be crucial. He had never intended to get emotionally close to Ava, she was simply part of his *work*, but she had him captivated from the first time that they met. Falling in love with a woman like Ava was inevitable.

Yuri left the Bolshoi by the back entrance that serviced the facility. A short walled road protected the area's security, with a staff parking area at the far end.

Moscow's icy night air bit cruelly as Yuri trudged out of the sheltered area to make his way up the walled road to the parking bays beyond. He thought he heard footsteps behind him and turned, but nobody was there. A black limousine had parked at the top of the road, blocking the way in and out of the parking area. This was a common occurrence; the inconsiderate rich parking where they pleased, when they pleased. Their arrogance irked Yuri, particularly as it now meant he would have to go back into the Bolshoi and find the usually non-cooperative owner to move it. Yuri turned and came face to face with two heavy set men. They were dressed in full length black cashmere coats and carrying baseball bats. One had a deep scar that split his forehead

151

and brow; the other was taller with thin lips and mean furtive eyes.

Yuri was no stranger to street fighting and his survival instincts immediately kicked in. He rapidly evaluated his assailants, ascertaining which was the weaker, should physical aggression be required. At the same time his eyes scanned his surroundings for an escape route. Yuri neither recognised a weak link nor a way out, other than to turn and run towards the limousine. But Yuri was not a runner. His inherent Angel skills would give him a chance at least, but the narrow road with high walls either side, gave him too little room to manoeuvre and avoid the swinging baseball bats. He needed to get the two men out into the open.

Yuri slowly backed off towards the car park. All the while his eyes flicked from one thug to the other, looking for an early warning of their attack. Every assault begins with the contraction of the aggressor's pupils. Yuri watched for that reflex, knowing that it could give him that split second advantage, perhaps enough to save his life. He was coiled, ready to attack like a viper with powerful finger strikes to their eyes. Blinding one, he was sure of, but blinding both was unlikely to say the least.

It was unlikely that Yuri would leave this fight unscathed. Some of their blows and kicks would inevitably find their mark, weakening him. Both men appeared to be right-handed, guiding his rapidly forming defensive strategy. Once he had disabled the first assailant, he could twist his body in anticipation of the other's attack. A heavy blow to his left arm was a sacrifice worth making, allowing him to counter attack, forcing his fingers deep into the man's eye sockets, blinding his opponent.

They were nearly at the car park. Yuri found it strange that the two thugs were making his withdrawal so easy. His heart dropped in sudden realisation of the trap set for him, when he heard the metallic click as Bortnik released the safety catch of his semi-automatic pistol.

Yuri naturally turned his back to the wall as the three men formed a semicircle in front of him, with Bortnik in the middle.

There was no way out for Yuri. Bortnik's pistol was aimed right between his eyes and the two heavies had their baseball bats at the ready. Bortnik appeared high on cocaine, shaking with sadistic anticipation of the pending blood-bath.

"You have made a very dangerous enemy Yuri Alexandrov. Now you must pay for that mistake. I have instructions to kill you slowly and painfully."

Bortnik sneered conceitedly, sure of his victim.

"My men have instructions to take their time killing you. They will break every bone in your body and you will hear and feel each one break. I will take the utmost pleasure watching you writhe in agony, begging me to kill you and release you from your pain. Finally, when I am ready, they will crush your skull and the last thing you will hear is my voice laughing."

Yuri just stared back implacably at Bortnik, his eyes drilling into his. Inexplicably, the leering fat man began to sweat profusely despite the sub-zero temperature. He tugged at his collar to suppress the feeling of suffocation, swiftly overwhelming him. There was something about Yuri that was unsettling him. He showed no fear, despite the odds, which was beyond Bortnik's experience; all before having cowered to his brutality. Yuri's stare seemed to penetrate Bortnik's very soul, unnerving him, such that he could not break free to look away and hide his fear. At last he broke, panicked and screamed out.

"Kill him! Kill him quickly!" Bortnik's voice sounded shrill in the cold, still night air as the baseball bats rose and fell.

-------------------------------------------------------------------------

Chapter 13

It was one o'clock in the morning, more than three hours later, when Demitri let Ava's slack body slump to the floor following a final bed-ending that she would never forget. He looked down at her disdainfully. She looked so much like her mother. It was like history repeating itself. The image of Anastasia's slender body hanging from the ceiling at the Metropol flashed through his mind, and he wondered how he would deal with Ava when the time came. But that was for another day. First, she had to deliver him the corpses of Callum Knight and the other Angel generals. That would leave the Matriarch Maelströminha and her sister Crystalita; exposed to be dealt with last.

Demitri left Ava there, seemingly unconscious on the floor. He didn't care and had to resist the temptation to kick this loathsome woman in the ribs out of contempt and hatred. Her conditioning and dehumanisation couldn't have gone better, he mused. Ava was now ready to murder whosoever he wished.

---------------------------------------------------------------------------

Ava was semiconscious and only vaguely aware of Demitri leaving. She lay naked on the floor for another two hours before she regained enough strength to drag herself back onto the bed. As a Shadow, Demitri had been blessed with literally super-human virility. It felt to Ava as if there wasn't a single place on her body that hadn't suffered one way of another from Demitri's relentless pounding and grip. He had been brutal, treating her more like a whore than a lover, but in truth, Ava had never known the difference. Indeed, she enjoyed the abuse as if she somehow deserved the punishment. Ava knew this stemmed from her lack of self-esteem and somehow the pain of brutal sex made her penitent. Katarina had been the only person that she had experienced loving sex with. She had never expected that from a man.

Ava struggled onto her back and winced at the pain of the manoeuvre. She had been sodomised, something that she had never allowed. Demitri hadn't sought her consent either. He had just taken her roughly without warning. He was too big a man for the act and had left her torn and bleeding. Ava needed to clean herself and change the soiled bedding. The effort of standing and walking to the shower room was excruciating for her. The tears of pain and shame rolling down her face were testament to that. Ava wondered how she could have let her standards slip so low as to have let him do that to her, and how she could ever face him again. Ava knew that she would though, and that it would be all too soon, particularly as she no longer had Katarina to watch over her.

The cool waters of the shower soothed and cleansed her, but the soap stung like a bee as she washed the vestige of Demitri from her. Ava's thoughts turned to Yuri and how disappointed and hurt he would be, fuelling one of her strongest emotions, guilt. It was past midday and Ava knew he would already be back at the Bolshoi. She decided to call him as soon as she had showered.

Ava towelled herself off in front of the full-length mirror and examined herself as she did so. There were black bruises all over her body caused by Demitri's powerful fingers gripping her, particularly around her pelvis and buttocks. Her breasts were also bruised and sore to touch and the inside of her thighs were marbled with marks from Demitri's hands where he had forced her legs apart. She looked like she had been raped by a convention of chimney sweeps, Ava surmised as she wrapped herself in the soft white towel, tucking it in at her cleavage. She took another to dry her long auburn hair and wrapped it in a turban, picked up her mobile and called the Bolshoi. As the phone rang, she remorsefully calculated what lie to tell Yuri.

"Bolshoi Theatre, good afternoon, how may I help you?"

The voice was Slavic and one that Ava didn't recognise. There had been many staff changes in the months she had been away.

"Is it possible to put me through to Yuri at the bar?"

There was an uncomfortable silence.

"May I ask who I am speaking to Madam?"

155

"Ava Kap... I mean Ava Thompson. Recently married you know how it is?" Ava cringed at her clumsiness. "I'm a close friend of Yuri's."

"Well I don't quite know how to say this but I'm afraid I have some very bad news for you. They found Yuri's decapitated body in the back yard this morning. I'm sorry, he was a friend of mine too and we are all devastated."

Ava felt like she had been kicked in the stomach. Nausea and giddiness swiftly overcame her and there seemed no air in the room to breathe. She should have been with him. It was the third time she had failed to save someone she loved. The feeling of guilt and uselessness was suffocating her as tears of remorse flooded her eyes. It took some time until Ava could speak. Finally, she latched on to a glimmer of hope.

"You said that he had been decapitated, so it could be somebody else then. Couldn't it?" It was more of a pathetic plea than a question.

"They found his papers, watch and car keys on his body. Yuri was still dressed in his work clothes too. There is no doubt Miss Thompson, no doubt at all. I am so sorry, really I am."

"Thank you," Ava mumbled and cut the call.

She felt totally stricken. The pain in her heart was unbearable, eclipsing the physical pain she had been suffering. Ava lay on the bed with her knees drawn up to her chest in the foetal position, sobbing her heart out. There was now only one person in the world that she could trust and who loved her; that was Demitri. She vowed she would never let him down and that she would love and protect him for the rest of her life, no matter what he asked of her. He was now everything to her; her whole world.

It was prayer time, Ava noted after some time. She would pray for forgiveness and pledge the rest of her life to do God's will and that of his prophets Mohammed and the Hydra.

---

Over the ensuing week, Ava dedicated herself to prayer and her work. It was the only way she could at least partly block out the grief and guilt she felt over Yuri's murder. At night though, when she was all alone, her demons came back to haunt her. They fed off her unhappiness and occupied the emptiness in her soul throughout the hours of darkness, just as Katarina had said they would. Ava craved sunrise when those demons would scurry away, but they would just lay in wait for the return of the night.

This particular morning was much awaited. It would be the day of reckoning. Leonardo had joined the team of scientists and literally did bring another dimension to the project and its avenues of investigation. They had determined that passage through the mirror and therefore the time-space continuum was entirely thought driven. Using the functionality of the portal demanded clarity of vision, far in advance of normal human capacity. Leonardo had that clarity of vision. For example, it was only Leonardo who could see the future because of his advanced skills of imagery and perception, whereas the rest of them could only make the mirror reflect the past through familiarity. Leonardo had already transmitted a thought that manifested itself in the mirror. It was happiness, an entirely abstract concept that had no connection with past or present and was therefore entirely fifth dimensional. The next step was to follow that or a similar thought into the mirror. Ava's job was to encourage Leonardo to do so, whatever the risk. Those were Demitri's explicit instructions to her. All of the scientists were expendable for God's greater glory it seemed.

The 19th of December, was to be the last day of Ava's secondment to the project. Demitri had set the date and told her that her next mission was to find out about, and get close to Callum Knight. For what reason, Ava did not know. What she did know, was that she had to convince Leonardo to make that journey today. Demitri was not a man who would accept failure.

--------------------------------------------------------------------------

Ava found the scientists in debate at the table, as was normal. They were used to her now and their greeting was more than cordial, but somewhat less than the goddess status of their first meeting. The reason for detuning their greetings was entirely honest. She had ascended in their appreciation from beauty to brain and their respect for her intellect was immense. Ava was now simply one of their peers.

She cast an appraising eye over Leonardo. He was a fifteenth century man of feverishly inventive imagination and unquenchable curiosity. He was born out of wedlock to a notary and his peasant lover, something quite notorious in its day. His intellect was, and still is, unsurpassed but he was a remote man. Leonardo looked older than his sixty or so years. He had long grey hair and an unruly beard that almost encompassed him, such that there was little of his face to show. Leonardo always wore a slouch beret, day and night, an idiosyncrasy of his that had become part of his identity. Behind all of this, Leonardo was a shy, kind and compassionate man; the sort a woman would naturally trust and confide in, but unlikely to fall for romantically. He was a man you would love to be your father and had an innocent fondness for Ava, as she did for him. They would spend hours in the evening exploring each other's minds and Ava found a degree of peace in his company. She had confided all her life's secrets and sought his guidance. Leonardo had been particularly interested and supportive when she told him about her demons that came to her in the night.

"I see dead people sometimes," Ava told him. "They are with me in my room at night and they want something of me, but I don't know what."

When she told him, Ava had shivered as if someone had walked over her grave and expected Leonardo to think she was mad and that her demons were all just nonsense, a woman's ramblings, but Leonardo's understanding of the universe, physical and spiritual, was second to none.

"Do not confuse theses apparitions with demons for they are not Ava, nor are you some fallen Angel. They are simply souls that have not found their way home to rest. I believe that these restless souls find solace in unfulfilled and unhappy people. When we are complete as people, then there is no place or space for them and so they move on."

Leonardo took Ava's hand. He was about to give her the direction and reassurance she desperately needed.

"Ava. When you find love, true and unconditional love, these spirits will leave you forever. They will leave because there will be no room for them in your life. The right man will complete you physically, mentally and emotionally and you will shine in his presence like you have never shone before."

Leonardo's manner was entirely fatherly. Ava wondered at the man's perfection as he continued with his advice.

"You have only experienced users Ava, men of a frail and manipulative nature. They will trap you and use your desires and compassion against you. Demitri is a user Ava. Beware of him because he will consume you. You will be like a bird in a cage and all that he will ever be able to offer you, is a bigger cage. Cast him out of your life and find your knight in shining armour and *joie de vivre*. Find peace Ava. Find yourself, know her and love her; then you will shine like never before and your demons will be gone."

Leonardo was Ava's rock now, particularly as Demitri hadn't spoken to her since that torrid night. Since then, she had only received instructions from him through her mailbox. Ava and Leonardo agreed on all things, well apart from his opinion that Demitri was a user and a cad. She could not accept anything other than that he was her saviour. All that Leonardo could do was to guide her and hope that she would reflect on his words one day and see the light.

Ava had grown to love this amazing man in a fatherly way. She was uncomfortable with Demitri's written instructions to encourage Leonardo to follow his imagination into the mirror, and into the fifth dimension. Ava had documented and shared with Demitri every experiment, every theory or idea and had spent much time recording Leonardo's thought processes which enabled him to access the fifth dimension. Demitri was now confident that he had enough recorded knowledge to risk Leonardo's life in proof of theory.

Ava was deeply at odds with this, particularly as everyone that she came to love was taken from her, but she could not deny Demitri, her master. Ava knew that Leonardo's journey into the fifth dimension would be a disaster, and that she would be sending him to certain death. Ava sensed that Leonardo had grown to love her and would do anything for her. Conversely, she knew that Demitri would never forgive her if she refused him. Ava agonised over this and finally conceded that it was God's will. She had pledged her allegiance to *Allah*, his prophets and Demitri. It would be done in God's holy name, she decided at last, trusting in him.

"May *Allah* forgive me," Ava muttered and set herself once again to prayer.

--------------------------------------------------------------------------

Emboldened by her prayers, Ava sought out Leonardo and asked him to come and sit with her.

Nobody should ever have to be put into the position, that by its very nature, would be perilous at best; potentially life threatening. Ava lamented that she had to do just this. She felt deeply ashamed, disloyal and sullied. Leonardo sat facing her. Even with age, his eyes were the brightest blue and alert, but with the softness of the philosopher. Ava had sensed from the moment they met that Leonardo had Angel blood in him. This explained why he was centuries ahead of his peers in terms of rounded intellect. The Angel race had undergone millions of years more evolution than humans and their skills were passed down through their genes, much the same as hers.

Leonardo searched Ava's face and could sense her inner turmoil. It was not just Ava's struggle with her conscience that pained her though, he deduced. He could see visible signs on Ava's flesh conducive to her having taken a beating of some kind. Ava felt Leonardo's eyes on her and her shame showed in her troubled eyes. He let the matter go, sensing that Ava would not want to talk about the cause.

This gentle man was a humanist. Above all he valued the basic and good qualities of mankind: compassion; love; faith; trust; honesty and loyalty. Leonardo could see that Ava was at odds with all these emotions, confused and lost. He looked into her eyes. They were normally blue but today they were marbled honey brown. Leonardo could also see that Ava needed a means of salvation, and so unbidden, he gave her that which she yearned.

"I have been thinking little one. Perhaps it is time for me to journey into the fifth dimension," he suggested.

Leonardo was another who had referred to her as *little one*. Ava wondered if she really was so pitifully vulnerable.

She knew that Leonardo had come to a monumental decision. If required, he would lay down his life to preserve hers. There was no bigger sacrifice, proof absolute of his humanity, his unconditional love for her. Leonardo had seen something in Ava that she couldn't begin to comprehend, which humbled her.

Leonardo held Ava's gaze, watching as the brown flecks in her eyes evaporated like the morning mist. He had freed Ava of her guilt at perhaps the cost of his own life. Tears of relief and gratitude welled in the corners of Ava's eyes until they broke free under the sheer weight of them, cascading down her face. She stood and came to him, kneeling at his side. Ava laid her head against his shoulder and Leonardo held her closely to him. For

Ava, it was the closest thing to a fatherly moment she had ever experienced, and cried heart-felt tears at the tragedy of that simple fact. Leonardo let the turmoil inside Ava abate before he imparted some words of wisdom.

"There are things that I must say to you lest my journey separates us. You must promise me that you will at least consider what I tell you."

Ava knew that Leonardo's reference to his journey separating them was a euphemism for his death and his selfless bravery squeezed her heart. He was the perfect man and she knew that she would lose him, just as she lost everything that was precious to her.

"I promise Leonardo," Ava lifted her head from his shoulder to meet his fond gaze.

"What I am about to say is vital for your future safety and happiness Ava," Leonardo's voice was earnest and fatherly. "You only have but one chance at life and the choices you make determine whether that is an abundant life of happiness, grace and fulfilment, or a life wasted. I can sense that there is no true love or romance in your life, only use and abuse by those who selfishly manipulate your good and giving nature to their advantage. As I have already said, these men are takers Ava. Beware of each and every one them, for they will consume you and use you up until you are of no worth to yourself or to them; nor indeed to any other whom you love, or even the children you may bear. Finally, when you are spent and your looks gone, they will discard you for another, and you will look back with great remorse on a wasted life."

Leonardo put his hand under Ava's chin and lifted her face until her eyes were level with his.

"Life is all about loving and being loved Ava, nothing more, and you only bank your memories and your regrets. You must learn to love yourself Ava, because until you love yourself you will not be truly able to love another. I see special qualities in you, but all that you see in yourself are imperfections. There will be a man one day who will be your salvation. Recognise him when he comes and embrace him. Hold on to him at all cost, for his love will be complete and all encompassing."

Leonardo looked through Ava's eyes deep into her soul. She nodded, physically agreeing with all that was being imparted to her, but Leonardo sadly realised that his words were wasted. Ava was a tragedy in the making; ill-equipped, emotionally handicapped and naively innocent in matters of the heart and life. She was her owner's puppet, his trophy, his chattel. Despite all that he had said, Ava would do whatever Demitri asked of her. Fear and guilt would be her driving force, then eventually pity and duty; two of the ugliest devices that any man can use to mentally imprison a woman. Leonardo sighed at the hopelessness and inevitability of Ava's dilemma. He kissed her on the forehead.

"Journey well little one," he whispered in despair for her life.

-----------------------------------------------------------------------------

Chapter 14

Yuri had his back to the wall. At a push, and with a little luck, he could have taken on the two bat wielding thugs, but the third holding a gun, changed everything. He could see by the glazed look in Bortnik's eyes that he was high on something, which might make his mind easy to overpower, Yuri assessed. Time was against him though. He had to get into Bortnik's head and quickly. Taking control of his mind was Yuri's only remaining chance.

"You have made a very dangerous enemy Yuri Alexandrov. Now you must pay for that mistake. I have instructions to kill you slowly and painfully."

Bortnik sneered conceitedly, sure of his victim.

"My men have instructions to take their time killing you. They will break every bone in your body and you will hear and feel each one break. I will take the utmost pleasure watching you writhe in agony, begging me to kill you and release you from your pain. Finally, when I am ready, they will crush your skull and the last thing you will hear is my voice laughing."

Yuri needed to keep eye contact with Bortnik and hold him in his stare long enough to penetrate his psyche. Bortnik unwittingly obliged by scrutinising Yuri's eyes for any sign of terror, something that he would have found immensely pleasing. He sneered at Yuri, as the thought increased his sadistic desires. When Yuri returned that gloating smile with pure defiance, without the slightest hint of fear, it unnerved Bortnik triggering a panic attack.

"Kill him! Kill him quickly!"

Bortnik's voice sounded shrill in the cold, still night air. He was suffocating and sweating profusely as he tugged at his collar to find air, but struggled to fill his lungs. Bortnik wanted to look away from Yuri but could not. Despite the baseball bats rising and falling, striking him relentlessly, Yuri didn't buckle. His eyes drilled into Bortnik's mind until finally he had the control he needed.

"Stop it!" Bortnik screamed, but his men were in frenzy. The blood lust was on them.

The sound of the gunshot in the confines of the walled street was deafening. The bullet entered the scarred man's head at the temple and exited through the back of his head, splattering his brains against the brickwork behind Yuri. His lifeless body slumped to the ground ending in a sickening thud as his head slammed into the cobblestones. The man's corpse twitched comically for several seconds before it lay still in the gutter. The second bodyguard looked back at Bortnik in complete disbelief. His thin lips were about to utter the word *why* but it never formed. Bortnik's second bullet took him high in the chest killing him instantly.

Yuri's survival instincts, combined with his genetically inherited skills stopped him succumbing to the nauseating pain, caused by the repetitive beating. Somehow he refused to slip into the comfort of oblivion. He knew if he lost control of Bortnik's mind for just one second, he would be a dead man. At the same time Bortnik tried to drag his drug-crazed mind back from Yuri's control, needing a super-human effort on Yuri's behalf to hold on to him. The battle of minds finally fell in Yuri's favour and he grabbed the pistol from Bortnik's pudgy hand.

"On the floor, face down!" Yuri coughed out the words, his cracked ribs made talking painful. "Do it!"

Bortnik awkwardly lowered his bulk to the ground obediently. Yuri's cover at the Bolshoi was blown now. He needed a plan. Even if he killed Bortnik, Demitri would seek him out. That was a certainty. He decided quickly that it would suit his purposes to be assumed dead, that way he could still keep an eye on Ava.

They were only yards from the limousine. Yuri crossed to it painfully, confident that Bortnik was unlikely to get up and run. It wasn't in him; the physical effort, or the courage. Yuri was thankful for his Angel abilities that had given him denser and more resilient bones. The pain in his ribs and forearm suggested that those areas had taken the brunt of the beating. The initial numbness, followed by intense throbbing was indicative of fractures at the very least. He had been able to fend off many of the blows, but inevitably some had penetrated his defence. The baseball bats had also tenderised his thighs and hips. Every pain was excruciating in its own right, and Yuri winced with each step he took towards the car. He popped the boot, immediately finding what he wanted; which was the snow shovel.

"If you were going to kill me, you would have already done it!" Bortnik spat out his words.

He struggled to his feet and stood there defiantly, glowering at Yuri.

"Big mistake fat man, not taking me seriously," he dismissed.

"Yuri squeezed the trigger, the gun spitting a bullet straight into the big man's upper thigh. Bortnik squealed like a stuck pig, his face growing redder by the second."

"Strip him naked!" he ordered, pointing at the corpse of the scarred man, the one that best fit Yuri's own physique.

Bortnik went about the task cursing as the bullet wound burnt each time he moved. Yuri stripped at the same time, the icy chill of the Moscow winter mercifully numbing his beaten body. He threw his clothes at Bortnik.

"Dress him in these!" Yuri demanded.

He began to dress in the man's clothes. The fit was good, which meant that the dead thug could also pass for Yuri, albeit cursorily.

"Take his chain and watch off and put these on him," Yuri tossed his own possessions over to Bortnik, along with the snow shovel. "Now hack his head off."

At first Bortnik looked back at Yuri in dismay, then realised his plan and why he was still alive. Yuri was in no state to have done this by himself. Bortnik began to shake with fear, as he realised that Yuri had only extended him a stay of execution. He resignedly hefted the shovel over his head and hacked at the scarred man's neck until his severed head rolled free.

"Put the head in the boot along with him," Yuri pointed at the body of the thin-lipped bodyguard.

Dragging the body of his man to the car was a monumental effort for an unfit, fat man like Bortnik, who was now encumbered by the gunshot wound in his leg, the task proved to be an impossible one. Bortnik looked like he was about to have a heart attack at the sheer physical effort required, forcing Yuri to assist him. Even together, the task was monumental. At last Yuri slammed the boot shut on its macabre cargo and turned to face Bortnik.

"Don't kill me!" Bortnik pleaded, sweating like the pig he was.

Bortnik felt sure he was looking into the eyes of his executioner, his bowels releasing out of sheer terror and the stench filling the night air. Yuri stepped back in disgust.

"You are only alive Bortnik, because I swore an oath to a close friend that I wouldn't kill you. That pleasure will be hers and hers alone."

"The Kaplinski woman?" he blurted.

Bortnik was open-mouthed in astonishment, which made him look even more foolish. It was his last effort at defiance and he laughed in the face of death.

"Bring her to me and I will show her the same compassion I showed her bitch friend and aunt!" he yelled.

Bortnik had found some spine at last and Yuri had to dig deep to contain his rage and not kill him there and then.

"You would do well to fear her Bortnik and may well wish you'd died here today with a bullet in your head, rather than anything that she may have planned for you."

It took all Yuri's effort not to squeeze the trigger and end his life there in the street.

"In exchange for your life you're going to give me your mind freely. Don't resist me Bortnik, or I will live with my conscience and forget my oath to the woman."

Bortnik's mind was easy to re-enter. His fear had eradicated any ability to think, let alone resist. Yuri had him controlled in a trancelike state in only a minute. For the headless body to pass for himself, Yuri had to erase all memories of the night from Bortnik's mind.

"You will ditch the body and head where they cannot be found and valet the car. You will believe that I am dead and accept that your men left your employment after killing me. Repeat that!" Yuri ordered, and Bortnik did, word perfect.

"When you have done that, you will report back to this dangerous enemy that I seem to have made," Yuri guessed that it was Demitri Papandreou, "and tell him you have carried out his orders to the letter. You will never think of this again, nor of the Kaplinski girl. Is that understood?"

Bortnik nodded his fat balding head which was now deathly white and beaded in feverish sweat. Yuri made him repeat his orders and Bortnik was once again word perfect.

"Now do as you have been instructed!" Yuri commanded.

Bortnik limped away to his limousine without looking back, unaware of what had just transpired, not even the pain in his leg seemed to encumber him on his mission.

The sheer effort of holding himself together had taken Yuri to the very point of exhaustion. He knew he needed medical help, but first he had to get the body back to the Bolshoi yard where he wanted it to be found, as if he had been murdered there. This would leave an easy and obvious trail for the police to follow and to naturally presume the identity of the body to be his. To achieve that, Yuri needed to somehow wrap the body, before dragging it to the yard; otherwise the dead man's blood would leave a trail. Thankfully, at that moment the heavens opened, washing the dead man's blood into the gutter and away.

Yuri cursed at the pain as he dragged the heavy corpse down the cobbled road, regretting letting Bortnik go before thinking his plan through. Every step demanded Yuri to dig deep to continue, thrusting away the nausea that would have him abandon the task. At last there, he checked his car keys were still in the dead man's pocket, along with his ID then dumped the body by the rubbish bins. He had just one thing left to do, before seeking much needed medical attention, which was to contact Callum Knight. He needed to tell him that his cover was blown at the Bolshoi and that Ava Kaplinski was alone and unprotected in the hands of Demitri Papandreou.

--------------------------------------------------------------------------

Leonardo sat in the recliner facing the old ornate mirror, considering his options. He wondered which thought to follow and whether to physically or mentally follow it through the portal. He decided at last that it would be safer to follow it mentally. After all it was a spiritual journey; flesh and bone were of no use or consequence where he was journeying to. At least that way there would be something left for them to bury when I get this all wrong; he mused and couldn't help but smile at the madness of it all. He wondered whether he was doing this act of madness for science or Ava, but was pretty sure that it was for Ava.

She was the daughter that he never had and in these few short days, had become more precious to him than life. There was something uniquely special about Ava that made her worth protecting. He also knew that she was not human but quite what she was, he didn't know. What was certain though was that Ava was an unwitting player in a very dangerous game, and the cards she held were a losing hand. If all that Leonardo could do was to give her an ace to play, then that might be enough to protect her; an old man's parting gift.

Albert, Isaac and Galileo stood supportively behind him as Ava came to kneel by his side. She took his hand and kissed it.

"You are a brave man Leonardo and you have my deepest respect," Ava hesitated and then added, "and love."

"To business then before I change my mind," Leonardo smiled back at her.

He didn't want the situation to become too emotional, as that clouded judgement and first and foremost he was a scientist. He looked at Ava as if for the last time.

"It will be the thought of your love that I will take into the mirror with me Ava, and I shall follow it to wherever it takes me." Ava's eyes flooded instantly.

As Leonardo gathered his thoughts, the mirror ceased to reflect their images and the room they were in. Ava had set cameras to record the event. That way, they could examine the reflections of the thoughts in Leonardo's mind more analytically later. There seemed to be a grey mist that swirled behind the glass and dozens of brief images flashed before them, half hidden in the mist of time. Ava could see that these were fond memories. They depicted loving moments of tenderness and smiles. She thought that some were likely to be of his parents at various ages through his life, and others of pets and friends. It was only briefly, but at one point she thought that she saw herself.

The images flashed by faster and faster, like the frames of an old nineteen twenties film flickering, giving the impression of movement until finally the mist cleared, replaced by a bright light in the distance with humanoid forms within. The light was so strong that it blurred the images, such that they appeared to be only grey shadows with vague outlines. Then it happened. Leonardo was inside the mirror looking back at them smiling. His mane of long grey hair and unruly beard looked like they were on fire because of the brilliance of the light behind him. Leonardo turned his back on his audience and walked towards the light without looking back. Finally, he was engulfed by that brilliance and was gone.

"But that cannot be," Ava whispered to the others. "I'm still holding his hand."

There was a shared feeling of religious awe. Galileo genuflected, making the sign of the cross. Leonardo was still sat in the recliner breathing peacefully with a benign expression on his face.

-------------------------------------------------------------------------

Leonardo found himself in a swirling mist looking back out through the old ornate mirror at the bemused faces of his colleagues. Although he was clearly in another world or another place, or even another time, he felt at peace. The happy and loving thoughts that had carried him through the portal into the fifth dimension were still with him, lifting his spirit. He smiled back at his colleagues, turned and walked towards the humanoid shapes silhouetted in front of him. The mist cleared as he approached the group and Leonardo had the strongest feeling of *déjà vu*. He had been to this place before, of that he was certain. Everything was exactly as Leonardo remembered.

"*L'ultima cena*," Leonardo whispered in religious awe, "the last supper".

The room they were in had a latticed ceiling and whitewashed walls, with heavy tapestries hung on both sides. There were three windows at the far end that looked out across the countryside to the hills in the distance. A trestle table was set for thirteen but only twelve of the seats were taken, and a coarse linen table cloth was spread, with bread and wine sufficient for all there. The man sat at the middle, clearly their leader, had long reddish brown hair and a close cut beard. He wore a red robe with a steel grey shawl thrown over his left shoulder. The six men sat to his left, dressed in colourful robes, were in animated conversation, as

171

were the five to his right. Only the second chair to the right of centre was empty.

"We have been waiting a long time for you Judas. Please sit with us, there is a place set for you."

The man with the reddish-brown hair pointed to the chair with a welcoming hand and a friendly smile.

Leonardo bowed respectfully and made the sign of the cross. The man welcoming him was Jesus Christ, and the men there were eleven of his twelve apostles. The scene was precisely as Leonardo had painted from his own imagination years ago. Now, somehow, he was living inside his imagination. Leonardo looked down upon himself. He now wore a blue and green robe, with open sandals, just as he had depicted Judas Iscariot in his painting of the last supper. In his hand was a purse filled with coins. It was impossible, but somehow Leonardo had walked into his own painting and become the traitor Judas who had betrayed his saviour for just thirty pieces of silver. Leonardo walked obediently to his chair. The weight of the silver in his hand felt as heavy as all the combined sins of the world. Leonardo was thankful when at last he could place it on the table. He intuitively knew why he was there. It was because he and the other scientists were about to betray mankind and open the fifth dimension, the world of imagination and possibility. He had become the traitor Judas Iscariot himself!

"Would you take bread and wine with us Judas?" Jesus offered.

His face was full of peace and love, even though he knew that Leonardo was on the cusp of forsaking him. Leonardo was perplexed, torn between his religious and humanitarian beliefs and the hard facts of science.

"Is this Heaven and are you Jesus Christ?" Leonardo asked with humility.

"I am no more Jesus Christ than you are Judas Iscariot, Leonardo. We are manifestations of your imagination and currently, of your guilt. You and your wise friends are about to

172

forsake the world and condemn it into oblivion. The decision that you all make when you return to your own dimension will either enable or avert Armageddon." *'Jesus's'* expression was benign and his manner epitomised love.

"Walk with me through time Leonardo, and let me show you all possibility."

Leonardo looked up. They were no longer in the painting and the apostles were gone. The mountains around them were steel grey and primordial against the stormy skies above. There was no vegetation and the mist around them tasted of sulphur. No birds flew and no animals roamed. The only colour was the red rivers of molten rock that streamed down the craggy slopes from the mouth of the volcano high above to the valleys below. Lightning struck around them and the thunder rumbled almost continuously. It was icy cold and the most hostile environment that you could ever imagine.

"This is *genesis*, the beginning of creation; a time when nothing existed other than infinite possibility and hope."

Jesus swept his hand across the sky like turning the page of a book. Somehow the landscape changed. They were still on the mountain but all was serene, the sun shone and the sky was blue. The steely grey rock was now covered in colourful lichen, and the valleys below were a luscious green, with goats grazing lazily. Birds of prey soared effortlessly on the thermal winds as they scanned the pastures for their quarry. The peace was disturbed as a lone goatherd whistled and drove his goats from their grazing down the mountain towards the settlement in the distance.

Again and again, Jesus swept his hand across the skies. Each time the scene changed. In one scenario, the valley below was littered with the bodies of men fallen on the battlefield, with birds of prey feasting on their uncovered faces. In another, there were monks filing up the narrow mountain footpath to a monastery that teetered impossibly on one of the lesser peaks. Jesus passed his hand across the heavens for the final time. This time the skies were black and the land a frozen waste from the legacy of a global nuclear winter.

"And *this* is the apocalypse, the end of the world," Jesus said mournfully.

In the darkness, Leonardo thought he saw a tear rolling down the side of Jesus's face.

"This, Leonardo, is what you bring upon mankind if you open Pandora's Box, and let the world into the fifth dimension."

Leonardo was shocked, desolate. His life's work was all about the search for knowledge and the betterment of mankind. This was a stain on his soul and he felt dirty.

"Do I do this?" Leonardo uttered the words in disbelief.

"You don't have to," Jesus replied, "not if you stop now. But there is one amongst you who holds the key to man's destiny. The future of us all depends on her conscience."

Leonardo intuitively knew that Jesus was referring to Ava.

"Come Leonardo; let me show you more of the wonders of creation."

The journey that followed literally took them out of this world.

When at last the revelation was over, the man that Leonardo had come to know as *Jesus* bade him farewell.

"It is time for you to return to your own kind Leonardo. If I was to give you a parting gift, what might that be?"

Leonardo thought carefully for a while before answering.

"More time would be the greatest gift a man could ever receive." Leonardo shook his head at the hopelessness of his predicament. "The lifespan of man is not enough for him to finish his work. There is much to discover and much to learn. What I have seen today, only begs more questions that need answers and there is no time," Leonardo lamented.

"Go in peace Leonardo, your friends are waiting for you."

The gentle man turned away and walked into the mist.

"Who are you if not Jesus Christ?" Leonardo called out in desperation.

"I am all men and then nobody," was his reply.

At once Jesus was gone, leaving Leonardo feeling bereft. He turned and instinctively walked in the opposite direction. At last the ornate mirror was in front of him, with his friends' anxious faces looking back at him. Leonardo took one more leap of faith and his spirit, his imagination passed through the mirror.

---------------------------------------------------------------------------

To those in the laboratory it was only moments later that Leonardo reappeared from the brilliance, walking confidently towards them. But this man was much younger, maybe twenty-five years or more. His hair was long black and silky and his beard cropped short. He had the physique and gait of a young man. A mischievous grin lit his handsome face. The image in the mirror began to fade until all that was left was the image of themselves.

"Oh, my God!" Ava gasped.

Once again Galileo crossed himself religiously. The image in the mirror was that of the four of them surrounding the recliner with a man in his early thirties asleep on it. They looked down from the mirror to the sleeping Leonardo, all of them astonished at what they saw. They were indeed looking at a young Leonardo, but now he wore a blue and green robe with leather sandals, clasping a purse of some kind. It looked heavy; Ava took the purse and opened it. There were thirty ancient silver coins inside. She looked at the others in incomprehension. Leonardo was totally unharmed and sleeping peacefully. It was Albert who finally broke the silence.

"Not only have we proven that the fifth dimension exists but we have discovered the fabled Fountain of Youth, the Holy Grail. The most sought after prize in Christendom!"

---------------------------------------------------------------------------

Leonardo slept for another four hours, completely exhausted by his journey. He awoke to a multitude of excited questions, but was not yet ready to answer them. His head was still in turmoil, trying to come to terms with his experience, an experience that would change him forever, both physically and mentally. They all recognised that change and gave Leonardo the space he needed. It was much later that evening before he was ready tell them about his journey.

"I have seen things that no man has ever seen," he began, "not even in their dreams. I saw the birth of a star and the end of the world. I walked with God and I talked to the Devil. I saw man at his best and man at his worst, and all things in between. I was in a place where all outcomes were possible, you only had to reach out and take your pick. The fate of all of us lies in that fifth dimension of imagination and infinite possibility. It is a place that no man should ever go to again, and should only be entrusted to those perfect beings that abide there. I want no part of this project."

The journey into the fifth dimension had clearly been a religious experience for Leonardo that had left a profound mark on him, changing his beliefs forever. They discussed the ethical implications of fifth dimensional travel at length through the night. Other than Ava they were unanimous in the belief that the project should be abandoned. It could lead to an *end of time* scenario, Armageddon. Ava was compromised by her deep love and devotion for Demitri, and truly believed she was enacting God's will.

At dawn Albert, Isaac and Galileo retired exhausted from the debate. They needed to rest and pack to return to their own times. Leonardo had slept most of the afternoon. That, coupled with his new-found youth and Ava's company, had left him rejuvenated. Leonardo had decided to enjoy every minute of this intelligent and beautiful woman's company.

"Do you believe in destiny little one and that you were always meant to be here, now?" Leonardo asked, cocking an intelligent brow.

Ava reflected for a moment before answering. Whilst she did so she analysed this extraordinary man. He was striking to look at and wore youth well. His face was handsome with long angular features, typical of the Romans, and his skin was tanned and shone with his new-found youth. He had lively blue eyes that danced below his broad intelligent brow. Ava could tell he was also feasting on her, drinking in every piece of her, knowing that he would never see her again after this day. His manner of speech was old fashioned, with the typical singing tones of the Italian Renaissance period, so kind upon the ear. It somehow drew Ava's eyes to the Cupid bows of his lips. This was becoming dangerous territory for a girl such as her and so she quickly diverted herself back to his question.

"Yes, I believe in destiny, but not in a pre-ordained way," she began. "I believe that we all have freedom of choice and that we exercise that choice to the best of our ability. In the end, it is the individual who determines the outcome, good or bad. We hold the key to our own destinies."

"Indeed, I believe that to be so too Ava," Leonardo agreed, "but powerful forces beyond our control do pull us together on occasions, to times and places where we can make those life changing decisions. It was no accident that our astral planes met and took us here Ava. We were blessed with the chance to meet each other and make a difference, to be different. It was a gift from the Gods that I believe only happens rarely and to the chosen few. When you are chosen and blessed in this way, you should take this gift and hold on to it at all cost and fulfil your destiny. But it will take all your courage Ava. Are you ready for that, and will you make the right choice when the time comes?"

Leonardo's blue eyes searched Ava's face for signs of the inner truth.

"But what is the *right choice* Leonardo and what am I choosing?"

"Our future Ava," he replied simply. "You hold the key to the destiny of all mankind and the right choice is simply having the courage to follow your heart."

Ava nodded respectfully, but she had no conception of what the wise old gentleman was talking about.

--------------------------------------------------------------------------

Scientists by nature are loners. It is a consequence of too much time spent studying and theorising and not enough interacting and socialising. None of them had been accustomed to working and living so closely, and it surprised them that they had bonded both as colleagues and as friends. They had found humanity and the true meaning of life. Much of that was through meeting Leonardo and understanding his philosophy on the human journey.

As they stood there in front of the old ornate mirror with their possessions packed, there was an atmosphere of deep regret, and that regret was double edged. Regret that they were departing to never meet again, a possibility denied them as they lived in chronologically and geographically different times and places. The second regret was that they had opened the fabled Pandora's Box that contained all the evils of the world.

According to the Greek myth, when Pandora realised what she had done, she hastened to close the container, but its deadly contents had already escaped with the exception of one thing; hope. Ava was now their hope, humanity's hope. Only she had the potential to right their wrong and close the door to the fifth dimension forever, before mankind abused the power that lay within. But Ava was naively unaware of her responsibility. The passage of time would ultimately prove whether Ava had the foresight and resolve to recognise and deliver that hope, or stand by and watch mankind descend into despair and destruction.

They had said their goodbyes to each other and were only waiting for Ava to arrive to release them back to their own dimension. She finally walked into the laboratory fashionably late, but they were all pleased that she had spent her time so productively. Ava had used that time to dress herself in her finest clothes, let her hair flow free, and applied her make-up precisely, each stroke of the lipstick and mascara reminding her of Leonardo's brush strokes. She wanted them to remember her as a woman.

Gone was the consummate professional with her white lab coat, tied up hair and flat shoes. Ava wore a long figure hugging floral red dress and high heels. Her shining auburn hair was set in a demi-wave which she had allowed to fall naturally past her shoulders. Ava's warm yet alluring smile was further enhanced by her red lipstick and perfect white teeth. Ava wanted their abiding memory of her to be that of a vibrant woman, and not just as a fellow scientist. Judging by their subtle nods of approval, Ava had succeeded. She crossed to them, entered their fold so that she was intimately close, and gave each in turn a heartfelt hug.

"I will miss you all immensely. You have become my friends; my family and I love you all dearly. If I ever unravel the mysteries of the mirror, I swear that I will visit. You have my solemn promise."

Ava wiped away a single tear as she took her place next to the portal. Albert came to her side holding his meagre parcel of belongings.

"I leave you with a heavy heart Ava. I have already been told that I will die in these next few weeks. It pains me that it will be without knowing whether I contributed to the opening of a doorway that leads to the destruction of mankind. How can my maker ever forgive me when judgement day comes?"

Albert seemed to have aged with the grim realisation of what they had done. All he wanted to do now was to go home and spend his remaining days with his faithful dog Lucy. He placed his hand on the mirror which vibrated to his touch. A mist began to swirl mysteriously behind the glass.

"Life is all about decisions little one," Albert embraced her in farewell." "The actions that you take, and the decisions that you ultimately make, may be pivotal to the survival of mankind!"

With that Albert stepped through the mirror, back to his own time, to his dog Lucy and to prepare to meet his maker.

"Albert! What actions, what decision?" Ava called out desperately after him but he was gone, lost in the mists of time.

Again, another had called her *little one* as if she had no inner strength or sound judgement at all. Was she really such an obvious 'fuck-up', she wondered?

Galileo took her hand, rescuing Ava from her thoughts.

"It has been a great pleasure meeting you and working with you Ava. You are a woman of great intelligence and fortitude, and I for one am confident in your discretion. When the time comes, you will execute that discretion to the better good." He lifted Ava's hand to his mouth, kissed it and stepped into the past.

Isaac was next. Ava could see that he was uncomfortable with goodbyes and had that stereotypical stiffness that older Englishmen are accustomed to possess.

"I bid you farewell Ava," his already long face set in his mane of hair, now looked longer still with the sadness of parting. "It has been an enormous privilege to work with you. What is done cannot be undone, but we may receive some form of absolution if the eventual outcome does not result in the end of humanity. We all have faith in your judgement Ava and you should consider carefully whether what we have discovered should be shared with the world. We all have our own destinies to fulfil."

With that said Isaac bowed his head in farewell and was gone, evaporated to some other time and place.

Ava suddenly felt burdened by these brilliant men's expectations of her. She was little more than the secretary to the experiment, but now the consequences of the outcome were apparently her responsibility. Ava was lost in the enormity of that expectation. Leonardo took Ava's arm and guided her to the table. They sat facing each other. He cupped her face lovingly with both of his hands.

"You are in turmoil Ava but you are not out of your depth. You have all the powers within you to put this to right if you so choose. I have faith that you will."

Leonardo's confidence was apparent but Ava's lack of faith and belief in herself gnawed at her consciousness.

"Why do you have such faith in me Leonardo? You don't know me. You talk of my *powers* but you have no idea."

"Do I not Ava? Do you not recognise that I too am an Angel and that I sense you?"

Ava nodded. "And I sense you Leonardo." There was the faintest sign of a blush from Ava, something outrageously out of character for her.

"Would you trust me with your mind if I trusted you with mine?" he asked holding her eyes with the softness of his.

Ava felt awkward. Her history was that of a harlot and if she agreed, he would know all her secrets; all of her sins.

"I will trust you if you do not judge me," Ava conceded.

They joined hands. She was surprised at the roughness of them for such a scholarly man, but amongst his many accomplishments, Leonardo was a sculptor. She wondered that those skilful hands had formed such beauty. Slowly their minds opened, allowing each to explore the other. Ava had never felt

181

anything like it. He entered her consciousness and she felt him exploring her thoughts and her memories. At first, she felt *violated* but then realised that the exchange and fears were reciprocal. Ava was suddenly swept up in his life, his art, his music and poetry. Most of all she was swept into his perfection. Leonardo truly was an Angel in every sense of the word, the most perfect being that she could ever imagine. His mind was in perfect balance and nothing like the train crash that represented her life. They were only linked in mind for minutes but in that time, they exchanged a lifetime of experiences. When the exchange was over, Ava realised that tears of pity were rolling down Leonardo's face, hanging in droplets from his beard. Ava lifted his hands to her mouth and kissed them.

"You are a wonderful man Leonardo," Ava said softly. "Don't cry for me. You see that I was lost and have lost, but Demitri has found me and I will be alright now," Ava's smile was both honest and innocent.

"I cry in part because of that Ava. You are making a pact with the Devil and you do not see it. Your life has been one of great suffering and it will end in this man's hands if you let it."

Ava let go of Leonardo and there was a sudden stiffness about her. She refused to accept what Leonardo was telling her. Sensing Ava's reticence, Leonardo backed off.

"Just stay aware little one. That is all I ask."

There were other things that Leonardo wished to say to her, but did not want to lose her receptiveness at the outset.

"The Bible tells us of the apocalypse and of the four horsemen. Beware of false prophets Ava. Beware of the Hydra for she is akin to the first horseman of the apocalypse, the *Antichrist*."

Ava baulked at the comparison. She had never mentioned the Hydra to Leonardo and felt betrayed that he had used her memories against her. Ava was furious!

"That is blasphemy! The Hydra sits at *Allah's* right hand along with Mohammed. They administer his will. How dare you!"

Ava's eyes had turned dark brown with rage at the insinuation, but the matter was too important for Leonardo to back down, even at the risk of losing Ava as his friend.

"Answer me this," Leonardo was commanding. "When did you find your religion Ava? How soon then afterwards did Demitri appear in your life?"

"That's not fair. It's irrelevant anyway." Ava felt trapped.

"Answer me!" he was now even more commanding.

"You have been in my mind Leonardo. You fucking tell me!" Ava's eyes were near black with rage now, papers began to lift from the tables and lights started to flicker.

"You have been a Muslim for just over six months Ava. Six months! And you have known Demitri for a few weeks only."

"And I have known you for less. Go back to your own time Leonardo da Vinci and go to Hell. You are no friend of mine!"

Ava turned her back and stormed out of the laboratory into her office, slamming the door behind her.

Leonardo sat for a moment holding his head in his hands in despair. Perhaps the world is not so safe in her hands after all, he lamented.

With a sigh of deep regret, Leonardo da Vinci stood and walked over to the old ornate mirror, placed his hand on it and stepped back in time. Leonardo went in the knowledge that he would spend the rest of his life never knowing if he had contributed to the end of the world or not.

--------------------------------------------------------------------

Ava was caught in a stand-off that she could not back away from. Her pride wouldn't let her. She watched through the one-way glass as a desolated Leonardo stood and left her life forever. The most perfect man that she had ever met slipped through her careless and un-purposeful fingers like the sands of time, never to return. Ava slipped to her knees in despair and lay on the floor sobbing.

What have I done? God forgive me what have I done? She had lost the only other man to have ever truly and unconditionally loved her.

----------------------------------------------------------------------------

When Ava woke, she was lying on the office floor, having cried herself to sleep there, but still she felt wretched and guilty. These pitiful emotions formed the backbone of Ava's life. She hadn't yet told Demitri about the success of their project. Imparting that news over a glass of Champagne with him, would go a long way towards healing her broken spirit. First though, it was prayer time. Ava had to show penitence for the blasphemous thoughts she had allowed to enter her mind. Ava needed to purge herself of any doubts that Leonardo had put there and re-affirm her allegiance to *Allah* and his prophets, particularly to the Hydra whom she had permitted herself to doubt.

After prayers, Ava took a shower and applied her make-up. The long floral red dress was still her preferred choice for the videoconference she was about to have with Demitri. Ava had decided that she would only impart the bones of their success at that meeting and save the best to tell him over an intimate dinner. She knew that he was in Moscow and that, after the amazing sex they had both experienced, he would be equally as desperate to see her. Ava has already convinced herself that their sex had indeed been amazing; to think otherwise would be an affront to Demitri and to *Allah*. Ava checked herself out in the mirror. Her auburn hair was big and shone red under the fluorescent bathroom light. She wondered whether the overall image was too red, as she had chosen red lipstick to compliment the red dress and hair. She smiled to herself lasciviously. Cock-sucker red they called it, and Ava wondered if Demitri would be so lucky. Not too red, she decided at length.

Ava straightened her dress and sat in front of her computer, angling the camera strategically to focus on her cleavage. A girl should always make one hundred percent sure of her man, she mused, clicked the conferencing icon and selected Demitri's link. It connected almost immediately.

"Ava, I have been expecting your call," Demitri's voice was music to her ears.

"Oh Demitri, it's so nice to see you and hear your voice. It seems such a long time and I have missed you so much," Ava fawned.

"It has only been nine days Ava, for God's sake," he pointed out clinically.

Ava played coy with him for a while but Demitri was not responding. She began to feel needy and foolish. She tried talking about their amazing sex and told him she couldn't stop fantasising about him, but his responses were simply matter of fact.

"Would you kindly get to the point please Ava, if there is one?" His tone was dismissive and impatient.

Ava was crestfallen, disorientated by his curt dismissiveness.

"Well um, the scientists have gone and..."

"Gone? Why did you let them go without consulting me?"

There was an immediate change in Demitri's manner that scared Ava. He was *really* angry now.

"They were finished with the project and didn't want any more to do with it," Ava was flustered. "It was their decision. I didn't tell them to go."

Demitri's expression was thunderous. He said nothing and just glared at her. Ava panicked and went into all the detail of the experiment to bring him out of his mood. It was the one thing that she did not want to do. That was supposed to be saved for their private time.

"Leonardo managed to transport into the fifth dimension and return. When he did, he was twenty years younger, maybe more. It was amazing. He saw creation and he saw the end of time. He said that he had seen things that no man should ever see. He had walked with the Gods but felt like an intruder there. Leonardo said that the fifth dimension was no place for people as imperfect as us. He said that to meddle would bring on Armageddon, the end of time."

Still Demitri was silent. Ava babbled on nervously.

"I have the video recordings and made copious notes. With the right subject, of suitable intellect, I believe we could recreate the experiment and repeat the journey."

Ava waited expectantly for the praise that she believed she deserved.

"Good work and good outcome," Demitri conceded. "I already have an appropriate candidate in mind for the next journey. Send me your notes and the videos and I will consider how we progress from there."

"But I thought that as you were in Moscow we could..." Demitri cut her off.

"Listen Ava, I'm a busy man and God's work cannot wait." Ava had visibly slumped in her chair at his rejection. She felt sick with the massive disappointment of the rebuff. "We have a golden opportunity to infiltrate the Angel organisation and take out their middle order leaders. This is your next mission and I have left full instructions in your mailbox. I see by your internet history that you have already been researching Callum Knight which is good, just as you have researched me," Demitri added accusingly. "He is currently in Moscow in dialogue with the Russian Foreign Secretary as a precursor to the emergency summit meeting to be held in Moscow next month, January 6th to 10th to be precise. He flies back to London Heathrow the day after tomorrow and I want you on that plane sat next to him. You will see when you read your mail that a first-class ticket has been arranged for you in the name of Ava Thompson. Unfortunately, we couldn't get adjacent seats but I am sure that you could use a little mind control to fix that."

Ava felt numbed by Demitri's coldness and simply nodded in reply.

"You will get to know him on the flight. I want you to show him how valuable you would be to the Angel organisation as a scientist, linguist and as a person with an all-round knowledge of global infrastructure and affairs. With that, and a little feminine persuasion, you are to infiltrate his team."

"Feminine persuasion?" Ava was horrified. "But that is for us; for you only."

"Don't play the naive virgin with me Ava," Demitri's tone was aggressive. "You have given sex away freely to all takers and on their terms. What I'm asking you to do is in God's name; to entrap the infidels and rid us of them. It is the Hydra's will that you do this and eliminate the Matriarch Maelströminha's generals, until you are in direct line of command to her. Then you will fulfil your destiny and rid the world of her and her sister; leaving the Hydra to reign supreme over the human race."

Demitri's vitriolic outburst was entirely unsympathetic towards Ava's clear and visible sense of disappointment. She looked wretched and broken. Ava sat there at her computer, sobbing her heart out. Demitri was suddenly concerned that he had perhaps pushed her too far and backed off a little.

"Then, when you have done all that I ask Ava, we will lie together and I will show you all that it means to be a woman, my woman. Trust me. It is our destiny."

Demitri could see that his final comment had placated Ava a little but her eyes were still jet black with the rage rumbling inside her. He realised that he had to tread more carefully now.

"In my mail to you are the names of the other generals that lie between you and Maelströminha. I want you to deal with them in the order that I have laid down. That is: Bud Lewinski after Callum Knight, then Ralph Robinson, Emanuel Goldberg, followed by Elizabeth and Ben Robinson. We already have basic plans for each but I am sure that a woman of your resourcefulness will have other ideas."

What Demitri was asking of Ava went far beyond her morals, principals and experience. She was furious with him for wrapping it all up as *God's* will, using her own guilt against her. Men seemed to be so good at doing that, she thought.

"Don't ever doubt that I love you Ava. You are precious to me and we will have our time together. Just remain patient."

It was hard for Demitri to make his smile anything other than wolfish but he hoped that he looked sincere. He terminated the call and turned to the pretty young blonde in his hotel room. She was naked, impatient with animalistic desire.

"Right, that's business over," Demitri assured the expectant young lady.

He swivelled his chair away from the dressing table and pulled his robe open. The girl's eyes opened wide with delight at what she saw and wider still when she impaled herself upon him moments later.

-----------------------------------------------------------------------------

Ava sat there unimpressed at Demitri's sheer audacity. Not only had he dismissed her out of hand, denied her the night of passion she justly deserved and craved for, he now wanted to transform her into a prostitute and murderess; all justified, as part of God's greater plan to expunge the Angel race from the face of the Earth. Momentarily, Ava allowed herself to reconsider Leonardo's words of advice. He had likened Demitri to the devil and the Hydra to the first horseman of the apocalypse, the Antichrist. "Beware of false prophets," he had said.

Ava quickly shut the blasphemous thoughts out of her mind; a black rage replacing them. All the pent-up emotion of losing

Leonardo and then being rubbished by Demitri, was building up inside her like the lava of a volcano trying to erupt and escape. Ava was building up steam like a pressure cooker and an explosion was imminent.

The phenomenon started with only the faintest stirring of the air around her, like a fan had been turned on in the room. Ava sat trancelike staring at Demitri's now frozen image on the computer screen. It had captured his last expression in what Ava could only describe as a smirk. Her fury was not just because of the smirk. Behind Demitri, in the background, she could just make out the naked legs of a woman. The frame of the screen had cut her at the thighs but it was enough to see that Demitri was a liar and a cheat.

The papers on her desk began to lift as the movement of air increased, becoming airborne, whipping around her like autumn leaves caught in a whirlwind. Ava was now in the centre of a vortex. The breeze became a gale. Pictures and charts ripped off the wall and got caught up in the debris of the maelstrom. Tables and chairs buffeted their way around the room, crashing into the walls and breaking into splinters. The fire sprinklers activated adding to the storm, likening it to a full-blown hurricane.

All the time, Ava's black eyes never left Demitri's image until finally the glass of the screen shattered into minute shards that immediately got caught up in the tornado swirling around her. With that painful image gone, the storm abated and the airborne debris came crashing to the floor around her. Ava's rage was replaced with something worse, a feeling of betrayal and great disappointment, both in Demitri and in herself. Her disappointment in Demitri was easy to reconcile. That was simply because he had rejected her again, just like he had done at the Bolshoi and again with the air hostesses on his Lear Jet. Her disappointment in herself however, was much more complex. She had once again allowed her faith to be challenged by letting doubts enter her head. To even think of the Hydra as a false prophet, and Demitri as a liar and a cheat, was unforgivable.

Perhaps he was doing God's will right now with *that* woman in the hotel, Ava thought, just as she must do with the men Demitri had selected for her to kill.

It was not for her to judge him. Ava decided, she would read Demitri's instructions then spend the rest of the night in prayer, seeking forgiveness for her sins.

Ava left the shambles that was her office for the laboratory and the workstation there. She logged on to the computer and set herself to work learning all there was to know about these men and women Demitri had told her to get close to and kill.

---------------------------------------------------------------------------

Chapter 15

22nd December 2015. Domodedovo Airport, Moscow

Yuri had kept a watchful eye on the premises of the Papandreou Research Laboratories for eleven boring days. In all that time, Ava had never left the buildings, nor Demitri enter them. He was becoming concerned that Ava had already suffered the same fate as Katarina and her aunt Alisa. Just before midday his heart leapt with joy. Ava appeared at the main gates with a generously packed suitcase and a cabin bag. His relief at seeing her alive was palpable, his heart pounding with the intensity of the love that he had for her. Moments later a long black limousine pulled up and she was gone.

Yuri followed the limousine at a distance, thankful that the registration number was not Bortnik's, but there were other oligarchs as bad as, and even worse than him, Demitri for one. As was typical, the windows were blacked out so he had no idea if she was alone.

Ava's destination soon became apparent when they left the confines of the city and took the AutoRoute towards the airport. Ava's baggage was further confirmation of her purpose. Callum had made it clear that he wanted to be notified as soon as Ava was on the move. Yuri placed the call.

"Callum Knight speaking," was his brief response.

Even without his name as an introduction, Yuri could not have mistaken his voice. Callum spoke with a perfect English accent, free from any regional colloquialisms and his tone was friendly but authoritative.

"Ava's on the move Callum, I'm following her now and pretty sure she's headed for the airport."

"Who is she with?" It was just the news he had been waiting for.

"I can't tell Callum, she's in a limo but they are ten-a-penny out here and I don't recognise the registration. Not Bortnik, that's for sure."

"Thank heaven for small mercies then," Callum said wryly. "By coincidence I have just parked at the Domodedovo Airport. I'm flying on the three o'clock out to London. Find out where she's going but don't follow her, she will spot or sense you a mile away. I can have one of our men placed on her flight within the hour. Thanks Yuri." Callum ended the call.

--------------------------------------------------------------------------

When Ava arrived at departures, she went straight to the British Airways check-in, joining the queue for the London Heathrow flight; scheduled for a three o'clock take-off.

A coincidence, Yuri wondered as he redialled Callum.

"Yes?" Callum was expecting the call.

"You're not going to believe this Callum, but she's on *your* flight!"

Callum reflected on that for a few seconds and quickly decided that it was far from coincidental.

"They have assigned her to me then. We always suspected they might one day, either me or Bud that is. We both fit the bill perfectly. Single and fatally flawed when it comes to women," Callum laughed ironically. "Perhaps we all deserve what we get in the end."

Yuri was immediately protective of the woman he loved.

"She's a good girl inside Cal, don't pre-judge her. She needs rescuing from herself as much as from Demitri."

Yuri's attempt to be professional and pragmatic got lost somewhere because of his deep love for Ava.

"I know Yuri; I have followed her life too. Perfect victim meets man from Hell and falls in love with him. It's the story of so many

192

women. They put up and shut up, always convinced that tomorrow will be better, but of course it never is. They find excuses to stay, but eventually they get used up, lose their faith, their looks and then lose themselves in drink or drugs. But one day, every one of them looks back with deep regret for a wasted life; if they even make it that far," Callum added as an afterthought.

Callum was a hopeless case himself when it came to women and his choice of them, so he was truly speaking from the heart and past experience.

"Don't worry Yuri she's special to all of us. If we lose her, then the whole world might follow. None of us can afford for Ava's life to become a train crash, even if she sees no value in it."

Callum's comment went some way to placating Yuri's fears, but he was also well briefed in Maelströminha's knowledge of the alternative futures of mankind that she had glimpsed in the mirrors. Only one out of thousands resulted favourably for both mankind and Ava. She was one of those girls who lived her whole life just one step away from the next tragedy. Each day she survived, was a blessing.

Ava was not a girl to count on, least of all to be mankind's saviour. They both knew that they were pretty much on *mission impossible,* but there was just a slim chance that Ava could pull through and fulfil her destiny; the mirrors had foretold that. Ava could be the *Angel of Deliverance* but it was much more likely that she would be the fourth horse of the apocalypse, whose rider was *Death.*

-------------------------------------------------------------------------

"Good morning Miss. May I see your passport please?" asked the smiley Asian girl at the check-in desk.

She went through the usual questions as she processed the baggage. It was Ava's best opportunity to secure the seat that she wanted.

"I have a friend travelling on the same flight today, his name is Callum Knight. Could you seat me next to him please?" Ava gave the girl a winning smile.

"I'm sorry Miss Thompson, but this flight is full and the seats are already pre-allocated."

Ava was one of the first in the queue, and so it was unlikely that the boarding card for the seat she wanted would have already been issued.

"But you could swap them over, couldn't you?"

"No Miss. I am not permitted to do that."

That was not an acceptable answer for Ava.

"Let me put that another way," Ava offered.

She held the pretty Asian girl's dark brown eyes with hers. Those golden-brown flecks danced mesmerizingly in their sea of blue such that the girl couldn't look away.

"You will find the seat allocated to Mr Callum Knight and swop the passenger name next to it with mine. Do you understand?"

Ava's voice was gentle but commanding. The young woman nodded in accord, smiled and went about her task.

"Here's your boarding card Miss Thompson. I hope you enjoy your British Airways flight to London with us today."

That was the first obstacle removed. Ava was now looking forward to meeting the man that she had read so much about, the legend that was Callum Knight.

--------------------------------------------------------------------------

When Callum took his seat, Ava was already settled and reading the in-flight magazine, or at least pretending to. She had watched him walk confidently up the aisle where he stopped and engaged naturally with the pretty blonde hostess, who appeared captivated and visibly preened at his attention.

"Yes, he is comfortable with women. Quite a charmer," Ava was pleased to observe.

The corners of her lips turned up into a knowing smile. Confidence was one of the key qualities Ava looked for in a man. It was a gift often mistaken for arrogance, but there was no arrogance about this man. She judged him to be about six feet tall, strongly set as opposed to muscular and he walked with an easy stride. When Callum came to sit next to her, he engaged with the usual courteous, "Excuse me, may I?"

"Of course, please," Ava smiled and pointed to his seat with her open palm in confirmation.

It was a very English gesture on both their parts. Ava watched Callum around the edge of her magazine as he got settled, using that amazing peripheral vision that women seem to have.

Good hair, strong jaw and lively blue eyes, were her first thoughts. Mannishly handsome features, nice teeth and easy smile, were her second.

So far so good, Ava mused. Callum was about to sit when he saw her purse on the seat. Of course, it was strategically placed there to initiate conversation. Ava wasn't a great taker of chances when it came to attracting a man.

"This can only be yours," Callum handed Ava the purse. "It is just that I don't remember buying one in that colour."

He had a mischievous grin that showed Ava that he liked to take a risk.

"I am terribly sorry, but I am afraid it's not mine," Ava countered. "Are you sure you didn't buy this colour?" Ava's grin was equally as mischievous.

"*Touché,*" he conceded, extending his hand to her. "Callum Knight, and you are?"

"Ava Thompson. Pleased to meet you Callum," she returned as they shook hands.

Ava had deliberately used his first name.

"I lost that round Miss Thompson, or perhaps I should call you Ava?" Callum raised a strong brow in the interrogative. "Whichever, it means that I still have to pay a forfeit."

"It's Ava, and what might that forfeit be?"

Ava angled her head towards him and put her forefinger to her chin in a teasing, questioning manner.

"Well I guess that means I buy the first bottle of Champagne."

There was definitely a *bad boy* twinkle in Callum's eye, and Ava so loved bad boys.

"Champagne in first class on British Airways flights is free Callum."

She made a point of using his given name again in their conversation. She had read somewhere that it was a valuable tool in developing relationships.

"Really? I didn't know," Callum shrugged. "Oh well, that will have to be the next time we meet then."

Ava laughed spontaneously, impressed with his easy conversation.

"You are smooth Mr Knight, very smooth and presumptuous. So, what makes you think there will be a *next* time?"

"Astral planes and destiny," Callum quipped.

"I will drink to that Callum, well that is if your offer of sharing a bottle of Champagne wasn't just a bluff." Ava fixed him with a raised and immaculately groomed eyebrow. "I do hope you are not one of those men who can't finish what he started."

Ava took the red lipstick from her purse and pouted as she applied it theatrically to her full lips. All through the exhibition Ava never took her eyes off his, it was part of her intended entrapment. Ava could never have known just how sexy Callum found that simple act. To him it was the quintessential demonstration of femininity. Callum pressed the service button on the console above them.

"You will find out that I am a man of my word and that I do not make idle threats or promises that I cannot keep," Callum's smile was confident and a little roguish.

Ava smirked, shaking her head as she put the lipstick back in her purse, perfectly aware that its application had caused the desired effect.

"What was that wicked smile all about?" Callum quizzed.

"That is really forward of you Callum. I was just wondering that, in the unlikely event that we did meet again, just how brave you might be?" she was mocking him and Callum knew it.

"And I was wondering that, *when* we meet, just how long you could resist before succumbing to my charms," Callum countered with an impish grin on his face.

Both were sparring with no intended arrogance. They had tested the water enough and dropped the flirtatiousness before it became crass. The door to the possibility of romance had been opened. Now time would tell.

-------------------------------------------------------------------------

Callum's eyes had picked out Ava from the moment he entered the first-class cabin. He had deliberately flirted with the hostess to get Ava's undivided attention. The ruse had clearly worked as he could see Ava looking covertly around her magazine at him.

She would never make a spy, he mused. Callum knew that it was likely that she had researched him and would have gained a little knowledge of his background. Callum though, had the advantage. He had maintained an interest in Ava's development several years after she was orphaned at the hands of Demitri. Even then it was clear to Shadows and Angels alike that Ava would be of strategic importance one day. The difference was that the Shadows had no idea that the Angels were aware of the existence of Anastasia Kaplinski's half-breed daughter.

Like Ava, her mother Anastasia had a fatal attraction for bad boys. She was an Angel of almost pure genetic origin, with only two non-Angel couplings occurring over the past five thousand years. When it became apparent that she was seeing Demitri Papandreou, Maelströminha herself had warned Anastasia of the dangers, but she was too headstrong and too in love.

It was a calculated mating on Demitri's part, and he was only interested in the child that resulted from that union. With such pure blood, that child could ultimately become a powerful weapon. Both sides had witnessed the revelations in the mirrors that coincided with the exact moment of Ava's birth. They knew that the new-born child would be pivotal in the outcome of an ultimate power struggle.

The first time Callum saw Ava in the flesh, was at her debut at the Bolshoi. That was nine years ago. She was twenty at the time and Callum had to confess that he had fallen in love with her from the moment he saw her. There was something special and unique about her. Ava had energy and grace, the like of which he had never seen in any other woman. Over the years that ensued, Callum had seen most of her important performances, and was there at the Bolshoi when she first played the double-role of Odette-Odile in Tchaikovsky's *Swan Lake* as prima ballerina.

Callum was there again in the September of last year when she played the part again to a full-house. The adulation that followed was unequalled in his experience and he was there applauding until his hands were sore. Ava had matured into full womanhood in that space of time and Callum remembered being lost in her perfection that night. Ava was oblivious to Callum's presence or even his existence, not to mention totally unaware of the love that he was harbouring for her.

"So, what brings you to London?" Callum asked as if he didn't already know. The lie would be interesting though, he thought

"Seeking work," Ava replied casually. "My employment at the Papandreou Research Laboratories in Moscow has reached an end with the successful conclusion of some dimensional studies."

Ava's reply was succinct. Demitri had told her not to elaborate or lie unnecessarily, as it was always detail that would trip you up and expose you in the end.

Callum already knew Ava was working at the laboratory for the Shadows and was surprised by her honesty. He wondered how he might turn Ava into a double agent, but that was for much later.

"Really? How fascinating. Are you a scientist?"

"In part, I have more degrees, in a diverse range of studies, than you might accredit."

This was another fact that would stand the test of scrutiny if Callum decided to investigate her background. Demitri had arranged for all the necessary document changes to be made from Kaplinski to Thompson.

"Dimensional studies sounds intriguing, can you be more precise?" Callum tested.

"That would constitute a breach of confidence with my employer Callum, which is contrary to my ethics. You must excuse me for not answering that."

Callum could tell this was not up for negotiation and admired her integrity. He let the matter drop.

"OK, so degrees or equivalents in what subjects?" Again Callum already knew.

"This might get tedious I am afraid." Ava went on to list the main ones. "Physics, particularly particle theory and quantum mechanics; chemistry; information Technology; world infrastructure; nanotechnology; biology; several languages. The list goes on."

Callum continued playing the game and gave Ava a look of disbelief.

"With respect Ava, but how is that even remotely possible?"

Again Callum knew the answer. It was a skill that several Angels of the Matriarch bloodline had in their arsenal.

"Photographic retention is part of the reason." Ava began, flicking through the first ten pages of the in-flight magazine before handing it back to Callum. "Ask me some questions and you will get some idea of my retention."

Ava smirked unashamedly.

"OK then, page eight. What is the title of the main article?"

"Holidays in Tuscany," Ava smiled an honest smile. "I just love Italy, don't you Callum? It's my favourite country in all the world and I will live there one day and be happy."

Ava looked lost for a moment. She had worked in Italy with the Bolshoi in her early twenties. It was there that she had met Katarina and the first time that she had fallen in love.

"Impressive," Callum praised.

It was a standard ability for one of Ava's bloodline though. Callum went along with the subterfuge.

"First sentence of the third paragraph," Callum challenged.

"This villa is nestled into the Tuscan hills, looking southwards over vineyards and orchards," she returned looking just slightly smug. "I remember many things Callum including reading an article about you in the GQ magazine."

"Really?" he raised a brow.

Callum was impressed. Ava *had* done her homework.

"You were a Major in the Parachute Regiment; a bachelor, never married. You have been romantically linked to a string of beauties, mostly *it girls* or work colleagues. You generally don't fare well in love and you have had your heart broken on several occasions. Your loves are dangerous sports and apparently dangerous women."

She fixed him again with a cursory glance, and that glance was of challenge and her message loud and clear. She continued.

"You are currently working as tactical advisor to the Prime Minister of the United Kingdom, an office that you have held for over two years and you are preparing for the forthcoming summit meeting in Moscow, my home town, don't you know? I rest my case and await your verdict your Honour."

The beautiful smile Ava gave Calum took his breath away, such that he had to fight to not get lost in her. It didn't help that Ava had chosen that exact moment to release the clip holding her hair, letting her long shiny and now black hair, tumble down. Eventually Callum found his voice.

"Wow, you seem to have me at somewhat of a disadvantage Miss Thompson. You haven't by any chance orchestrated this meeting, have you?"

Callum was back in control of himself which showed in his wolfish smile.

"Certainly not!" Ava lied easily. "It's just that when a man interests me I research him. You can take that as a compliment if you like."

"I like," Callum returned easily. "More Champagne?"

------------------------------------------------------------------

They chatted animatedly for the next hour, despite the necessary subterfuge between them. Callum had to disguise the fact that he knew all about Ava, and that she was being planted by Demitri as a mole in his organisation to spy on them. More than that, he had to disguise the fact that he was secretly in love with her and had been for years. Ava on the other hand had to lie about her life and her motives. She was getting to like Callum too fast, particularly given the ultimate objective of her mission. She had to put the thought of murder out of her mind and concentrate on the present only, the rest would be God's will.

Callum was the perfect gentleman, something that Ava had not experienced before which unbalanced her, challenging her mission objectives.

He is intelligent and attractive, she thought; attentive, funny and caring. Ava could see that Callum was a man who would cherish his woman and that he was a giver, not a taker. She wondered what it would be like to be in bed with a man like that. The thought immediately sent a rush of blood to the pit of her stomach, making her feel a little light headed. Those kinds of thoughts were always dangerous for Ava, and this was no exception. She felt her pulse quicken as her thoughts became ever more carnal. She imagined him kissing her and the feel of his stubble against her face.

"I need the bathroom," Ava declared out of the blue and left promptly.

She knew that feeling only too well and how quickly it could make a fool out of her. Callum was oblivious to the desire he had aroused in Ava and her sudden need to escape, but it gave him time to be pragmatic and reflect on the situation. He had hoped to be able to read her thoughts, but she was guarded against that.

Callum considered the situation. Knowing that Ava had been coerced by Demitri to infiltrate the Angel organisation, and if Yuri was right that she had been brainwashed and radicalised in Pakistan, then what for and what is she up to, he wondered?

Champagne had dulled Callum's senses a little, and the company of his dream girl, a lot. He forced himself to concentrate.

We can rule out the target as being me, he thought, because Ava's grooming started nearly twenty five years ago. Anyway, Callum knew that he wasn't a big enough fish for that, so her target had to be the Matriarchs. But how, he wondered?

It was a conundrum. The Angel organisation was structured so that they administered everything through their six generals, one of which was himself. This gave Maelströminha and her sister absolute protection. It was a system of governance that had afforded the Angels total anonymity and safety for generations.

Yes, their target had to be the Matriarchs. No doubt about it, Callum decided. He considered the old adage; *keep your friends close and your enemies even closer*. He had no intention of letting Ava out of his sight, and for more than one reason.

Ava returned from the bathroom, her smile engaging. Somehow, she seemed different to Callum; calmer and more serene perhaps. The look in Ava's eyes had softened for sure and her hair had been re-secured to the back of her head. Callum idly reflected that he preferred her with red hair and was just about to tell her so. He only just swallowed his words in time. There was no way Callum could have possibly known that she was previously a redhead, unless he already knew her. It would have been game over. Ava diverted him from his thoughts.

"Did you see the headlines in today's papers?" she asked, striking up conversation again.

"The one about the terrorist attack on the American Embassy in Paris by the so-called ISIS, you mean? Yes, I did. But I only skim read the headlines. How bad was it?"

Callum could also memorise detail at a glance. Islamic State, or ISIS as they had become known, were in the middle of a fierce campaign of international terrorism. He knew all about the attack but did not want to steal Ava's thunder.

"I only read the news superficially too." Ava was point scoring. "But I can tell you that there were twenty-one killed, eighteen injured and six unaccounted for. The bomb went off in the lobby just after six o'clock yesterday evening and took out most of the first floor. One of the dead was the famous American Ambassador, Charles Goldberg."

"I knew him. He was the brother of a close friend of mine, Emanuel Goldberg," Callum lamented with genuine sadness.

Ava picked up on his regret instantly and felt wretched.

"Oh Callum, I'm so sorry. How crass of me. I didn't know and now I feel stupid and clumsy."

What she said was the truth. Worse for Ava, was that she recognised the name Emanuel Goldberg as one of the other generals Demitri had instructed her to kill in God's name, making her feel even more wretched.

"Don't be Ava. You were not to know. Politicians live in a dangerous but lucrative world and go in with their eyes open. Destiny has a plan for all of us."

The word *destiny* touched a nerve in both and the conversation died for a while.

"This act of terrorism is just part of one of the three prerequisites to achieve global domination," Ava declared in a matter of fact way.

"You have a theory on global domination? Surely you don't think that a terrorist group such as ISIS can succeed and dominate the world. That would be naive of you." Callum was testing her.

"I am not naïve," Ava defended.

Her eyes had hardened and they seemed to change in colour too. She was clearly cross.

"Explain your theory then," Callum challenged.

He admired the girl's spirit; there was a business-like manner in Ava's tone as she continued, clearly annoyed at his patronising statement.

"Do you want the sugar-coated version?"

Ava didn't wait for his reply and delivered her theory with confidence.

"There are at least two superpowers on this planet that are struggling for ultimate control. And no, I do not mean ISIS, nor do I mean America and Russia. That is just old school rivalry and sabre rattling. These superpowers, or *organisations* to be more accurate, are currently faceless. Their anonymity is only temporary though, as they succeed in their goals by stealth."

Ava raised that beautiful brow again as she summed up Callum's reaction.

"Go on Ava, I am intrigued."

"To accept my theory, you first have to accept the principal that money is everything, because *everything* can be bought, including power and loyalty."

"Accepted," Callum agreed.

"Globalisation is the key strategy of the twenty-first century conqueror. First, you create an economy where self-sufficiency is no longer sustainable and then control the trading. This is already being done through conglomerates and oligarchs, who together hold the lion's share of global wealth. Then it is dog eat dog until you are left with only a few conglomerates. That is when the ultimate financial war begins as they fight it out until only one dog is left standing. That battle will be even more devastating than the two World Wars put together. There will be no regard for humanity, only money and the power that it buys."

Ava looked saddened as she visualised the impact.

"The world will be plunged into war, famine, disease, poverty and anarchy, as essential supplies dry up and banks cease trading. The financial apocalypse if you like, and we are already on the road to that. China already has four out of the top ten biggest and most powerful conglomerates in the world. All you need to do is unite these under one megalomaniac and the rest will either collapse or join them. So, with that you have the first of the three prerequisites, financial control of the world."

"Sound logic," Callum had to agree.

Globalisation falling under the control of a despot was one of his organisations deepest concerns. They already knew that several of the Shadow ruling Senators had positions within the Board of Directors of these conglomerates, one of whom was Demitri Papandreou.

"The second prerequisite is the control of the people. This is done in two parts. First through the media, including social media, they gain control our perception of everything and therefore control our minds and actions. The second part of controlling the people is through religion. This is where extremist organisations such as ISIS come into play."

Ava paused for a sip of Champagne. Callum knew exactly where she was going with this train of thought. ISIS was another Shadow run organisation.

"Give people fear and religion and you can control the masses. Unite the masses and you can control the Nation. The recent rise of ISIS is an attempt to incite the Americans into a land war on Muslim soil, fulfilling the Islamic end-of-time prophecy. Then the Mahdi, the Islamic equivalent to Jesus, unites the Muslims to fight a holy war against all those who oppose Sharia. After a fierce battle the Muslims will emerge victorious, according to the prophecy."

Ava subconsciously raised her hand to her forehead at her mention of the Mahdi, immediately confirming to Callum that she had indeed been indoctrinated. Ava continued eloquently.

"The gruesome decapitations of the Americans in Syria at Dabiq were entirely symbolic. Dabiq is where the scriptures say the holy war will take place. The murders were done there to incite the Americans to attack. But I agree with you Callum, ISIS is just a distraction that will serve to divert America and her allies from the greater goal, which is global domination. At the same time, those atrocities further enable the second prerequisite, control of the people through war and religion."

Callum was totally lost in Ava now. Her intelligence matched her beauty, and she exuded energy and youth. It was a heady cocktail for a romantic man like him. Despite Ava having amazingly expressive eyes, he found himself watching her mouth as she spoke. So kissable, he thought.

"The third and final prerequisite," Ava continued, perfectly aware that Callum was watching her mouth, "is control of the politicians, who are largely corruptible with either money or power. This is where the three prerequisites are entirely interdependent on one another. The first buys the second and the third. The politicians cannot govern their countries without world infrastructure, banking, food, employment and medicine, nor expect to be re-elected when they fail. The ruling conglomerate funds and enables all this and everybody is happy, just so long as the politicians do as they are told. QED, global domination and a New World Order complete in three easy steps."

Ava waited for Callum's challenge, or to rubbish her hypothesis, as men so often do to undermine a woman.

"Wow. That is one hell of a scenario Ava. Scary and very plausible. From *status quo* to Armageddon in three planned steps. What you have just described is exactly what *we* believe the Illuminati are doing right now, with the unofficial endorsement of the CIA."

Callum sighed at the enormity and almost inevitability of what Ava had recounted. She had summed up exactly what his organisation was fighting against. The Illuminati was a secret society led and funded by the Shadows, who were getting ever closer to their goal. It was a depressing thought.

"Can I have the *sugar-coated* version now please?"

"That *was* the sugar-coated version," Ava replied with a grin. "If you wanted the bitter version, I could have added the precursors to the *coup d'état* which are cyber-warfare, strategic chemical or biological releases, dirty bombs and more. All designed to cause fear and panic and destabilise governments.

I have studied all of them in detail Callum. Man's inhumanity to man is endless. Life has no value in the grand scheme of things. Money is the only valid currency and we are just collateral damage. Nothing has really changed since the days when the infantry was regarded as *cannon fodder,* before the officers and cavalry galloped in and took the spoils of war."

Ava looked coyly at Callum and then gave him the biggest smile.

"Should I get off my soapbox now?"

Callum was totally unprepared for what happened next. Ava put both hands behind his head and pulled his face to hers. The kiss was beyond urgent, although only lasting seconds. Ava pulled away from the kiss as fast as she had initiated it.

"I'm sorry, that was totally inappropriate of me. It must be the Champagne and the talk of power, it does something to me."

Ava blushed. It wasn't an act, not part of the script that Demitri had written for her to play out. She genuinely found Callum extremely attractive.

"You do something to me," she added shyly.

The last time Ava had used those words was on the night Katarina had been taken from her. She suddenly felt deeply saddened. Callum could see that Ava needed to come to terms with her emotions, and needed a few moments to compose herself. He sensed that it would be wrong to take advantage of her moment of weakness. Instead he kissed her briefly on the forehead.

"Go slowly little one. We have time."

Callum had already waited years for her and could wait a little longer.

Ava smiled thankfully back at him, not used to gentleness from a man, which was having the strangest effect on her. *Little one* again, she observed. It seemed to be a natural endearment from people who genuinely loved her. Katarina, Yuri and Leonardo had all called her that in precious moments, she recalled. Somehow Ava didn't challenge the fact that Demitri had not. Her subliminal indoctrination and radicalisation was deeply engrained and holding strong. Callum needed to divert her solemn mood.

"You have an amazing understanding of the intricacies and interactions of world politics Ava."

His compliment was genuine. Now was his chance to introduce the opportunity of a place in his organisation. Recruiting Ava was going to be a big risk, but an even bigger one to leave her out in the cold. At least he would be able to keep an eye on her and lead her onward to fulfil her destiny. Callum considered that maybe he could influence which one it might be; saviour or destroyer.

"Thank you kind sir. I deliberately kept the brief simple so that you could keep up," Ava teased, inciting him to chastise her.

"You do me an injustice. Let me finish my compliment if you can hold your concentration that long." Callum faked a hurt expression.

"You make me feel like a naughty child," Ava pouted and gave an equally fake sulk.

"Your qualifications are diverse and I do not doubt that you have more. Clearly you have shown me just a glimpse of your knowledge and intellect, but sufficient that I would be interested in having you work for us. In our line of work your photographic memory alone would make you a valuable asset. Would you be interested in an offer?"

Unaware that Callum was conscious of her deception, Ava decided to play it cool.

"Well I don't know. I was thinking of maybe taking a holiday for a couple of months, you know? Relax for a while and consider my options," Ava's tone was politely disinterested.

"Yes of course. How silly of me. Most presumptuous, please forget that I even mentioned it," Callum feigned. "Can I pour you more Champagne?" He could see the panic rise in her expression.

"No! Not the Champagne; I mean *yes* to that. I meant *no* to you forgetting about the job offer you made. Yes, I am interested in that."

It was probably the clumsiest sentence that Ava had ever put together. She caught the mocking look in Callum's eye and they both burst out laughing at her predicament.

"You bastard! I was just playing hard to get and well you knew it!" Ava shook her head and looked into Callum's smiling blue eyes. "You are an absolute bastard."

"I hope you always give up playing *hard to get* that easily," he quipped, only half-jokingly.

Callum was testing the water, but Ava was not going to make it quite that easy for him.

"In your dreams Callum Knight. What sort of girl do you think I am? Let's keep it to work. Tell me more about the job offer. What company is it?"

Ava had stopped Callum's flirting in its tracks, regaining the upper hand.

"Yes of course."

Callum already regretted his crass statement and wished that he could turn back the clock. He had waited so long for this woman and had nearly blown his chance in one ill-timed pass.

Ava's expression never acknowledged his apology, but inside she was secretly laughing. She was going to make Callum work for his pleasure now, and it was going to be fun. After all he deserved it for being so cocky and self-assured!

"Well we are not exactly a company, more of an organisation really. I can only give you a broad outline until we have you security checked," Callum bluffed for credibility's sake before continuing. "You mentioned there were at least two organisations battling it out for global domination, and on that premise you are quite correct. But there is another organisation that is not in competition, quite the opposite. That organisation, our organisation, exists to resist that global takeover and fight for human rights, free trade, democracy and peace."

He appeared sincere, Ava thought. Demitri had warned that the Angels would sell themselves as the good guys, but in reality were wolves in sheep's clothing. They were the infidels, those that the Mahdi would fight against in the holy war and fulfil the prophecy.

"Guardian Angels then?" Ava couldn't help the *double entendre*.

"Perhaps, and I've heard that one before, by the way," Callum gave Ava a crooked smile. "But we are just trying to keep things fair by staying one step ahead of the game. There is one particular organisation we need to keep in check whose name I cannot divulge until after your security clearance, but they are our enemy in no uncertain terms. They are ruthless and virtually unstoppable in this global race for absolute power. This organisation and ours have been literally at war with each other since before the birth of Christ."

Ava wondered what web of deceit Callum was about to weave. Demitri had told her that he would.

"To give you an example of their ruthlessness; one of the most despicable things that mankind has ever suffered was the

Catholic Inquisitions. The Roman Catholic ecclesiastical court, infiltrated and dominated by our enemy, literally forced their will throughout Europe for six centuries. All those who spoke, or even thought differently to the Catholic Church, were relentlessly sought out and branded as heretics. They were then tortured and killed in the foulest and most inhumane of ways."

Callum expected a shocked response but Ava was quite stoic about his revelation, which concerned him. He wondered just how deeply she had been brainwashed by the Shadows, and how much she had lost. Certainly, her trust had been compromised, but he feared that her humanity may also have been affected. He continued.

"The execution of this crusade was the perfect cover for our enemy to carry out their own agenda, the genocide of our kind and the legitimate removal of any opposition. Nobody truly knows how many were killed. Those records are held in the Vatican archives and privy only to a select few, but the numbers were probably in the millions."

Ava was conscious of Callum waiting for some response from her, but she was experiencing a personal crisis, and suffering another lapse of faith. Callum seemed to be totally sincere and plausible. He seemed like a man you could trust with your life although not necessarily your body, she had to concede. She had met many liars in her life and had to again admit that they were mainly men. Was he just another? She wondered.

Ava had senses, inherited from her mother, that gave her insight into people's minds, but men like Yuri, Demitri, Leonardo and now Callum, had an ability to shut her out which confused her. The one thing that they couldn't hide from her though, was their auras, that invisible light we all emit, though few can see. Yuri, Leonardo and Callum's auras were bright pink and light, normally associated with being loving, tender and sensual. Katarina had that same aura she lamented.

Demitri was stereotypically Shadow though. His aura was black, like Bortnik's and seemed to capture light and consume it. There was always darkness about their characters and cruelness in their dark brown eyes. Ava seriously doubted her own judgement, nothing stacked up. Then she remembered what the Mullah and her mentor, the old Imam, had told her when she was studying the *Quran* and *Hadith*. They warned her that, in moments of weakness, Satan would try and enter her body and prevent her from doing God's will and that she must deny him.

"The devil takes on many guises," the Imam had told her, "and you must turn to prayer each time you are tempted by him and supplicate yourself to *Allah*. He will make you strong so that you can continue in his holy work."

Ava decided she would go directly to one of the London Mosques as soon as they landed and pray for strength and forgiveness for her lapse of faith.

"Intriguing," Ava said at last and Callum looked visually relieved that she had responded. "I'm sorry I might have appeared distant, but I was considering all that you have said. It's most disconcerting to find out that the world is not entirely as you see it."

Ava's smile was perfectly professional; she was once again in control of her mind and her body.

"What exactly did you mean by *our kind* when you were talking about this other organisation and their campaign of genocide against you? What *kind* are you?"

Ava had the devil in her eye. She had caught him out, picking up on his indiscretion. Callum cursed himself for his sloppiness. It was no time to talk of Angels and Shadows. Ava's company and the Champagne were dulling his wits. He needed to divert that avenue of conversation.

"That will become clear after your security clearance is through." Callum procrastinated and Ava looked disappointed.

"You cannot tell a woman half a story Callum. You should know us better than that," she demurred.

With the decision made to pray for strength at one of the Mosques, Ava was ready to flirt again. After all, she had objectives and there was no reason why she shouldn't enjoy her work, she justified. Callum came up with an idea.

"If I photograph your passport, my organisation could have you vetted in a few hours. I would have invited you out to dinner tonight, only I see that I offended you earlier by my forwardness."

Callum looked a little uncertain of himself for the first time, prompting Ava to fix him with that arched brow again and a mocking look. She knew that she had him on the ropes.

"Were you not paying attention when I said, 'I do hope that you are not one of those men who can't finish what he started'?"

Callum looked nonplussed for a moment, and then grinned in realisation.

"You have won another round, haven't you?"

"Get used to it," Ava smirked, handing over her passport. "Where are we staying?"

"I always stay at the Savoy in the Strand."

That was something else that Ava already knew. Her investigations were proving fruitful.

"You can book me a room there then," Ava advised. "I will make my own way though, as I want to stop somewhere first. We can meet at the bar at eight o'clock. Don't be late, I will be hungry."

From the look that Ava gave Callum, she wasn't just talking about food.

"Two rooms of course?" Callum questioned.

"Of course; a girl has to keep a little mystery, wouldn't you agree?"

--------------------------------------------------------------------------

Ava left the mosque emboldened by prayer, but still could not get Callum out of her mind. She found him fascination and so sexually attractive, even though he wasn't her type at all. Not bad enough by a distance. He was much more the type that Katarina wanted her to meet; White Knight to sweep her up onto his saddle, riding away with him into the sunset, living happily ever after.

Poor Katarina, Ava thought. She is the one who lived in a fairy tale. White Knights don't exist. It was strange that Callum's name actually was *Knight* though, Ava pondered. Demitri will be my saviour, Ava reminded herself. And when I do all he asks of me, we will be together forever.

Ava was back on track, with a deadly mission to carry out and the resolve to do it. God's will be done!

-------------------------------------------------------------------------

Chapter 16

Callum was in his usual River View suite, looking out across the Thames towards the London Eye. He had sent the photograph of Ava's passport to Yuri to run a search on it earlier and Yuri had just called back with his findings.

"She checks out Callum. I have traced Ava Thompson's history right back to her childhood, including schools and further education. Police records show some minor misdemeanours but nothing more. She's had three jobs apparently and all taxes have been paid. Her security check suggests that she's as clean as a whistle."

Yuri had turned that information around in less than three hours.

"And a complete fraud," Callum added. "I would expect nothing less from Demitri Papandreou; his attention to detail is commendable. The man continues to strive for the total annihilation of the Angel race and is meticulous in his mission. He is a worthy adversary indeed Yuri. I want you to keep me informed of his whereabouts in case Ava opens the door to him when I'm not expecting it. I think the danger will come from him though; Ava will just be the facilitator."

"OK Callum. I will continue to monitor them both. The dangers associated with her infiltration for espionage purposes cannot be ignored. We should consider the benefits of using her as a double agent, or feed her disinformation to confuse our enemies."

"I'm hoping that it's the former. Feeding her disinformation will eventually get her killed. Stay in touch Yuri and thanks."

Callum ended the call with a pang of guilt, sensing that Yuri loved Ava too. He consoled himself with the fact that Yuri's love was relatively new-found; his was approaching the anniversary of a decade. Tonight he might demonstrate the magnitude of his feelings for her.

-------------------------------------------------------------------------

It was already seven o'clock and Callum had just an hour to get ready for the date of his life. Getting over Kayla had taken him a long time, but now at last, he was ready to offer his heart up again and risk it being broken. It was a risk well worth taking, he decided. Strangely, Callum really did *get* women and they *got* him. The sad thing from his point of view was that in his experience, women would so often sacrifice their own personal happiness, fulfilment and security for the whims and wants of an absolute bastard. Callum was convinced that Demitri controlled her mentally, emotionally and sexually.

Callum knew Demitri well enough to know that there was nothing that he would not do to manipulate Ava. He would make her indebted to him, dependant on him and responsible to him. Then he would use all of her emotions; love, compassion, loyalty, fear, guilt and pity to manipulate her to do his will. She would be his slave. He also knew that Ava would be dead in six months, either by act of suicide or murder. These women always were, and there had been many before Ava. She was the perfect victim.

He reflected on how his day had progressed so far. His charm and charisma had fallen far below his best whilst engaging with Ava. It was an alien experience for him to be anything other than totally focussed on his objective, but the belief that she could be his soul mate had distracted him. Bizarrely, this distraction had piqued his curiosity. He liked it, and the fact that she had totally bewitched him."

Callum knew of Ava's fabled sexuality and promiscuity. To bed her, would not be an achievement. He wanted more than that. Callum was a lover of women, and derived far more pleasure giving as opposed to receiving. Callum wanted all of her, mind body and soul. He believed in unconditional love and that a man lives to protect and cherish his woman, hence the many broken hearts. Ava was of another generation though, and had probably never experienced that kind of love and might shun his advances.

Callum could not read her at all and that was something else that he enjoyed. So many girls were transparent and bland. Ava was the epitome of womanhood; beautiful, intelligent, elegant, sexy and mysterious. He looked at himself in the full-length mirror as he pulled on his jacket, straightened his collar and adjusted the cuffs.

Not too bad for an older man, he thought. You don't win any more rounds tonight Ava Kaplinski or whatever name you want to call yourself. I'm back and I'm taking you by storm!

He grinned at his reflection, turned and went to meet the girl of his dreams.

---------------------------------------------------------------------------

Ava was at the London Savoy sat at her dressing table in suite 304. She had spent the last two hours preparing herself for her date with Callum. Well it wasn't really a date, rather a meeting to discuss a career opportunity. Anyway, it would turn out to be much the same thing, she decided. Ava had planned his seduction to the minutest detail. She knew exactly how she was going to get him back to her room, and exactly what she was going to do with him once she got him there. She could already feel her body relishing the possibilities.

Ava had chosen the little black dress with the halter neck to show off her svelte figure. After much deliberation, she decided to pile her thick black hair up, accentuating her long neck. Men had a thing about pulling bows, clasps and ties on a girl's clothing, and they were always aroused by a woman's neck, particularly when she knew how to use it to its best advantage. Ava had chosen dark brown eye shadow to pick out the brown flecks in her otherwise sky-blue eyes and, of course, bright red lipstick. She stood up and wriggled pulling the riskily short dress down over her stocking tops to remove any creases and gain a little length. Finally, she winked conspiratorially at her reflection.

"Boy you don't stand a chance!" she said aloud, smirking.

Ava turned, picked up her clutch bag and left her room.

---------------------------------------------------------------------------

Callum was already sat at the bar when Ava entered, fashionably late. He was dressed in a charcoal grey, crisp designer suit, white open neck shirt and brown Gucci shoes. Ava approved. A good-looking, suntanned man well attired never failed to attract her. It always annoyed her though at how much easier it was for a man to look good, compared to the hours of preparation that went into a woman's appearance.

Ava wanted to be sure that Callum would be sat waiting for her when she entered the room. Her work at the Bolshoi had given her the deportment and walk that never failed to turn a man's head. Callum was immediately captivated. That was the first part of her seduction checklist ticked.

"Ava you look stunning. I'm so glad that I decided to wait for you."

It was a gentle rebuke for her tardiness but Callum's smile showed Ava that she was forgiven.

"You can't look this good without spending a little time in preparation," Ava admonished.

Her smile promised everything. She was deliciously conscious that he had watched her lips for just a little too long. Game on! She thought. Ava also noted that Callum had already ordered her a gin and tonic without asking her preference. The bottle was still open on the counter and it was *Bombay Sapphire*, one of her favourite brands.

Presumptuous but spot on, she acknowledged and let the matter go. Anyway, she had to concede that she preferred men who took control. Ava leant forward to offer her cheek for a kiss and took the opportunity to smell him as she did so. There was no hint of cologne just the invigorating smell of clean man and that was just as she preferred it. Their banter was light and from Ava's part, flirtatious. She could sense Callum's growing interest as she drew him into the sexual undertones of her stories. That was the second stage of her seduction ticked off the list.

On his part, Callum avoided discussing his employment offer. That could wait, he thought. Tonight, he simply wanted to enjoy Ava's company. Watching Ava make a play for him was so much more interesting! She over-used her innuendos as the gin began to cloud her judgement, and her obvious attempts to let her knee brush against the inside of Callum's thigh, were a little too predictable. Callum pretended not to notice, an act that irked Ava, and forced her try even harder.

Evidently, she was more than a little interested. Callum smiled, amused at her predicament and continued to play it cool. He could tell that his apparent lack of sexual interest was disorientating Ava, making her babble a little too much. She had the upper hand twice on the aeroplane and now it was his turn. He watched Ava's perfect red lips as she talked and had to suppress his desire to kiss them. She was stunningly attractive, funny and deeply interesting. He could tell that the attraction was mutual and that he could press home his advantage, if he so wished, but *not tonight, Josephine,* he decided. She was far too precious to him than to risk all on a one night stand.

Callum had regained his composure and self-confidence, blissfully aware how attracted to him Ava was. The waiter summoned them for dinner and guided the striking couple to their table in one of the more private booths. Callum had requested this, again without consulting Ava. He had chosen to seat her to face the restaurant to enjoy the ambience of the five-star surroundings, while he contented himself with just the view of her and some outrageously expensive wallpaper. That was the only ambience that Callum needed.

"I've chosen the pan-fried scallops with lime and coriander for an *entrée* with a *Grand Cru* Chablis to compliment. I hope you approve?"

Callum's manner was easy and he was confident in his choice.

Damn cheek! Not consulted again, Ava thought, struggling to hide her annoyance. The problem was compounded by the fact that it was exactly what she would have chosen. Ava wondered how he could have known that.

Yet another man was taking control, and this was not included in her seduction plan! But then she couldn't have known how intuitive Angels could be. The Chablis was indeed spectacular with that fabulously characteristic flinty taste. However, the wine was a little too spectacular and Ava drunk it enthusiastically. She had issues with white wine, as it always affected her inhibitions. If she was going to make a fool of herself, it would always be after consuming too much white wine.

Ava was more than just a little light headed and thoroughly enjoying Callum's conversation. Her game plan was falling to pieces though. She had met Callum in the restaurant tonight to do as Demitri had commanded; to ensnare him, seduce him and finally kill him. Instead, she was falling in love with him which was a totally alien experience for her. Men were not for love, she reminded herself. Only Katarina had ever evoked that emotion.

Ava found that it was now her watching Callum's mouth as he spoke. His smile was easy, bright and endless. He was attentive and he actually *listened* to what she said, which was another thing that men just did not do. Ava could tell he was deeply attracted to her, but also that he was not an aggressor. She knew that Callum would not be so bold as to make a pass at her; he would leave that up to her. Ava suddenly realised that she was so lost in him, that she hadn't heard his last few sentences.

"Don't you think so Ava?" Callum asked. He could see that Ava was flustered and helped her out graciously. "By that I mean you should not pre-judge people."

Ava recognised this as a life-line and improvised her response.

"Quite so Callum and I am guilty of that myself tonight. I think that I may have misjudged you."

Callum took the Chablis from the wine bucket and topped up their glasses, still holding Ava's gaze.

"For the better or worse?" he asked.

"Better, definitely better," Ava flushed pink.

She was totally out of her comfort zone and felt completely exposed and vulnerable. It was a relief when George, the waiter appeared.

"And how was that for madam?" he asked politely.

"Divine," Ava replied without taking her eyes off Callum. "Simply divine."

The waiter cleared Ava's plate and recharged her wine glass with the last of the Chablis.

--------------------------------------------------------------------------

Ava had forgiven Callum for his presumptuousness ordering their entrées without consulting her, but then George arrived with the main course. Callum explained *his* choice for them.

"I thought we could share the chateaubriand, rare of course. And I have selected a rather delightful Malbec to compliment. I hope you approve?" Callum smiled warmly.

Ava was clearly enjoying the white wine so much that Callum felt a little guilty for not staying with the Chablis, but that would have been entrapment, he conceded.

Ava was still inwardly seething about Callum ordering for her again, but had to concede yet again that she liked this man to take control. Perhaps you would like to eat it for me too? You take too much for granted Mr Knight! Ava was tempted to say.

She had to force herself to bite her tongue and let the matter go. Again, Callum's choice was good though, which irked her even more. Her engaging smile showed none of her petulance though, and the main course was perfect, their delicate fillet steak, baked to perfection and the Malbec fuelled their mutual desires. Ava rummaged in her clutch bag for her lipstick.

Damn you for being so perfect, she thought as she applied the red cream theatrically to its best effect.

Callum enjoyed Ava's display of femininity which physically stirred him. She sensed his interest, which fuelled her own passion. Ava could feel her body preparing itself for him and the wait until they inevitably went to her bedroom, was becoming agonising for her.

"I'm feeling a little intoxicated Callum. Can we skip desert and you just walk me to my room?"

Ava's eyes were soft and inviting. Callum called the waiter over to sign the tab.

"Excellent meal and service, thank you George. We'll skip the desert tonight though."

With that Callum picked up Ava's room key and pulled her chair back as she stood.

The wine had affected Ava in the same way that it usually did. She was grateful for the gentle, yet strong support of Callum's arm as he led her out of the dining room, taking the lift to the third floor. Ava leaned against the cool steelwork, the sensation invigorated her, clearing her mind. For the first time in her life Ava was going to make the right decision. She was not going to ask him in, despite the fact that she had never wanted a man as much as she wanted Callum right then. He was already too special to her. She didn't want him to think that she was a tart, an easy lay and wondered how she was going to let him down gently. Shyness and modesty were such alien feelings for Ava. She was confused and in turmoil, lost in an unfamiliar feeling. Love she wondered? But that would have been ridiculous.

The lift doors opened on the third floor. Ava kept her own counsel as Callum steered her towards suite 304. He slipped the key into the lock, heard it click and then opened the door. There was an awkward moment, where neither knew precisely what to do. Reluctantly, Ava was about to make her excuses, a headache she had decided, when Callum took the initiative.

"We appear to be neighbours Ava," he pointed out, producing the key to suite 305. "I will bid you goodnight and perhaps we can meet for breakfast?" his smile was honest and charming.

"Err. Yes of course. That will be lovely." Ava was completely taken off her guard. She had not expected that.

"Good. Eight o'clock then. We still have much to discuss about your future employment." Callum kissed Ava on the cheek. "Goodnight then and sleep well." He left her with a boyish grin that masked his true desire.

Callum almost rushed into his room, while he still had the resolve not to attempt to seduce Ava. He closed the door, leaving a totally frustrated Ava, open mouthed, in the corridor. Several seconds passed before Ava regained her wits and entered her room. She closed the door behind her and leaned against it, deep in thought.

So many emotions were running through her head; confusion, anger, love and guilt. *Confusion*, because she had never met a man who made her feel so special and who clearly desired her, but had not tried to take advantage of her. *Anger*, because Callum had taken the initiative and the moral high-ground with his gentlemanly retreat. Ava would have dearly loved to have been the one who played hard to get, but he had beaten her to it. *Love*, because she was powerfully attracted to Callum in a way that she had never considered possible from a man before. Ava was completely infatuated with him and felt weak at the knees in his presence. *Guilt*, for two reasons; if she was so madly in love with Demitri, then how could she so immediately feel such deep love for Callum, an almost total stranger? Secondly, and worse, she was luring Callum into a honey-trap to forsake him and ultimately kill him. This assignment was for *Allah* and Demitri; a task that she dare not fail to execute to the letter.

Ava put that macabre thought out of her mind as it was unsupportable and so alien to her nature. They had exchanged telephone numbers during the evening. Ava reached for her phone; her mind engrossed with everything that related to Callum.

*You are such a gentleman for not taking advantage of me in my drunken state. Thank you. A x*

---

Callum closed the door to his suite and crossed to the window opposite. He had always found the view of London at night inspiring and thought provoking. Tonight, was no exception. On this occasion though, his thoughts were all about the girl he adored next door. With his natural Angel retention, Callum replayed every moment of their date, remembering all that they discussed; her smiles, her laughs, and her frowns. Callum was so intoxicated by Ava that he couldn't believe he had simply pecked her on the cheek and said goodnight. To have done anything else would have sullied the moment, even though he wanted her more than his next breath. Callum's reveries were abruptly ended by the message alert on his phone. There was only one person in the world right then that he wanted a message from. His heart leapt when he saw that it was from Ava.

*You are such a gentleman for not taking advantage of me in my drunken state. Thank you. A x*

Callum reflected on Ava's comment for a while. Gentleman, Angel or fool? He wondered.

---

Callum took breakfast at a little before eight o'clock, having already been for a run, down by the Thames, showered and read the morning paper. He had not slept much, but that wasn't because it had been a troubled night, it was simply because Ava was still coursing through his veins, the visions of her still vivid in his mind. Callum couldn't wait to see her again. He imagined that she would still be fighting off a hangover though, and would be most of the morning. At that moment Ava walked into the breakfast room looking radiant.

As she walked towards him, her smile reflected the genuine joy she was feeling at seeing him sat there. There was something entirely different about her demeanour though. She looked at ease with herself, and shone as some people are prone to do when they are deeply in love. Ava wore tight faded jeans, torn at the knees and a simple white cap-sleeve blouse that buttoned to her throat. Modest, Callum thought, but the cut was tantalisingly feminine. Her hair was loose and casual and she had armed herself with the habitual red lipstick and mascara. No more.

"Good morning Callum. I do like a man who is on time, and I for one am famished. What have you ordered for me?" it was a subtle rebuke.

"Actually, I haven't ordered for you. I thought you would like to choose your own breakfast," he returned as if it was remiss of him.

She had de-railed him in the instant.

"You didn't last night," Ava admonished, and waited just long enough to see the discomfort in Callum's eyes before adding. "Oh, don't ever let that stop you taking control. I loved it."

Ava positively beamed at him and Callum's momentary anxiety melted into a grin that split his face.

"You don't take prisoners do you?" the grin melted into a chuckle. "It is going to be fun getting to know you Ava!" Callum meant it.

"If you can't stand the heat, then stay out of the kitchen!" Ava scolded mischievously. "Speaking of the kitchen, what do you recommend?" she raised her eyebrow in the inquisitive.

"They do amazing Eggs Benedict, with smoked salmon and chives. It will tantalise your taste-buds Ava, I promise. Perhaps washed down with Buck's Fizz?"

Callum appeared so enamoured with his recommendation that Ava was unable to refuse.

"That sounds good to me Callum, but should we really be drinking on the job? After all, this is a working breakfast, my induction if you like."

Again, Ava fixed him with a feigned frown, but the sparkle in her clear blue eyes showed that it was only in jest.

"Fortunately, I'm the boss and what I say goes."

Callum's wolfish expression confirmed it would be a Champagne breakfast and one to remember.

Breakfast and discussions lasted until after midday. Ava was given a comprehensive overview of Callum's organisation and gained a greater knowledge of him as a man, and as a leader of men. Nothing that Callum had imparted though was anywhere in line with Demitri's account of whom and what the Angel organisation stood for.

Ava had to work hard at not being sucked in by what she had been warned were Callum's *lies*. She had fallen in love with the Devil himself, or so it appeared. Ava knew that she would have to separate her heart from the truth, treat them as entirely different things. If not, she would be ineffective as an agent for Demitri. Ava consoled herself with the fact that it wasn't something she needed to confront right now, and that maybe she could plead Callum's case later. He clearly was not the monster that Demitri thought he was. That was for another day though. Ava felt sure that, when push came to shove, she could convince Demitri of Callum's good nature. After all, Demitri was a reasonable man. Wasn't he?

Conversely, Callum was good at separating business from pleasure. They ate a light lunch and talked only of their lives and loves. Ava was at a disadvantage. She had to invent certain parts of her history, but managed to include her dance, even though she wasn't able to boast the Bolshoi. Callum showed his surprise and admiration graciously.

The afternoon flew by as Callum brought Ava up to date with current affairs in the Middle East. Again, Ava saw the difference between his and Demitri's account, finding Callum's version the most credible. The very fact that she had allowed herself to doubt Demitri was an affront to her God, *Allah*. Ava needed time alone later for prayer and penitence. She was losing her conviction, questioning her religion and even her mission. Ava knew that Demitri would kill her if she failed him and that *Allah* would damn her to an eternity in Hell.

Ava had a dilemma to address. She had a duty to perform and needed to pray for the strength to carry it through. Demitri would assuredly insist upon her completing her mission, and she needed God's strength to do so. It was after four o'clock in the afternoon when Callum reluctantly called their meeting to a close.

"If you haven't had enough of me, I would like you to be my guest for dinner tonight. Would you do me that honour?" Callum asked, a little uncertain of himself.

"I thought that you would never ask Callum, but I do hope this time you can finish what you started."

It was a challenge and the first flirtatious comment of the day uttered by either of them. Callum's heart soared. Ava calculated that she would have just enough time to bolster herself with prayer before then.

------------------------------------------------------------------------

They had arranged to meet at the bar at eight, giving Ava that time she needed to go to the local mosque and pray. She stayed for two hours, half of which was praying for forgiveness and strength, the rest praying to *Allah*, and his faithful servant on

228

Earth, Demitri, to spare Callum's life. She was certain that a forgiving God would hear her and grant her prayers.

When Ava walked into the bar to meet Callum, she looked nothing like she had the evening before. Knowing that Callum was a refined man, she had chosen to dress appropriately for him. Tonight, her figure-hugging white dress was long and feminine, cut modestly at the front and radically at the back. Anyone carrying just an ounce of fat would not have been able to wear the dress as elegantly as Ava did that evening.

Ava chose to have her hair up again, as it perfectly suited her choice of dress and red lipstick because Callum paid so much attention to her mouth. She tried to look demure when she caught sight of him at the bar, but her heart was pumping so hard that it made her feel a little faint. Speaking at this precise moment would have been impossible for Ava. She was relieved when Callum opened the conversation, giving her a few moments to calm her emotions.

"Ava, you look stunning," Callum acknowledged as he walked over to greet her.

Callum kissed Ava briefly on the mouth, which felt completely natural for both of them. The taste of this amazing woman lingered on Callum's lips, as he led her to the bar where her drink was already waiting.

"I decided to risk the Bombay Sapphire again. Was I right to do so?"

"Absolutely Callum, and thank you for the compliment." Ava raised her glass to his, the expensive crystal ringing out as they gently touched glasses. "To our successful union," she teased, holding eye contact.

"To pastures new," Callum's boyish grin was proof enough of his understanding of Ava's *double entendre*.

"Shall we eat? I'm ravenous!" Ava demanded. "What have you chosen for us? Whatever it is, remember that it has to fit in this dress."

"Ava you have the looks and figure that could carry off anything that you decided to eat!"

It was just the opening that Ava was hoping for.

"Perhaps room service would be more appealing this evening Callum?" Ava muttered huskily.

She glancing at her own cleavage invitingly, but that was as much to avert her eyes as to tempt him. Again Ava was experiencing shyness, something that she was unaccustomed to.

"That would be lovely Ava and my choice too," Callum confirmed, feeling the sudden rush of adrenaline that seemed to weaken him.

His yearning for Ava bordered on painful. To have spent all day with her, without so much as touching her hand, had been excruciating. He leaned across and breathed his words in her ear.

"I want you Ava. I ache to lie beside you," Callum's voice was almost a groan.

"God I feel the same Callum. We have to leave now. I can't contain the passion growing inside of me any longer." Ava's voice was breathless and her eyes ablaze with passion. "You can call room service later. Bring your drink."

Ava took the initiative and slipped her hand into Callum's, prompting him to stand. She led him to the lift with the confidence that Callum was struggling to find. He was grateful that she had made the transition to become lovers so simple and natural.

It seemed an eternity waiting for the lift to arrive. Ava couldn't risk looking at Callum lest her knees buckle beneath her. She wanted this rugged yet tender man inside her satisfying her carnal desires. Finally, the lift arrived, the doors opening, accompanied by the familiar ping. They entered attempting to hide their passion, yet desperate to share a kiss. As soon as the doors began to close Ava spun on her heels urgently pressing her mouth against Callum's.

"Ah. Nearly missed it!" The burly American and his stout wife bustled in, forcing Callum and Ava to the back of the lift. "Hate waiting for these goddamn things. You don't mind, do you?"

"Not at all; please be our guests." Callum exchanged an awkward smile with Ava.

The Americans got off on the first floor. Ava pressed her body against Callum as soon as the doors fully closed. Her kiss was urgent, wanting and her lips soft and inviting. Ava's tongue probed the depths of Callum's mouth, entwining, exploring and teasing. The kiss continued beyond the lift doors opening on the third floor, forcing Callum to half step out to stop the doors closing on them. As they reopened, he guided Ava into the corridor, still lost in the rapture of their embrace. Remarkably, their gin and tonics remained un-spilled.

"Find your key," Callum urged, taking her drink so she could search her bag. "I can't wait for you."

Callum feasted on the vision of Ava as she rummaged clumsily through her bag for the key. She looked young, fresh and infinitely desirable. He was overcome with the need to embrace her but his hands were effectively manacled by the drinks he was holding.

"I have to go to the bathroom first," Ava's plea seemed urgent.

She needed to slow things down. Ava didn't want to reveal quite how desperate she was for him, not yet. She wanted this to last the whole night, waking in Callum's strong arms, sated by their love-making.

-------------------------------------------------------------------------

Callum set the drinks down on the table, took off his jacket, draping it over the sofa before kicking off his shoes. He stood there awkwardly for a moment, unsure of how she should discover him. First, he lay on the bed, but thought that presumptuous and sat instead.

"Still presumptuous," he muttered.

Callum got to his feet again, but that still felt awkward, formal even. Decision made, he pulled two chairs up close to the table, setting them discretely apart. He arranged the drinks and sat in the one facing the bathroom door, wanting to see Ava the moment she stepped into the bedroom.

"Better," he murmured, "much better."

"Sorry, I needed a minute to compose myself," Ava looked abashed, "only I'm not used to caring about someone so much."

She averted her eyes and smiled nervously. Ava immediately noticed how Callum had arranged the room so that she wouldn't feel under pressure, and smiled in silent appreciation. Callum indicated the chair inviting her to join him.

"Thank you, kind sir," Ava smiled nervously.

Irrationally she momentarily thought of Katarina; how at last she was with her *knight*, even if only by name. Katarina would have approved though, she mused.

They sat, chatting easily, sipping at their drinks. Both had regained control of their passion but there was still that feeling of unfinished business between them. Callum, normally a confident man, was finding it difficult to make the transition from friendly chat to romance. Ava sensed that Callum was so clearly infatuated with her, that he had lost his nerve. She stood and smiled at him easily as she hitched her dress up to her hips, then straddled him on the chair facing him. Ava put her hands behind Callum's head and pulled his face to hers, kissing him reassuringly. The kiss was long, lingering and honest, just what

Callum's confidence needed. They broke for a moment and looked into each other's eyes.

"I liked that," Callum whispered, his eyes searching hers. "You can do that again, if you like."

Ava did, but this time with just a little more intensity. Her breathing quickly became urgent, as she struggled to keep up the momentum of the kiss. It was all consuming though, and far too precious to lose. The kiss was eternal. Her fingers searched for the buttons on Callum's shirt. Finding the one at his collar, she worked purposefully, unbuttoning each in turn, down his chest until finally releasing his shirt from his shoulders. Callum allowed the shirt to fall free, dropping to the floor. Again Ava kissed him passionately, running her fingers up his muscular arms to his shoulders. As she reached his broad chest, she allowed her fingers to gently tease his nipples, now erect from her attentions. She shuddered with anticipation. Callum's groans of pleasure heightened her own eroticism, tightening the muscles in her stomach. Ava reluctantly let their lips part, loving the proximity of this man, but needing so much more. As their eyes met, Ava's display of tenderness was replaced with a look of feral desire.

Callum sensed the change in Ava's demeanour. She was urging, almost pleading with Callum to take her. After so many years of yearning for her Callum was not going to refuse his invitation. His eyes drifted from the beauty of Ava's face, down to her heaving chest, her breasts rising and falling with each breath. Ava's dress had ridden above the line of her underwear and Callum's eyes naturally fell on her gossamer lace panties that barely covered her femininity. The vision consumed him, heightening his own arousal. He needed to remove that final obstacle; his want to have this beautiful and charismatic woman was all consuming. Callum needed to see Ava naked, and take her soon. Sensing Callum's desire to have her, Ava slipped off his lap and moved to the bed, letting him watch as she pulled her dress over her head, exposing her black lingerie and holdup stockings.

Callum undressed urgently, never taking his eyes off Ava as she lay there on the bed wearing little more than a knowing smile. She was eager but composed, more composed than he felt at that moment. Ava reached behind her back, releasing the clip of her bra, shrugging the delicate garment from her shoulders, avoiding the possibility of an awkward moment of her man's fumbling's. Ava's small, pert breasts were accented by hardened nipples that inevitably caught Callum's attention. She watched him admiring them, and was excited by his clear and unambiguous intentions. He smiled at her, acknowledging his gift, before burying his face in her breast. Ava exulted in Callum's touch, his stubble gently scratching her delicate skin, and his mouth taking in each nipple in turn, suckling briefly, before tormenting them gently with his teeth and tongue. Ava was herself already delirious with want and began to ease her panties invitingly from her hips. She was surprised and shocked when Callum's powerful hands suddenly locked around her wrists preventing her.

"No!" he said firmly. "That is for me to do. I want to watch your surrender Ava." Somehow his smile was both loving and wolfish in the same moment.

Callum hooked his thumbs in the waistband of Ava's black gossamer panties, drawing them slowly down her long smooth legs, his eyes never leaving hers, not even to look at her sex. For Ava it was just the sexiest thing. Normally her man would have been fixated on his prize, quite possibly oblivious as to whom she even was. When the garment was free, Ava naturally let her legs fall open, only then did Callum feast his eyes on her. The feeling of his gaze upon her was amazing to Ava, sensuous. He made her feel like a woman, loved and cherished. She wanted to reward him for his attention and she wanted it to be now.

"Don't make me wait any longer Callum. Please don't make me wait," she implored.

He covered her mouth again, kissing her deeply, her submissiveness telling him more than any words could convey. That kiss explored each other's mouths and minds. She could tell that Callum was an experienced lover, allowing her desperation to rise uncontrollably. Callum had lost his shyness now and was in total control. Ava ached for his touch, willing his hands to explore her body further. Her moans became louder, more intense, but Callum was not going to give her the climax she yearned for; at least not yet.

Ava's urgent responses began to propel Callum ever closer towards his own needs as his hands explored the body of the beautiful woman beside him, slowly teasing her with his tender caresses. She gasped as his hand at last passed gently over the strip of fine hair that inadequately covered her mound, shuddering in anticipation of his fingers and the thought of him exploring her. Looking imploringly into his eyes, Ava raised her pelvis from the bed to encourage him to do so. Her already erratic breathing caught in the moment of Callum's sweet invasion, his fingers mimicking their inevitable union. The feeling was so intense and Ava now so sensitive, that she brought her knees up and together, trapping his hand. She needed the intensity of the moment to pass. Now, at the very edge of ecstasy, Ava let her knees fall apart urging Callum to make her his. She kept her eyes shut, allowing her imagination to run wild. Ava opened her eyes momentarily, expecting Callum's eyes to be firmly focussed on her openness. He wasn't! Callum's eyes were still focussed on her face and the expressions he was causing, reading her desire. No man had ever been that attentive before.

The erotic thought of what Callum was about to do to her, sent Ava's heart racing, faster than she had ever experienced. God, I hope he takes me soon, she pleaded silently in her mind.

Callum's fingers were careful and purposeful, each gentle caress causing small explosions of colourful light to appear in her mind, a virtual meteor storm. The feeling was so intense that Ava had forgotten how to breathe. She was lost in him and what he was doing to her. When Callum's fingers finally circled around her clitoris, she climaxed instantly, every muscle contracting and releasing in regular waves. The colourful starbursts in Ava's mind began to merge until they became one single ball of brilliant white light. Ava screamed out in glorious ecstasy as her orgasm consumed her and clung to Callum as if her very life depended on it; her nails digging deeply into his back.

The contractions in Ava's lower abdomen spread, wracking her body, disorientating her such that she hadn't realised that Callum was now on top of her. She held his eyes imploringly as she succumbed to that ultimate feminine act of submission.

"Fuck me Callum. Make me yours. I will die if you make me wait any longer."

Ava's softness gave way to the hardness of his penetration. For the first time in Ava's life, she felt complete. She felt that their two worlds had collided, her hips rising and falling to match his thrusts, lifting her to ever higher levels of ecstasy.

Time seemed to stand still. Ava had no idea of how long they had been making love. All she was aware of was Callum's powerful rhythm, becoming more urgent as he approached his own climax, his eyes still locked on hers. Sensing the moment, Ava linked her legs behind Callum's back riding every powerful thrust. Her hands now gripped his hips, pulling him into her, urging him to come. When he did, the force of his passion drove her deep into the mattress and her mind into the heavens.

Ava lay back with her eyes closed for several minutes, blissfully savouring everything that had just happened. Neither spoke, words being unnecessary. At length, she became aware of Callum gently urging her onto her stomach, raising her hips until she was on her knees; his virility and stamina already recovered. She giggled expectantly and then gasped as he penetrated her from behind.

"God I love that," Ava murmured as she copied his thrusts, forcing herself backwards on him. "Don't stop. Please don't stop."

Ava was still aroused. The vivid array of lights darting in front of her warned that she was close to another glorious orgasm. Callum read the change in her, increasing the tempo of their love, whispering erotic words of encouragements, helping her fantasies. Moments later, Ava's back arched as she gasped out again in ecstasy, so lost in the moment that she was unaware that Callum had climaxed too.

Now satisfied and exhausted, Callum rolled Ava into the loving spoons position, planting little butterfly kisses on her cheek, neck and throat. At last, he turned her face to find the softness of her mouth. Their kissing had lost its urgency and now reflected the deep contentment and tenderness that both shared. Turning into Callum's arms, she held him to her, treasuring the aftermath of the best sex she had ever experienced. At last she realised that men didn't have to treat her badly to bring out her sexuality. She lay their feeling safe and loved, cherished. It was the first time in her life that Ava had ever felt that secure with a man.

The gentle and loving kissing continued long afterwards and Ava exulted in the feel of Callum's tongue on hers as it entwined and explored her mouth. It was just the most sensual feeling and she didn't want it to stop, ever. Callum was as tender and considerate a lover as Katarina, but could satisfy her in a way that Katrina never could. He truly was the White Knight that she had wanted her to find.

Suddenly a vision of Demitri's face destroyed her serenity and contentment. She could not disobey this man. At that moment Ava felt bereft, unclean and sullied. Her orders were to kill this amazing man. A man who could pleasure her like no other man had ever done before.

--------------------------------------------------------------------------

Ava woke up in Callum's arms, her cheek stuck to his chest. She lifted her head and winced. It felt like her ear was glued in place. Callum was sleeping peacefully, never stirring. Ava could just see the bedside clock over his muscular shoulder. It was nine-thirty in the morning. Thirteen hours had passed since they had entered her bedroom, and they had only slept for five of them. Callum had sexually pleasured her, one way or another, for eight hours, allowing her barely enough time to recover between sessions.

He was the most unselfish lover she had ever known. Callum had only allowed himself to come that once, the rest of the time was all about attending to her needs, giving pleasure in abundance. Callum had taken control throughout, something that she loved, turning her every which way he desired, but it was done to please her. He was gentle, inventive and used his hands and mouth expertly. It was heaven. Ava had never thought that it was possible for a man to take her to such erotic heights, let alone keep her there in ecstasy for hours upon end.

Ava sat up and examined her body. Yes, she felt royally fucked, but there were no bruises, scratches and more noticeably, no split lip! He had paid her breasts a lot of attention. "His little girls," he had called them, so they were a little sore but they wouldn't object to a little more attention, she decided and smiled lasciviously at the thought. Callum had boasted early in the evening that she would not be walking comfortably for a week by the time that they had finished.

Typical male exaggeration, Ava mused. It would only be three days at the most. But then she had not finished with him yet! She gave him the benefit of the doubt, hoping that he might be correct in his assumption of a whole week!

The thought of some gentle morning sex roused her and she looked at the sleeping Callum impatiently. Ava had needs, an itch that had to be scratched. She decided to give him the best wakeup call that a man could possibly wish for. She slipped down under the bedclothes with wicked intent.

--------------------------------------------------------------------------

It was after midday when they finally breakfasted. Ava was famished. They had only allowed themselves Champagne and sandwiches during the night. Time was limited and too precious to waste.

"God I had the most amazing time Callum," Ava enthused as she buttered the steamed kippers. "You are officially a sex God."

"A workman is only as good as his tools," Callum quipped. "And you do something to me, remember?"

He purposely used the same expression Ava had used on the plane and she raised her well-groomed brow in acknowledgement of his attentiveness.

"How am I going to go back to my old Rovers now that I have experienced an Aston Martin? You have ruined me for all other men Callum Knight!"

It wasn't just a throwaway compliment, Ava meant it.

"Stick around then," Callum suggested. "You could wake up to the same loving attention every morning of your life if you want to."

That wasn't just a throwaway comment either. Callum meant it too.

"I want," Ava demurred.

"Destiny still has a major part to play, little one. We will see."

Callum's voice felt full of irony. Ava was puzzled by his response, but didn't press the issue. She had no way of knowing that Callum had seen alternative futures in the mirrors with Maelströminha, nor that she had refused to reveal some of the details to Callum as they may prove to be self-fulfilling.

"It is too much information Callum," Maelströminha had said at the time. "And it will damage your life in ways that you cannot fathom. Trust me that it is better that you do not know."

Alternative futures generally didn't end well for Callum. He knew that Ava was perfectly capable of sacrificing her own happiness for a perfect bastard. She had such low self-esteem that if push came to shove, she would not value herself enough to fight for what she wanted, or indeed him. Ava sensed that Callum had regressed to somewhere dark and needed distracting from whatever that darkness was.

"What are you doing for Christmas?" Ava asked. It was only two days away.

"Stuffing a hot bird, I hope."

The look he gave Ava left her in no doubt as to what he meant.

"Good," was her response. "I don't like cold turkey."

She met his look with equal intent. The problem was that the thought of the innuendo had stimulated her. Callum sensed her anticipation.

"Checkout isn't till four o'clock Ava. Eat up, you will need the energy."

Ava had already learned that Callum did not make threats he couldn't follow through with. She crammed her mouth in preparation of what might follow.

"You will be my Queen," he added, grinning suggestively.

Ava knew exactly what that would entail; having read all about that position, but had never experienced it. She got even more excited as she pictured herself in the act. So much of Ava's sex was played out in her mind.

"Oh my God," was all that Ava could mumble. Her face was a picture.

--------------------------------------------------------------------------

Chapter 17

5th January 2016. Thirteen days later.

Ava spent the two weeks that followed both in paradise and denial. She had hardly left Callum's side, other than for prayer. Her prayers were for forgiveness. She had fallen head over heels in love with Callum and prayed for some justifiable way to spare his life. She had even talked with Demitri about it, but his wrath was possibly even greater than God's.

She had tried to distance herself from Callum, but Ava was the proverbial boomerang. Ava even tried hurting him, and then begged his forgiveness. She tried to make him hate her, but there was no hatred in the man. Every day they were together, Ava saw more perfection in Callum. His ability to love her, mentally and physically grew stronger each day. It was going to be like killing the most precious and perfect flower. Ava had been warned that the devil takes on many guises, and that Callum had been sent from Hell to tempt her. She must prevail. It was her duty and Ava turned to her God whenever she weakened. She had to keep reminding herself that she owed everything to Demitri and that he loved her, and that one day they would finally be together.

Ava reflected on the last two weeks. They had been a roller coaster ride for her. Callum had offered her the job, with a salary several times more than she had earned as prima ballerina and an expense account that was obscene. The money was of no importance though; nothing could compensate for the final act that she was expected to perform. Ava was to be Callum's personal secretary. Whilst undertaking this position, Callum and his team would train her in the arts of counter terrorism, strategy, espionage and intelligence. Most of Ava's days were spent monitoring covert conversations in the Middle East, and her nights spent mostly on her back in the company of her lover. Ava adored the nights!

Callum had explained the history of the Angels and the Shadows since they had colonised the Earth over five thousand years ago. This tuition went a long way towards helping her understand herself, and from where she had originated. Ava was certain though that Callum had changed the natures of the two competing races. It was the Angels seeking world domination and not the Shadows. After all she had heard it from the mouths of the Mullah, her mentor the Imam and Demitri.

Ava worked in a small select team. Intelligence emanating from the Middle East suggested that the Shadows had completed the design and manufacture of a dirty bomb, and that its despatch and deployment was imminent. Demitri had warned Ava that the Angels would pervert the truth. She remained sceptical as to this actually being a *Shadow* initiative. Ava did however believe that it was an ungodly act, that deserved to be stopped, whoever the perpetrator.

The intelligence had originated from an Iranian opposition group, the National Council of Resistance of Iran. They had disclosed the existence of a secret uranium enrichment facility at *Natanz*, and a heavy water reactor at *Arak*, suitable for making plutonium-based nuclear weapons. The site called Lavizan-3 was operated by the Iranian Ministry of Intelligence and Security, within a military compound and was off-limits to the scrutiny of the International Atomic Energy Agency inspectors. The Iranian regime continued to deny the facility's existence and insisted they were not a nuclear-ready state. Ava's job was to monitor all communications coming in and out of Lavizan-3 to establish the bomb's actual existence, dispatch and target.

Apart from Kayla Lovell, Ava had already met the team she was going to work with. Ironically, Kayla was the one she most wanted to meet. Ava had heard the hot-gossip about Callum's torrid affair with her from others in the team and felt jealous and threatened to say the least. Kayla would be one to watch Ava decided.

Bud Lewinski was an archetypical product of the American Military Academy, with a chest full of active service medals, which included the Purple Heart, awarded for being wounded in action. Lewinski's helicopter had been shot down in Afghanistan and he had spent weeks injured behind enemy lines. He was a

Green Beret, larger than life, a drinker and also a womaniser. Bud was a fearless man who led from the front. He was always the first man into action and the last to leave, and then only after securing the safety of his men.

Another, Red Jake was a bear of man who shared many of the same character traits as Bud. The only exception was his choice of women. They were from the low-life bars, clubs and often the streets, whereas Bud's women tended to be politicians, socialites or other officer's wives.

Then there was Sergeant Mike Jackson. At twenty-six, he was handsome with a quizzical look that made girl's hearts flutter. He had joined the army at the age of seventeen, spending most of his nine years of service in the theatre of war. Mike had completed three tours in Afghanistan, working covertly in villages. His swarthy looks and fluency in Arabic allowed him to pass unnoticed as an Arab. He followed those assignments by working in and around Syria, tasked with gathering intelligence on the deployment of ISIS and the elimination of their leaders, through targeted precision strikes. Although young by comparison with his peers, Mike was fearless, funny and just the man you would want to watch your back.

Craig Jamieson was selected as their medic, a man in his early forties, handsome with a broad forehead and bright blue eyes that exuded competence and confidence. Jamieson had the accolade of administering morphine and keeping each of his comrades alive, whilst the team was under fire on more than one occasion. Red Jake held the unenviable record of having been shot five times on active service, a badge that he wore with pride, *took one for the team*, being his catchphrase.

Each wound emboldened Jake's next operation. Craig marvelled at his total lack of fear, but secretly dreaded the day that would surely come, when Jake's luck would finally run out and the wound dressings and morphine would be replaced by a body bag.

Sean O'Malley was their helicopter pilot. The expectation was that the team, including Ava, would be dropped in the desert at some stage to disarm and liberate the bomb. Ava had quickly surmised that *liberating the bomb* was a euphemism for fighting tooth and nail for it. She consoled herself with the thought that she was with an experienced and battle hardened team. Strangely though, Ava never considered that the dormant powers within her could crush a small army if she only knew how to deploy them properly. This however was something that Demitri remained constantly aware of, and feared.

O'Malley, as he was always referred to, seemed to be harbouring a dark secret to Ava. He was a very private man, nervous at times, paying his mobile phone far too much attention. What she could never have known, was that he had a gambling addiction, constantly placing on-line bets. O'Malley had sold his soul to the Shadows some years ago in exchange for his gambling debts. His misery started when he lost control of his addiction, which he had kept from his family, always hoping for the big win that would make everything alright. The big win never came and O'Malley was about to lose everything: house, car, wife, kids and his career. It was then, when his life had hit an all-time low, that he was approached by the Shadow organisation. They had a solution. Money would never be a problem again. O'Malley knew that his debt would be called in at some point; everything comes at a price.

What Ava did know through her own senses, was that they all shared a common denominator that linked them all. They were all from the same bloodline, all Angels. What Ava could not know, was that the only team member she had yet to meet, Kayla, was not.

Ava was both scared and confused by what she was learning. *Scared*, because it brought her suddenly and violently into the reality of the new world she now lived in and *confused*, because nothing was making any sense to her. Demitri had assured her that the Angels were the aggressors, but that didn't add up. If indeed that was so, then who was killing the Angels? Ava wondered.

She had already witnessed two recent murders within the Angel organisation; those of Bart Jeffries and Larry Madison. Both were supposed to join their team. Apparently they had been murdered to prevent them doing so. Nothing was stacking up. Ava turned as usual to prayer to assuage the doubt that was building up inside her.

Bart Jeffries was to be their logistical specialist, and Larry Madison their nuclear scientist. Both travelled together from Heathrow Airport to join them in London. Tragically, both were found dead, along with their driver, only a few hundred yards from the Savoy. All three had sustained a single gunshot wound to the head. The death of their two comrades threatened to put plans to intercept the dirty bomb into disarray.

The team was scheduled to fly out to RAF *Akrotiri* in Cyprus on the 13th of January, three days after the emergency summit meeting in Moscow. There simply wasn't enough time to organise and brief replacements. Ava's role in the operation was escalated to include nuclear expertise, in line with her research education. Kayla would take on the logistical and administrational responsibilities, which as the junior member, were supposed to be Ava's duties. This deeply concerned Ava. She believed that Kayla would resent Ava's necessary promotion, allowing ill feeling to fester between them from the outset. It was only Ava's broad scientific experience and photographic memory that had made this last-minute change and the continuation of the mission remotely possible.

--------------------------------------------------------------------------------

Ava spent her last hours before her flight to Moscow, studying activation mechanisms for nuclear devices, particularly Permissive Action Links, or PALs as they are more commonly referred to. In all probability, the dirty bomb would be activated by the enemy shortly before their team found it, in some last-ditch attempt to fulfil their mission. That was at best. Worst case was that Callum's team would be walking straight into a nuclear explosion. It made every day seem precious. Anti-tamper systems were Ava's biggest fear. There were literally scores of schematic diagrams to study and memorise. The survival of the whole team could depend on Ava's mental ability to recall that plethora of information.

Callum had left for Moscow three days earlier to prepare for the emergency summit. Ava missed him enormously; mentally and physically. She had never had sex on a daily basis before and now her body seemed to depend upon it. Ava rejoiced in the fact that she would be meeting Callum that evening at the Metropol Hotel in Moscow. Dangerous thoughts and ideas entered Ava's head. She knew that he would be as desperate to see her as she was to see him and decided to give Callum a treat. He loved to see her wearing lingerie and hold-ups. *It did something to him*, apparently. That was exactly what he was going to discover when she slipped her coat off in his room that evening. Coat, underwear and nothing else! The erotic thought of how he would respond to her seduction consumed Ava, and she quickly became lost in her body.

-------------------------------------------------------------------------------

It was eight o' clock in the evening when Ava walked into the lounge of the Metropol Hotel. The bitter cold outside had chilled her to the bone and her feet felt like blocks of ice. She hadn't dressed properly for the Moscow winter, the cold being the price of her vanity.

A real passion killer, Ava thought and decided to have a coffee to warm up before going to Callum's room; otherwise he would have shuddered at her touch; and not the kind of *shudder* she had planned.

Whilst her coffee was being prepared, Ava took the opportunity to go to the bathroom and freshen up. She locked the door, slipped off her full length red coat and looked at her reflection in the mirror. Ava wore a one piece black and white polka dot dress with a high neck, cut to below the elbows and above the knee. She took the hem, pulled the dress up over her head in one fluid motion, revealing red underwear and matching hold-ups. Ava was perfectly aware that Callum preferred that she kept her stockings on and idly wondered why he found this so exciting.

She washed, quickly fixed her makeup and brushed her long black hair. Ava was tempted to let the mental subterfuge drop and let everyone see her red hair, but she was in Moscow now and close to the Bolshoi. Ava could easily be recognised by the police who frequented the establishment and decided to keep up the black hair disguise. She purposely folded her dress, dropped it in her bag and pulled on her red coat, grinning at her reflection lasciviously, pondered what Callum's reaction would be.

"Good plan Stan," she whispered and left the room.

Ava returned to the crowded lounge now feeling highly aroused. The thought of secretly being almost naked beneath her coat, and that the people around her hadn't the faintest idea, was exciting. As Ava sipped at her coffee, enjoying the warmth, she found herself smiling at strange men, imagining how shocked they would be if she shrugged off her coat, exposing herself there in the lounge. Ava's anticipation had become urgent and all-consuming, such that she couldn't think of anything else other than having Callum. Ava ached for him. She needed him. Now warmed through, Ava took one final sip of her coffee and headed for the elevator.

As she approached Callum's room, Ava couldn't help but smile at the memory of previous visits to him in various hotel rooms. She smirked at the naughtiness of her plan. Ava's heart pounded in her chest with sheer excitement, knowing in her heart that Callum would be feeling that same heady mix of anxious exhilaration. When Ava reached the room, she took a deep breath to steady herself and knocked. She was going to gift herself to Callum and fulfil as many of his fantasies as she could, knowing that he would naturally reciprocate and fulfil hers.

The wait seemed like minutes, not the seconds that it actually took for Callum to open the door. He met her with his usual beaming smile. Ava could tell from the look in his eyes that he wanted her more than anything in the world. As she walked into his room, Ava could feel Callum's eyes feasting on her, taking her in from head to toe giving her the most sensuous feeling. Ava imagined that Callum could probably visualise what she was wearing beneath her coat; the usual black and white dress that she found comfortable to travel in, and the usual black lace underwear. She smirked at the naughtiness she was concealing from him and couldn't wait for Callum to unwrap her and see the look of surprise on his face.

The instant the door closed Ava was upon Callum, her mouth planted firmly on his, the sensuousness making Ava go weak at the knees. She reached up taking the back of Callum's head and pulled his face to hers, urging his tongue deeper into her mouth. Callum responded hungrily, devouring her but all the while his strong hands gently framed her face, as if to him she was the most precious and fragile thing. The desperation of their kissing quickened their pulses and Ava found it difficult to catch her breath. The wanting within her burned low in the pit of her stomach. She stopped the kiss abruptly, smiling wickedly at him, pulling the tie on her coat to reveal herself. The look of wonderment on Callum's face was reward enough for Ava and she had never felt more woman than she did at that moment.

Callum looked down at Ava, lost in her beauty, overwhelmed by the generous and most sensual gift she had given him. His eyes feasted on her red lace lingerie and sheer hold-ups before returning to the blueness of her eyes. Ava bit her lip in response, those eyes pleading with him to take her as she trembled in anticipation of his caress.

--------------------------------------------------------------------------

Ava woke the next morning to the sound of a man's electric shaver coming from the bathroom and immediately felt bereft. She had fallen asleep whilst anticipating the pleasure of their gentle morning sex and felt cheated. Callum was up and getting ready for the summit.

"Callum!" she called out petulantly. "I need you!"

"So, does the Prime Minister honey. Taxi picks us up in an hour."

"Jesus!" Ava shouted and threw the covers off. They had overslept. Ava bustled past Callum in the bathroom. "Mind if I pee?"

"Be my guest," he said naturally.

They had become comfortable in each other's company. Ava already knew that she loved Callum deeply and totally, and tried not to think about how their love affair would end. She looked guiltily down at her knees, unable to meet Callum's eyes.

"Is something on your mind little one?" Callum was always intuitive to her moods.

"No," she lied. "I just wish we could spend the morning in bed together."

"I seem to remember that you ground yourself into oblivion last night. Don't you ever have enough sex?" Callum questioned, shaving his cheeks and jutted-out chin. He cast a mocking glance at her.

"Never and I will prove that to you tonight if you have the stamina." The look Ava gave him left Callum in no doubt that a challenge had been issued.

"The summit will go on until after midnight and we need to be back there again at eight in the morning honey. Plus, we have to fit in a couple of meals..."

"Humph!" Ava was more than a little annoyed. "Then I will just have to ride while you sleep." They both knew that she meant it.

---------------------------------------------------------------------

Despite Ava's misgivings, the five days of the summit went well romantically and their emotional bond was becoming ever stronger. Ava was in deep turmoil though. Acting as Callum's secretary prevented her from following her accustomed prayer regime. It was only through prayer that Ava could keep her focus on the mission that Demitri had given her. That resolve was waning fast. Ava knew she needed to reinforce her spirit and determination through supplication as soon as the summit was over. She managed to secretly email Demitri daily with any new occurrences and observations. Amongst other things for example, were state secrets and reports, including the whereabouts of Callum and his team. Ava would never have known, but the assassinations of Bart Jeffries and Larry Madison, were as a direct consequence of her leaking the information of their travel itinerary to Demitri. Ava was also unaware that, since the death of those two agents, her messages were being monitored by Callum's organisation, and that they were completely aware of their content and recipient.

Following the murders, the Angel organisation's knee-jerk reaction was to shut down the operation, but the operation was of far greater importance than the loss of two lives, and crucial in avoiding the deployment of a small nuclear device, not to mention the pressing probability of Armageddon. They were gambling everything on Ava completing one of her alternative destinies; the one that ended in the salvation of mankind. They had no choice but to carry on and watch her more closely. Limit, or at least control, the information she was a party to. Forewarned was forearmed.

It was the final day of the summit. Ava had left Callum and Bud with the President and Prime Minister to wrap up their discussions, giving her eight hours to herself and a chance to visit the local mosque. She spent two solid hours there praying for strength, forgiveness and understanding. Then at the end, she guiltily asked *Allah* to forgive Callum and to remove the fatwa that the prophet Hydra had placed on him through Demitri.

Once again, bolstered by prayer and hope, Ava left the mosque to return to the hotel. She checked her phone for messages and the new message light was pulsing. There were only a few people that messaged her these days: Callum, Demitri and occasionally the Mullah. It was Demitri. Despite having waited days for him to contact her, she felt disappointed that the message was not from

Callum. Ava immediately begged forgiveness from *Allah* for her betrayal and muttered a prayer in Arabic.

"*Rabbi inni zalamto nafsi faghfirli.* Oh, my Lord. I have indeed wronged my soul!"

Now repentant, Ava opened the message.

"*Ava. I am staying at the Metropol, suite 206. Come to me now. I need you.*"

She noted with great disappointment that the message was not signed off with a kiss.

------------------------------------------------------------------------

Demitri had kept Ava under surveillance throughout the summit. The dozens of pictures spread across his dressing table were testament to that. They showed a woman deeply in love, and not those of his agent doing her duty. Demitri was enraged. Furious! He grabbed the photographs, ripped them apart and tossed the pieces onto the floor, all the while pacing frenetically around the room.

"The bitch!" he spat the words out venomously. "The traitorous fucking bitch!"

The bottle of whiskey he had drunk had not assuaged that rage. Instead the alcohol had fuelled it. Falling in love with her assignment was not part of his plan and completely unacceptable.

"Bitch!" he yelled again, heaving the empty bottle at his angry reflection in the tall mirror.

The collision of glass on glass caused a cloud of shards to be sprayed into the air. Pieces of mirror and bottle flew randomly around the room, before settling where they landed. Ava needed re-indoctrinating. He had sent her the text message over two hours ago, and still she had not arrived at the hotel.

"She's probably still in the arms of her lover, fucking his brains out!" Demitri screamed out despite no one being within earshot.

At that moment his mobile rang. He recognised at a glance that it was the Hydra's number. Demitri realised that he needed to control his temper before talking to her. She would not be amused at his loss of control and he was already out of favour because of the whole Kaplinski episode.

"Hydie, sweetheart, where are you? I've missed you so much," he cooed, all sweetness and light.

"Bored with your little Russian whores then are you *agápe mou?*"

It wasn't so much an accusation on the Hydra's part, as an acknowledgement of Demitri's sexuality. For a man like Demitri to live apart for months on end without the satisfaction of a woman's body, was impossible.

"You know that there are none that can hold a candle to you *agápe mou.* You have always known that."

Demitri's sentiment was at least honest and the Hydra was sure of him. Their sexual compatibility was legendary. Of course the Hydra had her own indiscretions too, but Demitri had the good grace not to expose them.

"*She* is with you, isn't she?" The Hydra had a sixth sense.

"No but she is on her way," Demitri confessed.

There was a brief but agonising silence. The Hydra was the only person in the world that Demitri was truly afraid of, both intellectually and physically. She was blessed with perfect Shadow abilities and could crush him if she so wished.

"I would have you kill her Demitri, but we need this genetic abomination to fulfil our needs," the Hydra's tone was impatient.

"I am bored of this political deployment of a nuclear device Demitri. What do we achieve in comparison to opening up the fifth dimension? And what happens if the bitch-whore is killed in the fallout? Don't risk her Demitri. If there is the remotest chance that she will be in danger, then get her out. Bring her back to your research laboratories and get me access to the fifth dimension. I will end this five thousand year war with the Angels in minutes."

Demitri needed to sound upbeat but he was still in that dark place. He had to dig deep to do so.

"But darling we have invested too much time in deploying the nuclear device to stop now. Besides the fifth dimension project is without guarantee of outcome." Demitri chose his words carefully so as not to incite her anger. "I will find a way to extract the woman, should the situation require."

There was a sound at the door, rescuing Demitri from further interrogation, but alas not from the Hydra's wrath.

"*Agápe mou*, I must go. The woman has arrived." Demitri instinctively held his breath.

"If you don't kill the bitch as soon as this is over, I will kill the pair of you!" she screamed.

Hydie Papandreou ended the call with Demitri left in no doubt that she meant every word.

---

As Demitri crossed to the door to let Ava in, the images of her with Callum, so happy together, were burning like coals in his mind. It wasn't that he loved her or wanted her; he didn't. But she was his possession, his chattel. It was that another dog had the scent of his bitch and that she had the audacity to love him. Normally, he would have killed her, but he didn't have that luxury. Well not yet anyway. For now he would just punish her. Make her pay for her treason.

---

Ava stood outside Demitri's room, her emotions confused; sexual anticipation, fear and guilt. She knew that the sexual anticipation was because sex was almost inevitable. He had denied her for so long. Fear coursed through her veins. She was petrified of him. Demitri had a dark side that was always lurking just below the surface and it terrified her. Demitri was rough, without conscience or compassion. He exuded power and control and had the blackest aura around him she had ever sensed. But even so he was sexually appealing she had to concede. Guilt wrenched at her soul. Ava was about to betray Callum. She knocked on the door with the greatest trepidation. It seemed to take forever for the door to open, deepening Ava's anxiety.

"Come in Ava," Demitri's words were spoken without soul. She was prepared for the welcoming kiss that never came. "Take off your coat and come and sit on the bed next to me. Tell me about the summit."

The bed? Ava thought. Why not welcoming drinks in the lounge area first? It made her feel like a tramp. Just business and sex, Ava lamented. Although Ava was undeniably in love with Callum, Demitri was her saviour. She was indebted to him and had a duty to perform. Demitri had told her that they would be together afterwards, and she still believed in him. Ava fought back her fear and began her summary.

"The hot topic, as I have already told you, was terrorism and the current threat of a dirty bomb. All the usual nations pledged support for the international initiative tabled by the Americans, except Russia of course, who sat on the fence as usual."

Ava paused for Demitri's response, still disappointed that he hadn't even asked her how she was, let alone welcomed her, which was in stark contrast to the loving and caring attention that she had received from Callum in abundance. It made her doubt why she was there at all and not with Callum instead. Ava dug deep and reminded herself that she had sworn allegiance to Demitri and *Allah*. The words of the old Imam filled her mind and bolstered her resolve.

*Satan will try and enter your body and prevent you from doing God's will and you must deny him!*

Ava's moment of weakness had passed. She pushed all blasphemous thoughts from her mind and listened to Demitri attentively.

"Excellent! That is just as I had hoped," Demitri enthused.

Ava noted that it was the first time that he had looked excited since she walked through the door.

"Did they speculate where that bomb might be deployed?" he added with clear elation.

"Tel Aviv," Ava said simply.

"Intuitive," Demitri gave her a wry grin. "I want them to find it. The Mullah will be there waiting for them."

"It's our bomb then?"

Ava was shocked. She had assumed that it was a known terrorist group.

"It is an Angel trap Ava, a carefully planned Angel trap. I will feed you the communications from Iran for you to listen in to. They, along with your perfect insight, will lead you along the route the bomb will take to Tel Aviv. You will impart that knowledge to your team and look a hero in their eyes Ava."

*But not for long sweetheart*, was his private thought.

Ava felt the cold chill of dread go up her spine, knowing that she would be sending her friends to their deaths.

"Why would we do that Demitri? Why would we kill indiscriminately?"

Ava could see that her question had angered Demitri and her body tensed at the anticipation of his wrath and a probable beating.

"Have you learnt nothing woman!" His black eyes burned with rage. "The Angels are our enemy and must be wiped off the face of the Earth; the scriptures demand it to be so. The Hydra demands it!" Demitri was vitriolic. "Make no mistake that their intention is the same, and they oppose *Allah*. You have a duty as a chosen jihadist. Our world is made up of hostile unbelievers whose sole purpose is the destruction of Islam. It is no time for you to become sentimental."

Demitri was furious, losing control. Just in time, he saw the stricken look on Ava's face and realised that he had taken his tirade too far. Of course he didn't give a damn about her feelings, but he did care about losing his control over her. Demitri fought back his anger and altered his approach.

"Ava, forgive me. It's only that I have missed you so much and I'm worried about you being with that man. You are precious to me you beyond all else, you know that, don't you?" Ava nodded and wiped a tear from her eye. "Please do as I ask and trust me," Demitri added in false tenderness.

Ava smiled weakly.

"I do trust you but it's so hard, and I know these people as my friends now. They seem good and honest to me. It's just so confusing, that's all. Please forgive me."

"There is nothing to forgive Ava," his tone was softer now. "Let me explain everything. You have earned the right to be made privy to our intentions".

His placatory words caused the stiffness and defiance to leave Ava's body.

"The bomb planned is small and it is not indiscriminate. Any loss of life is only intended to be small, but the political statement it will make will be huge. If we can link the bomb to the Angels by

256

getting them there and exposing them, then international feelings will harden against them. They will then be recognised for what they are, a covert terrorist organisation; wolves in sheep's clothing."

Demitri smiled at Ava winningly and continued.

"*Allah* will decide if any of them should perish in the explosion. It will be his will, and his alone. You should feel comforted by this that the burden you feel right now, will transfer to *Allah*."

Demitri looked at Ava knowingly and grinned wickedly.

"Enough of business, I know what you really want; what you need."

Demitri slid his hand up the inside of Ava's thigh, under her dress, up to the warmth of her sex.

"Has she been missing her man?" he asked.

Involuntarily, Ava pressed her knees together at his invasion, Demitri sensing her rejection.

"Don't you dare deny me you Angel-fucking whore!"

The force of his slap split Ava's lip and momentarily knocked her senseless. He shoved her on her back, took two handfuls of her delicate dress and ripped it off, leaving Ava in her sheer underwear, confused and vulnerable.

"No Demitri! Not this way; please!" Ava sobbed. "Not this way."

She looked up at Demitri in shock and disbelief, still begging him to stop. His second slap was even more powerful than the first. Her nose exploded under the impact and blood gushed down her face and neck.

I was wrong to deny him, Ava thought guiltily. It is my fault, not his. I deserve this. She began to mumble in Arabic. Her prayer was for forgiveness. The words bolstered Ava as she resigned herself to endure the painful and disgusting rape that was already happening to her.

---------------------------------------------------------------------------

Ava was still in shock when she returned to her room. Callum was due back in another three hours, enough time to tidy herself up, she hoped. Even the walk to the bathroom was excruciating and Ava winced with every step. She turned on the vanity mirror light and looked at herself.

"Oh my God!" she gasped and burst into tears.

Ava's face and hair were caked in blood. One eye was half closed and swollen; her nose was fat and her lip split. Even with Ava's amazing powers of regeneration, she would look much the same when Callum returned. Ava needed a plan. She couldn't let him find out that it was Demitri, or they would kill each other for sure. More than that, Ava couldn't expose Demitri as he was her saviour, the man who had watched over her for years protecting her from her benefactor. She was his to do with as he pleased and she was wrong to have angered him. Ava decided that she would use most of those hours before Callum returned in prayer to be a better and more faithful woman.

She ran the bath, lacing it with oils, perfume and antiseptic. As she lowered her bottom into the hot water Ava gasped and instinctively cupped her genitals with her hands to protect the raw tissue. Sex had never been that painful before and her unusual dryness had damaged her. It seemed that her infinite wetness was for Callum and Callum alone.

When Ava was calmer and able to call upon her teachings and the old Imam's rhetoric, it became clear to her that her brutal assault really wasn't Demitri's fault. He had a duty to punish her in God's name, she decided with absolute certainty. She had made him angry by allowing the devil within her to cloud her judgement and vowed that she would be wet and wanting of him next time they met. Ava stared at the wall, still in shock, and quite subconsciously began to scrub his stain from her body as if it would also cleanse her soul. Ava was oblivious to the fact that she was repeating the same nursery rhyme that Katarina had all those months ago, when she was about to be raped.

-------------------------------------------------------------------------

Callum's meeting with the President and Prime Minister had gone well. He and Bud had been given carte blanche in exchange for their absolute guarantee that their team would mobilise to intercept the dirty bomb within three days and succeed in their mission. It had been made categorically clear to them that, should they fail, their existence and any connection with the United States or the United Kingdom would be vehemently denied. They would be disavowed.

On the drive back, Callum agonised about how he could keep Ava in the team and effective, without jeopardising the safety of the others. To set her free would result in the Angels having no influence on her choice of any alternative destiny. It was a conundrum. If he redacted Ava's responsibilities, she would become suspicious to the fact, wondering if they suspected her as a double agent. They would lose her. All he could really do was watch events unfold, be honest with his team, and watch each other's backs. Under the circumstances, it would be interesting to see how Ava and Kayla got on, he thought wryly.

It was eight o'clock in the evening when Callum arrived at their room, looking forward to their first romantic dinner in nearly a week and the tender loving that would follow.

"Honey I'm home," he called out stepping into the darkened room. "Oh, sorry are you asleep?"

"Please don't turn the light on!" Ava said a bit too urgently. "I've got a migraine."

The truth was that she still looked like she had been in a car crash. Even with Ava's uncanny power of regeneration, her face and body would not repair for some days.

Callum came to sit beside her on the bed. Ava lay still with her face mostly concealed in the pillow. He stroked her temple gently with the back of his hand.

"Will you lie with me and hold me for a while?" Ava asked. "I'm sorry but we can't make love."

Ava was still raw and bruised and couldn't bear to be touched.

"That's OK. I need a well-earned break anyway." Callum made light of the situation.

He stripped and slid into the bed naked beside her. Ava lay on her side with her back to him, her knees tucked up towards her stomach, holding herself in a protective position. Callum nestled into her and brought his knees up under hers, tenderly reassuring, giving them the closeness they both desired. Callum naturally cupped a shapely breast with his left hand and buried his face into Ava's neck, placing little butterfly kisses there. He could sense that she didn't want to talk and so they lay there in silence. It was twenty minutes later that Ava finally spoke.

"I love you Callum. Whatever happens I want you to know that."

Callum could tell that Ava needed to talk. He loved her so much that he just lay there and listened. She continued.

"It was you who made me love you Callum. I didn't ask you to, and I didn't have any choice, you simply made it happen." Ava sighed deeply. "You are so perfect Callum; a perfect gentleman, perfectly charming and a perfect lover. How could any woman not fall in love with you?"

Minutes passed before Ava spoke again.

"You should leave me Callum. I will only hurt you and cause you pain if you stay. I'm not worthy of your perfection. I don't want to break your heart but I will if you don't go. I destroy everything that is precious to me. I always have and I always will."

Callum leaned over and kissed Ava on the cheek and on her closed eyes. He gently drank the tears she was crying off her face. For the first time, he saw the deep split on her lip and the dark bruising under her eye, but said nothing. Ava clearly didn't want to talk about her ordeal.

Callum sadly conceded that Ava was indeed, albeit through no fault of her own, tragic. He held her closely to comfort her, until at last she fell asleep in his arms. Callum had a rage burning inside him. He knew that it was Demitri who had abused her. One day their paths would cross. Callum vowed to repay everything Demitri had done to Ava and more.

---------------------------------------------------------------------------

When Callum awoke, Ava was already gone and no trace left of her ever being there, only a note that read:

*Callum,*

*Sorry to leave without saying goodbye, but I have something personal to do in Moscow. I will catch up with you in London.*

*Ava* ☺

It was the first of five cruel denials that a woman uses when she wants to leave her lover, triggering unwelcome memories of Kayla Lovell. Kayla was the last of a string of women to break Callum's heart, a dark-haired, dark-skinned African-American beauty of amazing sexuality. Callum adored her and let her too deeply into his heart. He failed to see that Kayla was a woman for a season, not for life and was still suffering from her rebuff. He had loved her far too much to see the ice in her heart, just as he had now failed to see the ice in Ava's. The first of Kayla's five cruel denials was the substitution of a kiss at the end of a message for a smiley face. Eventually those disappeared too, he lamented.

The second cruel denial, was when Kayla stopped letting Callum see her apply her lipstick and then not to let him see her wearing it at all. In Callum's opinion, letting a man watch a woman put on her lipstick was one of the greatest gifts a woman could bestow a man and ironically one of the worst things she could deny him.

Kayla's third cruel denial was when she took away her smile, possibly the cruellest denial of all. He remembered how he used to love looking at her mouth when she talked and smiled.

The fourth was when she denied him her loving glance and spontaneous loving conversation.

The fifth and final act of cruelty, was when Kayla had denied him her presence; the final *coup de grace*. She had been cold and brutal throughout her clinical campaign of rejection and now he was going through it all over again with Ava. He could sense it. The problem for Callum was that when he fell in love, he fell hard, and getting over Ava would take a very long time, Callum knew this from bitter experience, if at all.

He had several hours to kill before leaving for the airport. They were going to be the longest and emptiest hours he had spent in a long time.

--------------------------------------------------------------------------

It was four o'clock in the morning when Ava woke. Callum was dead to the world. Ava allowed herself five minutes just to watch his face while he slept. Ava knew that she would never see him at peace again, or maybe even alive. She packed silently and went to the bathroom.

Ava looked in the mirror, assessing herself. Her split lip was healing well and there was only the faintest touch of yellow left from the bruising under her eye. Miracles of her half-breed abilities she thought. But there was something missing. She looked like a woman without a soul, and it was visible. Ava's decision to erase Callum from her life and out of her heart had come at a monumental price. Ava knew that she would never be happy and fulfilled again and that those spirits that haunted her

262

at night would come flooding back to fill the void of their love. She had decided to devote herself unconditionally to Demitri and do his will. Her wants and needs were inconsequential in comparison to the importance of his demands and her duty to *Allah*.

Ava picked up her toilet bag and turned off the light just as she had doused the burning beacon of their love. She walked over to the sleeping Callum and kissed him gently on the forehead. He moved at her touch and Ava held her breath until he was settled again.

"Goodbye my love," she whispered. "I'm sorry, you don't deserve this. I have condemned myself to a living Hell and you to death. How could you or any God ever forgive me?"

The metallic lock clicked as Ava closed the door on Callum and everything that they had shared, also closing the most perfect chapter of her life.

--------------------------------------------------------------------------

It was ten o'clock in the morning on Thursday 7th January, eighteen hours since Ava had last seen Callum. She was hurting more than words could say, mourning his loss, which left her feeling empty to the pit of her stomach. The emptiness consumed her, even more than her self-loathing.

It didn't feel the same sat at the bar of the Bolshoi drinking Dirty Martinis without seeing Yuri's smiling face; watching his reflection in the mirror behind the bottles of spirits. Ava was lost in her own misery, a *femme fatale* that brought death and misery in abundance. To make matters worse, there was nothing that Ava seemed to be able to do about it. She had asked *Allah* for guidance, but her prayers fell on deaf ears, encouraging death as opposed to love. Tonight, she would willingly give *Allah* another soul to torture eternally; Bortnik's.

Ava was depending on Bortnik still being a creature of habit. She couldn't remember the last time he had not come in on a Thursday night after the show, and confident that he would not recognise her now. She had continued with her illusion of black hair and had added some subtle facial changes, such as black lipstick, heavily made up eyes and over-accentuated eyebrows. Bortnik's mind was weak. Ava was confident that she would be able to control his thoughts, since discovering and practicing her latent abilities in Pakistan.

Ava didn't need to wait long. Within the hour, Bortnik's corpulent frame filled the doorway. His lecherous, predatory eyes urgently hunted the lounge; fat lips almost tasting the air in search of his next sexual encounter. Ava noticed that he had employed two new bodyguards. They were huge, with tailored black suits barely managing to cover their muscular bodies. They were not the *heavies* that she had hoped to reacquaint herself with. She had hoped to take her time exacting her revenge on those bastards. Regardless, these new bodyguards would provide her with sufficient sport to make up for the disappointment, and guilty by association.

Ava smiled at Bortnik over the rim of her Martini. He received the invitation loud and clear, waddling over to her like a dog on heat.

"Hello my lovely!" Bortnik's face was uncomfortably close to hers. "I haven't seen you before, and I always notice beautiful women."

Ava remembered that same stale vodka breath and words of greeting. She leaned forwards despite the nausea building in her throat so that he could look down her cleavage.

"Hello handsome. Are you going to buy me a drink?" Ava feigned being slightly drunk, leaning even closer to whisper in his ear. "Only I find myself a little short of funds." Her smile was conspiratorial, alluring. "It's a Dirty Martini, in case you hadn't noticed."

Ava's smile promised the Earth with the Moon as a side-dish.

"A woman of your beauty should never be poor, my lovely."

Ava wanted to scream. It was that ugly possessive term again, but she fawned over him instead.

"Are you going to offer me a job then? I certainly need one."

Ava's wink conveyed that sexual favours could possibly be granted; for a price. Bortnik smiled, rapidly assessing the business opportunity.

"Are you propositioning me?" Bortnik feigned shock.

"Of course not!" Ava flirted. "I doubt that you can afford me anyway."

The game was on.

"How much is it you think that I cannot afford, my lovely?"

Ugh those words again! Ava cringed inside. She could have killed him there and then, but instead she continued to play along.

"Five hundred thousand roubles," Ava held his arrogant stare, "for ten hours of the best sex you've ever had sweetheart."

"Half a million? I want to fuck you not buy you *sweetheart*."

"Suit yourself. There are other men here who *can* afford quality pussy. Go find yourself a cheap hooker and forget the drink."

Ava turned her back on Bortnik, knowing from personal experience, how much rejection maddened him.

You are going to pay for that later *sweetheart*, he said to himself.

Bortnik decided he would pretend to accept the price. After all, his men would take the whole amount back off her before they dumped her body in the river; or maybe a trash bin.

"Make it a round million for twenty hours! Give me the best personal attention you have ever given to any customer. Nothing is off the menu. You do anything and everything I want." Bortnik leered at Ava, almost drooling with anticipation.

"For a million roubles, you can have any part of my body that your heart desires." She gave him a lascivious smile.

"Oh, I intend to, my lovely. I intend to."

Bortnik took out his wallet, obscenely stuffed with notes of five thousand roubles denomination. He peeled off twenty and stuffed them down Ava's cleavage ensuring that his pudgy fingers brushed her nipple. It took all of Ava's self-control not to pull away in disgust. Instead she encouraged him. The thought of killing Bortnik helped her to focus her mind, allowing her to tolerate the clumsy manhandling.

"Oh, yes big boy. My little girls want your touch so much, they want to come out and play. Do you want that?"

Ava cupped her breasts and pressed them together trapping Bortnik's hand. She was immediately consumed by guilt and remorse. It was Callum who had called her breasts his 'little girls', and Ava felt that she was desecrating this memory. Ava disguised her motive as she pulled away.

"Not so fast big boy, this girl can count," she grinned at him knowingly. "Twenty notes make just ten percent of the asking price. We can call it quits for the little nipple tease if you like?"

"That's just a down payment on your arse sweetheart. You'll get the rest at my hotel." He nodded at his men. "We are leaving."

-------------------------------------------------------------------------

Bortnik steered Ava into the back of the limousine as his new guards took their seats in the front. He needed to brief them.

"Sweetheart, there's Champagne and glasses in the minibar. Pour us drinks my lovely. I just need a minute with my men."

He tapped on the driver's window, which opened on his request. Bortnik spoke softly so that Ava would not hear.

"I'll give the bitch her money and enjoy twenty hours of her professional expertise. She's yours after that. I just want my money back and I don't want to see her around again. Do you understand me?"

"Perfectly Sir."

The driver winked at his colleague sat in the passenger seat. Working for Bortnik had its perks.

Ava's abilities included heightened hearing. She had heard every word of Bortnik's exchange. It was unnecessary though, as Ava also had the ability to read his thoughts. Bortnik was a dull-witted man for a Shadow, probably attributable to his repeated alcohol abuse. He was an open book to her. On the ride back to his hotel, and even with the loud music, Ava could hear his men gloating about what they were going to do to her. The men had even agreed who was going to abuse her first. They talked of previous rapes and the killings of Bortnik's numerous prostitutes, as if they were animals. That was enough for Ava to confirm that there would be three killings that night, not just the one.

As soon as Bortnik's limousine arrived at his hotel he took Ava straight up to his room, leaving his guards parked outside to idle away the next twenty hours. The brief journey had been a nightmare for Ava, as Bortnik seemed to have more arms than an octopus. Fortunately, she managed to please him with her breasts, only narrowly avoiding the violation of his pudgy fingers.

Taking the lift to the eighth floor provided no respite. Bortnik forced his mouth on hers, which was even more unbearable. Ava diverted his head to her breasts as a more preferable alternative.

He's not going to make it to the bedroom, Ava thought, as he rubbed himself urgently against her.

The bell pinged, signalling their arrival at the eighth floor.

"Is this our stop?" Ava distracted him.

The doors took too long to slide open, but at last she bundled Bortnik out into the corridor.

"Slow down tiger! We've got nearly a whole day." Ava looped her arm in his. "Show me your lair lover boy."

Bortnik fumbled in his pocket for the room key. He struggled to open the door to the suite, his mind set on one thing and one thing only; sex. Ava noticed that Bortnik was sweating profusely, his acrid scent pervading the corridor. Ava hated men like that. They disgusted her. He disgusted her. The door eventually succumbed to Bortnik's clumsiness and at last he spilled into the room, immediately unfastening his trousers. He was way past desperate.

Ava calmly locked the door. There was no way she was going to let this despicable man leave the hotel room alive.

"Easy tiger show me the colour of your money first. Then you can have everything you want."

Bortnik grunted in annoyance at the unnecessary delay. He walked over to the wardrobe, shedding his jacket and loosening his tie as he went. Inside was the safe. He punched in the numbers and pulled out an envelope.

"Here. Keep the change." He tossed Ava the envelope.

It was already open. Ava quickly flicked through the notes, judging that there were significantly more than a million roubles inside. She smiled appreciatively back at Bortnik.

"Grab a handful of those neck ties darling; I need to slow you down."

Bortnik obliged. When he turned around Ava was already in her black lace underwear.

"Get naked!" she ordered and Bortnik obeyed unquestioningly. "Quickly!" she demanded.

Bortnik eagerly did as he was told and looked a fool, hopping around on one leg, trying to remove a stubborn sock. It was immediately evident to Ava that domination was one of Bortnik's fetishes, and an opportunity too good to miss.

"Don't keep me waiting, you bad boy!" Ava commanded.

Bortnik hurried and was naked in less than a minute, stood there in front of Ava with a hard on and a handful of ties. He looked ridiculous she thought. Fat and ridiculous, but she humoured him nonetheless. The bed had ornate brass head and footboards with vertical bars, suiting Ava's purpose ideally.

"Lie down, you naughty boy," Ava said firmly but teasingly, "and spread your arms and legs."

Bortnik knew what was coming and loved being tied and teased. Minutes later, Ava had him spread eagled on his back and tied securely. She went briefly to the bathroom and returned with a box of tissues and baby oil. His piggy eyes opened wide with delight. She straddled him, sitting across his chest, too high for him to touch her with his penis, though he arched his back impossibly trying to do so, and too low to bury his head in her crotch. His inability to touch her was driving Bortnik mad. He craned his neck forwards just to get the scent of her.

"Do you know what I'm going to do with these?" Ava asked coyly, shaking the box of tissues and opening the bottle of baby oil.

"You're going to wank me off?" he blurted out in eager anticipation.

"Close but no cigar sweetheart."

Ava poured some baby oil onto a handful of tissues, then with the other hand, reached behind her and cupped his testicles.

"Mm, you have a full load! That really is impressive fat man. Bet you're proud of them."

Ava had a flashback to that night at the Bolshoi when Bortnik had viciously pinched Katarina's cheek until it bruised. He had held his genitals in his big fist then and boasted, "There is plenty in here for the both of you." That was Bortnik's first big mistake.

Ava gave his soft genitals a playful squeeze, very nearly sending him over the top. She returned her attention to the oil-soaked tissue.

"Do you remember me Bortnik?" Ava's voice was calm and serene.

Bortnik looked confused. Somehow, this woman was familiar but the throbbing in his groin was too distracting for him to concentrate.

"No. Should I?"

"Oh, yes sweetheart, you really should," Ava's tone was ice cold.

She began to wipe the black lipstick and eye makeup off her face with the oil-soaked tissue. His puzzled expression continued even when her face was rid of the mask. Finally, Ava let his perception of her black hair change until it shone naturally red in the lamplight.

"Ava Kaplinski!" Bortnik's face twisted in horror as he strained at his bindings, trying to free himself.

Ava reached behind her again and cupped his testicles. This time there was nothing *playful* about the squeeze, and Bortnik screamed out in agony. Ava maintained a vice-like grip for a full twenty seconds, until Bortnik was close to losing consciousness. She released him but the sickening pain did not abate.

"For pities sake woman, stop!" he sobbed.

Ava was relentless and she squeezed again, but even harder this time.

Watching Bortnik's trauma brought back the memory of the man who had raped her as a child at her mother's house. Ava remembered how she had killed the bastard and how much it had aroused her. The violence brought out the bad girl in her that she

270

had managed to suppress for so long. Ava slipped her hand inside her lace panties and discovered with no surprise that she was already soaking wet. Her fingers found her spot immediately and Ava began to work herself, squeezing Bortnik's testicles in the same rhythm as her fingers. His screams augmented her pleasure until at last they both briefly lost consciousness, but for entirely different reasons.

I must be well and truly fucked up, Ava had to concede.

"You are such a bad boy turning me on like that sweetheart. So bad, that I'm going to give you a little reward," she cooed, slipping of his chest.

Ava crossed to the window and opened it. She needed the cold night air to clear her head, so that she could focus on torturing Bortnik. Ava looked out. The two bodyguards were leaning casually against the limo smoking.

"Boys!" she called out to attract their attention.

They looked like bookends, Ava thought randomly, dressed in their ill-fitting dark suits. Both were stocky and muscular, with close-cropped fair hair and both smoked. It would have been hard to tell them apart, she mused. Ava reached behind her and took off her bra. Cupping her shapely breasts in her hands, Ava leaned out of the window, fondling them provocatively. She wanted to be absolutely sure that they would come up to Bortnik's room when the time was right.

"Me and your boss are having such a good time. I bet you wish you were up here fucking me too. Perhaps he will let you. After all, he has paid me enough."

Ava blew them a kiss, tore the thin nylon cord from the Venetian blind and waved it at the men.

"He's going to tie me up now, so I'm going to be helpless. Can you imagine that?" she teased.

Leaving the window open, Ava returned to Bortnik and straddled him. He was still groaning in agony and struggling frantically against his ties. She casually looped the nylon cord around his testicles and pulled the cord uncomfortably tight. Bortnik screamed out in pain and terror.

"Now then, we can't keep the boys waiting, can we?"

Ava's voice displayed none of the rage that was inside her, which scared the hell out Bortnik.

"What are you going to do?" his voice was shrill with panic.

"Well that all depends on what you did to Katarina and my Aunt, doesn't it? An eye for an eye, as they say," Ava whispered the words menacingly in Bortnik's ear.

Ava gave the cord a playful little tug and Bortnik squealed like a stuck pig.

"I don't know them!" he screamed, his voice going up an octave.

"Let me refresh your memory then Bortnik. Several months ago, your two thugs laced our drinks at the Bolshoi and took us back to your car. You molested Katarina and were going to rape and kill her, until some man stopped you at gunpoint. That is all I remember because of the drug. Now you tell me the rest, if you want to save your balls."

"I'm not telling you anything you bitch-whore!" Bortnik's rage had finally surpassed his fear.

"Sorry fat man that is the wrong answer."

Bortnik watched in horror as Ava wrapped the cord around each of her hands to give her extra purchase.

"Say goodbye to them fat man!"

Ava jerked her hands apart and castrated Bortnik in an instant. His agonising screams were deafening, loud enough for the bodyguards to come running, just as Ava had intended. Bortnik thrashed his torso from side to side in a futile attempt to escape. Eventually, he slumped motionless in exhaustion, whimpering like a whipped puppy. Ava picked up the sorry parcel from the sheet, shoved it in Bortnik's mouth and held it shut, pinching his nose so that he couldn't breathe.

"Come in your own mouth for a change, you fat bastard. And you can suck on those in Hell!" Ava spat out the words in contempt.

Bortnik rapidly turned purple, as his body starved of oxygen and his eyes bulged from their sockets until he looked every inch the pig that he was. It only took a minute before those piggy eyes were staring sightlessly at the ceiling. Bortnik was dead. Katarina and her aunt Alisa were finally avenged.

There was calmness and serenity about Ava as she looked down on Bortnik's bloated corpse. Randomly, she dipped two fingers in his gaping wound and drew parallel lines of blood down both her cheeks, sucking the blood dispassionately from her fingers afterwards. As Ava left the bed, she looked distant, as if in a trance. She could already hear the heavy footfalls of the bodyguards running down the corridor towards her and turned the key in the door to the open position and left it ajar. She had every reason to want them to enter. How else might she kill them otherwise?

---------------------------------------------------------------------------

Bortnik's bloodcurdling screams were deafening even out in the street. The two bodyguards looked up to the open window in disbelief. It was definitely a man's scream, not the usual terrified screams of a woman.

"Christ! What has she done to him Vlad?" one of the musclebound men cried out in disbelief.

He flicked his half-burnt cigarette into the street and pulled his gun from its shoulder holster. They both knew that one of the girls would get the better of their boss one day. The second guard also drew his gun as they ran to the hotel entrance. Weapons concealed in the folds of their jackets; the men crossed the lobby to the lift. An old couple were about to get in, when Vlad shoved them rudely out of the way, without explanation. The old man was about to protest, when he caught a glimpse of the butt of a pistol. He grabbed his irate wife's arm and bundled her towards reception. Vlad pressed the call button for the eighth floor.

"Whatever that bitch has done Alexei, she's going to die badly. I never heard a man scream like that before."

At the eighth floor, the suited men exited the lift with pistols at the ready and raced down the corridor to Bortnik's room. The door was open invitingly, which seemed strange.

"The bitch has already fled," Alexei presumed as he eased himself into the room, pistol hand extended. "What the fuck?" he gasped.

Vlad followed cautiously. As hard and as violent as these men were, they had never seen such a macabre scene. Bortnik was lying on his back, spread-eagled, and tied to the four corners of the bed with neck ties. The white sheets were soaked in the brownish-red stain of his blood. It was clear to see that Bortnik had been brutally castrated and that something had been stuffed in his mouth. Ava stood implacably by the bed in her knickers, on the very edge of her sanity. Her body was smeared with Bortnik's blood, stripes painted down her cheeks, like an Indian squaw.

"Holy fuck!" Vlad gasped.

Even though Ava looked harmless, he had his gun arm pressed forward, shaking as he approached her.

"Get on the floor, face down!" Vlad's voice was almost panicked.

Quite what he was going to do, Vladimir wasn't sure; he just needed that implacable stare that drilled into his psyche, to stop. It was unnerving him.

"No!" Ava's voice was defiant, but devoid of emotion.

"Do what he says!" Alexei ordered, also unsure of himself.

Ava just stood there smirking back at the two brutish men. To Alexei's absolute dismay, Vlad turned to face him and pressed his pistol into his forehead. Alexei stepped backward until he was against the open window.

"Vlad! Vlad! What are you doing?"

To his horror, Vlad wasn't even looking at him. His eyes were locked with Ava's.

"Vlad!" he pleaded.

It was only the slightest of nods on Ava's part. Still without looking at his comrade, Vlad pulled the trigger and sent Alexei cartwheeling out of the window, crashing down onto the limousine below. Still emotionless, Ava nodded her command and Vladimir put the barrel of the gun in his mouth and pulled the trigger; his last thoughts, plastered over the wall behind him.

Ava sat on the bed next to the body of Bortnik. She drew her knees up to her chest and began singing a nursery rhyme. It was once again that same nursery rhyme Katarina had sung in the back of Bortnik's car, when all this madness began.

------------------------------------------------------------------------

It was the sound of police sirens that finally brought Ava back from that dark place she had regressed to. She looked around at the carnage in the room as if for the very first time. Ava tried to comprehend the scene. Bortnik was dead, naked and lashed to the bed, lying in a pool of his own blood; his severed genitalia filling his mouth. A suited man lay by the open window, with the back of his head missing. Blood and tissue was grotesquely splattered up the wall and curtains. It all seemed familiar, but surreal. Ava stepped over the corpse to look out of the window to the street, eight floors below. The limousine's hazard lights were flashing, with a man's body heavily indented into the roof.

Ava gasped as she replayed the macabre scene in her mind, the police sirens getting ever louder as she did so. The reality shocked Ava into consciousness and out of the inertia that bound her. She was a triple murderess, and that was only today. Ava had to get away before the police arrived. She dressed quickly, catching a glimpse of herself in the mirror as she slipped on her dress, her body was covered in Bortnik's blood and her face painted in it. Ava had no recollection of doing that to herself, and the sight of her own image revolted her, making her gag. There was no time to shower. Instead Ava sponged her face, so as not to risk unwanted attention walking out through the lobby.

The limousine was parked at the back of the hotel. There was the slimmest of chances that it wouldn't have been discovered yet. Ava quickly rummaged through the pockets of the dead bodyguard and found what she was looking for; the ignition key. She grabbed her shoes, picked up the envelope with the roubles in it and walked out of the room.

"Working girl," she mumbled, by way of justification.

The corridor was empty and the lift still on the eighth floor. On the ride down, Ava slipped her shoes on and took a few deep breaths to compose herself. When the lift doors opened, she walked confidently through the lobby and out into the street, just as the police arrived. Resisting the temptation to run, Ava walked briskly towards the back of the hotel and the parked limousine. The night air still had that wintry chill from the unseasonal north-easterly winds coming in from Siberia. A frost had already covered the sidewalk, making the short journey in heels treacherous. As Ava rounded the corner, mostly in a skid, she could see the limousine with its warning lights still flashing. Miraculously, nobody had come out to investigate, but then this was Moscow. You could be killed in the streets here, without a passer by stopping to attend.

The bodyguard was firmly set in the roof of the car, needing all of Ava's considerable strength to pull him off. He landed with a sickening thud on the pavement, but that was of no concern to Ava. The man was a self-confessed rapist and a murderer, getting just what he deserved. The damage to the roof was so great, that when Ava got in, she had to open the window to crane her neck out to see. After kicking her shoes off, Ava started the powerful

V8 engine, selected the gear and drove sedately out into the back streets, towards her hotel, hazard lights still flashing. The cold night air on Ava's face quickly numbed her thoughts and she was grateful for that respite.

The adrenaline rush of the last two hours abated, leaving Ava exhausted, both physically and mentally. Her thoughts turned to Callum and how she had forsaken him, making her feel guilty and morose. Ava had avenged the murder of Katarina, but that only brought back painful memories. Ava remembered Katarina's words of warning. They were so prophetic, so true of how she had treated Callum.

*'You need a man Ava; you really do, but not a man who just takes. You need one who gives in abundance; a man who can love you unconditionally, cherish you and bed you; your own knight in shining armour. He is out there. One day he will find you Ava and he will make you shine so brightly.'*

Ava now knew that Katarina was talking about Callum and that she had gone on to warn her.

*'He will come and he will win you Ava, and you will shine as bright as any star. You will feel so right in his company and so happy and free, but you will push him away and your demons will come flooding back to fill that empty place in your soul.'*

When Ava had asked why she would do such a stupid thing, Katarina had simply replied that she didn't love herself enough to have him.

Ava was so lost in her reverie, that she didn't see the truck pulling out of a side road in front of her. She stamped on the brakes, but her shoes had gone under the brake pedal. Ava tried to swerve, but it was hopeless. The big limousine wasn't built for agility and straight lined on the frosty road, ploughing into the side of the truck, crumpling right up to Ava's knees.

The sudden impact knocked the air out of Ava's lungs, leaving her gasping for breath. Although she hadn't sustained any mechanical impact to her head, Ava was concussed. The sudden deceleration had caused her brain and other soft organs to impact her skeleton. She was dazed and hadn't noticed the smell of gasoline. Moments later the fuel ignited on the hot exhaust. In her confused state, Ava just watched the flames dancing in front of her, mesmerised by their beauty. It all seemed surreal as the fire quickly engulfed the car. Ava was unaware that her door had been flung open and of someone dragging her out. Seconds later, the tank blew. All Ava could feel was the agonising pain of her skin burning from her legs before oblivion rescued her.

-------------------------------------------------------------------------

Ava woke in a white room with cream curtains, the smell of antiseptic and a thumping headache. It was daylight and the clock on the wall read two o'clock.

Where am I, she wondered and how did I get here? It was daylight outside, so that meant two in the afternoon. She had been unconscious for twelve hours, Ava deduced. She tried to piece her last hours together. The memories of killing Bortnik came flooding back to her, a sadistic smile turning the corners of her mouth. She remembered driving the limousine and the truck pulling out, then nothing. Ava tried to get out of bed.

"Ouch!" she cried out in pain, as the catheter pulled in her private place.

What's that for? She wondered. Ava noted that she was also on a drip and attached to a heart monitor. She felt extremely groggy, like she had been drugged. There was a service bell and Ava pushed it. Moments later a plump smiley lady, in a starched blue Sister's uniform, entered the room.

"Welcome back to us," she beamed, putting her hand on Ava's forehead. "Good, your temperature's going down nicely. Nurse will come in soon and change your bandages."

"My bandages?" Ava was off balance.

"Yes." The Sister felt a little awkward at the way she had introduced the situation. "Your legs sustained first-degree burns in the accident but they are healing nicely. Apparently, you were very lucky. A man pulled you out only seconds before the petrol tank exploded. If he hadn't, this would be an entirely different story."

Ava reached under the bed covers, discovering the bandages that came to the top of her thighs.

"I don't feel any pain," Ava puzzled. "How bad is it?"

She prepared herself for the worst while the Sister seemed to be considering what to say.

"Well at first we thought it was very bad indeed, but you seem to have an extraordinary ability to heal. Either that or we misjudged your condition on arrival, which is possible I suppose. We were more concerned about your long period of unconsciousness. Anyway, to answer your question, you are on morphine for the pain. Doctor says that your recovery is progressing nicely, and that he is pleased with your rate of recovery. The bandages can probably be removed in another three or four weeks, based on your unusual ability to heal."

"What, unconsciousness? How long have I been here then?" Ava felt close to panic.

"This is your third day Miss Thompson." The Sister let Ava come to terms with this piece of news before continuing. "You are in a special private hospital for burns and trauma. After your accident, you arrived here with a Major Knight who stayed at your bedside until only a few hours ago, having to leave to catch a flight to Cyprus. Major Knight said that when you awoke you would want your personal things. He brought them for you. They are in the cupboard by your bed. He also asked that I contacted him the moment you became conscious, so I will be able to relay the good news now."

Callum had stayed by her side for three days. Ava considered that for a few moments.

"He must love me so much," Ava said to the Sister excitedly. "Tell him that I..." Ava suddenly remembered the last time that they had spoken, and swallowed her spontaneous joy. "No, just tell him that I am well."

"As you wish." The Sister couldn't help herself and added disdainfully. "But I think he deserves a lot more than that."

The Sister turned and walked out of the room, clearly not impressed by Ava's display of cold heartedness. After she left, Ava burst into tears of remorse and guilt, wondering what kind of a monster she was.

Ava had callously rejected the man who truly and unconditionally loved her, only to subjugate herself to a man who wanted to take all he could from her, abuse her and give nothing in return. Leonardo had warned her that Demitri would use her until she was useless to him, and to herself. Ultimately moving on and discarding her. But Demitri was who she was meant to be with, Ava was still sure of that fact. It was *Allah's* will. She had to forget Callum and be faithful to Demitri, no matter what that meant, or cost.

Ava needed to get a message to Demitri. He would be angry with her for not contacting him sooner. She checked her bedside cupboard, assuming that Callum would have included her laptop in her personal possessions. He had. Ava logged on to the hospital's Wi-Fi and clicked on Demitri's icon. The icon displayed 'Available'. She opened the video call.

"Ava, I thought you had dropped off the face of the Earth. I told you to update me daily. I am not amused. Explain yourself!" To say his tone was off would be an understatement.

"I'm sorry Demitri, but I had a car accident and..." Demitri cut in.

"And what information do you have for me?"

Not even a *how are you*? Or *are you OK*? Ava noted with disappointment.

"Callum has left for Cyprus; probably with the remainder of his team, scheduled to meet Mike Jackson and the Mossad agent, Ben-David there. They are going in preparedness only, waiting on further intelligence. The last I heard, was that they still do not know exactly when the package is due to leave Lavizan-3 or its destination. But that was three days ago," Ava paused for some kind of an acknowledgement. None came.

"Then I want you to give then the information that they need Ava," Demitri was matter of fact and insensitive. "I will send a communique from the nuclear facility to the Mullah Ismael Alansari for you to intercept. It will give the hour of departure, precise route and destination."

"Why would we do that?" Ava asked. It made no sense to her.

She was glad that the conversation was via a video call and not in person. The last time she asked a question like that, Demitri had brutally beaten and raped her.

"To draw the Angels into my trap of course. When they're all together, I will arm the bomb remotely myself. That will give them ten minutes to disarm it. Without you there, they won't have that skill and will die trying."

Demitri laughed openly at the thought of the team's predicament and the likely head-count.

"We will take out two generals, six senior Angels and maybe a squad of soldiers in one strike. There will be abundant Angel DNA throughout the area, implicating them in the atrocity."

Demitri was in rapture and Ava, horrified.

"But only two of them have a fatwa against them, the others are innocent," Ava pleaded. "What about the Mullah? He is your friend and he helped you to free me?"

"And expendable," Demitri added. "All Angels are included in the fatwa. They are all infidels. Yours is not to question Ava, it is to do what you are told."

The look in Demitri's eyes told Ava that her opinion was worthless and unwanted.

"Look at the situation positively Ava. There will be two generals you will not be required to kill yourself." He looked cruelly at Ava. "Anyway, I cannot miss this opportunity because I am still not certain of your devotion to *Allah* or to me enough to fulfil your orders. So, for that reason alone they all must die. Their blood will be on your hands, not mine."

Demitri loved twisting the truth, playing on Ava's guilt and pity. She was so easy to manipulate that way. It was pathetic.

"I will do as you ask," Ava confirmed with a heavy heart.

She had become used to being regarded as worthless.

"Good. I will be in London as soon as this is done and I want you to return to me. Remember that you belong to me. I saved you from the madrassa and your sponsor. I adopted you when you had nobody to turn to Ava. Always remember that, and that I love you."

Demitri smiled falsely at her. She was so easy to convince; so faithful.

"You must reward me with your obedience and chastity Ava, unless I require that you give your body in pursuit of advancing our cause. Is that clear Ava?"

Ava felt like a little girl being punished for being naughty.

"Yes Demitri, I understand," she confirmed, resignedly.

Callum left Ava recovering in the hospital just four hours earlier, but it already seemed an eternity to him. Now he sat miserably in the VIP lounge at London Heathrow, waiting for his colleagues to board their chartered jet to Cyprus. Callum felt guilty about leaving Ava at the burns unit alone, still unconscious, but their squad numbers were already at a critical low. He couldn't back out, or else there would be no mission. Callum felt the darkness of despondency.

Ava had shunned him in Moscow and he had not been able to understand the reasoning behind her decision. She had clearly taken a beating and didn't want to talk about it. Callum could only guess that Ava had seen Demitri and that he had become territorial; read the riot act perhaps. But his misery was more than that. Callum was in love with Ava and it hurt him to see her lying there. The doctor had told him she was out of danger, and that the coma was probably her way of dealing with the shock. Callum also knew the Angel regeneration ability would allow her body to heal without scarring, so that wasn't an issue. The real problem was that Callum didn't believe that Ava could withstand the mental scarring she had suffered over the past several months.

Callum used the lounge Wi-Fi to check his mail. The first message was from the Sister at the hospital, sent less than an hour after he had left:


*'Good news Mr Knight. Ava is awake and in good spirits. We should be able to treat her as an outpatient in a couple of days.*

*Kind regards,*

*Marion Joyce'*

Callum was elated, but his elation was tempered with the fact that he had missed her awakening. He wished he could have been there to hold her. The second message was received some hours later. It read:

*'Callum.*

*I have been catching up with the telephone traffic coming out of Lavizan-3. There was a call made from Amir Salemi, Head of Special Projects there, to the Mullah Ismael Alansari. Salient points are:*

*Package leaves Lavizan-3 at 1730 hours tomorrow*

*Arrives Taybad at 0700 hours the next day*

*Brief rest stop at the intersection of Routes 97 and 36 services*

*Arrive Herat International Airport, Afghanistan at 1500 hours local time*

*Destination is probably Tel Aviv. Package is leaving as part of a convoy. Military support capability is unknown*

*All times are Iran Standard Time*

*I have sent the message to our assurance department for an authenticity check, they will call you personally.*

*Regards,*

*Ava.'*

"Pretty formal," Callum had to concede, "and not even a smiley face this time let alone a kiss."

It was another step in Ava's *denial process* to expunge Callum from her life. He was crushed at her insensitivity and cruelty. His deletion from her life was just like Kayla had done. History was repeating itself.

---------------------------------------------------------------------------

Chapter 18

Less than seventy-two hours after leaving the summit meeting, the Prime Minister and President's task force were on board a chartered Lear Jet, headed for the Royal Air Force base at Akrotiri in Cyprus. Bud sat with Kayla Lovell, looking through the latest intelligence on the whereabouts of the dirty bomb and various interception possibilities. Callum and Red Jake were in discussion about which Shadow agents were most likely to be responsible for the dirty bomb initiative, where they had been last seen, and particularly any that had recently visited the Middle East. Two names came up immediately, the Mullah Ismael Alansari and Amir Salemi. They agreed that Demitri Papandreou could be added to that shortlist, as the mastermind behind the plot.

Craig Jamieson sat alone, organising the essential medical supplies, while Sean O'Malley researched put-down and refuelling opportunities for the twin-engine Chinook helicopter in Afghanistan. All on board were actively contributing to the success of their mission.

Callum was now certain that, barring the possibility of disinformation, the bomb would be transported overland from the nuclear facility, Lavizan-3, in Iran to Afghanistan. From there the bomb would be flown to its destination in Tel Aviv. This was based on Ava's latest intelligence, and the bomb not having the Iranian government's formal endorsement, something made patently clear at the recent summit. The Iranians could not afford to have the bomb traced back to Iran.

Theirs was a depleted force, since the murders of Bart Jeffries and Larry Madison, further compounded by Ava's eleventh hour accident. The remaining member of the task force was Sergeant Mike Jackson, who was already based in Cyprus, having been stationed at the Dhekelia garrison as part of a rapid response team, kept in constant readiness for just such an occasion. He headed an experienced six-man squad, made up of Royal Marines, RAF Regiment and a single Mossad agent, Ben-David. The Mossad was an Israeli Government department, responsible for intelligence collection, covert operations, and counterterrorism. With their support, it was possible to achieve almost anything in the troubled Middle East.

Half way through the four-hour flight, neither Kayla nor Callum had properly acknowledged the other's presence. Whenever Callum was occupied or looking the other way, Kayla couldn't help herself from secretly watching him. Kayla had her regrets. She had several lovers on the go that could collectively satisfy her body, but they came nowhere near to satisfying her mind. Callum was the only man she had ever loved that could do both. She wished she could have replayed their time together, but knew it would have been hopeless. Their relationship would simply have ended the same way, she conceded. Kayla needed her conquests too much then, but wondered if all that had changed.

Callum had been ignoring her for his own reasons. Kayla had hurt him too much. He couldn't trust himself not to fall for her again, particularly after having just been dumped by Ava. It was going to be difficult working alongside her but he, no *they*, had to be professional about the operation. Other people's lives, and probably their own, would depend on the success of their mission. Professionalism dictated that he had to fix this, nip it in the bud, before their recriminations affected the dynamics and performance of their team.

"It's been a long time Kayla."

Callum gave her a lopsided grin and presented his hand. The smile that went with it was little more than cordial. Kayla left her seat avoiding the hand and offered him her cheek instead. Callum reluctantly accepted and kissed her.

"A little more than two years I guess." Kayla's smile was more giving.

Callum felt like his heart had been physically squeezed. He didn't need to guess. It would be two years and three months at the weekend. He thought he was over her, but clearly that was not the case.

Kayla was statuesque in appearance, almost Amazonian, with a commanding presence. She was five feet nine inches tall, athletic and slim. It was only when you met her eye to eye that you could truly appreciate the beauty of the woman. Kayla was an African-American with a tantalising mixture of Italian, Caribbean and English blood, that brought out the character traits of all those nations; sometimes too much so. She was a perfect storm in the making.

Kayla had dark brown, nearly black hair which she mostly wore up, giving her a secretarial look. She often wore glasses to enhance that image but didn't really need them. When you looked into those dark brown eyes, you could see that she didn't suffer fools gladly. Now, they were soft and kind but could darken into a black rage instantly when provoked. Those eyes also suggested she was capable of all sorts of mischief, something Callum was more than accustomed to. Kayla had soft African features and an amazing pout with possibly the most kissable lips ever. She was a woman you would cross at your peril. The world was black and white to Kayla, as were her moods.

Callum had fallen for Kayla from the moment he first saw her. She was confident, funny and outrageously sexy; a man's dream woman. But she was a paradox. Within that tantalising mixture of bloods were both Angel and Shadow genes. She was another half-breed, blessed or cursed, with the same awesome powers that Ava possessed.

Callum needed to divert any conversation to their mission. He knew from bitter experience how easily she could manipulate him.

"How much of a brief did you guys get before you left the States?" he asked easily.

"Enough to put us all on the same page Callum. We already knew who the players were. Assuming our *intel* is right, and we've no reason to doubt your boys at the listening station in Cyprus or *Ava's*."

Kayla said Ava's name in the strangest way, almost sarcastically, before continuing.

"If so, the bomb appears to be ready to transport by road from Lavizan-3 to the Herat International Airport in Afghanistan. One of our satellites should be able to confirm its departure when the time comes."

"That's pretty much it Kayla," Callum agreed.

Kayla was always up to speed; Callum never doubted that she wouldn't be. He checked his watch. They still had another hour and forty minutes before landing, just enough time to knit all their intelligence together and get the bones of a plan in place. Callum summoned the team.

"OK everybody, let's group up now, pool knowledge and form a plan."

The configuration of the jet was far from ideal to get the six of them comfortably together for a dialogue. They overcame the problem by having three sat facing forwards and three kneeling on their seats to face backwards. Callum opened the meeting, but control would naturally fall to Kayla, their strategist, once the base information was disseminated and understood.

"So, to recap; *Ava* has had a breakthrough," Callum began.

He said Ava's name with an equally strange intonation, territorially in fact. Callum instantly regretted doing so, particularly when he saw the look of amusement on Kayla's face. She had drawn *first blood*.

"We now know that the bomb will be loaded in twenty two hours at the Lavizan-3 facility in Arak, 1600 hours GMT tomorrow. That is 1930 hours Iran Standard Time. The enemy will travel east, driving through the night resting just before the Iranian/Afghanistan border at Taybad. That will be about twelve hours later at 0700 hours, the following morning. They will be in convoy, but we have no idea at this point of numbers or arms, rendezvousing at Herat in Afghanistan, at approximately 1500 hours that afternoon. Their cargo flies out from there to an unconfirmed destination."

Callum paused for any questions but there were none. He continued.

"The drive from Taybad to Herat is nearly five hours, so they will have only rested for three. That my friends, means that the enemy will be tired and dull witted at that time and place, but we cannot assume that they will not be on their guard for any signs of trouble."

It was Bud who spoke for them all.

"Can we trust the intelligence?" It was a relevant question.

"Can we trust *Ava*?" Kayla interjected in a similar tone.

It was a cheap shot and Kayla's turn to regret what she had said. She continued, usurping Callum's briefing.

"Ava intercepted the information today," Kayla confirmed, coming to Ava's defence. "It seems that she's not very good when it comes to convalescing."

Kayla grinned winningly at Callum without the slightest hint of sarcasm. She hoped that her comment would be taken as an olive branch. Callum's expression showed that it was not. He continued to answer Bud's question.

"We all know that there is a question mark hanging over Ava, but she had the intel run by our assurance department for verification. The information appears genuine as far as we can tell at the moment, but we have to remain open to the possibility that the Iranians, or the Shadows, might be leaking disinformation for us to pick up."

Kayla gently placed her hand on Callum's arm as much in placatory manner as affection. Her touch brought back a storm of bitter-sweet memories that took away Callum's power of speech.

"I'll carry on from here if you don't mind Callum."

Kayla's smile was fleeting but lasting in Callum's mind. She began her address in authoritative manner.

"At this stage, Tel Aviv being the package's final destination, is unconfirmed but it is the most likely of three; New York and London being the other two. The size of the device dictates that heavy loss of life is not the objective, so it must be politically motivated. My guess is that the purpose is to further destabilise the Middle East. For that reason I am also favouring Tel Aviv as the target detonation."

There was a general nodding of heads supporting Kayla's theory.

"We also know who the perpetrators are. This has Shadow endorsement at the highest possible level, the Hydra herself. Delegation is through Demitri Papandreou, her confidant and long term lover, then out through the Mullah Ismael Alansari and his cohorts. Their choice of the Mullah also underpins why I think the target is Tel Aviv. His network of terror extends out through Palestine right into the heart of Israel."

Callum had recovered his composure and challenged Kayla's logic. They were already acting as a team and not as rivals.

"If Tel Aviv is indeed the target Kayla, then why would they head east to Afghanistan when they could go west though Iraq directly into Israel?"

"Good question but the answer is simple Callum. There is too much American involvement in and around the airports there. Besides, Herat and Yasser Arafat International airports are safe havens for the Shadow organisation. They have immunity there and can load their deadly cargo free of any custom control or scrutiny."

Kayla paused to let them consider that.

"If we fail in our mission and allow the enemy to get the bomb into the air, then it's likely we will lose track of the consignment. So we have forty-one hours to intercept that convoy before it gets to Herat."

It was pretty much as Callum had deduced, but he knew Kayla well enough to know that she hadn't finished.

"Go on Kayla," he encouraged.

Kayla smiled at Callum's intuition. He had always been able to read her intentions.

"That said we need a fall-back plan. If for any reason we fail to intercept the convoy on the ground, and we all agree that its probable destination is indeed Tel Aviv, then we need to plan an incursive intervention at Ben Gurion airport to take control of the aeroplane on the runway." Kayla looked directly at Callum for a response.

Callum couldn't help watching Kayla, particularly her mouth as she spoke. She was the consummate professional; vital, beautiful and probably the best lover on the planet, one to give Ava a run for her money. Unfortunately though, she was also the least faithful. Kayla was wearing her lipstick again, something that she had cruelly denied him. Callum knew it meant one of two things. Kayla was either totally over him, or she wanted to open old wounds.

"Callum?" she prompted.

"Yes," he said at last, "it is a credible alternative should the situation demand it. I will call ahead to Ben-David in Cyprus. He could have his Mossad boys mobilised in a matter of hours. Airport operations are bread and butter stuff to the Israelis. What about New York and London, Kayla?"

"Too many airports to cover and too little time to guarantee success. What we could do though, is to broadcast our own disinformation." Kayla had a mischievous look in her eye. "Get the FBI and the SAS mobilised at the New York and London airports as a diversionary tactic and leak the information to the media. Make them think we know they're coming. That will force them to the Tel Aviv option, where we will secretly be lying in waiting."

Clever girl, Callum thought. It was that clear, simple but effective logic that made Kayla the best in her field. Callum endorsed her suggestion.

"Agreed Kayla; good plan. I'll leave the logistics to you, if that's alright?" The question was rhetorical.

It would have been Bart Jeffries' job, had he not been murdered in London. They all sensed the moment and there was an awkward but respectful silence. Callum broke it.

"OK, moving on then. Shaun, we have forty-one hours and counting before we need to intercept the parcel at Herat. How are you going to get us there?"

Shaun had already considered his options and was ready with the answer.

"It is sixteen hundred miles from Cyprus to Herat, outside the operating range of a Chinook." O'Malley had a lovely southern Irish accent that was easy on the ear. "Better we take a jet out from RAF Akrotiri to Kuwait, sure it is. Then onwards to Herat by Chinook."

O'Malley, a reserved man not used to public speaking, looked through his notes while he spoke. He found team meetings and being put on the spot stressful. Strangely though, in the theatre of war, he could fly his Chinook devoid of any emotion, even under enemy fire.

"I have already filed the flight plans and the jet and Chinook are both prepped and on standby. I just have to confirm the departure time is all." O'Malley cleared his throat nervously and continued. "Flight times are five hours to Cyprus, one hour changeover, and then eighteen hours to Herat, including re-fuelling stops. I've advised Ben-David and he will rendezvous with his squad in Kuwait, so he will."

"Good work Shaun." Despite his nervous exterior Callum knew O'Malley would be on top of his game when it mattered. "So, two more hours on this flight from 41 leaves us 39. Less 24 in transit, leaves us 15 hours for final preparations, transfers and sleep. That agenda doesn't leave us much latitude for set-backs," Callum observed.

"It's worse than that Callum," Kayla corrected. "That assumes we arrive and go straight into action. It won't happen that way. We need to be there six to eight hours beforehand for reconnaissance, and to take a measured tactical approach. Whatever plans we make beforehand will change dependent upon local conditions and any set-backs that you mentioned."

She was right and it was a rare oversight by Callum. He was still distracted by thoughts of Ava and grateful Kayla had pointed out his omission in a non-point scoring manner. He smiled at her in recognition. Kayla continued.

"We land at Akrotiri in less than two hours at 2000 hours local time. I suggest we call ahead and have Mike Jackson and his squad meet us there ready for immediate departure. Any kit we are short of for the mission can be supplied by Mossad when we rendezvous with Ben-David in Kuwait. That way, we will be a little ahead of the game."

The strategy made perfect sense and met with unanimous agreement. They would be leaving for Kuwait at ten o'clock that night. Callum turned to Craig Jamieson.

"What's your state of readiness Craig?"

"I have requisitioned all I need to set up a combat field hospital in the Chinook, and have confirmation that it is all waiting for us at Akrotiri. No issues." Craig's response was succinct and to the point.

"You better have some whiskey in there too Doc, you know I have a bad reaction to morphine," Jake interjected.

His statement wasn't a joke or bravado. Jake could tolerate huge amounts of pain as long as whiskey was close to hand.

"Packed and ready to go!" Craig grinned back at the burley sergeant. "I'm sure you only get yourself shot to get a bottle of the stuff down you."

Craig's jibe wasn't too far from the truth and Jake laughed a belly laugh.

"Excellent work Craig. I never doubted that you wouldn't be ready for action," Callum interceded. "Let's just make sure the lid stays on the bottle, shall we?"

Callum had lost too many men over the years in operations such as this and felt the weight of his responsibility to keep them safe.

The team spent the next hour strategizing and running through *what if* scenarios. The truth was though, that they couldn't put much of a plan together until one of the space satellites had picked up the convoy. Only then would they know the scale of the situation, and that wouldn't be for at least another twenty-four hours, when the package left Lavizan-3 in Iran.

Callum checked his emails shortly before landing, hoping for something from Ava. He had immediately written back after receiving her mail informing them of the intercepted telephone call. Callum had congratulated her and gone on at great length about matters more personal, ending the message wishing her a speedy recovery, to stay safe and that he missed her. He signed off, "*I love you Ava x.*" Until then, he hadn't received a reply and felt shunned and despondent. At last the message alert chimed. It was Ava and his heart lifted.

'*Yes thanks, will do. Same to you and all of the above.*

*Ava.*'

What the fuck? '*Same to you and all of the above?*' Callum was furious at Ava's insensitive remark.

It was dismissive, cruel and insulting. Callum knew these few glib and uncaring words would stay in his head for a lifetime. He felt hurt and couldn't resist replying immediately, even though silence would have been more powerful:

*'And what is that supposed to mean Ava?'*

Her response was instant this time:

*'We had an affair. It's over. It was good while it lasted. Get over it!'*

Callum was devastated. His whole world crashed in on him just from reading that short and brutal message. He was thankful that he had the mission to concentrate on and couldn't afford this diversion, not right now. Callum pressed Ava out of his mind. His men's lives would depend on his focus and professionalism.

---------------------------------------------------------------------------

When Ava pressed 'send' her heart seemed to stop beating. She desperately wanted to cancel the message, claw it back from out of the ether, but it was done. Ava felt sick, bereft and guilty. Callum didn't deserve that. He didn't deserve her, bitch that she was, but Demitri did.

"I'm a heartless woman for a heartless man," she mused, speaking the truth out loud.

Ava reached for the vodka bottle and poured herself a large tumbler full. It was the first of many to follow, as she drunk herself into oblivion. Ava was hoping to find solace in her bottle of dreams.

The transfer from the RAF troop-carrier jet to the Chinook helicopter at Kuwait International Airport was undertaken with military precision. They were on board and loaded in less than twenty minutes. Shaun O'Malley lifted the collective increasing the power to the rotors. His feet skilfully manipulated the pedals countering the torque from the rear rotor, before easing back on the cyclic lifting the lumbering bulk of the Chinook into the air. The helicopter headed east north east towards Herat, Afghanistan. Minutes later, they had left the sprawling outskirts of the city behind them and were out into the desert. Just a few sporadic dun-coloured dwellings were testament to the fact that man could endure the oppressive heat and arid conditions of this unforgiving land and eke out a living.

The roads below them had been crafted from the rock and sand by myriad wheels, snaked their way across the featureless landscape. Occasional cars and trucks passed below, kicking up dust clouds that hung in the limpid air for several minutes afterwards.

The air in the Chinook was stifling and oppressive for the team now strapped into their bench seats, with their shirts stuck uncomfortably to their backs. Each was deep in thought, conscious of the peril that lay ahead. It was clear to all that the Shadows would gladly settle for the death of a force of eleven key Angels plus a half-breed, rather than a town full of peasants. There was a better than evens chance that they were being drawn into a trap, and that the intention of the bomb was to eradicate the assault squad.

They had made good time and were ahead of schedule, both on the first leg of their journey to Kuwait, and now as they flew towards Herat. Good news had just been received from the satellite tracking station in Cyprus, confirming that the convoy consisted solely of a single covered truck and two Jeep outriders. Video footage and satellite images had shown four men in each of the Jeeps, both with 50mm machine guns. There were only two in the truck with thermal imaging showing none under cover.

"They appear to be travelling extremely light," Callum informed his unit. "Ten versus eleven; we out man them and have the element of surprise."

"And three of them will have their hands on the steering wheels, leaving only seven of them effective," Sergeant Mike Jackson added.

Although only in his late twenties, Mike's face was tanned and hardened by years spent in the desert. That, coupled with his black hair and fluency in Arabic, had enabled him to pass as one of them in the villages, where he had worked covertly in counter terrorism. Mike had joined Callum and his team at Akrotiri, with his squad of four. Chas and Joey were from the RAF Regiment, devoted brothers, who had joined the Regiment a year apart. They had been inseparable throughout their service and each owed his life to the other on more than one occasion. It was their back-watching and total commitment, one to the other that had been their salvation. Mike knew that if he was to lose one in combat, he would probably lose the other, either in support of his brother or in mindless, blind revenge.

Then there were Zak and Rudy, both Marines and dangerous men on and off the battlefield. They were a wild pair in their late twenties and highly charged with testosterone. Mike dreaded them going off-duty, as it invariably meant he would have to negotiate their release from the local gaols the next day. These two lived for danger and were totally fearless.

Mike Jackson would have felt comfortable taking this convoy on with just the five of them, but with eight active men, a medic, pilot and Kayla, the chance of a successful interception was in their favour. Kayla was one of the finest markswomen he had ever seen. More dangerous was the fact that she appeared to derive great pleasure sighting on an enemy before squeezing the trigger, ending that enemy's life. When they went into action, she would be there right alongside them. It was Kayla who came up with a proposed change of strategy.

"Boys I've been rethinking this in light of a less substantial enemy force than we had been anticipating."

Kayla had their attention immediately. She always managed that. It wasn't because of her beauty, and she had that in abundance, it was because of her mind. She was always ahead of the game and the team respected her for that. In fact, they were often prepared to risk their lives on her judgement calls, often changing tactical positions based on her advice. Kayla had unique powers of perception, premonition even, that was inherent from her mixed Angel-Shadow genes. She, like Ava, had experienced strange happenings in her childhood. The difference was that Kayla had control over them right from the outset, although not necessarily over when it was right or wrong to use them. She was dangerous in that respect, and also had trouble with controlling her dark side. Kayla continued.

"I think we should bring the attack forward and take them at Taybad," she began. "If they are on schedule, and we can adjust the plan to suit any satellite updates on that, then they are scheduled to arrive there in the morning at 0700 hours. They will be dead on their feet from their punishing drive through the night and have scheduled only three hours sleep to recover. If we hit them two hours later at 0900 hours, they will be disorientated waking from deep sleep and we can kill them in their beds."

"I don't like this," Callum said, tugging thoughtfully at his chin. "Not your revised plan Kayla, I don't mean that. Only it's as if they are inviting us to take the bomb. The whole operation feels too easy. It smacks of another Shadow trap."

"It probably is," Bud added. "But what do we do? If we don't go in, they detonate it somewhere, killing goddamn hundreds, maybe thousands. And if we do attack, then there is a high probability that we could end up kissing our own ass's goodbye!" He folded his arms dramatically.

"No, there is no choice," Callum conceded shrugging his shoulders. "We have to hope for a quick kill, so that they don't get a chance to arm the bloody thing."

"OK," Kayla began, "so we agree. I'll hand you to Callum for the battle-plan as it's more his territory."

Kayla could easily have put the plan together, but that would have undermined Callum's authority. He noted the appropriate act of subordination with an approving glance.

"So, down to the detail then." Once again Callum was thinking on his feet. "We should arrive at Taybad at around 0500 hours. That's two hours before the convoy gets there, but I need to confirm that with O'Malley."

"Confirmed," O'Malley's Irish brogue rang out from the cockpit intercom. "Maybe a little before then with this tailwind."

His words were positive and jovial, but O'Malley was hiding a sinister secret from them. He had received a message in Kuwait from Demitri, the man he had sold his soul to in exchange for his gambling debts to be wiped off.

'*Drop your cargo and leave',* it had instructed.

O'Malley had no choice but to obey, otherwise his family would be dead the same day. He lamented that the road to Hell was often paved with good intention and that he would surely meet the devil himself one day soon. Callum continued.

"Thanks Shaun. OK then, we will still have the cover of darkness at 0500 hours, but not for long. Sunrise is at 0640 hours, so we need to be in position by then. O'Malley drops us two miles to the east of Taybad and we run in from there. I estimate that will take thirty minutes max, giving us a little over an hour for reconnaissance and to find cover."

Callum knew that the two-mile jog to Taybad with weapons and full combat kit, weighing sixty pounds in total, over desert terrain, would be arduous. It was however essential. Many ill-planned missions had failed, simply because of the will to get too close too quickly to save the hard work of a march. Their sixty pound loads were justified by the need to carry water and a significant amount of ammunition. They had no means of knowing in advance whether there would be reinforcements at their chosen rest stop. The characteristic thumping beat of the Chinook's twin rotors can be heard for several miles in the still desert air and would give them away, if they chose to set down closer.

"We know the convoy will be coming in from the north on Route 97, resting for three hours, and then heading out east to Herat along Route 36. When we arrive at that intersection, we split into two squads. One sweeps around to the north and the other to the south, regrouping on the west side. We are looking for anything military or suspicious. Then we pool knowledge and finalise plans."

Callum looked towards Kayla who had the strangest look in her eyes. He had seen *that* look before and knew just where her mind was. She needed diverting.

"Kayla. Download me a detailed plan of Taybad. I want to get a feel for where else they might choose to rest if our intelligence proves wrong, and where we can fall back to, if it all goes tits up. Our *Alamo* if you like."

Kayla nodded and smiled knowingly at him.

"We set up Craig's med centre now, here in the Chinook." Callum directed his next comment to their medic. "I want you to stay on board Craig. I can't afford to lose you. Jake and me are both trained in combat casualty care and will bring any injured back to you if we can't deal with them in the field, or call you in; is that clear?"

Craig nodded and gave Jake an accusing look.

"Try not to get yourself shot this time then Jake. You might have medical duties to perform on this one."

There was a loud guffaw in acknowledgement of the fact that there was so much truth to the comment. Jake beamed back proudly. He was the kind of a man who would put himself in the line of fire, taking a bullet intended for a comrade in arms, then go on to kill the man who pulled the trigger. Callum looked at his watch.

"OK, touchdown in four hours let's move it!"

-------------------------------------------------------------------------

# Chapter 19

Mullah Ismael Alansari sat uncomfortably in the passenger seat of the three tonne, dun coloured military truck. The two jeeps, painted in the same drab livery, were riding at point and behind. They were still three hours away from their rest stop at Taybad and the Mullah was in a foul mood. His ancient bones felt every jarring undulation during the hot punishing ride through the desert, a sign that he was no longer a young man. He knew that he had been sent on a fool's errand. Demitri had organised the convoy and only permitted ten men, including himself, to guard one of the most politically sensitive and physically devastating devices ever transported.

It made no sense to the Mullah, except it made total sense, he pondered. Total sense, if your objective was to let the device fall into enemy hands, that is. The Mullah was nobody's fool and certainly was not going to be Demitri's. He hawked the desert dust up from his lungs and spat it out of the open window, a token sign of his resentment for his employer. Demitri and that whore wife of his have sacrificed me, he decided and spat again. There was no true honour amongst the Shadows; it had always been about survival for the powerful ruling elite.

I will survive this, the Mullah vowed, and I will have you and your bitch dead inside the month.

It was perhaps an optimistic statement, given the power and vengefulness of those who had betrayed him, but there was yet to be a man who had survived the Mullah's oath.

He sat there seething, but the time for revenge and retribution would have to wait. He needed to focus on the events unfolding before him. His survival and escape depended upon it. The Mullah had an amazing ability to anticipate the actions of his enemies. The current situation revolving inside his head asked; if he were Callum Knight, where would he choose to intercept this destructive cargo? The Mullah rapidly deduced that Demitri would have made sure that the Angels were able to intercept intelligence leaked to them, revealing the route that the bomb would be transported along.

It has to be at Taybad while we are sleeping, he concluded. His parchment skin crumpled into a grin, exposing his gapped teeth. If I were Callum Knight, I would choose to kill us there too, but I will be waiting for you; in *Allah's* name I shall be waiting!

The Mullah Ismael Alansari knew exactly what to do. However he had no way of knowing the true destructiveness of the bomb he was transporting.

--------------------------------------------------------------------------

"Prepare for landing!" O'Malley's voice called out above the din of the rotors.

To order, the squad quickly gathered their weapons and kit whilst exchanging the usual pre-action banter; none more so than Red Jake.

"I hope you've packed your sandwiches and drinks children, 'cos this is going to be one hell of a tea party!"

"Bet you brought a bottle Jake, you usually do," Mike Jackson quipped.

While the others used their nervous energy in trivial one-upmanship, Callum used the remaining moments to confirm his brief to medic and pilot.

"Craig. I will radio ahead of any casualties so you are prepared. O'Malley. Get out of here and out of earshot. Come in on my call. I will let you know the pick-up point when we know what we are up against, OK?" Callum got the thumbs up.

The Chinook touched down for less than thirty seconds, the heavy rotors kicking up a dust storm as the squad exited from the tailgate. They were immediately being caught up in that storm, shielding their eyes as they made their way out of the downdraught. Callum stayed briefly to confirm some last-minute details with the pilot, before setting off with his men at a fast jog eastwards towards the intersection.

His cargo of soldiers safely unloaded, O'Malley lifted the collective and increased power to the rotors. The lumbering Chinook shook with the torque of the heavy rotors and lifted off. O'Malley took a bearing to take them away in the opposite direction. He had already spotted a likely place to put down. A place where had had something dreadful to do. His heart was heavy with guilt for that sin.

The moment O'Malley set the craft down, Craig busied himself with the final preparations for his trauma unit, never seeing the rifle butt that came down heavily on the back of his head, splitting the skin wide open and fracturing his skull. Craig Jamieson's body convulsed for a few moments on the Chinook floor, and then laid still, his unseeing eyes staring back at his traitorous friend. O'Malley dragged the medic's lifeless body to the side door and shoved him out, his corpse landing face up in the sand.

"Holy Mary, mother of God, please forgive me," O'Malley pleaded and genuflected, as if that might absolve him of his sin.

He returned to the cockpit slowly, as if in a trance and took his pistol from the dashboard and the photograph of his family from his top pocket. It was his favourite and one that he carried with him everywhere. He kissed their images. They would be safe now and unburdened by shame.

"I'm sorry!" O'Malley blurted, before putting the gun barrel in his mouth.

He tried for all he was worth, which was little, to pull the trigger, but he wasn't even brave enough to do that. Sean O'Malley burst into tears of shame and buried his face in his hands.

After some time, he took one final look at his much loved and loving family. With his jaw set in determination, O'Malley increased the throttle and pulled back on the collective. His mind was set. He took the Chinook upwards as fast as the laws of science permitted, needing to get this over with, while he still had the resolve. At twenty thousand feet, O'Malley cut the engine and grabbed the photograph, holding it lovingly to his chest as the Chinook dropped out of the sky.

---------------------------------------------------------------------------

Callum heard the explosion in the stillness of the desert air. He didn't believe in coincidences. It was an odds-on certainty that the Chinook had been taken out by a surface to air missile. If that was the case, then their presence had been anticipated. It *was* a trap!

He couldn't turn back. Apart from the successful outcome of their mission, he had the lives of those with him to consider. Tears of sadness and anger burned Callum's eyes as he ran on through the desert, ever aware of the enemy that surely must have been behind them.

Callum focused his anger on the job in hand. It was now even more important to him that these despots died tonight, all of them; those in the deadly convoy and those murderers behind him, who had taken out the Chinook. Callum swore that he would not leave this desert until justice had been served, their deaths avenged.

The ground beneath the squad's feet was loose scree, giving way as each team member moved forward, sucking at their boots, making each pace more gruelling than the one before. They were all supremely fit, barring Jake. Pride and sheer belligerence kept him at the front of the squad though, acting as point man for the mission. Stealthily, but with haste, the team moved onwards towards their objective; the intersection.

The squad arrived at the rendezvous in a little over twenty minutes, some breathing more heavily than others. Only Kayla still looked fresh, but she had a genetic advantage over the others. Kayla possessed the brains of an Angel and the stamina of a Shadow. Callum began to share his concerns.

"I guess you all heard the explosion?" There was a sombre nodding of heads. They had all arrived at the same conclusion. "We must assume that they are both killed and hope to God that they are not. We cannot now assume that there is a helicopter to pick us up and will have to improvise when it comes to our escape."

Kayla touched Callum's arm compassionately.

"I'm sorry Callum, but it's not an assumption. They are both dead. I felt them pass." Sixth sense and premonitions were common to her.

Kayla's eyes were soft and kind. He felt empathy encompassing his body. It was an ability she seemed to possess. Callum believed that this ability could also allow her to devour his spirit and break his heart into little pieces though, if she so chose. Callum needed to push aside any feelings that he might have for his men lost in battle, and indeed those for Kayla, to the back of his mind. Now was a time to lead. Callum's eyes scanned the horizon. Intelligence reported a truck-stop three hundred yards to the south along Route 36. The eyes on the ground confirmed this.

"The truck-stop ahead is the focus of our search." Callum pointed at the truck-stop in the distance. "We sweep around it maintaining at least eight hundred yards separation, then re-group on the east side. You all know what we are looking for. Jake, you take Kayla, Chas and Joey to the north. Bud, you go with Zak and Rudy to the south. Keep your eyes open for enemy approaching from the rear."

They quickly regrouped into their teams as Callum continued.

"Mike, we will manoeuvre directly into the truck-stop, or rather, I want you to."

Callum opened his rucksack and pulled out a pair of white baggy pants, followed by a three quarter length white shirt. Sandals, a wallet and a coarse linen bag completed the disguise. The final items taken from the rucksack was an AK47 assault rifle with folding stock, the weapon of choice of the local population.

"To be more precise, I want you to penetrate the truck-stop whilst I maintain over-watch from the car park. You have money and papers in that wallet. I want you to check in and carry out surveillance from the inside. Only use your weapon in an absolute emergency. There are two clips of ammunition. Communication must be kept to a minimum." Callum passed over a tiny radio receiver with built in transmitter. "Put this in your ear. I will keep you informed of our enemy's arrival or any changes to the plan."

"Relax Callum. It's my day job, a walk in the park," Mike assured his team leader.

He was no stranger to carrying out covert activities behind enemy lines, relying on his wits far more often than he cared to remember. Mike began to take off his battledress, removing any piece of clothing or equipment that could betray his cover, while Callum continued to outline the operation.

"Bud. Once you have infiltrated from the south, I want you to form a perimeter around the truck-stop making use of whatever cover you can find. Once our enemy are inside, Mike will keep us updated on their movements, disposition and capability, but only if he is safe to do so." Callum turned back to Mike. "Maintain operational silence unless compromised. Once you assess that the time is right, transmit directions for a safe approach or come in and join us. It's your decision. At that time we will move in and kill them in their beds."

Callum's brief was succinct, devoid of emotion. They were there to complete a mission. Death was an inherent risk that they all accepted, and could come at any time, and from any direction.

\------------------------------------------------------------------------

Ava lounged at home, her laptop balanced on a padded tray. The morphine was losing its effect and the pain from the burns was excruciating. There was still another hour to go before her next medication was due. Ava simply couldn't wait that long. She tried to transfer her thoughts out of her body, her normal method of escape. This time though, she was suffering too much heartache and anguish for the transference to make any difference. Ava desperately missed Callum. Only love can hurt this, she thought ruefully.

Ava tried to picture Callum on his assignment in the desert, less than a day away from the end of his life, helpless and uninformed. She wanted to warn him, wanted to let Callum know that it was a trap. Tell him to run; run back to her! It would be so easy for her to save his life, but *Allah* would not permit it and Demitri would *never* allow nor forgive it.

Ava agonisingly waited, watching the hours tick away until Callum's death was finally confirmed. The solution was so simple, and yet also impossible. All she needed to do was select Callum's icon on her phone and message him. Ava swigged another generous measure of vodka. Bortnik was dead. The only person left to hate was herself. Right now, there was nobody that she hated more in this world than Ava Kaplinski.

--------------------------------------------------------------------------

The convoy laboured into the truck-stop at Taybad at a little after seven thirty in the morning. Morning had broken on yet another cloudless and increasingly aggressive hot day. The Mullah extracted himself from the cab of the truck, muscles taut, aching from sitting in the same position for hour upon hour. In fact his whole body ached, a constant reminder of his age. He hadn't spoken a word to the driver in eight hours and the tension between them was palpable. It mattered not to the Mullah. The man who had driven him eight hundred miles would be dead within the next couple of hours.

--------------------------------------------------------------------------

Callum watched as the three dun coloured military vehicles pulled into the parking area, tyres scrunching on the hard packed dirt, before finally coming to rest. Nine men gratefully clambered out of the vehicles, relieved that at least this section of their arduous journey was over. They were desperate to get some warm food in their stomachs, before collapsing into bed for a few hours of restful sleep. The last man to leave was the Mullah. Callum recognised him instantly. This was a man who had survived countless attempts on his life, allowing the faithful to believe that he was invincible. On numerous occasions, when his followers had been slaughtered, either by ambush, or from a missile strike launched from a predatory drone, the Mullah had evaded death, disappearing into the surrounding dunes as if he himself was made of sand. Callum noted how the Mullah struggled with fatigue as he negotiated the high step of the truck to the ground.

"Succumbing to your age at last then, you old dog," Callum whispered to himself. "But you are still worth twenty men I would wager."

Callum knew that this old dog of war had the ability to kill them all if the operational plan was flawed. Before the Mullah had the opportunity to put any more of his men in the ground, Callum swore that he would bury the old man first. As the Mullah walked to the rest area, the stiffness seemed to leave his body with each passing step until he looked as spritely as any young man. Callum couldn't help but admire the resilience of the old cleric.

Once the Mullah had disappeared inside the building, Callum spoke softly into the microphone attached to his headset.

"Team leader to covert one. All tangoes are in the nest. How copy?" A single click in Callum's earpiece indicated that his message had been received. "Team leader to teams Alpha and Bravo, I am checking target vehicle to ascertain package. How copy?"

A momentary pause was broken by "Alpha team copy, standing by." Followed by, "Bravo team copy, standing by."

Callum emerged from between the two parked cars he had used for cover. Using other vehicles and the natural environment he stealthily approached the canvas covered truck, remaining hidden as much as he could, crouching to reduce his profile. Callum lifted the tail flap and looked inside. There was a single wooden crate, no bigger than an office desk, lashed to the sides of the truck. He removed a portable Geiger counter from one of his belt pouches, switched it on, and passed the machine over the crate. The audible crackle and the visual confirmation of counter's reading confirmed the presence of the device. He whispered confirmation to his team.

"Team leader to all teams. Target is red. I repeat target is red."

Callum replaced the tail flap and retraced his steps, returning to his previous position, concerned by the lack of security surrounding the bomb.

---------------------------------------------------------------------

Mike was positioned at one of the tables towards the rear of the café, his back to the wall. The Turkish coffee was thick, black and sickeningly sweet. He sat there stirring never intending on drinking it. Despite all the years Mike had spent covertly in Arab villages, he had never acquired a taste for the drink. The earpiece was pushed deep into his ear, hiding it from all but the closest of inspections. To any onlooker, Mike appeared to be minding his own business, but his peripheral vision noticed everything around him.

Nine men entered the establishment, dusty from the long drive in their semi-open vehicles, checking in noisily, placing their orders for food and drink. The Mullah was the last to enter, making ten in total, but his posture and demeanour were markedly different. He carried a carpet bag concealing an MP5 light machine gun and his personal SIG Sauer pistol. His furtive eyes scanned the room, resting momentarily on each of the travellers there. Mike felt the Mullah's eyes burn into him. He continued stirring his coffee, ignoring the Mullah, until the act felt awkward. Mike had stirred the drink enough. Further stirring would appear unnatural. He picked up the coffee and downed the sickly drink in one, concealing his revulsion at the nauseous taste and texture. The rangy old man finally looked away and Mike breathed a sigh of relief. He knew the Mullah was a legendary and ruthless killer and his death would have been a certainty had his identity been questioned.

Satisfied with the security of his surroundings, the Mullah checked in at reception before taking a seat in the café, detached from his men.

Mike sauntered over to the counter and ordered a portion of Bademjan, a local aubergine and tomato stew. He joked with the barista before returning to his table with a plate full of the aromatic dish accompanied by a Barbari flatbread. Mike knew that the Mullah and his men would be tired and keen to retire to their rooms. He would not have to wait long, he was reasonably sure of that.

Mike watched as their room keys were lifted from the keyboard and memorised each as they were allocated to the men. They were billeted in rooms 8, 9 and 10, with three men in each. Only the Mullah was afforded single accommodation; room 11. Gradually the nine men retired to their rooms, but the Mullah stayed on at his table for another hour. At last he stood wearily and approached the receptionist. A heated discussion developed that resulted in the young man reluctantly handing something to the Mullah. The wiry old man turned away and left the café, presumably heading towards his room.

-----------------------------------------------------------------------------

When the Mullah entered the café, his men were already checking in at the reception area. He looked around and appraised the men there, as was his habit. It was a habit that had ensured that he had been able to live a long life to date. One man in particular had drawn his attention. For the moment he could not quite understand why this man seemed out of place. He appeared to be relatively young, maybe in his late twenties. The Mullah looked more closely. His dress suggested that he was potentially a cleric, possibly middle-class, but certainly not one that he was acquainted with. He immediately pondered over the cars parked outside that he had meticulously memorised. None of which caused him any reason for concern and none would be of the kind that a middle-class cleric might use. The Mullah noted that the man subconsciously stirred his coffee for a long time before drinking it in a single gulp. In fact there was nothing in the way that the young man dressed, looked or acted that should have been cause for suspicion. But something was wrong about him. Maybe it was the way he drank the coffee? The Mullah pondered. That was not the Arab way. Coffee is a drink to sip and savour, not swig like the Americans and Europeans do.

As the man in question rose and walked over to the counter he spotted a tiny piece of plastic embedded in the man's ear.

I have you! The Mullah exulted. This was no cleric. The enemy had tracked him. American or European, it made no difference. Every instinct in the Mullah's body urged him to remove the SIG Sauer from the carpet bag and execute the man at this very moment. He paused, considering the situation. If the man was wearing an earpiece, then he was not alone. He had postulated the chance of an ambush here before beginning this journey, but the longer the journey continued, the less likely the Mullah believed his theory to be. The old sage wondered who had supplied these infidels with the intelligence, allowing them to find him. He already suspected the answer. Demitri had leaked the intelligence. Demitri was sending them all to their deaths.

The Mullah took a chair at one of the tables, silently considering his options. He waited for his men to retire, allowing them sufficient time to fall asleep, contemplating his response to this situation. An hour passed before he decided on what action he would take. He rose from his table and approached the reception desk. The young man looked up from his paperwork and enquired how he could assist the old man stood in front of him.

"Give me the master key to the rooms" the Mullah's demand was authoritative.

"*Iinaa asif sayidi*, but I cannot. I have to go with you and…"

The Mullah removed his identity documents and thrust them in front of the receptionist's eyes. The young man, now recognising the man stood in front of him, stopped mid-sentence. He fumbled under the counter and proffered the key, bowing his head as a mark of respect.

"Don't do anything stupid," the Mullah hissed through gapped teeth, leaving the café for the accommodation behind.

The Mullah knew with absolute certainty that to stay would be to die, either at the hand of Callum Knight and his task force, or through Demitri detonating the bomb remotely. He had no intention of being within fifty miles when that happened. The old war dog removed the SIG Sauer from his carpet bag, screwing on a silencer. He slipped the key silently into the lock of room 8, listening at the door. His sharp hearing was rewarded with the sound of snoring. They were asleep. The Mullah turned the key and slipped into the room taking a cushion off one of the chairs. He buried the silenced barrel into it and spat two bullets into the first man's head then proceeded to the others. In less than twenty seconds all three were dead. He repeated the executions in each of the other two rooms, closing the door behind him after shooting the men.

Satisfied that each door was re-locked, the Mullah made his way to the fire exit at the back of the premises. It was on the opposite side to the car park and quiet. The Mullah knew that the building would be surrounded, but not how many there were. It was a chance that he had to take if he wished to survive. He moved silently, miraculously evading the enemy within, and as he had done so many times in the past, disappeared quietly into the desert and melted into it.

--------------------------------------------------------------------------

Demitri Papandreou sat in his study at his luxury homestead in Thessaloniki, looking at the satellite images in front of him. It was live video footage of the truck-stop in Taybad and the surrounding area, enhanced with thermal imaging technology. The Hydra sat in her white silk dressing gown next to Demitri, her head on his shoulder. Both had gloated, as the Chinook dropped Callum's squad at a distance, to afford them a stealth approach, imagining their fear and trepidation as they skirmished into the unknown towards the tuck stop. The thought of their inevitable fear gave Hydie Papandreou a sexual frisson and she naturally nestled even closer to Demitri.

Both had exulted when the satellite picked up the murder of one of Major Knight's team, thermal imaging showing the body of a man supine and motionless in the sand, long after the Chinook took off. It was clear that O'Malley had kept his side of the bargain, when the Chinook subsequently dropped out of the sky, repaying his gambling debt in full. The scenario unfolding was riveting watching and clearly physically exciting to the Hydra.

They watched the unsuspecting arrival of the Mullah and his convoy, who Demitri was certain had no idea of the trap he had set for him, nor the potency of the bomb.

"He will be just another man to die and be consumed by the desert, Hydie," Demitri said dispassionately to his woman.

Thermal imaging showed the positions of each of Callum's squad as they lay in wait, watching the nine men and Mullah Ismael enter the buildings. The Mullah was the only one recognisable, but that was down to his dress and the way he moved, rather than any kind of facial recognition.

"There look, between the cars!" Demitri pointed with excitement.

They could see a man crouched watching the Mullah and his men as they disappeared into the truck-stop. When they were out of sight, the man stood and moved with stealth towards the truck, using whatever cover he could find. He looked around then lifted the tail flap.

"I'll bet my life that's Callum Knight, Hydie. We have them, Hell's teeth we have them!"

Demitri's grin was sadistic. He was going to make sure they suffered before he killed them, very much like a cat playing with a mouse, only ending the torment when boredom set in.

"Are you going to detonate now *agápe mou*?" the Hydra asked.

She subconsciously licked her lips in anticipation of the massive blast that would obliterate the truck-stop, nearby towns and much, much more.

"No not yet my darling, not until they have shown their hand and I can be sure of exactly what they hope to accomplish."

The Hydra looked positively disappointed. She was an impatient woman by nature.

"We may have to wait a couple of hours yet my darling, before they all regroup. I want them to know that they cannot disarm the device nor out-run the blast, and that their death is imminent, never to see their loved ones again.

The thought of so much death continued to excite the Hydra. She kissed Demitri passionately, her need building inside her like a storm ready to break. They were quickly too lost in each other to notice the Mullah slip through the back door of the truck-stop and disappear into the desert.

--------------------------------------------------------------------------

It was two hours later when Sergeant Mike Jackson returned with the layout of the truck-stop, and precisely which rooms the terrorists occupied. His first-hand knowledge and that extra detail, was what might make a difference when they were in the theatre of war. Callum organised his men into two squads and moved in towards the walls of the café and residential area. It was broad daylight but thankfully there were few vehicles parked and nobody outside of the building. Mike, now back in military fatigues, took the lead as was natural. Although Bud outranked him, none there had Mike's Middle East experience in this type of raid. Jake followed, with Zak and Rudy falling in line to bring up the rear. They made their way clockwise towards the back entrance of the block, moving silently, keeping low and using whatever cover they could find. Callum, along with Kayla, Chas and Joey, circled in the other direction in similar manner, meeting at the back door. Mike had already made sure that it was unable to be locked before he left, having broken off the jam where the mortice would otherwise locate.

"OK men to recap," Mike whispered. "Go down the corridor. Take the first left, then their rooms are the first four on the right, numbers 8 through 11, the Mullah billeting in 11."

He had already surveyed his room and determined that the doors were flimsy and would give at a single barge made with conviction.

"Thanks Mike. Bud and Jake, you take room 8; Chas and Joey, 9; Zak and Rudy, 10. Kayla and me will take the Mullah in room 11. Your job Mike is to kill anyone who gets through us."

Callum had chosen Kayla to act as his back-up against the Mullah. Although it might appear counter intuitive to take a woman into the most dangerous of the killing fields, Kayla had mental skills and kinetic abilities that made her the obvious choice. Nobody had yet taken on the Mullah and survived.
Callum took the lead, the squad stealthily progressing down the corridor, their pistols held in the classic two-handed Weaver grip, enabling rapid and controlled fire. They stopped in pairs outside their allocated rooms, with the heaviest members at the front. Callum gave a silent three finger countdown and the teams simultaneously charged the doors as the third finger fell. As expected the doors gave easily, the teams bursting through them, emptying their guns into the beds. When silence fell, Callum

became aware of the sound of guests screaming and fleeing from the building, and the pungent smell of cordite. The Mullah's bed was empty. Callum sensed imminent danger and swivelled on his heels, expecting to see the Mullah's rangy frame and sun parched face braced in the doorway with a rifle aimed at them. The others collected in the corridor with looks of consternation on their faces.

"They were already dead!" Jake lamented, clearly disappointed. "Shot through the head while they were sleeping."

"The Mullah was not in his room either," Callum added. "He must have executed them, but why, and where is he?"

The premises were already empty. In this volatile land where death was always a possibility, all had evacuated in panic at the sound of gunfire. Callum took the opportunity to brief his squad.

"OK, here it is. We must assume the Mullah is still in the game and a danger to us. He is a prolific killer and can take us all on alone if he so chooses. Do not underestimate him, he can literally rise from the sand in front of you and disappear just as quickly. We form a square, facing outwards and retreat to the truck; flanks being Chas and Joey, to the West and Zak and Rudi, to the East. I will lead with Kayla. Mike, you bring up the rear with Bud and Jake. If the Mullah is still here, that is where he is most likely to attack from, so be alert! If anything moves shoot. You don't get a second chance with this man. Be warned or ignore at your peril!"

They were aware of the legend relating to the Mullah and his fabled abilities. The idea of a vengeful assassin rising from the sand filled them with supernatural trepidation. Callum continued.

"We need to take a closer look at that crate, and examine the device. Jake, find the keys to the Jeeps and Truck. We will exit by road. Remember, no one gets left behind."

That was an unwritten law. Comrades in arms always brought back their dead.

Callum, Bud and Kayla took several minutes to assess the wooden crate, before gently prising the lid open, exposing its deadly cargo. Callum only had rudimentary knowledge of nuclear devices and wished now, more than ever, that Ava was with the team. Her knowledge would have been crucial to disarming the device. Without warning, the lights on the consul flashed up. The group looked to each other, uncertain as to what had precipitated the event, but knew without doubt that something was dreadfully wrong. Click. The timing mechanism flashed and the LED display began to count down. Ten minutes. Ten short minutes to oblivion.

----------------------------------------------------------------------

Demitri watched the satellite transmission as Callum and his squad exited the building in box formation, moving forwards towards the truck, each covering the other. They clearly expected some resistance, which never came. A minute later, two men and a woman entered the truck.

"It is done Hydie. They have killed the Mullah and his men. The trap is set."

Demitri showed little concern that he had sacrificed the Mullah in the setting of this trap. The old cleric had been a reliable resource, nothing more. Mission complete, he was now expendable.

He took the PAL activator, or Permissive Action Link, from his desk and punched in the twelve-digit activation code. Demitri paused for one tantalising moment, looked down and hit the send button.

"Ten minutes is all you have to wait now my love. Do you have any final requests before you see the fireworks?"

The lascivious look in Hydie Papandreou's eyes suggested that she did.

----------------------------------------------------------------------

"Jesus!" Bud cried out. "What did we just touch?"

"I don't think we touched anything Bud. It's been activated remotely, probably by the Mullah. Now everything makes sense. This has been a purposely designed trap from the outset," Callum said wryly. "Go with Kayla in the Jeeps and get the Hell out of here now while you still have a chance. I'll see how lucky I can get here. Now go!"

There were immediate protests by all, but it was a direct order from their commander and they conceded, leaving reluctantly, shaking hands in symbolic goodbyes. The chances of Callum surviving were minute and his men's were already uncertain.

"Go!" he insisted.

Kayla was the last to leave and jumped down from the tailgate, calling out one final sentiment.

"I love you Callum. I have always loved you." With that said, she was gone.

Callum heard the Jeeps start, engines racing as they screamed out of the car park heading north; tyre tracks and a dust trail evidence of their hurried departure.

They could still make it out of the range of the blast and fall out, Callum judged, as the time display rolled down to nine minutes. He re-examined the bomb mechanism. The wires and cogs meant nothing to him. A line from a classic movie came to his mind.


*'I should have cut the red wire...'*


Callum needed to let the timer tick down as long as possible to give his team the best chance of surviving the blast. Then he would need to choose which wire to cut. Life or death decided by a random decision. He cursed the bad luck of Ava's accident. She had meticulously studied nuclear device schematics, and her knowledge would have tilted the odds of success in their favour. Kayla had picked up on this fact. Moments later her commanding voice made Callum jump.

"Call Ava on your satellite phone now!"

Kayla had turned back to help the man that she loved. She couldn't leave him there to die alone.

"But I told you to..."

She cut him off.

"Shut up arsehole and call her. Then give me the phone."

---------------------------------------------------------------------------

Ava hadn't stopped drinking for two days and poured herself yet another vodka. She was searching for oblivion, but no matter how much she drank, oblivion denied her. The detonation of the bomb was scheduled for today, almost at this hour. Soon, the man that she had fallen in love with and her new friends would be blown off the face of the Earth. Ava had the power to stop it but not the resolve. Instead she had facilitated it. The guilt, shame and grief she now felt was unstoppable. Ava wanted to die.

The phone rang. It was Callum's satellite phone.

"Callum! Thank God."

"It's Kayla," she corrected coldly. "I'm with Callum and we have less than eight minutes to disarm a dirty bomb. No time to explain, but we share some abilities and skills. We need your help, your knowledge. Do you understand?"

Valuable seconds passed as Ava fought with her conscience. To save them would mean the betrayal of Demitri and *Allah*. To not help would be a betrayal of Callum, mankind and her personal beliefs outside of her religion. It was a conundrum.

"Ava, for God's sake!" Kayla shouted down the phone.

"What do you want me to do?" Ava's words were slurred.

Kayla cupped the mouthpiece. "Jesus Christ Callum, she's drunk." She returned her attention back to Ava. "Let me share my mind with you. Use my eyes to see this bomb and then for Christ's sake, tell us what to do."

"I've never done it like this, only face to face with eye contact. I can't..." Ava was on the verge of panic.

"Yes you can Ava!" Kayla cut in. "Concentrate and take control of my mind."

Ava fought away the alcoholic haze that was befuddling her, until she could feel Kayla's thoughts knocking at the door of her consciousness. Their connection was more through Kayla's honed skills than Ava's, which were still in ascension. The images of Ava's room faded, until she could see her lover's face clearly.

"Callum!" she gasped.

Kayla was looking at him and Ava could see his image, plain and clear.

"Oh Callum," Ava was lost in relief and guilt.

Kayla switched her gaze to the bomb, not wanting to encourage any eleventh-hour reconciliation.

"Right Ava, what do we do?" Kayla looked at the bomb from all angles to give Ava an overview.

"Seven minutes and counting Ava!" she reminded her firmly.

Ava searched her mind for the schematics that she had committed to memory.

"Oh, my God Kayla, this isn't a dirty bomb!" Ava was shocked. It wasn't at all like the device Demitri had described. "The device is a complete thermonuclear weapon. This won't kill hundreds it will kill tens of thousands, maybe hundreds of thousands after the fallout."

Kayla and Callum exchanged a glance that needed no words to explain. It was the realisation that the others would never out-run a thermonuclear explosion. They were all going to die unless they somehow disarmed the bomb.

The sudden realisation that Demitri had lied and employed an indiscriminate weapon of mass destruction and not the relatively impotent dirty bomb was immediately sobering. Ava's anger at Demitri's lie focussed her mind and her thoughts suddenly became crystal clear.

"The PAL activator has opened a circuit allowing the battery packs to charge the capacitors in the detonation box. That's the black rectangular unit below the digital display." Ava clarified, speaking quickly. "When the counter gets to zero, it opens the circuit from the capacitors to the detonation unit. This ignites a conventional explosive, probably cordite, sending a uranium bullet down that short barrel below the detonation box into its uranium target at the other end. This creates a supercritical mass and a big bang."

Ava was thinking on her feet.

"You have two choices. Either you bend the barrel so the bullet jams in the barrel and can't reach its target, but it's made out of titanium, so that won't be easy. Or you disconnect the wires that connect the capacitors in the detonation box, to the firing cap at the end of the barrel. That is if you can find them."

Kayla repeated Ava's words as they arrived as thoughts in her head to orientate Callum.

"Five minutes," Kayla announced, as much to herself as to the others. "Bending the barrel is out of the question Ava. We haven't got adequate tools. We have to cut the wires, but I can't see any leaving the capacitors to the firing cap. It must be hard wired or something."

"Can you gently lever off the rubber cup that covers the firing cap?" Ava suggested. "That might expose the wires going into the cordite, but don't short circuit them or it will detonate."

The intensity of the moment and the sheer concentration of sharing her mind with Kayla had given Ava total clarity. She was back to her calculating and analytical self

"Callum's working on that now. Four minutes Ava."

Callum had already opened the small toolkit from his field webbing and spread its content. A multi-screwdriver, pliers, a pair of snips and an adjustable spanner were all he had to disarm this thermonuclear device.

Meagre tools indeed, he mused as he worked off the rubber cap with the flat end of the screwdriver.

"Kayla," Ava began as an afterthought. "Look for any wiring that doesn't seem to fit in with the standard of workmanship of the bomb. It could have an anti-tamper system added as an afterthought."

"There's what looks like an earth wire attached to the cowling of the detonation box." Kayla observed. "It's not properly terminated, just twisted around a nut and bolt."

"Don't touch it!" Ava's thought arrived almost as a scream in Kayla's head. "It's not an earth. It's a circuit. If you had stripped the cowling and gone in that way, it would have been game over."

"Three minutes Callum," Kayla advised.

She watched Callum's hands closely, so that Ava could see exactly what he was doing. The anxiety was beginning to take effect on Callum now. His hands were shaking and the sweat dripped copiously from the tip of his nose.

"There Ava look. A red and a blue wire; which do we cut?" Kayla stammered her words, a sign of the stress that they were all under.

"Uh, I wasn't expecting that," Ava admitted.

She quickly scanned the memorised schematics in her mind. They all showed white and black wires.

"I don't know, I would only be guessing," Ava admitted.

"Great!" Kayla's response was said in such a way that suggested the lack of knowledge was all Ava's fault. "Think Ava, think!"

A pregnant silence ensued between them while Callum tried to fathom the dilemma facing him.

"Two minutes remaining," Callum observed. "Are we going to take a vote?"

It was his attempt at irony, but there was no reply from either woman. Ava was already praying to her God and Kayla just sat down on the bench seat in resignation of their almost certain demise.

"OK, I am cutting now," Callum smiled fatalistically, as he closed the snips around the red wire. "Let's hope it's not another *grab the cat* moment." It was gallows humour that would only have made sense to another who had watched the movie.

-------------------------------------------------------------------------

Demitri and the Hydra watched as the two Jeeps sped off to the north, leaving Kayla Lovell alone in the car park. Clearly, she had changed her mind and chosen to die with her old flame, Callum Knight. There were just eight minutes remaining on the display of his PAL activator when Kayla re-entered the truck. It would have been pointless her leaving with the others anyway he mused. They were expecting a dirty bomb, not the thermonuclear device they now had to deal with. Out-running a device of that magnitude was impossible.

Killing several high-ranking Angels was a deserved bonus for his meticulous planning, Demitri reflected. A thermonuclear bomb detonated on Iranian soil, would cause an international shock wave that would tumble governments. The Iranians would automatically think it was an Israeli attack, and America would immediately raise their threat response level, concerned over a Russian escalation and vice-versa. As icing on the cake, Demitri could distribute satellite images showing Callum's involvement

325

immediately prior to the explosion, and cast international doubt as to the credibility of the Angel run organisation. It was just the global destabilisation they needed as the precursor to total Shadow domination and a New World Order.

The minutes ticked by as he and the Hydra watched the truck in gruesome awe. Since assassinating Larry Madison, the nuclear expert, Ava was the team's only specialist with the knowledge capable of disarming the bomb. She was out of the equation, since her car accident, and so Armageddon was inevitable. Demitri counted down the final seconds.

"Five, four, three, two one…"

The anticipation, coupled with the sexual tension, was a heady mix. Hydie bit her lip expectantly.

The moment of detonation passed and Demitri immediately flew into a rage. He shoved the Hydra off him, stood and stomped heavily around the room like a wounded bull in the ring.

"What the fuck?" he cried out, and then stopped suddenly in realisation. "It's that bitch whore, Ava Kaplinski. She must have talked them through disarming the device. I'll kill her!"

"Not so fast, *agápe mou,*" the Hydra comforted her man. "She's still useful to us. Make the woman kill Callum and her other friends first. That will punish her more than death. Besides, she is the key to the fifth dimension," the Hydra added with a winning smile.

-------------------------------------------------------------------------

Chapter 20

22nd January 2016. London Savoy Hotel, The Strand.

Only eleven days ago, Kayla left her family home in the States, where she had been nursing her sick father. Now that felt a lifetime ago. Since then, life had been a roller coaster of excitement and danger. Kayla loved danger. She was a girl who liked to go out of her comfort zone and into the lion's den, just to see if she would come out alive. Seven days ago, when they were in the desert disarming a thermonuclear bomb, was as close to death as Kayla had ever come, and the experience had excited her mentally and sexually. After the bomb had been disarmed, it had taken all Kayla's self-control not to rip off Callum's combats and pleasure herself on him there and then. Kayla still had the *hots* for Callum and knew she always would. That near-death experience had only served to awaken and reinforce that carnal passion.

Kayla realised she had been a fool to cheat on Callum, ultimately losing her man. Now she yearned to win him back. On their return from the desert, Kayla had tried every trick in the book to entice him into a sexual liaison, but he had resisted every attempt. The fact that Ava had totally rejected Callum, despite his advances on her, made it the right time for Kayla to pounce and reclaim him.

Kayla sat perched on the window sill in her suite at the Savoy, trying to get a signal by pressing her phone against the glass. She was expecting a call from Callum that she dare not miss. Her body needed him too much to risk missing his call, so she was standing by expectantly. Even the thought of Callum gave her shivers of expectation that came in waves, running up from the base of her spine to her neck. They flushed her face and hardened her nipples, giving her goose bumps. Only thoughts of Callum had ever done this to her. No other man came close to thrilling her that way. It took her back to the very beginning of their love affair.

At that time, Kayla worked in their New York offices and Callum in London. Although they had exchanged emails of a business nature, they had never met. It was on a videoconference over three years ago, that they finally did. Kayla remembered being knocked out by his looks and persona. She was in her late thirties then and Callum in his mid-forties. He was one of those men who oozed confidence and competence; a man with charisma and presence. When Callum talked, everyone listened because he always had something meaningful to say.

But Callum was a listener too, with great soft skills. Apart from that, he was just about the sexiest man Kayla had ever seen. She remembered how her ovaries felt squeezed at the sight of him, as if she was trying to make herself fertile for him. The one thing Kayla did know was that she had to have him, and from that moment forwards that is exactly what she had set out to do. Kayla smiled as she recalled how she had openly preened in front of him; the pouts, hair flicks and a multitude of other affectations, all to catch his attention. She felt a little ashamed that she had also used her psychic talents to probe his mind in an effort to prompt his affection. Well, a girl can't take any chances, can she? Kayla had justified to herself at the time.

Kayla found excuses to send emails personally rather than through the company protocols. She occasionally let them get a little flirtatious, which seemed to meet with his approval and resulted in the occasional slightly inappropriate message in return. Kayla was grooming Callum, but he never realised it. In one email, she had referred obliquely to something that had made her nipples harden. She knew exactly what she was doing when she sent it, and how the risky message might affect him when he received it. From that day on Kayla had captured her man. Only a week later, Callum had arranged for her to take on some research work in London. The rest was history.

Their affair lasted nine tempestuous months, but Kayla had already started straying. She needed her conquests, or at least she thought she did. Kayla had got heavily involved with a Texan oil tycoon who treated her badly, but she always thought she could change him and make him a better man. She thought the same about all her trashy conquests that followed. Leopards rarely changed their spots though, and Kayla came away badly bruised and disillusioned after each sordid affair.

Recently Kayla had got to know about Callum's passionate affair with Ava, as everyone did. Worse still, she knew that Ava was stunningly beautiful and a real threat. Kayla regretted and was deeply jealous that the hot gossip that used to be about them, was now about Ava and Callum. She would have given her back teeth for her relationship with Callum to be back as it had been at the very beginning.

The fact that Callum and Ava had broken up, was good news for Kayla. She knew that he would be recovering from yet another broken heart, and also knew that Callum wouldn't risk having her break it again. He very nearly didn't survive the last time she left him. Strange, Kayla thought, that such a strong and robust man could become so vulnerable when he gave his heart. Callum couldn't love by half-measures. He dedicated his whole heart to each and every relationship. In simple terms, he was a one woman man.

Perched there on the window sill awaiting Callum's message, was becoming hard on Kayla's back. She decided to lie on the couch and stretch out. Kayla was in great shape and looked svelte and feminine lying there. She had innate fashion sense and generally chose classic clothes that enhanced her physical attributes. Today though, Kayla had chosen an almost casual look for Callum; tight fitting blue jeans and white fitted short sleeved T-shirt. She was a size 10 but with a generous bust, that was accentuated by the fitted cotton of her T-shirt. Kayla noted that the dark ovals of her nipples showed through the stretched cotton shirt. She would use that asset to her best advantage, when he arrived at the room.

Kayla lay there reminiscing about their first encounter. She had spent a couple of weeks seducing him through a well thought-out programme of suggestion, teasing and innuendo. At one time, after a few glasses of wine, she had confessed her sexual feelings for him in an email. It read:

*'I imagined you on top of me fucking me and feeling small and vulnerable underneath you.'*

She smiled as she remembered what he had said in reply about their mounting passion:

*'I sense a storm coming on Kayla and it will be tempestuous. And there will be fallen fruit. And that fallen fruit will be you and I will consume you!'*

It was so Callum! Later, when he had experienced Kayla's insatiable sexual appetite, he changed that to:

*'I liken you to a Caribbean hurricane Kayla; warm, wet and dangerous!'*

Callum was wonderful with words, she recalled. He had said at the start, that he would get inside her head, seducing her in prose. And that was precisely what he had done, but it was a mutual seduction. The erotic memories of Callum were beginning to have a physical effect on Kayla. He had already won her even then, on paper, and in chemistry.

It had been five weeks since Kayla last had sex, something unheard of for her and she was hungry! She knew from their mission in the desert, that Callum was in abstinence too. Kayla imagined that she was the water in his oasis and that her passion would end his drought. She imagined him cupping his hands as if she were cool waters and putting her to his lips and quenching his thirst on her. She imagined Callum on top of her, fucking her, and her feeling small and vulnerable beneath him. The thought of Callum making love to her made her whimper and cry out.

"God I want you Callum!"

At that moment the message tone bleeped on her phone.

*'Be there in five. What room number?'*

No kiss at the end. Kayla noted with disappointment.

She had to concede that she was the one who had started sending him messages without kisses over two years ago. Only now did she realise just how much that must have hurt him.

Kayla replied with just the room number and a kiss, sprang up from the couch then ran to the bathroom. She needed to make sure that she looked her best for him. Kayla critically appraised her reflection in the mirror. She probably looked better now than she did five years ago. Kayla was a Capricorn, and according to the astrological profiles, Capricorns can appear to get younger as they get older. This was certainly true about her. Kayla put this down to many things, one of which was finally being comfortable in her own skin. At last Kayla knew who she was, what she wanted and most particularly, what she didn't want. That particularly meant men who were takers and brought nothing to the party. Callum was different; a man in a million who knew how to treat the whole woman, who knew how to satisfy her mind and her body; and God did he know how to satisfy her body! She noted that her mirror image was flushed with anticipation. This was one night she couldn't bear the thought of disappointment.

Kayla took the makeup brush and lightly brushed her dusky skin. She had inherited the almond shaped brown eyes from her Italian ancestry, that and a great complexion that still shone with youth. Kayla remembered that Callum loved her well-groomed eyebrows which accentuated her brow line. She had already spent time meticulously plucking and pencilling them. Callum was a man who appreciated and rewarded beauty. He paid attention to detail, and the effort that it took to achieve. Kayla knew that, if this reunion went well, he would reward her for her labours one hundred-fold in the form of the best love-making imaginable. She also remembered that when they made love, Callum seldom took his eyes off her face. That was another reason for her to look as perfect as was practically possible for him. He was a man who *read* his woman and played them, based solely on facial expressions. Callum knew the precise moment to take a risk and when to back off. He was a powerful, yet gentle lover. Kayla was sure of one thing though, if this did indeed go to plan, then she would be royally fucked by morning. She just couldn't wait!

And finally the lippy, Kayla thought; one of woman's most potent tools of entrapment.

Kayla selected the colour and pouted her full lips. She would normally wear plum in the day as it suited her dark complexion, but for Callum it had to be red. He was a man drawn to a woman's mouth and Kayla needed to be sure of his kiss. If she could get him to watch her mouth and kiss her, then getting him in bed would be a natural progression of that kiss.

She decided to wear her dark brown hair wild; which suited her mood right now. She took one final look at herself, pulled her T-shirt down and settled her breasts into it with her hands. She noticed that her nipples had hardened again testing the elasticity of the cotton.

"Standing to attention as required. Good girls!" she praised out loud.

She was more than ready. A wicked smile crossed her lips as she turned away from the mirror, sensing Callum at the door. Her heart pounded in her chest at the delicious anticipation of his touch, her groin throbbing with unbridled desire. This foxy lady was fully armed and dangerous!

---------------------------------------------------------------------------

Callum turned his silver BMW into the parking bay at the hotel, knowing that the risk he was taking was crazy. He had resisted Kayla's obvious advances all week, but had finally agreed to meet her socially for old time's sake. He had suggested the restaurant as a safe and neutral location, but had finally relented and agreed to meet Kayla in her room for drinks. Kayla was a woman who always got her way and never much cared how she got it. She also had special psychic and mental skills that Callum was never sure that she used fairly.

Was I coerced, he wondered, or do I just fancy the pants off her? If he was being honest with himself it was probably a little bit of both, he decided.

Callum knew he had to resist her though, because it had taken him over two years to recover after their last break up. He knew with certainty that she would leave him again if he allowed any relationship to get that far. Kayla had that same heady combination of Angel and Shadow genes that Ava possessed. By nature she would always struggle against her dark side. Just a drink, Callum vowed, taking the elevator to her floor.

Kayla opened the door to him before he even knocked, having the ability to predict things, another weapon in her impressive arsenal. Callum wondered just how much freedom of choice he had in this date that he had reluctantly conceded to.

"Callum!" Kayla gushed.

She took him by the hand and led him into the lounge area. What Kayla really wanted to do was kiss him, but the door was still open and he might have run for his life. Two glasses of Bollinger were already poured. Kayla handed one to Callum.

"To us," she toasted, with *that* look in her eye.

Callum knew Kayla of old and knew exactly where this was heading. He had to derail her and quickly.

"Cheers Kayla but there is no *us*," Callum was as firm as he could be, but there was uncertainty in his voice. "You made that clear over two years ago."

Ouch! Kayla thought. The truth hurt. Kayla was far from beaten though. Besides Callum's voice had no conviction and she had always known how to play him.

Use your assets girl, she prompted herself.

Kayla had strategically left her purse on the coffee table beside the drinks. She diverted the conversation to trivial matters to take away the impact of Callum's painfully true accusation. When she felt the conversation had been sufficiently banal for long enough to relax him, she played her trump card.

Kayla nonchalantly picked up her purse, taking out the red lipstick and compact mirror. She continued talking as she removed the cap. Half way through her next sentence, Kayla paused, pouted and began to apply the bright red lipstick theatrically. Like most women, Kayla had that feminine ability to take in all things around her without seeming to look. Her eyes appeared to be looking at herself in the mirror, but she was watching Callum for signs of interest.

Kayla's plan worked. Callum's eyes were fixated on her mouth. He loved her mouth, he always had. She was fast reaching the limit as to how much of the red cream her lips could take. Kayla stopped and glanced down to locate the cap on the lipstick whilst strategically eying the new-found bulge in Callum's trousers.

Yes! She exulted but the word was only a thought.

Kayla replaced the lipstick and mirror in her purse whilst continuing with her boring topic, pretending not to notice Callum's predicament. Kayla nonchalantly put her thumbs in the waist band of her jeans and pulled them up wriggling her hips enticingly as she did so. She reinforced this sensual display of her femininity by pulling her T-shirt down, enhancing the shape of her breasts and the prominence of her now painfully erect nipples.

The trap was set. Kayla went in for the kill, while Callum was so obviously physically distracted.

"You haven't heard a word I've been saying have you Callum?" Kayla accused, feigning hurt. "That's one of the silly reasons it all ended between us."

Kayla had strategically placed the blame of their parting on him. Callum could see that she was close to tears and felt suitably guilty and repentant. Her performance was worthy of an Oscar. To be fair, Kayla had chosen a conversation of such banality that, even without the sexual distractions, Callum would have been hard pressed to remember a word.

"Kayla, I'm really sorry. That was rude of me. Please forgive my inattentiveness." Callum had big puppy-dog eyes.

She let the moment hang in the balance for just long enough to make Callum start to panic. Judging her timing to perfection, she extended her arms towards him.

"Hug?" she asked, with a theatrically trembling bottom lip.

Callum had no choice and accepted her embrace gallantly. Kayla pressed herself firmly into him.

"Why Mr Knight; what is all this about?" she gasped and slipped her hand between their groins. "Oh my God Callum! I had forgotten what a big boy you are."

Before Callum had a chance to excuse himself, Kayla pressed her mouth urgently against his and increased the pressure of her hand on him. Callum's protest simply fell away at her touch. He tightened his hold on Kayla's slim waist, drawing her into him. Kayla's skilful hand assured all else. Their kissing was intense and it was kissing that had been their *glue* that bonded them. Kayla was desperate for Callum to touch her, but he was well practiced in their game of love and denied her, as she knew he would. All she could think of was Callum's hardness and the throbbing in the pit of her stomach that was driving her crazy.

Callum slid his strong hands down the slimness of Kayla's back to the roundness of her bottom, gripping the firm flesh. Kayla had the most perfect bum Callum had ever seen, let alone felt. He remembered the first time they had made love. Kayla had rolled out from under him onto her hands and knees, looking back at him wickedly over her shoulder. He remembered how she had just the biggest *come on* smile ever, shaking her booty provocatively, whilst laughing back at him. It very soon turned out that Kayla didn't have enough breath in her to waste on laughing. The memory of that erotic encounter turned Callum on ridiculously, reinforcing his want to have her.

Callum brought his hands back up to Kayla's T-shirt line, loitering there long enough to unbuckle her jeans and pull them off her hips. He ran his hands up underneath the stretched cotton of her shirt, over Kayla's well-formed abs until he had both her breasts cupped in them.

"God you've got amazing breasts Kayla. I had forgotten just how wonderful they are," he murmured into her open mouth.

Callum began to work her nipples gently with his thumbs. They responded eagerly and hardened still more as they sensitised, sending their secret messages down to Kayla's groin inflaming her passion. She needed him to touch her there and remembered how his skilled fingers could release her. The ache in her groin was becoming unbearable. Kayla framed his face with her hands, and then pushed him away to arm's length, so she could study his face.

"Touch me Callum, I want you so much," Kayla implored.

It was clear to Callum from the look in Kayla's eyes that she was desperate to make love. She needed release. Callum turned Kayla slightly away from him to allow his hand to slip inside her jeans and panties, over the fine coarse hair that covered the mound of her pubis. Kayla instinctively shuffled her feet apart; inviting Callum's touch and trembled with the sheer anticipation of his sweet invasion. At last Callum's purposeful fingers gently found their goal and Kayla cried out, almost in pain at the intimacy of his caress.

"Oh, my God Callum, Don't stop, please don't stop."

Kayla couldn't breathe. Her entire perception of the world at that moment was just Callum's touch. Then it happened powerfully. Kayla screamed out as she was lost in the ecstasy of the moment. Her legs went from under her and Callum had to take her full weight in the hand that was pleasuring her. The sudden pressure of his grip sent Kayla into spasms of rapture, her moans becoming guttural, almost animal-like.

Kayla no longer knew where she was. It seemed like she was floating in the air as Callum carried her over to the King-sized bed. She was still in glorious confusion and unaware of Callum raising her hips to drag her tight-fitting jeans from under her. They caught hopelessly at her feet. Callum was still tugging at them urgently when Kayla came back to full consciousness. She smiled up at him, sensing his urgency, and kicked the troublesome jeans free, leaving her in her black lace panties and white T-shirt. Kayla sat up and pulled the shirt off over her head, the action raising her breasts until they were free of the cotton before springing heavily back with a single bounce. Callum gasped at that little show of femininity. Now sure of the outcome, Kayla lay back appreciating his eyes feasting on her, smirking provocatively.

Somehow, Callum was already naked and Kayla wondered how long she had been lost in her orgasm. He was knelt between her knees with his generous manhood standing high and proud. Kayla felt small and vulnerable, just as she had fantasised, laying there in her flimsy panties spread before him. Callum looked her directly in the eye and not at her vulnerability, reinforcing her memory that he was the only man she had ever made love to that did that. He was a man who knew the importance of winning a woman's mind and how completely she would give her body afterwards if he did.

Kayla was charged with expectancy, knowing that this was one of Callum's favourite erotic moments. He slid his thumbs under the sheer fabric of her panties at her hips and drew them slowly off her. Kayla raised her pelvis to help him free them and now she was exposed and prone to him. Callum only glanced at her womanhood, noting that she still preferred Brazilian. There was a devilish smile on his lips. She grinned back, knowing what he was thinking. He had told her that every woman had a special look in her eyes at that moment of sweet surrender, when she gave up her panties; her last line of defence before her fate was inevitable. It was a look that could encompass many feelings: expectancy, excitement, guilt, want and love. Every woman had it and Callum found that expression so sexy.

Callum would normally play his woman slow at this stage, kissing her breasts and teasing her nipples before planting little kisses all the way down to her pubis. The musky smell and taste of a clean woman was an aphrodisiac to Callum and he loved to skilfully reward her with his mouth to prepare her body for him. It was something that Kayla loved too, particularly by Callum, who knew just how to excite her. But he knew that events had already gone too far for Kayla, even for that delicious luxury.

"Make love to me Callum, please. I want you inside me."

Kayla's voice was husky and demanding, her pupils big with lust as she spread her legs wide to encourage him, in that act of total submission. She needed him to make her his woman and wanted their lovemaking to be hard and urgent. Kayla pulled Callum's head to hers with one hand and consumed his mouth whilst guiding his manhood into her with the other. His penetration was slow and continuous until it felt to Kayla that he was touching her womb. She gasped.

Callum began slowly and rhythmically, taking each penetration to its fullness. Kayla could immediately feel those little contractions in the base of her belly that were the harbinger of her orgasm. They grew in intensity with every powerful but tender thrust. Callum watched Kayla's face, as he always did, looking for the signs of her journey. Her mouth stayed open and her eyes distant as she forgot to breathe. When each breath finally came, they were forced gasps and little moans to the rhythm of their love. Callum could see from her expressions that she was building fast, no longer aware of anything except the sensation of him inside her. Her eyes had lost their focus, staring directly into paradise. Kayla was somewhere else, out on some astral plane.

Callum was quickly reaching his own limits too, as he quickened the pace of his lovemaking to suit Kayla's journey. At last she screamed out, her body convulsing with the enormity of her climax. Only just conscious, Kayla desperately finished the act of procuration by grabbing Callum's hips, pulling him deep inside her, locking onto him, trying to milk the seed from him. When Callum's release came, it was like an explosion. More than two years in the wilderness of her love culminated in that moment for him and his fulfilment was immense. Kayla felt Callum's body go rigid with the intensity of his release. She looked up at him. Every muscle in Callum's arms, chest and neck bulged with the effort of that moment, his face twisting in divine agony. Finally he collapsed, totally wasted and spent on her breast. Kayla wrapped her legs around Callum and encompassed him in her loving arms.

"You are mine again Callum," Kayla murmured in his ear.

She closed her vagina tightly around his manhood, so as not to waste a single seed. This was the man she wanted for eternity.

-------------------------------------------------------------------------

# Chapter 21

Ava had lived every day in despair, since defying God's will by helping Callum and Kayla disarm the bomb. Her assistance was contrary to her instructions as a jihadist, and abhorrent to her God. She knew there would be no divine forgiveness, no place for her in heaven and certainly no forgiveness from Demitri. Ava had tried prayer, but she felt that the spirit of *Allah* no longer dwelt in her soul. She had been abandoned, cast aside to spend eternity in damnation.

Demitri hadn't contacted her in nearly a month, and Callum had given up on her. The office was purgatory too, watching the love between Callum and Kayla blossom. She had to steel herself not to burst into tears every time she saw them together. Ava still loved Callum with all her heart, but Demitri had ordered her to engage only in essential work-related conversation. She had watched Callum's despair mount by the day and could see that he was heart-broken and felt betrayed; forsaken.

Ava was hurting him desperately, but could do nothing to ease his pain. It was breaking both of them. All Ava had now was a master who despised her and wanted to control her. She had been attracted to yet another despicable man, and had spurned Callum, emotionally destroying the most perfect man that she had ever met. Ava knew that she had committed Callum to a lifetime of pain and sadness, and hated herself for her weakness and infidelity. She couldn't even blame him for turning to Kayla. He craved solace as much as she did.

Kayla was naturally guarded and off-hand around her, as any female rival would be, but there was something more deeply rooted. When Ava joined minds with Kayla in the desert, they both had an insight into each other's psyche. Kayla's experience of mind-sharing was infinitely greater than Ava's, resulting in Ava inadvertently allowing Kayla access into her personal and secret life. One of those secrets was her association with Demitri. Ava had no way of knowing just how much knowledge Kayla had gleaned from her. She dreaded that it might include the planned murder of Callum and other senior Angels. The fact that she was still considered as a part of the team, suggested to Ava that Kayla had not totally penetrated the darker recesses of her mind.

Ava was caught up in a cycle that she could not break. She worked by day and drank by night. Drinking was no longer a pleasure. It had become a necessity for her to survive the day and brought on the narcolepsy she desperately needed to help her escape into oblivion at night. Her migraines were now almost constant, brought on by her unhappiness and denial.

When Ava made herself up in the morning, she could see her beauty waning. There was no longer any sparkle about her. She had lost the shine that Callum had brought out in her. Demitri had made her bland and dull. Ava was suffering the depths of misery and despair. Even her demons had sensed her new-found weakness and massed to haunt her at night, giving her no respite. She thought of Katarina, her truest girlfriend and mourned her.

Katarina had always worried that Ava would eventually press her own self-destruct button one day, and that was exactly what Ava was doing now. The message alert sounded on her phone. She looked at the display, half-hoping it was Callum. It was Demitri.

*'Meet me now at the Savoy. Usual suite.'*

No, more than that. Ava thought about messaging back saying, Fuck you! But instead she capitulated, just as she had always done to the men who had controlled her life. Ava hated herself for being so weak.

-------------------------------------------------------------------------

The taxi dropped Ava outside the Savoy. She reached inside her bag, surveying her surroundings as she did so. Nobody was looking at her. She unscrewed the cap of the vodka bottle and took three big swigs, shuddered and re-capped the bottle. Ava rummaged deeper in her bag, her fingers wrapping around a small aerosol mouth-freshener, squirting copious amounts into her mouth. Emboldened by the rush of alcohol, she walked through the hotel entrance. Ava felt sick, not just through alcohol abuse, but because she had lost her identity, self-respect and her hope. Worst of all, she had lost Callum.

Ava was no longer aroused by the thought of meeting Demitri. She was no longer afraid of him either. Nothing mattered anymore. He could kill her if that was what he wanted, at least death would be a release. She had made the decision to simply obey him, tolerate an un-fulfilled life, deeply regretting what might have been. Ava knew that she would never shine again. She knew Callum would never again hold her in his strong arms, pleasuring her like no other man ever had or could.

The elevator stopped at his floor. Ava walked the twenty painful steps to Demitri's room. She took a deep breath to steel herself and knocked. It seemed to Ava that she stood there waiting for an age. She wondered how unimportant she must be to be left there waiting like a fool. At last the door opened. Demitri spoke, already with his back to her.

"Come in," his voice showed no affection.

He waved her in dismissively. Ava obliged. She always *obliged*.

Ava stood there in the middle of the room, waiting for Demitri to at least offer to take her coat. He didn't. Ava shook the coat off onto the bed, and then sat there beside it. She glanced around the room. The bed was dishevelled. There were female cosmetics on the dressing table. He hadn't even bothered to hide them and there was the sound of a tap running in the bathroom. She felt sick.

"So, Ava, it has been a month. What do you have for me?" Demitri's manner was business-like.

Ava ran through the events immediately following the failed bomb attack, hoping that they would not implicate her. Much to her relief he said nothing. Ava updated him on the whereabouts of the key Angels and their current activities. She finished her report by focussing on their suspicions that the Shadow organisation were carrying out experiments into fifth dimensional travel. The only thing that interested him was her comment on the fifth dimension.

"How would they know that unless you told them?"

His words were was nothing less than an accusation. Ava had no energy for his disdain. She replied as if disinterested.

"Apparently Maelströminha glimpsed it in her mirrors, after our scientists returned to their own time. There has also been a new archaeological find of previously unseen documents, written and authenticated in Leonardo da Vinci's own hand. They refer to the experiment we performed in detail."

Ava's response was also delivered in a business-like manner. There was nothing more he could do that would make her life any worse.

"Of course," Demitri conceded. "We transported them here and changed their experiences, which changed history."

He no longer suspected Ava of treason, well at least on this subject, but her infidelity still angered him. Without seeking her consent he pushed Ava backwards onto the bed where she froze, scared and sickened by Demitri's clear intent. Without resisting, Ava let him humiliate her again, hating herself throughout her disgusting ordeal. Afterwards, without an affectionate word or a kiss, Demitri pulled up his trousers and crossed to the bedside table.

"I have something for you," he announced, removing a small glass phial from one of the drawers and handing it to her.

"What is this?" she asked frowning, but unable to look at him through her shame.

"That Ava is a fast-acting, tasteless neurotoxin. Ingestion brings on death in minutes by arresting all muscular activity. You are to entice Callum Knight to your room at the Waldorf Hilton. You will seduce him there with the pleasure of your body, something that you have never had issues with," he chided. "You will drink Champagne with him to dull his wits and administer this poison, knowing that you are doing God's will and my will. Afterwards you leave and my men will tidy up after you."

Ava looked devastated, but that meant nothing to Demitri. She meant nothing.

"But I can't..." Ava began.

The backhanded slap Demitri viciously delivered made the last one that Ava received seem like a caress. It bloodied her mouth and sent her spinning, half conscious, across the room. She sat there dazed looking back at him. His jaw was jutted out in rage and somehow familiar to her. Ava had the biggest sense of *déjà vu* that she had ever experienced. This had happened to her before, somewhere in some other time or some other life. History was repeating itself. Ava was almost at the point of realising who Demitri actually was. It was like a word being on the tip of your tongue, but elusive such that you just can't find it.

"You bastard! I will kill you for that," Ava growled, spitting out a mouthful of blood.

A black rage brewed rapidly inside Ava like a storm, borne out of the pure brutality of Demitri's assault. Her eyes blackened with hate, a precursor of her readiness to kill. The lighting in the room began to flicker and crackle, until the bulbs exploded into clouds of dust. Panes of glass cracked in the windows and the fire sprinklers burst into life, cascading water everywhere, drenching them. Ava's black hair hung in wet rat's tails down her face, her eyes burning like coals, drilling into the psyche of the man she now hated. Ava was in a killing rage, oblivious to the terrified screams of a woman in the bathroom.

Demitri had stupidly lost control, driving Ava too far. It was the one thing that he could not afford to do. Demitri was no match for a vengeful Ava. She could kill him in a hundred different ways if she but realised it. Demitri was on the back foot, needing to act fast.

"Ava, my darling I am so sorry. Oh, God what have I done to you? Please forgive me. I am under such pressure from the Hydra. It was so wrong of me to take my frustration out on the one I love."

Demitri was literally fighting for his life. He knelt beside Ava and put his arms around her, looking soulfully into her eyes. Slowly the blackness of Ava's eyes faded to dark brown. Demitri knew that he was safe, but continued to hold her for some time. Ava was numb, staring disbelievingly at the phial in the palm of her hand.

"I will do as you ask," she said with finality, "and then I don't want to see you ever again."

Ava, now defeated, cold and soaking wet, stood and walked robotically out of the room, without picking up her coat or looking back at Demitri.

---------------------------------------------------------------

It was a cold February night. Ava made the journey back across London dressed only in her grey pencil skirt and white blood-splattered blouse. She was chilled to the very bone, but the numbness of her body didn't come close to comparing to the numbness inside her brain. Ava was traumatised, empty and broken. She let herself into her apartment, closed the door behind her and dropped her purse on the bed. Ava was still in deep shock, functioning rather than being in control of her senses. She ran the bath, pouring in a generous amount of bath cream, before adding most of a bottle of antiseptic, wanting to cleanse herself of this man; every action carried out as if in a trance. Ava looked at her reflection in the bathroom mirror, ashamed of what she had become. Ava had let Demitri degrade her again, without even putting up a protest. She hated the weak pathetic woman staring back from the mirror with a passion. Even in Ava's weakened state, that passion was enough to shatter the glass into a thousand pieces, sending the shards scattering across the floor.

Ava undressed, dropping her clothes randomly to the floor. She walked to the bath, shredding her feet on the broken glass, but felt no pain. Her face was devoid of expression as she stepped into the almost scalding water. She took the shower hose off its cradle, unscrewed the shower head and adjusted the mixer tap to hot. Ava spread her legs and inserted the hose, flushing the residue of the man out of her. She wanted no trace of him left inside her. The scalding water caused her excruciating internal pain. Ava bit her lip grimacing as she continued. She took the loofah, soaped it and scrubbed her skin until it was raw. Ava still felt unclean, scrubbing herself again, then again until the bath water was cold and pink with her blood.

Ava had fallen into the abyss of despair. There was no retreat for her now; nobody to turn to. Dejectedly she reconciled herself that she would do God's will and kill Callum Knight, just as she had been commanded. Ava had also made the monumental decision to take her own life and face the wrath of God. Without Callum, she would have nothing to live for anyway. Ava needed to rediscover her beauty, become attractive to Callum once more. She picked up the vodka bottle, took one last copious swig and poured the rest down the sink.

"The sooner this is over, the sooner I can end my life," Ava told her image in the mirror, devoid of any feeling.

She was emotionally barren. Demitri had taken away everything; her family and friends, her identity, dignity, compassion and now her soul. There was nothing left for Ava to lose.

-------------------------------------------------------------------------

Ava was a different woman when she arrived at the London offices the next day, bright, cheerful and conversational; all in direct contrast to how she had been, and indeed actually felt. Kayla was immediately alert to the danger signals, taking up as much of Callum's time as was reasonably possible.

Unsurprisingly, she was exceptionally cool towards Ava, sometimes plain rude. Conversely, Ava countered Kayla's rejection with beaming smiles, offering support wherever possible. Despite Kayla's best efforts, she was unable to divert all of Callum's attention. There were times when it was entirely necessary for Ava to consult with Callum in order to do her job, which gave Ava some head to head time with Callum, where they both sat closely viewing the same data.

"I'm sorry Callum, for everything. I have been in a bad place," Ava looked soulfully into his eyes. "I have a very controlling boyfriend, you see. He is jealous and extremely possessive. I know he doesn't love me; he just wants to own me and use me. In his eyes, I belong to him, that's all there is to it. There is no Ava Thompson. She has no identity. He took that from me. I don't even know who she was, and he will make sure that I never find her."

Ava looked down at her hands, unable to hold eye contact with Callum. It was the shameful truth.

"You got so close to helping me find myself Callum, so close. I was almost there. I almost broke free of his manipulation." Ava looked completely forlorn. "But his control is too powerful. He uses my emotions against me, and I don't love or believe in myself enough to take back what's mine."

"Is he the one who hit you when you left the summit meeting in Moscow?" Callum already knew the answer.

"Yes," she shrugged.

Again it was the truth. The tears that rolled down Ava's face were honest and painful, testament to her broken heart. Callum put a comforting arm around her. Ava nestled her face into his shoulder, seeking solace.

"Thank you, Callum. I have missed your tenderness so much." Ava pulled away smiling bravely. "But now we must work."

Kayla watched Ava's play for Callum over the top of her computer screen. To say that she was spitting fire was an understatement. With the greatest of difficulty, Kayla bided her time until Ava left to go to the restroom, and then went straight over to Callum.

"Watch her Callum. There is something dangerous about her. She's harbouring a dark secret." This was not a simple case of female rivalry, Kayla meant every word. "That day in the desert, when we shared minds, Ava was holding something back from me. It involved you and it wasn't love that I sensed; it was danger. Don't be a fool Callum. Always remember that you are my man again. Please don't break my heart just because I broke yours."

Kayla went back to her desk glaring at the returning Ava. She was still fuming.

Throughout the day, Callum had felt trapped. It should have been heaven having two of the most beautiful women on the planet vying for his attention. But it was Hell. He had real concerns that the rivalry could turn into a cat-fight and, with the kinetic powers that both women possessed, could so easily become a fight to the death. Eventually, Ava decided she had won enough ground for the day and backed off. It was strategically done to give her the moral high ground, which once again galled Kayla.

The next day passed very much the same, as did the next. Ava was slowly regaining Callum's interest. He was in a dilemma because he loved both women. *Sophie's Choice*, he mused.

It was fortunate for Callum that Kayla had to go away on business the next day. He was still wrestling with his conscience when Ava made the decision for him. They were sat together at her desk.

"Callum," Ava began, out of the blue, "I have to go away. I can't work this close to you and I can't come between you and Kayla."

Callum was about to protest but Ava silenced him by putting her finger on his lips.

"I must Callum. Besides I am already spoken for and I cannot let him down."

"Even though he beats you?" Callum felt angry and bereft.

"Even so," Ava whispered fatalistically, "even so. I love you so much Callum. I don't want to leave you, and I can't leave you, not until we have made love just one more time, in the knowledge that it will be our last. I want to treasure every second of that memory and hold it in my heart forever."

She looked at him with unfeigned sadness. Genuine tears of regret flowed down her cheeks as she set the honey trap that would end his life.

"Will you sleep with me tonight Callum? Please?"

-------------------------------------------------------------------------

Ava vacated her apartment, renting a suite at the Waldorf Hilton. Demitri had specifically directed that Callum's murder should take place at a hotel where his men could *tidy up* afterwards.

It was sick. Demitri talked of murder as if life had no importance. Ava was confused. She had spent a lifetime believing that God was all-forgiving, that he guided humanity towards peace and its better side. It seemed to Ava now that this was only half of the doctrine. The other half was holy war, death and destruction. What price peace? Ava wondered.

Callum had agreed to go to Ava's room, even though he was uncomfortable with the infidelity. He was essentially a faithful man, but he needed closure too. Their romance had not ended in a satisfactory way, or through one or the other falling out of love or straying. The separation had been excruciatingly painful for both of them, describing it in terms akin to bereavement. They needed to part on loving terms. From Callum's viewpoint, he couldn't fully commit to Kayla until he was at peace with Ava. He was due to arrive at seven that evening, which gave Ava another two hours to bathe and get ready.

Ava stripped and stood appraising herself in the full-length mirror. She had now fully regained the weight lost through attrition during her incarceration in the madrassa. That pleased her. But Ava regretted the loss of muscle tone, the result of not dancing for so many months. Ava wondered if she would ever dance again, sighing, knowing that she never would. She had chosen death over future. Vainly, Ava also lamented that she would not be looking her best when they discovered her body after committing suicide. Strangely it mattered to Ava how they would find her. She began to think about what would be fitting. First tough, Ava had to murder Callum. This was a duty bestowed upon her by a vengeful deity.

Ava filled the free-standing, roll top Jacuzzi bath, emptying the complimentary bottle of Molton Brown body wash into it. She let the bath fill deep and hot until the bubbles were as high as the rim, and then stepped in, one long elegant leg after the other. She lowered herself in, holding her breath as her body became accustomed to the heat, then pressed the 'start' button, relaxing as the powerful jets of water massaged her body.

Ava lay in the hot soothing waters, formulating her plan. She wanted their last union to be perfect, something for them both to take with them to eternity. Ava quickly decided that she had to divorce her mind completely from the terrible task that she was about undertake, else her resolve completely abandon her as Callum wrapped her in a blissful embrace. Ava had always been able to compartmentalise things, even disassociate herself from pain; as she had done whilst being lashed in Pakistan. She would need to draw heavily on that talent tonight.

Ava placed a bottle of Dom Perignon on ice, deciding the best course of action would be to poison his final glass of the sparkling wine, and wondered if there was enough poison for two of them. She decided not. Ava wanted Callum's death to be as quick and as painless as possible. Besides, she wanted to hold him while he took his final breath, making his death as peaceful for him as was possible. Ava had also made the decision that she would indeed take her own life, but not immediately afterwards. She deserved to suffer the anguish and guilt of her murder. To die so soon afterwards would be a quick release, a coward's way out. Ava knew that she deserved to suffer for her crime and suffer badly.

After bathing, Ava sat in front of the dressing table mirror in her black lingerie, drying and styling her hair. She had chosen to put it up, knowing how much Callum delighted in her neck. Ava imagined him placing little butterfly kisses there, shuddering with the sheer ecstasy of the thought.

Ava took the greatest of care making her face up. Callum was a man who appreciated beauty, and it would be her image that he took to eternity with him. She wanted to look perfect for him on their last night together. Callum had often commented on how important full and well-shaped eyebrows were on a woman and meticulously plucked them to perfection. He had also explained that used well, how important eyebrows were in the seduction process; how they framed a woman's eyes and drew a man to look into them. Ava applied her mascara with utmost precision to maximise her appeal. Finally, she knew that he would watch her mouth, because he always did. Ava pouted and applied the red paste, following the contours of her full mouth.

Her makeup now perfect, Ava slipped on a simple grey wrap dress with a tie waist. That won't stay on for long, she mused and her smile became a positive grin. Ava was doing a good job of diverting her mind from the stark reality of the situation. She was about to murder the man she loved. It was as simple as that. No matter how beautiful she might look on the outside, it could not compensate for the ugliness in her soul.

-------------------------------------------------------------------------

At ten minutes to seven, Callum entered the hotel, almost in a daze. His mind was in turmoil. Erotic and beautiful thoughts of meeting Ava were sullied by the guilt and treachery of cheating on Kayla. This guilt was irreconcilable. Crossing the lobby to the lift, Callum tried to force the guilt from his mind. He could not escape it though, knowing that Kayla would discover his infidelity. Nothing remains a secret from a woman of her abilities. But Callum needed to see Ava this one last time; he needed to hold her, to kiss her and to give and take pleasure from her. He needed to watch her face go through those glorious expressions of ecstasy that fascinated him and touched his soul.

Callum needed Ava. It was as simple as that. Callum didn't know how he would handle never seeing her again. That grief would surely follow, but at least they would make love in the knowledge that it was their last time, savouring the moment and locking it away in their hearts.

Callum walked down the corridor towards Ava's suite, shaking with nervous anticipation; his heart thumping in his chest. Callum took a deep breath to settle him, before knocking on the door. When Ava opened it, Callum was not prepared for the greeting that awaited him. Ava reached out, cupping the back of his head with her elegant hands and urgently pressed her mouth to his. Their kiss was long and passionate, tongues entwined; each tasting and exploring the other, reflecting their long abstinence and mutual love.

Still locked in that lover's embrace, Callum steered Ava back into the bedroom, kicked the door shut and backed Ava against it; their passionate kiss unfaltering. With her mind already focussed on the end game, Ava's fingers went purposely to Callum's shirt buttons, until at last she had freed him of the troublesome garment. Ava desperately wanted to feel Callum's skin on hers. She tugged urgently at the waist tie of her wrap dress, until at last it released. Shrugging it to the floor, Ava recalled her earlier thought that the wrap dress wouldn't last long. Not long at all, she smiled wickedly, certain that Callum had not even seen it. Ava reached behind her back to release the clip on her bra, the black lacy adornment falling to the floor, exposing her small but perfect breasts.

Now naked, except for her black panties and holdup stockings, Ava pressed herself hard against Callum. The feel of skin on skin was electrifying, sending goose bumps up her back, neck and arms. Ava felt more alive at that moment than she had ever felt, aching for Callum's touch; aching for him to take her. She needed him naked and broke their kiss to fully undress her man. Free now of his clothes, Ava felt Callum's hardness against her soft body and groaned at the image that it placed in her head. Callum lifted Ava's leg until she was in the classic tree position of Yoga, open and vulnerable. His eyes were predatory, demanding; his body willing and able. It was all that Ava wanted, all she needed and all that she had planned. Meeting Callum's eyes with equal want, Ava pulled her lace panties to one side, guiding him inside her. Her breath stopped. Just for a moment her world stopped; their union being all consuming. Ava rode the waves of ecstasy as Callum made love to her until at last she collapsed, breathless and sated.

Still lost in the aftermath of her ecstasy, Callum swept Ava up into his powerful arms as if she was a child and carried her to the bed. He pulled the covers aside and gently laid her there. Ava looked up at him trustingly as he removed the last of her underwear. There was mischief in his eyes though, and Ava wondered what he had planned for her. She also wondered at how Callum had always made her feel safe and respected, whatever those wicked intentions were. Ava felt suffocated by her love for Callum. Terrible thoughts of what she must do to him tonight suddenly consumed her, blighting that special moment. Ava knew that she had to keep her objectivity to perform the heinous act that she had so meticulously planned, and chased those dark thoughts from her mind.

God's will be done, she reminded herself. The dread and guilt was all consuming though and contrasted so completely with the emotions she was feeling.

"You look sad little one. Let me please you," he observed and grinned.

Ava immediately knew Callum's plan, and what he meant by *please you*. Making no objection, Ava parted her legs to encourage him. As he lowered his mouth to pleasure her, Ava bit her lip in anticipation of what was to follow. In her mind, this was the most intimate of all sexual acts and Ava did not allow all her lovers to pleasure her in this way. However, she had no hesitation permitting Callum. She knew instinctively that he would treat her with the gentle respect required. Ava could feel his cool tongue touching her intermittently with kisses, and her body responded to the delicious sensation. Ava's fists clenched as she struggled to cope with the intensity of the sensation, tugging at Callum's hair to guide him. Involuntarily, Ava clamped his head between her thighs as her orgasm heightened, crying out in delight as the divine feelings swept over her body. She flushed red as the heat rose from within her and she laid still, content from his wonderful act and one of the best orgasm of her life.

With his customary smirk, Callum moved up the bed to kiss Ava on the lips, his tongue feasting hungrily on hers. Ava's own sweet taste still lingered in his mouth and her musky scent, on his breath. It stirred glorious feelings within Ava and at that moment, she felt the sexiest woman alive.

After that, the hours passed too quickly for Ava, fluctuating between that caring gentle sex, to urgent powerful sex, and then all things in between; only pausing to cuddle and kiss, before it would start over. Ava was delaying the inevitable, but had to finally concede that it was time to do her duty. Silent tears welled in her eyes. She was filled with remorse that this would be their last encounter.

"I need to pee and bathe Callum. Do you mind?"

She sat on the edge of the bed looking down at him lovingly.

"Feel free Ava. I can't promise that I won't mess you up all over again though," he grinned boyishly and Ava left him with a false smile.

The menacing vision of Demitri entered her head, along with the stark realisation of the mission that she had to fulfil; her duty to *Allah* and his prophets.

Ava left the comfort and safety of their embrace, now feeling alone, vulnerable and disgusted with herself. Thankfully it was cool in the bathroom in comparison to their warm bed, allowing Ava to compose herself. She leaned against the chill of the tiled wall. It was refreshing and served to focus her mind. Ava looked at the *'his' and 'hers'* sinks beneath the mirrored wall, its poignancy hitting her in the chest, knowing *his* would never be used. Ava ran the hot water into the bath, emptying another complimentary bottle of Molton Brown body wash. She needed to remove the intoxicating smell of sex from her skin and rid the delightful images of Callum from her mind. They were the Devil's temptation, just as the old Imam had warned her of.

Ava plunged into the bubbly bath, whilst the hot water continued to pour. She sat cross-legged in the lotus position, taking the brief opportunity to focus her breathing and mind. After a few minutes, she relented and lay back, submerging her head in the cleansing water. With her eyes closed and ears under water, she was unaware of Callum standing in the doorway watching her, noticing the effect that a lifetime of dancing had taken on her body. Her long and slender legs were flexibly tucked under her and her hip bones rose out of the water with the bubbles tantalisingly hiding her modesty. Her stomach was flat, slightly concave. Callum moved closer, intrigued by the small pool of water that had collected in her belly button. He had the ridiculous urge to kneel beside her and drink it but Ava's eyes flew open.

Ava was unnerved at being watched. She much preferred to be the observer. By the time Callum reached the bath, Ava had already sat up. He perched on the side of the bath and ran his hands across Ava's shoulders and up her neck. As he did so, he massaged away the tiny knots until she visibly relaxed.

Callum stepped into the generous sized bath and sat down behind Ava, easing her backwards to lie against him, his tanned skin touching her pale body. He had her small breasts cupped innocently in his hands. They chatted about light-hearted, unimportant things such as commenting on the size of the shower gel bottles. They reflected on the difference between London and Moscow's weather, reminiscing about Ava's embarrassment at leaving the bar so urgently, obviously to make love. She could tell that he was watching her intently, feeling perfectly at ease. The more they spoke, the more Ava enjoyed his company. Callum had completely distracted her from her mission, from the *real* world

Ava suddenly felt light-headed. The combination of the heat of the water, the Champagne and the aftermath of their amazing sex had made her feel quite strange. She needed space to think.

"Go back to bed sweetheart. I need the loo then I will pour us a drink." Ava's smile was thin.

Callum obligingly left the bath, water cascading from his lean body. He took a bathrobe from the peg, kissed Ava tenderly on the forehead and returned to their bed. He had never felt more satisfied, more complete than he did right then, wondering what he could do to make her stay forever.

--------------------------------------------------------------------------

Ava stepped out of the hot bath, still feeling faint and nauseous. She crouched to steady herself, and then lay on her back on the tiled floor; the coolness of the ceramic quickly bringing her mind back into focus. Ava lay there for several minutes, formulating the final, deadly acts of her plan, her mind now set on her duties. Ava stood, took her robe and pushed the bathroom door fully shut. Taking her toilet bag from the sink unit, she rummaged inside finding the deadly phial. Her hands trembled almost uncontrollably. Looking into the mirror, her reflection was that of a murderess and a traitor. Ava hated herself, knowing she could end it all now, either by just walking away or by taking the poison herself. But Ava had sworn her allegiance to Demitri, and pledged an oath to their God, one that she could not break. Ava looked her reflection in the eye and spoke out loud her vow to that heartless God.

"When this is over you are no God of mine. You can take your hate, your manipulation and your prophets and go to Hell where you all belong!"

The last remaining remnants of Ava's radicalisation and brain-washing at the madrassa kept her tenuously on track to complete her mission. The mirror shattered at the intensity of her hate, distorting her reflection so that she resembled the monster that she felt.

"Honey are you OK?" Callum's inflection showed concern at the sound of breaking glass.

"I dropped a tumbler Callum, don't worry," she lied. "I am coming in now."

Ava slipped the phial into the pocket of her gown. When she returned to the room, Ava's emotions were on autopilot. She needed to execute the plan without recourse to her own feelings.

"Champagne my darling?" Her smile showed nothing of her intent.

"Is the Pope a Catholic?" Callum replied with a grin. The religious connotation was not what Ava wanted to hear right then.

Ava took the Champagne flutes from the bedside table, filling them at the minibar. She took the phial from her robe pocket, breaking the thin glass neck. Ava looked over her shoulder to check that her actions were hidden. Callum was beaming back at her lovingly, crushing her heart in a way that caused her to look away. Ava emptied the poison into his glass, giving it a swirl. She forced a brave smile, before turning and walking over to him. Callum was still smiling at her as she sat down beside him. Ava handed him his drink as casually as she could.

"Cheers," she offered. "Do you remember the first time we made love and you raised a glass and said *bottoms up*"? Ava forced a smile.

"Vividly!" he grinned wolfishly. "And you said that it would be more customary, and certainly more gentlemanly, if I was to save that position for later. Well I did."

Callum winked at her knowingly. Ava had to clear her mind of that treasured memory to focus on what she had to do.

"Yes, well. Bottoms up and down in one lover," Ava encouraged.

They clinked their glasses together and downed their drinks swiftly. Ava immediately took Callum's glass, placing them both on the bedside table before lying down beside him. She looked eternally sad.

"I want to hold you Callum," Ava's voice sounded like a plea.

She put her arms around Callum and embraced him lovingly, his head resting on her breast. Ava gently stroked the hair at his temple, soothing him. They lay silent for a while. Callum's face was turned to the side so that he couldn't see Ava's. If he could, he would have seen the silent tears flowing in copious rivers down her cheeks.

"I'm cold," he said at last.

Ava pulled the covers over him, starting to shush him, rocking him like a baby.

"I feel so strange."

Callum's words slurred as the neurotoxin began to take effect on his muscular system. His breathing quickly became irregular, until he had to fight for each precious breath. Ava turned his face to hers, so that he could watch her as he passed into eternity. She gasped when she noticed that he no longer had a blink reflex. The last words he spoke were almost inaudible.

"What have you done Ava?" his eyes were staring blankly into space.

"I'm sorry Callum but it is God's will," she choked out the inadequate words, wondering what kind of God could condone this.

Callum wanted to tell Ava something, but his voice was so feint that she had to put her ear next to his lips to hear him.

"I have always loved you Ava. I will always love you." Callum hadn't finished what he wanted to say. He took one last painful rasping breath before quietly uttering. "I forgive you Ava."

Those words of undying love were Callum's last before slipping away peacefully in Ava's arms. She recalled the lines from one of

Rumi's poems, taught to her by the old Imam in Pakistan. Rumi was a thirteenth century Islamic scholar whom Ava had great respect for. She spoke the words as Callum moved between worlds:

*'Out beyond ideas of wrongdoing and right doing,*

*there is a field. I will meet you there.'*

---

Ava lay there with Callum's lifeless body in her arms for several hours. She was in a state of deep shock and hadn't noticed that he was now cold to the touch. Ava had talked to him all the while, as if he was still alive and listening to her. She related each and every precious memory they had shared together to his unhearing ears. Finally, when there were no more tears to cry, she slid out from underneath him leaving Callum in the stiffness of rigour.

Ava never looked back at him after that. She just gathered her possessions and packed them in her valise, picked up her mobile dutifully, selected Demitri's name and wrote the simple message:

*'It is done. Waldorf Hilton, London. Suite 2010.'*

---

Demitri and the Hydra were still locked in a lovers' embrace following an evening of intimacy. The message alert sounded on Demitri's phone. He read it and smiled. Nearly thirty years of planning had gone into Ava's grooming and tonight it had paid dividends. Callum Knight was dead at last; others would follow.

"*Agápe mou*, the Kaplinski girl has finally completed her assignment. Knight is dead!" He kissed her cheek enthusiastically. "Next I will get her to utilise her charms to gain Bud Lewinski's affections."

The Hydra put her hand on Demitri's arm as if to hold him back.

"No, my love, that is no longer the way forward."

Hydie was a wise woman and Demitri waited for her council.

"That would only be wasting precious time. Our hold on Ava Kaplinski is barely tenuous. The shock of what she has just done is likely to make her question everything in her life. She will eventually shake off the chains of radicalisation and the sham of her religion. Ultimately, she will conclude that none of the acts that she has been tasked with were God's will and that it was our manipulation. We cannot afford for the rage inside her to mount and feed her powers. She would become unstoppable, almost as powerful as Maelströminha herself."

"So, what is the way?" Demitri asked, easing himself onto his side so that he could look at her face.

"For now, we bring her in from the cold, back to your research laboratories. Kayla Lovell would *read* her soon enough anyway and kill her. Ava could not keep such a dark secret from her. Tell Ava to prepare the lab for me and I will come and meet her there. Once she gets me access to the fifth dimension, I can change the world in moments. Create my own version of reality, a reality where all Angels cease to exist. Genocide of the Angel species will be immediate and final."

Demitri listened, watching as the Hydra's face transitioned from sublime beauty to burning fanatic. When Hydie Papandreou was in this frame of mind, she was a woman to fear; even the cups on the bedside table jangled on the saucers trembling with the sheer kinetic energy of her malevolence.

--------------------------------------------------------------------------

Ava walked aimlessly, hour upon hour, through the streets of London, numbed by the atrocity she had committed. Temperatures through the night had dropped to below zero, but Ava, dressed only in her office suit and blouse, was oblivious to the cold. Nothing could penetrate into the dark place that Ava had regressed to.

Dawn broke at last, flooding Ava's surroundings with a soft yellow light. Dawning usually brought with it a feeling of renewal and hope, but Ava was beyond hope. She had committed a sin, not holy retribution as Demitri had described the murder, but an unforgivably foul and evil sin. Ava couldn't find any way to justify what she had done. For the first time ever, she was glad that her mother was dead and wouldn't have to face her with the shame of the atrocity that she had performed. Life had no value to Ava now. There was no point in her existence. She hadn't even got the credibility of being a mother herself and to have brought something beautiful into the world. Ava felt ugly in spirit and a curse to mankind. She had searched for a mosque throughout the night, in the desperate hope she could redeem herself through prayer. When at last she found one, there had apparently been yet another terrorist attack in Paris, by the so-called ISIS. Ava read the billboard. It proclaimed that:

*'Islam condemns all forms of extremity, murder and attacks on innocent people. The Quran tells us that those who kill a single man, is as if they killed all of humanity, and those who revive but one, is as if they revived all of humanity.'*

These simple words damned Ava to Hell. She had taken Callum's sweet life, justifying the murder as doing God's will. How could she be so stupid, she wondered?

These are not the words of a murderous doctrine, Ava considered, and not in the spirit of the teachings of the old Imam at the madrassa.

Ava found no solace in prayer. Those words of peace and reflection on the notice haunted her as she continued to wander without direction. Somehow, her aimless meandering took her to Waterloo Bridge. Ava looked out across the icy waters, then down to the powerful currents and eddies below. They seemed to be calling to her. Ava was already climbing the railings as the message alert sounded on her phone. She looked at the text. It was from Demitri:

'*Well done Ava. I am so proud of you. Meet me at my research laboratories in Moscow the day after tomorrow. I will reward you then x.*'

A kiss, she mused, finally a kiss.

Ava climbed to the top of the railings, balancing there precariously for a few moments, looking down into the deep water of the Thames. She tossed the phone into the water, watching as the brilliance of the screen sank into the murky depths, wishing that it was Demitri sinking instead.

"I will see you in Hell first!"

Ava screamed out her last words of defiance and jumped into the black turbulent waters. The powerful current drew her inexorably down, taking away all the pain and suffering.

-------------------------------------------------------------------------

## Chapter 22

It was ten o'clock in the morning. Kayla sat alone in the London office drinking her third cup of coffee whilst opening the morning mail. She hadn't slept well, hardly at all really. The little sleep she did manage was deeply troubled. Her dreams were vivid, always a sign to her that something had gone terribly wrong, or was about to. These dreams were invariably harbingers of bad news. Kayla was filled with dread, particularly as neither Callum nor Ava had turned up for work. Both were meticulous time-keepers and this didn't bode well. She had tried calling them on their mobiles and emailing them, but without success. By eleven o'clock, she was certain that something was wrong. Kayla contacted the police for any information concerning road traffic accidents or breaking news, but there was nothing.

The fact that both were missing was also a massive cause for concern. She knew that Ava still harboured attraction for Callum and would stop at nothing to rekindle their relationship. There had to be more to come about that, she lamented.

Both of their cars carried tracking systems, so she logged on to the tracking software and ran through the last eighteen hours movements, starting with Ava's car. She was the first to leave the office yesterday at 15.12 hours, arriving at the Waldorf Hilton at 15.46. The car had stayed there until 01.16 hours the next morning and then the tracker had stopped functioning. She made a call to the hotel, asking them to check whether the car was still parked there. It was not.

Kayla placed another call to their Internal Investigations department to track Ava's car using the metropolitan CCTV cameras, then ran through the data generated from Callum's tracker. Callum had left the office just over three hours later at 18.16 hours, arriving at the Waldorf Hilton at 18.48. The enormity of the situation hit Kayla like a punch in her stomach, initially stunning her, before the feeling turned to nausea. She felt like she was about to throw up.

"You fucking traitorous bitch!" she cursed aloud, violently sweeping everything off her desk. "I'll kill you when I find you!"

Kayla meant that literally. She continued to monitor the data on Callum's tracker. His signal had also ceased transmission, but a little later at 01.25. Again, she called Internal Investigations to search for the car. Kayla's first and irrational thoughts were that they had run off together but, if they had, they wouldn't have deactivated the trackers. They would simply have abandoned their cars. No, there was something far more sinister about this situation. She needed help. If they were in danger, then even minutes could make a difference. She needed some high-level support. Nobody was better placed to give this than Emanuel Goldberg, the current head of MI6 and personal friend of hers and Callum's. She dialled his number. He picked up on the third ring.

"Goldberg speaking," his voice matched his affable nature.

Apart from being head of MI6, Emanuel Goldberg was the most senior of the Patriarchs in the Angel organisation. As such, he enjoyed the confidence of Maelströminha herself, with whom he consulted on an almost daily basis.

"Emanuel, I'm so relieved you've answered. I'm so scared and need your help."

All the words were rushed out in a split second, underlining the enormity of Kayla's fear.

"Steady Kayla, take a breath. What is it?"

"Callum and Ava have gone missing. Well at least I think so." She added, still holding on to hope.

Kayla felt a little foolish at having made such an early presumption, but Emanuel's acute Angel abilities had also sensed the disappearance.

"You are seldom wrong Kayla. I have learned to trust your instincts over the years."

Emanuel had been like a father to Kayla during those confused adolescence years. He was a gentle giant, with a mane of curly white hair and smiling blue eyes. Emanuel was attentive and forgiving, but fair and just. Exactly what Kayla needed when she was first experiencing the sheer magnitude of her psychic and telekinetic abilities. The onset couldn't have happened at a worse time for Kayla, her hormones being totally out of control. To compound Ava's precarious situation, her father was suffering the early stages of an illness and in no fit state to guide her. Emanuel had counselled Kayla through this period and dealt with the carnage that she had caused during her teenage mood-swings. Their closeness had endured the test of time. Kayla felt secure and comfortable in Emanuel's presence, enough to let the tears fall. Despite this, Kayla tried to maintain a pragmatic approach.

"They left the office about three hours apart yesterday. Both rendezvoused at the Waldorf Hilton." Kayla's voice caught and she only just managed to hold back a sob.

Emanuel detected Kayla's turmoil. He knew that she was in love with Callum and that her love was reciprocated, lamenting how young lovers always managed to torment each other so. Kayla battled through what she had to say.

"It appears to have been a lovers' tryst. Afterwards they both left the hotel at around half past one in the morning, or at least that's when their trackers stopped responding. After that, their cars seem to have dropped off the face of the Earth."

Kayla had more to say but Emanuel stopped her in order to process the information he had received to this point.

"Kayla. First, you don't yet know if it was a lovers' tryst. You can only suspect that it was. Don't let that cloud your judgement. The cars' trackers clearly stopped at the time you say, but they may not have left the car park until much later. You should consider that the registration plates may have been changed, allowing them to leave the car park undetected. Get them to re-run the CCTV data and look for all cars of their type and colour, whatever the registration. This will greatly enhance your chances of finding them." It was good advice. Kayla continued.

"I have asked the police if there have been any accidents or incidents involving either of the vehicles, or Callum and Ava. The police have already confirmed that they have not. However they have put out an all-points bulletin, but so far nothing," Kayla naturally used the American idiom.

"That's good Kayla. I can augment the search utilising my men and resources and send a team down to the hotel to check the room out for any clues or DNA."

Although Emanuel had not insinuated it, Kayla immediately imagined soiled bed sheets. The painful thought of the aftermath of their lovemaking made her go faint, once again turning her stomach.

"Thank you, Emanuel; I can always count on you. It's just that I can't." Kayla choked, unable to finish her sentence.

"You can't what Kayla?" Emanuel's heart went out to her. He sensed where she was going.

"I can't *sense* him anymore. I know that he's already dead."

At that point Kayla broke down in inconsolable tears. Emanuel also shared these skills. He sensed the loss too. Several minutes passed before Kayla had recovered enough to speak again.

"I will kill that bitch when I get my hands on her!" Kayla swore.

Emanuel had no doubt that Kayla was capable of following through on her threat.

"You cannot Kayla, you don't have that luxury. Ava still holds the key to all of our destinies. To kill her would be to kill us all," Emanuel pointed out firmly.

They were sound words of caution. Kayla knew it. She kept her own counsel. Kayla wasn't ready to let go of her anger though, nor in truth her plans of vengeance.

"We always knew that there was a massive risk; Callum as much as any of us." Emanuel pointed out. "Maelströminha had seen little chance of any favourable outcome for him in her mirrors, whatever the scenario."

Emanuel could tell that Kayla needed his company to get through this and offered support.

"Shall we meet for lunch and compare any progress; my club perhaps?"

"Of course," Kayla replied, "that would be lovely."

----------------------------------------------------------------------

Yuri had kept a covert vigil over Ava Kaplinski since the night of his faked murder. His only respite was when she was with Callum, who could also provide that safety. Even that was no real respite though. He could see that the couple had fallen deeply in love with each other, which was heart-breaking for him. Watching the woman he loved from afar, was singularly the most painful thing Yuri had ever suffered in his life. In comparison, the beating he took with the baseball bats was just a minor discomfort. Yuri still took joy in the occasional glimpse of her, which made his heart swell impossibly and his pulse race. She had recently broken up with Callum and Kayla was on the scene again. This turn in fortune had given Yuri hope, a second chance to win Ava's heart when everything was over. That single thought was sufficient to boost his flagging morale.

It felt bizarre to Yuri that he was looking out for the only woman on Earth who could possibly save the world from destruction, a woman who was totally oblivious to her own importance and destiny. The only thing he knew for certain, gleaned from Maelströminha's divinations, was that should the battle to save the world ever be fought, it would take place in Demitri's research laboratories. Or at least that was what the current images of the future foretold.

As Yuri understood it, if the fifth dimension was breached, then any intruder would have the potential to manipulate outcomes, perception and create new possibilities. The order of things could change almost instantly, according to the intruder's whim. Maelströminha had described it as akin to the performing of miracles; similar to when Jesus had fed the five thousand with just five loaves and two fish. It mattered not whether you believed the religious connotation, but the principal of creating something out of nothing was a massive part of the reality behind the fifth dimension. Yuri had asked Maelströminha if she herself could access the fifth dimension and prevent the catastrophe from happening. Her answer both surprised and humbled him.

'*Dearest Yuri, do you not think that I have not thought and agonised about that? And what then would separate me from them, if I chose to take up the mantle of dictator?*'

He remembered she had looked at him, serenely calm. She was a creature of total perfection.

'*I must trust that there is goodness in all of us and that goodness will prevail, otherwise we are already beyond salvation. You Yuri must do your part, as Ava must do hers. Trust in her and protect her, so that she might one day fulfil her destiny.*'

At that point Maelströminha's image in the mirror faded away but her almost religious presence remained with him for hours after.

Yuri had parked across the road from their London offices, waiting for Ava to leave work. She appeared at the door at a little after three o'clock and drove straight to the Waldorf Hilton. Yuri followed several cars behind Ava, watching out for vehicles that either kept up with her, or otherwise acted suspiciously. There were none. She parked in the hotel car park and went straight inside. Yuri waited for two minutes, and then went in to check out the lobby for any suspicious characters. Again there were none. Yuri returned to the car park and photographed the number plates of every car there and up-loaded them to the Angels central data base. Within a minute, he received confirmation that none of the vehicles presented any known risk. He returned to his car and settled down for his usual long wait until the morning.

A couple of hours later, and to his complete surprise, Callum pulled into the car park. Yuri slouched in his seat. This was unexpected and the worst possible news. This must have meant that their love affair was back on. Every second that passed after that felt like an eternity to him.

-----------------------------------------------------------------------

At a little after midnight, Ava appeared at the hotel entrance with a small bag in her hand. Yuri had just been joined by his colleague Joe, who was to relieve him for a few hours. They ducked down to lower their profiles, so as not to be visible to her. Quite surprisingly, Ava didn't walk into the car park, but turned left in the direction of the Aldwych Theatre. Joe started the engine and pulled away, following her from a distance. Yuri immediately noticed that something was wrong. Ava was a ballerina with classic posture and deportment. What he saw now was a beaten and broken woman; slouched and walking mechanically with no apparent purpose.

Callum has dumped her, was Yuri's first thought, and immediately regretted his selfishness. It was unworthy of him. Ava crossed the road several times between there and Holborn. Yuri cringed at each crossing. She was totally oblivious to the traffic. Even the sound of car horns and the irate abuse of the drivers, went without any recognition.

Yuri's brief was absolutely clear, 'follow but do not engage'. It was painful for him. He did however request paramedic support to be available in the event of a tragedy. Ava seemed to have no direction, no plan. She stopped at the billboard in front of a Mosque in Holborn, where she stood motionless for some minutes. Eventually, she turned and merged with the other worshippers entering the Mosque. Less than an hour later, Ava left much as she went in, almost catatonic. If she was seeking comfort from her God, then she had found none, he lamented.

Yuri knew that Ava's religion was a sham, something forced upon her by others. She had no idea of the love that Islam preached, only the hate that the false prophets expounded. He had reason to be further concerned about Ava's mental state. The temperature was well below zero. Despite not wearing a coat, Ava wasn't in that typical huddled position that seems to bring comfort against the cold or adversity. In fact there was nothing about Ava that resembled her former self. Yuri turned to his partner Joe, a young recruit and another Angel, looking for some fieldwork experience.

"Ava's lost it Joe. Something has happened; something sinister. I can feel it. More than that, I keep receiving fragments of her thoughts. She has lost control of them and they aren't making any sense. She's repeating something over and over again, to the exclusion of everything else."

Joe was a *lesser* Angel, one who had many dilutions of his bloodline and therefore unable to pick up on Ava's thoughts.

"What's she saying?" he asked.

"I'm not sure," Yuri replied, still puzzled. "It can't possibly be, but it has the rhythm of a nursery rhyme."

Ava walked south down Chancery Lane, past Temple Church to the embankment. She turned right and walked westwards along the river to Waterloo Bridge, then turned onto it towards the south bank, stopping at mid-span. They watched incomprehensively as Ava put her bag down, seemingly to gaze out across the Thames. Much to their alarm, she began to climb onto the railings.

"Jesus Joe, she's going to jump!" Yuri shouted in panic.

Joe pressed down the accelerator and sped towards her, now teetering on the top rail. She appeared to be looking at something in her hand, her phone maybe, Yuri thought. Whatever it was, she tossed it into the river. Just as they skidded to a halt next to her, Ava jumped. Yuri was two seconds too late.

"Get her bag!" he yelled, dragging his coat off as he ran.

Yuri vaulted the railings in one fluid move, desperately in pursuit of the woman he loved.

--------------------------------------------------------------------------------

Ava was immediately consumed by the icy blackness of the Thames, unaware of how she had got there and hadn't intended to jump. It was just that, on the spur of the moment, jumping seemed to be the right and only thing to do. She had not made any effort to protect herself in the fall and had therefore landed badly, concussing herself, driving the air out of her body. The strong currents drew her down into their murky depths and bowled her along with their power. Ava was violently channelled to a powerful eddy that spun her around and drove her up to the surface momentarily, before consuming her again. Finally the peaceful darkness of oblivion came over her, mercifully removing all of her pain and guilt.

--------------------------------------------------------------------------------

Yuri angled himself to land feet first, his eyes scanning the choppy water as he fell, hoping to spot the woman he had loved for so long, but she was gone. The coldness of the winter water took Yuri's breath away, numbing his brain, the very second he surfaced; Yuri began swimming powerfully downstream to make up valuable distance already lost between them. Just for a second Yuri thought that he caught a glimpse of something white on the surface just feet in front of him but then it was gone. He duck-dived, pulling himself down with his strong arms in the hope that it was Ava. The shock of coming face to face with her was a million to one chance, especially in the depths of the Thames. Yuri gasped, losing valuable air. He grabbed Ava with one arm and clawed at the water with the other, kicking for all he was worth, his lungs screaming. When they finally broke surface, he sucked in precious air, along with a mouthful of water, and choked for several more valuable seconds while he orientated himself.

Yuri could see that Ava wasn't breathing. He needed to get her to land quickly in an attempt to resuscitate her. Yuri estimated that the ice-cold water would keep Ava's vital organs alive for a maximum of five more minutes. That was his window of opportunity to save her, just five precious minutes. He struck out diagonally across the current, towards the north bank of the Thames, next to Blackfriars Bridge. Yuri swam as if his own life depended on it, his heart nearly bursting with the effort. He could see a mud bank that had accumulated at the side of the bridge, where he could land her. The current was obliging, swinging them past Blackfriars Millennium Pier and onwards towards the bridge. Yuri had to give one last desperate push to reach the bank and landed Ava there.

There wasn't a second to lose. He quickly checked Ava's mouth for obstructions. Thankfully there were none, but her lips were blue and her pupils dilated and staring. Yuri took off his digital watch, shining the display directly into her eye. There was an immediate contraction of her pupil. This was an alleluia moment for Yuri. Ava was still alive! He worked quickly giving thirty heart compressions followed by two breaths into her mouth. At the same time, he used his Angel skills to locate the dying embers of Ava's mind, in an effort to pull her back from the abyss. There was no response, none. He repeated the sequence over and again but still nothing.

"Ava! Come back to me. I need you!" he shouted pitifully as a last futile gesture.

Yuri looked stricken, a broken and desolated man. Ava was dead. After all she had been through, he had failed her. Yuri felt the enormity of that guilt crushing his chest, so that he could barely draw a breath. He closed Ava's eyelids over her sightless eyes for the final time and then kissed her cheek. He continued talking to her softly as if she could still hear him, running his fingers lovingly through her matted hair as he did so.

"You will never know how much I have loved you Ava and for how long. You will never know how much I have worshipped you, waited for you and hungered for you. These things you will never know."

Only then did Yuri truly feel the coldness and loneliness of his despair. He was knelt at Ava's side, looking up to the heavens with his arms outstretched.

"Why?" he beseeched, as if God could help him.

Yuri shivered. It was a mixture of the mind numbing cold and a supernatural chill. He closed his eyes and cupped his face in his hands, then cried for the first time since he was a child. Yuri was in shock. In his delirium, he imagined that he heard Ava's voice.

"I do know that you love me Yuri. Deep down I have known it for a very long time."

Yuri imagined Ava's arms around him, comforting him. He felt her soft kisses on the backs of his hands that were still covering his eyes. It seemed real, too real. Yuri slowly took his hands from his face, afraid to look. He thought for a moment that Ava was there kneeling in front of him, but that couldn't be.

"Thank you for caring Yuri. I felt your love and it brought me back from the brink." Her smile was tender and loving. "You gave me a reason to fight."

Yuri reached out to touch the apparition in front of him. To his surprise his hands found substance.

"It can't be." Yuri didn't dare to blink and risk her disappearing, losing her again. "Ava?"

He had underestimated Ava's Angel resilience, which was far stronger than his own abilities.

"Yes Yuri, it is me. Thank you." Ava looked puzzled and then asked. "I thought you were dead, that Bortnik had killed you. Does that mean I'm in heaven?"

"No, it means that I am," Yuri corrected and really meant it.

It was too cryptic for Ava's numbed mind. She simply kissed him gently on the lips.

"I'm cold; will you take me home? I don't want to be alone, not for some time."

Yuri's face lit up as he smiled back at her, reaching out to touch her again just to make sure that he wasn't dreaming. He searched his pocket, relieved to find that his phone was still there, and that he had bought the waterproof sports model.

"Pick us up on the north bank Joe; we are next to Blackfriars Bridge. Have the heater on full blast and there's my bedding in the boot too. Call one of our medics and get him to come to my apartment immediately. Ava needs checking out."

"Got that Yuri; will be there in five."

-------------------------------------------------------------------------

Ava remained silent on the journey back to Yuri's apartment. She was still frozen to the core, but at least she was dry and huddled in blankets with Yuri cuddling her. The cuddle was as much for Yuri's benefit as for Ava's, conducted under the ruse of friendship and the need to keep her warm. Joe glimpsed them in the rear-view mirror. Yuri's besotted smile said it all, and Joe couldn't help but chuckle. From Ava's perspective, all she would ever remember about the journey would be feeling safe again.

The medic was already waiting for them when they arrived at Yuri's apartment. It was James Bull, a friend of many years. His initial appraisal was that Ava did not appear to be in any immediate danger and directed that she should relax in a hot bath, with her limbs outside, before giving her a thorough examination afterwards. When she retired to the bathroom James took the opportunity to talk to Yuri alone. He looked grave, as doctors usually do.

"Even without closer examination, I can tell that Ava is suffering from acute shock Yuri. She has been through some kind of emotional trauma and appears to be taking time out in self-defence. Can you think of anything that might have caused that?"

"No, well nothing new that is. It's quite possibly common knowledge, but Callum and Ava were lovers. They split up a while ago for reasons unknown, and Callum has picked up his relationship with Kayla again. That seemed to have brought back Ava's interest in him, and she's made a play for him ever since. Whether that's caused her anguish or not, I couldn't say. You would have to ask Callum, or her."

"I intend to, have no doubt about that Yuri."

James tugged at his chin in thought. Although he was only in his early thirties, James was old for his years and took nothing for granted. He continued with his assessment.

"But I don't think that alone would have caused her condition. Ava's deportment, the look in her eyes and her apparent isolation, is more akin to suffering a road traffic accident or bereavement, than a lost love. Is there anything else?"

"Well, as you will have already heard after the debrief following our mission in Iran, Ava is closely linked to Demitri Papandreou, the most powerful of the Shadow Senators. There could quite easily be something going on there," Yuri suggested.

"Has she got her phone?" James asked, considering the Demitri connection. "We could run a check on her calls over the last twenty-four hours."

"No, that's in the Thames. I have her bag with her laptop in it though."

"Does she know you have it?" James raised an inquisitive brow.

"No, and I don't suppose she'll give it another thought. Ava has barely commented on being alive, let alone worry about something like that James."

"Good, I'll take her laptop and have her SIM card and hard drive checked out. It's not quite as good as her phone, but we'll get an insight to what she's been up to. I can get it back here by mid-afternoon," James confirmed.

He left to check on his patient and Yuri took the opportunity to pour himself a large Vodka. Purely medicinal, he assured himself.

Yuri fell into his armchair and slouched there, dog-tired. His heart and mind were still racing, through adrenaline comedown and the enormity of the situation he now found himself in. Yuri's clothes had all but dried on him, but he still felt the chill of the icy waters. He needed to get Ava bathed, checked out and put to bed, before he could even begin to think about his own needs. Yuri swilled the vodka around the glass and downed the drink in one, its warming effect flushing his body. He breathed out a deep sigh of satisfaction. The situation was unreal, he had the love of his life in his apartment, but broken and in bits. Once again, Yuri struggled with his conscience, both ethically and emotionally. His brief was to watch over Ava, not to fall in love with her. She was his work, not pleasure and besides, Ava was his boss's woman. None of that helped though, Yuri was too deeply smitten.

James returned an hour later and sat with Yuri, who by then was enjoying his fourth vodka. James could see that Yuri was also suffering from mild shock and needed help. He searched his bag and found the pills he was looking for.

"I want you to stop drinking and take these." James handed Yuri the medicine. "They are the same as I have given to Ava, but you are on half of the dose; two every six hours for the next twenty-four."

Just in case the alcohol ban was immediate, Yuri took the initiative of downing the glass in his hand. James continued.

"Ava is already asleep and I don't expect her to awaken until well into the night, so you can afford to get yourself some rest too. When did you last sleep by the way? You look dreadful."

"Thanks Doc. You know just how to make a man feel good," he rebuffed, giving James a wry grin.

Yuri was confused by the combined effect of tiredness, vodka and Ava. He had to think hard about the question before formulating some kind of an answer.

"Well I was up at six o'clock yesterday morning to watch Ava as she drove to work. Then as I was changing shifts with Joe, it all kicked off. So, I guess about twenty-nine hours in all."

Yuri was clearly running on a mixture of adrenaline and vodka.

"OK, take a shower and straight to bed then." James took Yuri's glass and gestured for him to get up. "Meanwhile, I'll get Ava's laptop checked and back to you as soon as I can. I'll need a key to your door though, because both you and Ava will be dead to the world."

James paused to consider what he needed to say.

"Look Yuri, you should know something. Kayla has raised an alarm. Callum has gone missing and she suspects that Ava is involved." He let that piece of news sink in. "You know she is seldom, if ever wrong Yuri. We all want you to be careful."

"But that is ridiculous James. Ava couldn't possibly hurt Callum; she's so obviously in love with him."

Yuri's tone was entirely defensive of the woman he had loved for some considerable time.

"Maybe so," James replied, "but humour me and be careful anyway. OK?"

With that James left the apartment, leaving Yuri somewhere between deeply troubled and heaven.

-------------------------------------------------------------------------

Yuri awoke to the smell of cooking bacon, still befuddled by the effect of the sleeping tablets, vodka and the induced stupor of sleep. It took some time before he had pieced it all together, deducing that it was James cooking breakfast, back from running a check on Ava's laptop and SIM.

He looked at the clock. It was six in the morning, almost a day since he had pulled Ava out of those freezing waters. He still felt groggy and confused. Christ! What did that mad Doctor give me? Yuri wondered, struggling to put any thoughts together.

He swung his legs over the side of the bed and stood in his briefs, stretching in front of the full-length mirror, studying himself critically. Although now in his mid-thirties, he was probably in the best shape of his life, he decided. Yuri wasn't a man who had to spend hours in the gym; he didn't need to. He was blessed with Angel genetics that gave him natural muscularity. Yuri made a mental note though; more cardio vascular exercise was needed. That lifesaving swim in the cold, turbulent currents of the

Thames was almost too much for him. His lack of absolute fitness had nearly lost Ava, and he could never have lived with that.

Yuri walked out through the lounge into the kitchen, inelegantly scratching his body as some men do in the moments immediately after waking, and came face to face with Ava.

"Jesus! I'm so sorry Ava," he gasped, pulling his hands out of his pants, turning and leaving abruptly, in huge embarrassment.

It was just what Ava needed and she laughed out loud.

"Don't leave on my account!" she called out after him, and then added. "Nice bum by the way!"

Ava laughed mercilessly. It really was just what the Doctor ordered. She had woken early and spent several hours going through all that had happened in the last thirty-six. The first three of them were just sobbing her heart out, lost in pain and despair. After that, there were no more tears to cry. All that was left was remorse and guilt. Finally, Ava could focus on the truth or at least the truth as she perceived it. She had reached the point of epiphany, at last realising that the dreadful thing she had done, was somehow programmed into her. It was as if she had no choice in the matter at all. Come to that, Ava wasn't even aware of having made any decisions of her own since leaving the Bolshoi months ago, none. Everything seemed like it was preordained.

That thought had a tenuous connection to her last conversation with Leonardo da Vinci. He had reminded her that she only had one chance in life and that she needed to make it count. Leonardo had gone on to say that she hadn't found true love, or someone who would love her unconditionally; that she only ever encountered men who used, abused and manipulated her. It was as if Leonardo was referring to someone in particular, but Ava was still too blinkered to see. She remembered that she was affronted by the insinuation at the time, blocking it out of her mind until now.

Why would I do that, she wondered, and deny myself such good advice?”

Then Ava remembered her very last conversation with Leonardo; the one where she had told him to go to Hell.

*“The Bible tells us of the apocalypse and of the four horsemen.”* Leonardo had said. *“Beware of false prophets Ava. Beware of the Hydra for she is akin to the first horseman of the apocalypse, the Antichrist.”*

Ava recalled that she had been furious with Leonardo, and called his words blasphemy. Ava again wondered why she hadn't trusted in the advice of the most learned man to have ever walked the planet. Finally, she considered Leonardo's parting challenge.

*“When did you find your religion Ava, and how soon afterwards did Demitri appear in your life?”*

Am I really such a fool? Ava questioned. Have I been manipulated?

Once again Ava was teetering on the very edge of that epiphany, but the devils of her indoctrination came storming in and turned her blasphemous doubt into guilt and supplication. She began to pray for forgiveness for her trespasses. Demitri still had that insidious control over Ava, despite all that had happened.

*“Rabbi inni zalamto nafsi faghfirli.* Oh, my Lord, I have indeed wronged my soul!”

Ava repeated these words one hundred times, until she felt healed in spirit.

I have done God's will as ordained, she justified.

With that, Ava once again felt emboldened, able to compartmentalise what she had done in God's holy name. The dreadful murder that she had committed was now justified and filed away. Ava knew she had to prepare herself for Demitri's next demand, swearing that she would see it through to the end, whatever the task. She was a jihadist! The old Imam had told her so.

In the last hour before she got up, Ava pondered the conundrum that was Yuri Alexandrov. She knew that he was an Angel and immediately feared that Demitri would order her to kill him too. Her mind went back to the night at the Bolshoi where Yuri had that face-off with him, remembering the murderous look in Demitri's eye. There was absolutely no doubt in Ava's mind that if they had fought that night, it would have been to the death.

Ava wondered why Yuri was still alive. That was not the way of a man like Demitri. Then she realised that the body was found without a head, along with numerous documents and possessions that only *suggested* that the corpse was Yuri's. Clearly Yuri had faked his own death! Ava couldn't begin to imagine what that might have involved, but she was impressed with his resourcefulness.

"Clever boy Yuri and here's me thinking you were *Mr Average!*" Ava said out loud, clapping her hands with glee. "At least you might be one that I can save from God's will."

She had two major obstacles in front of her though. The first was to somehow warn Yuri to remain dead. He already knew that she was somehow involved with Demitri, so explaining that might not be too hard. The second, possibly an insurmountable problem, was to convince Kayla that she had nothing to do with Callum's murder. Given that Kayla was significantly more advanced in her mixed Angel abilities than Ava, and that she also had the ability to read her, would be a tall order at the very least. Ava knew that she wasn't sufficiently advanced in her kinetic skills to take Kayla on in a fight. She would have to outsmart her and knew that her life would ultimately depend on this.

If I was Kayla, I would kill me and enjoy every moment, Ava admitted to herself. This could turn out to be the cat fight of the century, she lamented.

Ava knew that she needed to call Demitri. She remembered him messaging her just before she jumped into the Thames, saying that he wanted to see her at his research labs the day after tomorrow. Ava worked out that she had lost a day, so that meant tomorrow. She urgently needed her phone and had the hazy recollection of throwing it into the river. The SIM in her computer also contained her address book, she remembered with relief, then realised that she had either left it on Waterloo Bridge, or jumped into the river with it. Normally, she would have had no problem recalling all the names and numbers, but her trauma seemed to have blocked out much of her memory. At that moment Yuri returned, more appropriately dressed in a white towelling gown, carrying the valise that James had left in the hall.

"I thought you might need this Ava," he said, placing it proudly on the kitchen table.

Ava's expression was as if she had just won the lottery. Her computer, with all her notes and address book, would be in there. She crossed over and hugged Yuri, burying her face into his upper chest, shocked at the hardness of the muscles and his manly smell. These were things that normally sent Ava into a state of confusion, but right now it just felt safe. Eventually she spoke but stayed in the embrace.

"I thought you were dead Yuri that Demitri had killed you, and I grieved deeply for you. I can't tell you how much it means to me that you are alive and here to comfort me. I'm all alone now and need your love and protection." Ava meant every word.

She felt Yuri tense at the mention of Demitri's name. He tried to bite his tongue, but it was too much for him.

"And who do you think left you all alone Ava?" Yuri's voice was harsh and Ava's reply, furious.

"How dare you! You know nothing about him. Butt out of my affairs or I'll..."

Yuri cut her off and pushed her away to an arm's length, his eyes drilling into hers.

"Or you will *what* Ava. Kill me too?"

Ava froze like a rabbit caught in the headlights, wondering how Yuri could possibly have known that she had killed Callum. Or did he just guess, she wondered?

"Don't be ridiculous!" Ava defended, unconvincingly. "I love Callum. I could never have done such a terrible thing."

"Who mentioned Callum's name? I didn't Ava. What have you done?" Yuri demanded, his heart sinking.

In that mind numbing moment, Yuri realised that the love of his life was a murderess. Tears of despair welled in his eyes until they could no longer be contained and ran silently down his face. He had to at last concede that Ava was beyond salvation. She looked guilt stricken. There was no need for her to confess, as her face guiltily revealed the truth. Ava panicked and pressed her mouth against his urgently to buy time, her mind racing to find a solution. She felt Yuri's love and confusion in that kiss. He was depleted and helpless. It was her opportunity.

Ava began to use the power of her mind to soothe him. He was already lost in grief and the kiss, unable feel her probe his mind. The demonstration of her deep and enduring love further opened his mind to Ava, until he had no mental capacity of his own. The kiss lasted for a full ten minutes. By then, Ava had created a whole new version of that fateful night, one that Yuri would swear on his life to be true. More importantly, it was one that he could swear to Kayla as being God's truth when the time came.

------------------------------------------------------------------------

Chapter 23

It was a little after four o'clock in the afternoon when Ava paid the taxi driver and walked through the portals of the Papandreou Research Laboratories, London Plc. Although the livery and the name-plaques were the same as Moscow, the premises were in stark contrast. The Moscow laboratories had been built in a modern commercial style of construction, perfectly bland and uniform in appearance, whereas those in London were architecturally old-world and magnificent. Ava went to the security gate where the guards clearly expected her arrival. After a brief security check, she was issued her pass and taken to the Computer Science and Artificial Intelligence section in the main body of the building. The transition from the outside to the inside of the building felt like she had travelled forward three hundred years in time. Everything was space-age in appearance, white or stainless steel, hi-tech and futuristic, or simply foreign to her experience, creating an environment exactly how Ava imagined the study of robotics and artificial intelligence might be carried out. When Ava arrived at the sliding steel door that led into the 5D sector, she looked directly into the iris recognition scanner. There was click of a solenoid switch and the door opened silently on its tracks, letting her in.

The facility was not too dissimilar to the one in Moscow. There was a small office with accommodation to the side, and one-way windows, looking into the laboratory. A magnificent ornate mirror commanded the wall in front of her and Ava noted that it was similar to, but not the same as the one in Moscow.

Demitri stood facing Ava, oblivious to her presence. She could see that he was talking to a slim and elegant woman, sat cross-legged in a chair in front of the ornate mirror. The woman had her back to Ava and was in animated conversation with Demitri. She had a long neck and amazing shoulders and had chosen an open-back dress to accentuate those attributes.

Even though Ava couldn't see the woman's face, she instinctively knew that she would be strikingly beautiful. She noted that

Demitri was looking at her in a way that he had never looked at her and was instantly insulted and jealous. Despite Demitri's brutal and loveless sex, Ava still regarded him as her man. She needed to bring her body under control and focus. Ava had a good idea that the woman in the chair would be the prophet Hydra herself and was in awe of her close affiliation with *Allah*. It took several minutes before Ava had sufficient composure to press the button to open the door and enter the room.

"Ava!"

Demitri sounded genuinely pleased to see her, which gave her the confidence boost that she so desperately needed. Unusually, Demitri crossed over to Ava, meeting her half way. He embraced her in something approaching a warm manner, another first. In fact it was the biggest demonstration of affection that he had ever shown. Ava found his manner disorientating to say the least.

"Let me introduce you to our Supreme Senator, the Hydra. But I think we are all close enough that you can call her Hydie."

It was no accident that the Hydra still sat with her back to Ava. She had done so as a deliberate display of her supremacy, which was immediately recognised by Ava. Hydie Papandreou stood, almost regally and turned to face her. The woman's presence and beauty stunned Ava, rooting her to the spot. It was as if she had been petrified, just as in the legendary fables of thousands of years ago, when the mythological Hydra had turned her adversaries to stone.

"Miss Kaplinski, I'm so pleased to meet you at last. Demitri has talked so fondly about you."

Her smile was expansive and about as sincere as a second-hand car salesman, giving an unwary buyer his personal guarantee.

Again it was no accident that the Hydra had addressed Ava formally. She walked towards her then stopped, securely annexing herself to Demitri, linking her arm with his in a possessive posture, looking lovingly at his face, making a clear and unequivocal statement to Ava.

"We have business to discuss Miss Kaplinski, which is why you are here. I want you to take me through every step of the process that enabled da Vinci to access the fifth dimension." The Hydra's face was a perfectly plastic mask of cordiality.

Even without Ava's perceptive powers, she would have sensed the aggression in the Hydra's conciliatory address. Ava shuddered at the thought that half of the genes in her body, were of Shadow origin. Ava suddenly felt sullied and confused. She was expecting an almost religious experience at their meeting, but instead it was as cold as the Siberian wind.

Hydie Papandreou did look like a goddess though. She had the body of a dancer, deportment of a queen and the looks of a film star. But that palled into insignificance because of the sheer magnitude of her presence. Even the mighty Demitri looked a mere boy in her company. She filled the room. The Hydra's eyes never left Ava's, they just narrowed and darkened. She somehow tossed her mane of black hair nonchalantly such that it heaped, giving her the menace of a lioness. Ava naturally gave way in subservience to the alpha female and began her summation.

"I have recorded everything. We have conclusions based on bounded assumptions, facts that support the feasibility and a long list of concerns. Perhaps to be safe we should start with those?"

"And maybe we should simply get on with it Miss Kaplinski," the Hydra said tersely. "I am perfectly capable of forming my own opinions."

Ava caught the flare in the Hydra's eyes and responded submissively. This was the prophet, a woman chosen by *Allah* himself. It was not for Ava to pre-judge her, nor to argue against her wisdom.

"Indeed. We will begin with the facts, then table our conclusions and discuss the way forward." Ava was humbled.

Submission was exactly the right reaction for Ava to show and consequentially the Hydra's attitude changed in an instant.

"Ava, we will have such fun unravelling the mysteries of the fifth dimension together. It will be such an exciting journey and achievement. Together, we will bring such peace and happiness to mankind. Think of the wars we could avoid; the pain and suffering, disease and hunger that just simply won't happen. *Allah* has entrusted us with the key to the universe and, with your help Ava, I will use it wisely."

The Hydra's oration was worthy of the most credible prophet, but the change from *we* to *I* did not go unnoticed by Ava. None of her scepticism showed in her response though. Ava was finding it enormously difficult to take her eyes off the Hydra's perfect face as she spoke. Her beauty was mesmerising and her mind, commanding. The factors combined to make all that the Hydra said plausible. Ava was being groomed and she barely realised it.

"There is much to go through, um Miss..." Ava was still unsure of how to address the Hydra.

"You can call me Hydie. After all we are set to be best girlfriends are we not? And we already have so much in common."

Hydie Papandreou squeezed Demitri's arm as she looked up at his face, implicating him.

Ava saw Demitri's body stiffen at the discomfort of her statement. In fact, he looked scared of her. It was the first time Ava had seen this man appear weak and it nauseated her. Perhaps he wasn't the dark and powerful crusader she thought he was. Perhaps nothing was as she thought. Ava gathered herself and continued.

"*Hydie* then, thank you." Ava smiled equally as falsely. "When would you like to begin?"

"Now," Hydie replied in matter of fact tone, "all I want from you are your notes, electronic files and any videos. I have a quick uptake. We will reconvene at eight o'clock tomorrow morning, if that is alright by you?"

The Hydra's smile was false. She didn't wait for any acknowledgement from Ava.

"Good, that's settled then. I expect you have things to attend to Ava, so we will bid you goodbye."

Ava was taken aback by the suddenness of the dismissal, and fumbled her way through.

"Yes, of course. Indeed. I will leave my hand-written notes in the back office along with the file paths to my folders. Thank you for your time."

Damn cheek of the woman, was Ava's actual thought, as she smiled thinly back at her.

Ava left the room without even looking at Demitri. The walk out of the laboratory to the safety of the office seemed endless. A rage was building inside Ava like a storm. At last she was beginning to realise that she had been used and abused, manipulated, just as Leonardo had suggested. Ava entered the sanctuary of the small office, closing the door behind her. Instantly every light bulb and electrical appliance in the room exploded through the sheer electrostatic charge generated by her mounting rage. Ava looked at her reflection in the mirror and hardly recognised herself. Her face was twisted in rage and her eyes were black. The mirror shattered as she turned her malevolent gaze towards Demitri and the Hydra. They were looking in her direction, prompted by the explosion within the room, but couldn't see her, because of the one-way glass partition. With a deafening crash, it shattered, leaving Ava and the Hydra locked in each other's stare. Ava saw something in the Hydra's eyes. It was fear.

For the first time in her life, the Hydra knew that she was dicing with a power infinitely more potent than her own. The realisation that she had awoken a sleeping giant chilled her to the bone. It was what they had always feared. When Ava turned defiantly and left the office, the Hydra almost buckled at the knees with relief. She spun around to face Demitri, turning her fear into anger at her hapless partner.

"You dickless waste of fucking space! Where the fuck was your input?" the Hydra screamed venomously.

There wasn't much Demitri could say or do, so he took the middle ground; another mistake.

"She knows her duties and will be back in the morning, you will see *agápe mou*," Demitri assured, but unconvincingly.

"Fuck you Demitri. I gave you license to bed the whore and you couldn't even do that properly. She's slipping away from us right when we have our goal in sight. Tomorrow I could be ruling the world but for your incompetence. Sort it!"

---------------------------------------------------------------------------

By the time Ava arrived outside Yuri's apartment, she had all but calmed down. There were however, myriad questions without answers flooding her brain after her encounter with Demitri and the Hydra. Ava felt she had lost the best part of a year of her life with little or no explanation. She knew the answers lay somewhere deep within her consciousness, but denial was currently the strongest of all her emotions, and the route to any of those answers was consequentially blocked.

She turned the key to the door of Yuri's apartment and immediately felt safe. The lights were on, so she knew that he was home. The tone of her voice proclaimed her delight.

"Yuri! I'm home. Where are you?"

"It's just me here, you murderous fucking bitch!" Kayla appeared from nowhere, looking more than dangerous.

"What are you doing here Kayla?"

Ava's surprise was only surpassed by her fear. This was one confrontation she really did not want.

"I've come here for some answers before I kill you," Kayla hissed.

They stood toe to toe with their eyes locked together. Before Ava even had a chance to blink, Kayla back-handed her across the face with all the force of her birth right. It was a blow that could never have come from a normal woman, its magnitude sent Ava spinning across the room like a rag doll, crashing into the wall behind her and concussing her. That violent act brought with it a supernatural feeling of *déjà vu*. The last time Ava had been hit that hard across the face, was by a tall dark stranger when she was only five years old. Ava spat out a mouthful of blood that misted the white wall next to her. The assault reignited Ava's anger, which was brewing like a storm inside her. She stood shakily, and then concentrated on focussing that anger. Ava began to prowl around the room circling Kayla like a wounded lioness assessing her quarry for any weakness.

"Why did you kill him?" Kayla spat the words out.

She was livid, but it was still only conjecture at this time. The police hadn't found a body to support Kayla's suspicion, but Callum's death was an absolute certainty to her. She could no longer sense his presence. Up until then Kayla had always been able to; always. It was just another of those in-born abilities that she possessed.

"Kill who, Yuri?" Ava lied easily. "Why would I do that? He saved my life remember?"

"Not Yuri, as well you know Ava Kaplinski. Yes, we all know that you are her. We have always known. Callum knew it too, before you killed him. Even your name Thompson is a lie!"

Ava was in range again and Kayla struck out as fast as a viper. This time Ava was ready and sidestepped the attack. As she did so, she brought her leg up in a high kick, honed by years of dancing experience, catching Kayla squarely under the chin, driving her front teeth through her bottom lip. The wound opened and bled profusely, running down Kayla's chin onto her white blouse, maddening her.

"You fucking bitch!"

Kayla lashed out again and again but Ava was light on her feet, narrowly escaping each assault. Finally, Kayla's clawed hand raked the side of Ava's face, gouging deep channels in the soft flesh. Ava flew at Kayla in blind frenzy. The weight of her charge drove them across the room, sending them tumbling over the coffee table to the floor, tearing at each other's hair; biting, gouging and punching.

Ava broke free. She needed to put some distance between them. Ava was losing badly in close combat, as Kayla was significantly more streetwise than her. Ava had never had cause to fight in the refined environment of the Bolshoi, but she was learning fast, managing to get two more kicks into Kayla's face before Kayla charged at her like a wounded bull in the ring, maddened by the stabbing of the picas. The charge took Ava off her feet. She landed badly with Kayla on top, clawing at her face. Inevitably, Kayla finally got Ava by the throat and began to choke the life out of her. In the passion of the moment, neither had called upon their inner skills. It was just an old-fashioned girl on girl bitch fight.

At last Ava was beaten, getting exactly what she deserved for her sins and gave up the struggle for life. Ava wanted her last word to be sorry but the darkness came too soon for that small pleasure.

--------------------------------------------------------------------------

"What the hell are you doing?" Yuri yelled, grabbing Kayla by the wrists. "Stop it you're killing her!"

Yuri released Kayla's vice-like grip on Ava's throat, leaving Ava motionless on the floor.

"She's dead," Yuri wailed.

He was knelt beside Ava in uncustomary panic.

"No, she isn't! Just unconscious more's the pity. I can still hear the bitch's black heart pumping."

"Why did you do this?" Yuri asked in disbelief as he cradled Ava's bloodied head in his hands.

"A life for a life, or should have been. She killed Callum."

Kayla's response was matter of fact with no hint of emotion or remorse for what she had done to Ava.

"She didn't Kayla, she couldn't have done. You've got that wrong. I saw Callum leave the hotel ten minutes before Ava. He headed west and she walked the other way down to the Aldwych. I know, I followed her and she never left my sight."

Yuri's defence of Ava sounded wholly sincere. It was exactly what Ava had made him believe.

"Are you sure? It has to be her," Kayla challenged.

She looked at Yuri in disbelief, horrified at what she had almost done.

"Positive! I couldn't be more certain. You should clean yourself up and go Kayla. I don't think it would be a good idea for you to be here when Ava regains consciousness."

Kayla nodded in silent agreement and went to the bathroom. She turned the light on and looked at herself in the mirror.

"Jesus Christ!" she exclaimed in shock.

Kayla's face was ripped to pieces. Blood from the gaping wound in her mouth had matted her hair, covering her neck and chest, through the wild antics of the fight. She looked demonic, like something out of a horror movie. Kayla was thankful for her mixed genes that would allow her skin to regenerate and fully recover. It would take a couple of weeks of looking a mess like this though, she lamented. Kayla took off her blood-soaked blouse and examined her body. Everything hurt. Ava had punched, kneed, bitten or kicked her everywhere. Kayla even whimpered at her own gentle touch, as she explored herself.

"Fuck, that bitch can fight," she murmured, sponging the caked blood from her face.

Yuri had left a used shirt in the bathroom. Kayla dressed herself in it, turned the light off and left. Ava was no longer on the floor, where she had left her. Kayla instinctively spun on her heels to check that she wasn't behind her, ready to strike. Thankfully she wasn't. Relieved, Kayla quickly searched the apartment and found Ava lying, still unconscious, on Yuri's bed with him tending to her.

"Tell her I'm sorry," Kayla said reluctantly and left the apartment.

---------------------------------------------------------------------

Ava had fared no better than Kayla. She gradually awoke, enveloped in Yuri's arms, completely disorientated. She tried to raise herself on to her side then screamed out in sheer agony.

"Easy Ava, stay still and rest a while," he comforted.

She didn't need telling twice. Ava felt like she'd been hit by a speeding truck, and lay there for some time piecing everything together. The last thing that she remembered was a look of pure hatred on Kayla's face as she strangled her. Yuri must have intervened just in time, Ava deduced. The fact that she was still alive meant that Kayla must have left convinced by Yuri's account of what had happened that night at the hotel. Ava decided to test the waters.

"Yuri," she murmured into his shoulder. "Kayla said something about Callum being murdered. Please tell me that is not true."

"We don't know Ava. He's gone missing under mysterious circumstances. Kayla thought that you were the person responsible, until I told her that you never left my sight from the moment Callum left the hotel." Yuri kissed her on the forehead. "Oh, and she asked me to say sorry for her, for what that's worth."

Silent tears streamed down Ava's face as she re-lived Callum's murder; no longer sure that it was God's will after all. When there were no more tears left to cry she whispered to him.

"I hope he turns up OK."

Ava buried her face in Yuri's shoulder, wishing that Kayla had finished the job and killed her. Death was the punishment that she deserved, for committing this heinous crime.

Ava lay with Yuri for an hour before feeling strong enough to clean herself up. She ran a bath and soaked in it, sponging her wounds. Ava could not get the flash-back of the tall dark stranger who hit her as child out of her mind. The intensity and reality of the fight with Kayla had somehow given her renewed perspective. The memory was vivid now. She could recall every detail of the room, including the twisted expression on her mother's face as she died. Ava could remember everything except her assailant's face. But even that hung on the very edge of her consciousness, almost ready to be revealed. The whole experience was like a word perched on the tip of your tongue but just out of reach, or a familiar smell that takes your mind back to an earlier time and place, except you just can't place exactly where. His face had nearly formed in her mind so many times, but Ava would lose the image right at the point when it was crystallising.

Ava returned to the bedroom dressed in Yuri's white silk robe, lifted the bed cover and slid in. The sheets smelt of him. Ava inhaled, savouring the safe manly scent.

"Can I stay with you tonight Yuri, only I couldn't bear to be alone?" She was unable to make direct eye contact. "I don't mean for sex, although that might follow one day. I just want you to be close to me. You are all I have in the world now Yuri and I need you to be my constant."

Ava blushed at the child-like nature of her plea. She felt vulnerable and her need for protection was real. Once again, Ava randomly thought of Katarina and something that she had once said. Something that dear Leonardo had also inferred:

*'You need a man Ava; you really do, but not a man who just takes. You need one who gives in abundance; a man who can love you unconditionally, cherish you and bed you; your own knight in shining armour. He is out there. One day he will find you Ava and he will make you shine so brightly.'*

"Are you my knight in shining armour Yuri? Is it you?" She looked at his face searching for the answer.

"I am all and everything you want me to be Ava, but for now just close your eyes and sleep."

-------------------------------------------------------------------------

When Yuri woke in the morning, Ava was gone. She had left a note on the pillow; it read:

*'I have just one thing that I must do, and then I will be yours if you want me.*

*Love Ava xx*

*(PS I found an old phone of yours and have put my SIM in it for now - hope you don't mind xxx)'*

396

Chapter 24

It was seven forty-five in the morning, when Ava entered the office in the 5D sector of the Papandreou Laboratories in London. To her surprise, all the electrical equipment had been replaced along with the one-way glass mirror. Efficient, she thought then went about organising her data.

Ava had decided that she would do this one last thing for Demitri; help get the Hydra access into the fifth dimension and then quit. She was no longer afraid or indebted to him. As for his God and the prophets, she had no time for them either. Ava knew that she was already beyond redemption, and had made a pact with the Devil to claim her soul. Ava was sat in front of the computer when the Hydra entered. She was alone.

"Good morning Ava," the Hydra began. "Oh, my God your face, what happened to you?"

It was an unnatural show of concern on the Hydra's part. Ava recognised lip service when she heard it.

"It's of no importance or relevance, but thank you for your concern anyway," Ava's response was equally false. "I have everything ready for you. What did you make of my notes and synopsis?"

The Hydra placed her clutch bag on the desk, draped her coat over a chair and sat down elegantly, rewarding Ava with a false smile. She wore an expensive dark grey suit with a pencil skirt, white blouse and black Charles Jourdan high heels. Ava noted that, other than the red lipstick and eyeliner, she wore no other makeup nor needed any. Ava felt at a disadvantage, particularly as her appearance suggested that she had only just managed to survive an encounter in the lion's cage. The one thing she really didn't need right now, was to be sat next to this immaculately turned out, beautiful woman.

"I have read everything, watched the video recordings and considered your conclusions and recommendations thoroughly. You have done a good job of presenting your findings Ava, and I know that much of the success of the project is highly attributable to you. I was particularly intrigued about da Vinci returning as a much younger man, even though it was only his mind that made the journey into the fifth dimension, not his body. What did you make of that?"

It was the start of a lengthy conversation which explored all boundaries. At the end of the session Ava was impressed by the Hydra's intellect and innovative thought.

Beautiful *and* intelligent, Ava thought with just a hint of jealousy.

It was the middle of the afternoon before the Hydra relaxed in the reclining chair in front of the old ornate mirror. She was ready to take her first excursion into the unknown.

"It's not the same mirror as in Moscow," Ava commented in case this would make a difference.

"No, you are quite right Ava, it is not. We have procured a number of them, costing many lives obtaining each. They are precious beyond measure. It is only in visual appearance that they differ though. The science behind them is exactly the same. Their ability to allow one to transcend dimensions gives the user unlimited power to change destiny."

That was all Ava really needed to know about the mechanics. What she was hugely concerned about, was the Hydra's readiness and even her suitability for such a journey and such power; let alone the ethical aspect of the project in the first place. Ava recalled Leonardo's own words after his pioneering journey into the fifth dimension. He had said that:

'He had walked with the Gods but felt like an intruder there and that the fifth dimension was no place for people as imperfect as us. He said that to meddle would bring on Armageddon, the end of time.'

Ava could not let those words of wisdom go unspoken.

"Hydie," she began cautiously. "Leonardo had grave misgivings over the ethical nature of this project, as did the other scientists. He said that to meddle would bring about Armageddon, the end of time. That is why they all left."

The Hydra flared on Ava.

"Then they were all fools. It is man's duty and destiny to reach for the stars, to be one with the Gods. They were relics, old men absorbed in their own theories and self-righteousness, pompous and shackled by their own pious beliefs. Damn them all to Hell!"

The Hydra's eyes possessed the same zealous look in them that the old Imam's had displayed at the madrassa in Pakistan, making Ava's blood run cold. Another warning from Leonardo rang in her ears, one that she had completely dismissed at the time as blasphemous:

*'The Bible tells us of the apocalypse and of the four horsemen. Beware of false prophets Ava. Beware of the Hydra for she is akin to the first horseman of the apocalypse, the Antichrist.'*

Ava once again teetered on the edge of an epiphany, but the shackles that bound her were still holding tenuously. She desperately felt the need to divert the Hydra's mission until she was more certain of the outcome.

"Perhaps, I should travel there first and you observe me, learning from my errors," she suggested. "As Supreme Senator and a chosen prophet of *Allah,* your life has far more value and importance than mine." Despite Ava's misgivings, the offer was made sincerely.

The Hydra's laugh was disparaging.

"What? Do you really think that I would entrust you with infinite power; a half-breed like you? That is my birth right, mine for the taking. No, that is *not* the way this is going to proceed. If da Vinci found the way into the fifth dimension, and survived it, then you can be sure as Hell that I can."

That was the end of the matter, the subject clearly not up for further discussion. The Hydra considered Ava for several moments, sensing the change in her mood. She needed to maintain Ava's cooperation, if only temporarily. Once she had entered the fifth dimension, she could create her own reality, one with no place for Ava Kaplinski!

"Ava, I do apologise. That was rude and insensitive. You must forgive me, only I have dreamt of this moment for so long. I have so many gifts planned for mankind, that I can no longer stand the waiting."

For the first time the Hydra's smile appeared sincere. Ava succumbed to the façade.

"Well, if you think the time is right, then I must concede," Ava capitulated.

She had decided to see this through whatever. It would be her parting gift to Demitri, much as she had planned. Ava continued helpfully.

"When Leonardo went through the portal, he used the emotions of hope and love as the conduit to open the dimension. We all considered those *soft* emotions to be the safest. That was based on the belief that if he never came back, that he would remain in a world full of love and hope."

Love and hope? The Hydra mocked silently. Power and domination will be my thoughts! Her spoken words were conciliatory, though.

"I couldn't agree more Ava and those will be mine too."

They spent the next thirty minutes in silence, while the Hydra placed herself in an almost trancelike state of meditation. Although her eyes were closed, they danced beneath her eyelids as she went into a self-induced dreamlike state. Ava held her breath for the both of them. At last the reflection of the room in the mirror began to fade, replaced with the swirling mists of time, just as before.

Through the mist, Ava could make out vague human shapes. They seemed to be in various attitudes of distress. Some cowered, as if being beaten and others held their heads screaming out in pain. The images flashed and changed so fast that Ava only got an impression of their meaning. Together though, they seemed to portray something out of *Dante's Inferno*. 'The nine circles of Hell'.

Ava looked down at the Hydra. Her eyes were closed but she was no longer calm, instead she appeared to be in deep distress, convulsing. Ava was deeply concerned and about to bring her back to consciousness, when the Hydra suddenly relaxed and went still. Ava looked back up to the mirror, just in time to see the Hydra disappearing into the mist. Instantly the mirror became active again. This time the images were not vague and ethereal. They were like news footage on videotape, the images on the reel flashing by in the blink of an eye, thousands of them. Each depicted war or catastrophe, pestilence or suffering. Some seemed to be rooted in the past, others more current, or even futuristic. It was as if the mirror was running through all of the world's events; past, present and future. The theme was always the same though, death. Death on a biblical scale, Armageddon!

"God help me what have I done?" Ava cried out, terrified.

The walls in the laboratory seemed to twist and deform. Cracks appeared and the ceiling seemed to ooze blood. Ava thought she was hallucinating, but her senses told her otherwise.

Leonardo's voice called out to her, seemingly across time and space. In reality though, it was just the memory of his parting words to her:

*'It was no accident that our astral planes met and took us here Ava. We were blessed with the chance to meet each other and make a difference, to be different. It was a gift from the Gods that I believe only happens rarely and to the chosen few. When you are chosen and blessed in this way, you should take that gift and hold on to it at all cost and fulfil your destiny. But it will take all your courage Ava. Are you ready for that and will you make the right choice when the time comes?'*

She had asked Leonardo what the right choice was and he had replied simply:

*'Our future. You hold the key to the destiny of all mankind and the right choice is simply having the courage to follow your heart.'*

Ava hadn't understood the message at the time, but now she did. Suddenly, the floor beneath her seemed to crumble, reminiscent of an earthquake. She ran to the cabinet of instruments on the far wall, the few yards seeming to take an eternity. Just as she arrived, the cabinet crashed to the floor, spewing its contents in all directions. Bizarrely, the floor was no longer tiled; it was constructed from rock and soil. Ava rummaged amongst the metalwork until she found the scalpel she was looking for.

The laboratory was gone. There were no walls, no ceiling and no recliner. Instead, there were craggy mountain peaks, clear blue skies, and a natural marble slab with the Hydra dressed in black laid across it. The whole thing was surreal. They were totally alone on the top of a mountain. The lesser peaks around her gave way to rolling hills and fields that stretched out as far as the eye could see. Birds of prey circled lazily on the thermals above her, and a lone wolf watched furtively from atop a boulder, just a stone's throw away.

Something in the distance caught Ava's eye, perched on one of the lesser peaks. It was as if a mirror had caught the sunlight, reflecting it back to her. She looked more closely and could see that the source of the light was a woman dressed in gold, carrying a baby. The woman stoically looked back at Ava, but there appeared to be no threat about her. She seemed to be calling out to Ava, somehow reinforcing her resolve for what she needed to do. Ava looked down at the scalpel in her hand, then back at the woman dressed in gold. Ava thought she discerned a nod, but wasn't sure.

Ava turned away, looking across to where the unconscious Hydra lay, dressed symbolically in black. She looked at her own attire in wonderment. Ava no longer wore her pressed suit, blouse and the heels that she habitually wore to work. Instead, she was dressed in a simple white, cotton shift dress and her feet were bare. The scene suggested that Ava now had a role as a priestess and the Hydra, her sacrifice to the Gods.

Ava walked slowly over to the naturally formed altar, as if in a trance. There was no feeling of compassion or guilt for what she was about to do, only the inevitability of the act; the fulfilment of her destiny. Ava placed her hand on the Hydra's forehead, holding the blade to her neck. Her eyes flew open accusingly as Ava drew the blade across her throat and the look that she gave Ava was one of pure hatred and contempt. As the blade passed through her carotid artery, the Hydra's life's blood spurted in a fountain, mimicking her heartbeat, coursing over Ava's hands and arms. As her life dwindled, the wolf let out a ghostly howl. The Hydra was no more.

-----------------------------------------------------------------------------

Ava awoke with a start. She was back in the laboratory, lying on the floor, still wearing her work clothes. Inexplicably, the room appeared exactly as it had done previously, with no signs of the destruction she had witnessed. Ava was shocked and horrified when she saw the recliner with the Hydra's bloody corpse lying in it. Her eyes were wide open. The expression on the Hydra's face still portrayed the hatred and contempt she had for Ava in that final moment of her life. Her sightless eyes seemed to be staring at Ava in that same accusing manner.

Ava looked down, gasping in horror at the blood-soaked scalpel in her hand, proof that she had murdered the Hydra, her fresh blood still dripping from the blade. Ava raised her free hand to her mouth in horror at what she had done; unintentionally smearing the Hydra's blood across her lips and chin. The metallic taste of the blood made Ava gag. She suddenly felt faint and dropped the scalpel as if it was suddenly red hot. Ava leant against the wall for support, trying to gather her thoughts and make sense of everything, but it made none. The sequence of events was much the same as it had been with Leonardo, except for the horrific images of death and destruction.

The Hydra couldn't have gone in to the fifth dimension with thoughts of love and peace, Ava realised. What followed was out of a fantasy movie and just couldn't have happened, or could it? She wondered, looking again at her bloodied hands and the deep gash in the Hydra's neck.

A phone rang out, distracting Ava from her thoughts. She didn't recognise the tone and went straight to the Hydra's bag, guessing Demitri would be checking on progress. But the phone wasn't hers. Ava suddenly remembered that she had borrowed Yuri's, and transferred her SIM card to it. She checked the number on the display. It was unknown to her. Ava was about to cancel the call, when her curiosity got the better of her.

"Hello, who's calling?" she asked cautiously.

-----------------------------------------------------------------------

# Chapter 25

The two men sat cross-legged on the Persian carpet in the old Imam's Bedouin tent, smoking from the old copper shisha, the sweet smell of hashish filling the limpid air. It was considered as *haram* under Islamic dogma and not permitted, particularly for men of their ilk. But neither the Mullah nor the Imam were entirely the religious men that they purported to be. Both had gone into hiding since the Hydra and Demitri's plan of mass murder had failed. They both knew that Demitri would look for revenge and eventually extinguish any trail that led back to him, which included them. The Mullah was himself a resourceful man, but Demitri enjoyed the protection of the Hydra. It would only be a matter of time before they became Demitri's victims; to sever all links between him and that international incident. The Imam poured the Mullah a traditional Arabian coffee from the ornate pitcher. It was flavoured with saffron, as was their preference, and the mixture of aromas was pleasing to them. Mullah Ismael took a fresh date from the bowl in front of him, examined it thoughtfully, and then popped it into his mouth, the act appearing to help focus his mind on more pressing matters; in this case Ava Kaplinski. The soft fruit burst in his mouth, the sweet juices exciting his palate, seemingly confirming the decision that he had made.

"I will call the Kaplinski woman," he confirmed, swallowing the fruit.

"It is a risk old friend," replied the Imam. "She is still heavily under his influence and love is blind. The woman could so easily refute what you say and inform Demitri. He would then re-double his efforts to find us and we would be dead inside the week."

The Mullah took another big draw from the shisha, holding the sweet fragrance in his lungs for a full half minute before exhaling and replying.

"And if we don't take that risk old friend, we will be dead inside of a month." That was also likely to be true. "So all we are really risking is a few weeks."

They remained deep in their own thoughts for some time, both respectful of the other's meditation.

"I will call her now," the Mullah declared at last.

Producing a mobile phone from one of the folds within his white robe he selected Ava's number and called it. The phone went unanswered for some time, such that the Mullah was about to terminate the call, when a woman's voice tentatively answered.

"Hello, who is calling?"

"Ava it is I, Mullah Ismael. I trust that I find you well disposed?"

His was a typical Arab greeting; polite but spoken without sincerity, particularly from the mouth of someone such as the Mullah.

"I have no time or inclination to pass niceties with you Mullah. What do you want?"

Even though Ava had just cause to speak to him in that manner, it angered the Mullah. It was against the Arab culture for a woman to be insolent. He couldn't however afford for Ava to hang up, and so he controlled his anger, continuing.

"I have something grave to impart; something that you need to know Miss Kaplinski."

"Get on with it then!" Ava ordered.

She was impatient, regretting answering his call in the first place. The Mullah paused for maximum effect and then delivered his world-changing missive.

"It is only right I inform you that the man who killed your mother was the same man who arranged the killings of your aunt Alisa and your friend Katarina. He was also your sponsor at the

407

Bolshoi and the one who sent you to me at the madrassa, in Pakistan. That same man became your employer and lover. His name is Demitri Papandreou."

The Mullah cut the call, not caring to hear what reaction his information had caused.

Ava rocked back on her heels as her world came crashing in on her, collapsing at the sheer magnitude of what the Mullah had implied. The shock of the news paralysed her. It was brain numbingly foul and disgusting. Ava's nervous system suddenly went into uncontrollable spasms and she writhed on the floor as if fitting. There seemed to be no air in the room such that Ava struggled to breathe, vomiting copiously, gasping desperately for a precious breath to sustain her, but denied by the next retch and then the next. Ava eventually passed out as her lungs failed to sustain her, giving her some momentary respite from the agony of the truth.

When Ava regained consciousness only minutes later, her mind was clear, crystal clear. She lay there replaying her life, returning to the point when she was just a five-year old child at their hotel room in Moscow. Ava remembered her mother returning with a tall, dark and handsome man and that she looked radiantly beautiful and happy, laughing and touching the man fondly. She remembered feeling side-lined, jealous and had consequently played up, being sent to her room accordingly, where she had cried herself to sleep. Then Ava recalled waking to the frenzied screams of her mother and running into her room. The vision of the man strangling the life out of her naked mother was indelibly printed on her mind and she sobbed at the painful memory. But now that man, the man who had so brutally murdered his mother had a face. It was undeniably Demitri. Her brain had blocked him out of her memory for so long, but now she could clearly see the joy in the man's eyes as his hands extinguished her mother's life. He was smirking back at her with that strong chin of his jutted out aggressively. She now remembered screaming at him to make him stop.

"Leave my Mummy alone!"

Ava's pathetic defiance was met by a vicious blow across her face to silence her. She even remembered spitting out three of her baby teeth. The blow had sent her spinning, half conscious across the room, slamming her against the wall, where she remained, traumatised, too scared to move. Now Ava again felt crushed by the guilt of watching as her mother's frantic thrashing slowed until she became still. Ava recalled how the man had dragged her mother's naked and limp body to the centre of the room, where he had strung her to the ceiling with a rope he had pulled down from the curtain. Demitri's last act was to kick the bedside table into the middle of the room. None of that had made any sense to Ava at the time, but now she knew why. It was her father's last cowardly deed to implicate her mother in the act of suicide. Now Ava remembered her father leaving without so much as a glance in her direction; such was Demitri's loathing for her, his daughter.

Ava's brain flashed forward from that first distressing memory, through to her years at the Bolshoi. She recalled every letter that Demitri had sent her, not one of them conveying any love or affection. Next, that last night at the Bolshoi with Katarina, where they were drugged and abducted filled her mind. Ava remembered every sordid moment of that too, right up until the moment when they were rescued by a gun toting dark stranger. All she had seen of him before she lost consciousness was his back and his strong jaw line, which again was undeniably Demitri.

Ava gagged at the final confirmation as she relived the disgusting episode of her rape that followed, lying naked on her back in her bedroom with a man's face above hers, dripping sweat as he violently thrust in and out of her. His face was angled upwards so that all she could see again was the line of his jaw and a well-formed ear. That face had seemed familiar at the time. Now she knew with absolute certainty that she had seen it in some other bedroom at some other time. It was apparent to Ava that this *other bedroom* was that from her childhood memory. Beyond a shadow of doubt, her rapist was Demitri.

What kind of man could rape his own daughter and then take her to his bed as his lover? Ava wondered, feeling abused, dirty and defiled.

As painful as all of these events were, the thought of her aunt and Katarina being murdered and probably raped too, was unbearable. She wailed in pain at the images that these thoughts created in her mind, knowing that they had been abused and murdered because of their close association to her. Ava was convinced that, in effect, she was to blame for each and every one of these atrocities. She rolled on the floor holding herself, in a vain attempt to protect herself from the agony. Ava concluded that their murders would have been ordered directly by Demitri, as a way to control her actions and to isolate her. Bortnik would only have been his weapon.

Worst of all, was that she had obeyed Demitri's instructions, enticing and murdering Callum, the only man that she had ever truly loved up to that point in time; a man who had trusted and unconditionally loved her. That made her every bit as culpable as Demitri, maybe worse, because she had murdered someone she loved. Ava couldn't bear to live with that despicable act now, particularly as she could no longer fool herself that the murder had been carried out in God's holy name. Ava irrationally reasoned that she was as much of a monster as Demitri, and deserved to die for her sins. She had already taken four lives in almost as many months; the man at the madrassa, who had flogged her, Bortnik, Callum and finally the Hydra. Ava wondered how many more there would be, if she was allowed to continue her worthless life.

Ava stood shakily, accidentally stepping on the scalpel as she did so. She looked down at the surgical blade. Somehow the bloodied blade called out to her to pick it up. She obeyed the mystical call and sat on the edge of the recliner, looking at her reflection in the old mirror. There was no colour in her face, apart from the smear of the Hydra's blood across her mouth. Her eyes were lifeless and she seemed to have aged ten years. If there was little to live for before, there was nothing now. Ava put her left hand on her forehead just as she had done to the Hydra and reached across her throat, the other hand pressing the scalpel into her neck below her left ear. She felt no pain, only the wetness of the blood as it gushed down the smooth white skin of her neck. Just as she was about to end her existence by drawing the knife across her throat, Ava uttered her last words.

"Please forgive me Mum for not being there when you needed me."

----------------------------------------------------------------------

"That is not the way!" the woman's voice was firm and reassuring.

Ava's eyes flew open in surprise. A petite woman, dressed in a gold robe, was stood beside her. She carried a naked baby on her hip with one arm and held Ava's scalpel hand in a vice-like grip with the other. The woman was immensely powerful, which was incongruous to her appearance. Without any apparent effort she prevented Ava from carrying out the suicidal act. That such a slight woman could have such strength was unnatural, but then there was nothing natural about where they were, or what she had done. Somehow Ava was back on the mountain. She recognised the woman immediately, as the one who was there before; the one who had apparently consented to Ava's killing of the Hydra.

Ava was now sat on the marble slab, the sacrificial altar, and once again dressed in the simple white dress with her feet bare. She released her hold on the scalpel and the strange woman cast it aside. The blood from Ava's wound continued to flow copiously down her neck soaking the white cotton of her dress.

"Let me," the woman's voice was lyrical.

She leaned forward and kissed the open wound. Immediately the blood ceased to flow, and the skin of her neck regenerated, not a trace of the scalpel's cut remaining. The mysterious woman ran her hands over the claw marks that Kayla had gouged in Ava's face and her skin slowly restored, leaving her with a perfect complexion. Ava touched her skin in wonderment at how the woman's restorative abilities far exceeded her own.

"Am I in heaven?" Ava asked innocently, for the second time in only two days.

"Perhaps," replied the young woman taking her hand. "It depends on your point of view. All things are possible here."

Wherever this place was, Ava felt completely at ease in the company of this woman. She exuded peace and tranquillity. Ava felt no rush to talk. Somehow this strange being had already melded with her mind, communicating with her. The experience of holding hands seemed to reinforce that mental bond. With each passing minute, Ava gained a greater understanding of who she was, and more importantly, what she was; where she had come from and how she had come to this point in her life. She now realised that so little of the path that her life had taken had been through her own freedom of choice. By the end of their communion, Ava no longer felt like a murderess, just the conduit for someone who had manipulated and abused her since childhood.

Ava was fascinated by this woman. She appeared to be in her mid-twenties, svelte, but femininely so, and curvaceous. Childlike features were accentuated by big bright blue eyes. Her hair that hung like a thick rope over her shoulder was a lustrous black. She had an amazing smile, which lit up her face, bringing a feeling of joy and serenity to the beholder. All the time the infant, a little girl, had been watching and appraising Ava. At last she gave a beaming smile and held her arms out to be picked up.

"May I?" Ava asked, as if they were already close friends.

"Of course," replied the woman. "But she might be sick on you, I've only just fed her."

It was such a natural exchange between women, in such an unnatural situation. The whole essence of humanity reduced Ava into tears of happiness.

"I don't mind," Ava assured. "She can pee on me too if she wants, I just need to hold her right now."

They both laughed, carefree; two women at complete ease with each other.

"Be careful what you wish for Ava!"

"Oh, she's so lovely," Ava enthused. "You must be so proud of her. What's her name?"

Ava asked running her fingers through the child's soft golden hair.

"I am eternally proud of her Ava; her name is Niquita."

"A beautiful name for a beautiful little girl," Ava enthused, and then added. "Are you Maelströminha?" Ava was sure that she had to be.

"Thank you. Niquita was my grandmother's name, and yes I am Maelströminha. Call me *May* though. It will be easier for you."

"I thought so! Callum spoke so highly of you but at the time I thought he was lying. I was under Demitri's influence and control you see."

Ava wiped a tear from her eye with her free hand at the mention of Callum's name. She recovered her composure distracting herself by concentrating all her attention on the baby.

"Oh, you are so adorable Niquita. I want a baby just like you." Niquita touched Ava's face almost in understanding and giggled.

"In the balance of all probabilities you will have two children Ava, a boy and a girl; the girl first."

Ava looked at Maelströminha quizzically.

"How could you be so sure of that? We never know how lucky we are to be."

"Since the improbable fulfilment of your destiny, I have consulted the mirrors and the signs suggest that this will probably come to pass."

"Will I be happy?" Ava asked with some trepidation.

She realised that any attempt to glimpse future events, no matter how trivial they might seem, could be extremely dangerous.

"If you choose to be happy Ava, then you will be. But that is something you have never been good at, is it?"

Maelströminha's expression suggested that Ava should ask no more on the subject. Ava became pensive while she considered all that had passed.

"Are we in the fifth dimension?"

"We are in the place of consciousness Ava. Some call this existence Heaven, but it could just so easily be considered to be Hell. Everything depends upon what you bring here. The fifth dimension is a place of peace and justice unless the balance is upset. The responsibility of that continuity fell upon you Ava. You have brought with you something that is extremely rare and precious, that gift is hope. Hope was the last thing that remained in Pandora's Box after she released all of the evils of the world. You alone have averted Armageddon Ava. *You* were humanity's hope. The chance of your success to accomplish what we needed was almost a statistical impossibility, but somehow you prevailed."

Maelströminha kissed Ava thankfully on the cheek, and the kiss touched Ava's soul. Niquita broke the mood by reaching out demandingly to her mother.

"She's hungry again. Niquita is *always* hungry," Maelströminha rolled her eyes in mock despair.

She took Niquita, placed her on her hip and reached into her robe releasing a breast. Niquita took the offering eagerly and suckled contentedly. It was another entirely natural display of motherhood and openness that touched Ava deeply. She had been told about the legend of Maelströminha a dozen times, both from Angel and Shadow perspectives. Apparently, she had control over the powers of nature on a biblical scale. Ava had imagined the woman as an Amazonian warrior, not at all like the slip of a girl in front of her, breastfeeding her baby.

"May, something about the whole situation and course of events puzzle me." Ava began. "If only a fraction of the legends surrounding you are true, then you could have killed the Hydra at any time, couldn't you?"

"Over the millennia, I could have killed her more than a hundred times Ava," May confirmed. "But that would have been an abuse of my power, making me no better than the Hydra herself. We are *guests* on your planet Ava and have always attempted to help mankind steer itself to the better side of their nature. We have never dictated or forced the outcome, contrary to the Shadows philosophy."

"So you may be considered as guardians of humanity's destiny then?" Ava offered.

"Perhaps," May fixed Ava with a critical eye. "But do not liken us to Gods. We are not Gods. Our origin dates back over a hundred million years, and our abilities are more advanced than humanity can comprehend. But they will. One day, if humanity and civilisation survive that long."

The words *if humanity and civilisation survive that long*, were poignant, making Ava reflect on how precariously balanced the future was. She had very nearly failed humanity, only narrowly averting Armageddon. May's words broke her reverie.

"Your skills and abilities are derived from ours and those of the Shadows. You haven't yet realised even a part of them Ava, but they are there, and you must use them wisely once they manifest themselves. To have them is a great responsibility. You will either be blessed or cursed by them."

May almost let the moment pass but judged that Ava was strong enough for the truth and probably needed to hear it.

"Your mother was *blessed* by the gift of her birth right Ava. She achieved some amazing things in her short life and was as dear to me as you are now. Unfortunately, she had a weakness for bad men. Does that sound familiar?"

May cocked an accusing eye at Ava but it was not meant as an insult, just as a matter of fact and a warning. Ava bowed her head and nodded in agreement.

"Your mother eventually sought my counsel, but was not strong enough emotionally or physically to give Demitri up. She was too deeply in love with him, despite herself. Even when he took her life, your mother couldn't summon the rage inside her to hurt him."

Maelströminha knew that what she had said would hurt Ava. Consolingly she put her arm around her. That simple act seemed to draw away the pain and Ava marvelled at the powers of this complex and evolved woman. It was also very poignant. Ava heeded the message. Twice Ava had failed in the same way. She had failed to unleash her rage and save her mother, and had again failed when Katarina was being abused and ultimately killed. The message was loud and clear.

"But I don't have any real control of my abilities, nor do I know what others potentially lie dormant inside of me," Ava admitted.

It was a plea for help. Ava knew that she needed to know more about the powers within her, if she were to seek justice against her father.

"Ava, we have joined minds and I have left you the key to unlock your true potential. You will find your powers soon. All you need is purpose, clarity of vision and imagination. The universe has infinite possibilities Ava. We have the skills to explore that possibility and choose the one that we want. The mirrors give you access to everything. Remember that."

Ava had been thinking about May's first comment and needed to know the meaning.

"The first thing you said to me when I was about to take my life was, *this is not the way*. What did you mean by that and what is *the way*?"

Ava asked the question but had already begun to piece together the answer. May's response was cryptic.

"If you cut open a pear and it is bruised, do you discard the whole pear; or do you just cut away the bruised flesh? Or if a horse is lame; do you destroy it, or put it out to pasture to heal?"

May's questions were rhetorical. She was merely setting the scene for what she wanted to impart.

"You too were imperfect Ava, but you are whole once more. Can you not see that you don't have to destroy the whole to remedy the part? You shared the same bowl as a rotten apple and were tainted by it; that is all. Let me ask you a question Ava. How would you protect the rest of the fruit in the bowl?"

It was a simple question, but with profound implications.

"I would remove the rotten apple," Ava replied.

"Demitri is that rotten apple Ava. That is *the way*."

---------------------------------------------------------------------------

Their conversation lasted sometime. At last, it was getting dark and there was a chill in the air. Ava hadn't noticed until just then, as she had been so deeply absorbed. She was about to point out that the baby would be getting cold, but when Ava looked, Niquita was already swaddled in a blanket. Ava never saw it happen, nor knew where the blanket came from. She simply accepted it as another of the *infinite possibilities* that May had talked of. May curtailed their conversation apologising gently.

"I'm sorry, but's it's getting late and I must return you to your own place and time."

With true heart-felt affection Maelströminha hugged Ava goodbye.

"One last question May," Ava was still consumed with curiosity. "You said you could have killed the Hydra a hundred times over the millennia. How is that possible?"

"How old do you think I am Ava?" May looked a little coy.

"Twenty-five, perhaps less," Ava guessed.

"Try adding five thousand years to that and you would at least be close," May laughed, smiling at Ava's shocked expression. "I am the last of two original colonial Angels with pure Angel blood."

Ava looked totally shocked and amazed. May continued.

"I'm now in the latter third of my life Ava. From here onwards we Angels age quickly. Our DNA gradually loses its power to replicate. So you see I have waited an *extremely* long time for the arrival of Niquita."

"No way!" Ava gasped, but knew that what she was being told was the truth. Further reflecting, Ava timorously questioned Maelströminha. "So, what can I expect my life expectancy to be?"

"You are very much an uncharted territory Ava, the offspring of a third-generation Angel coupling with a first-generation Shadow. I am unable to predict precisely how long that you are likely to live, but it will be extremely long compared to your expectations and that of mere mortals."

"A-m-a-z-i-n-g!" Ava lingered long on the word.

"It is amazing Ava, but this longevity brings with it much heartache. I have seen earthly friends come and go over my lifetime and will outlive my husband by many hundreds of years at least, and Niquita will lose her father very early into her long life. My only advice to you is to enjoy each day to its fullest, and bank your memories, for they are precious beyond all else."

It really was time to part and May left Ava with one final thought.

"Remember that the passage to your future happiness lies in the mirrors and their ability to take you back to the past. You must be aware that you cannot meet your other self wherever or whenever you decide to travel, nor even be close in time and space to your alter ego. You cannot coexist in the same proximity, it would destroy you both. I have already told you that there are infinite possibilities, infinite outcomes. You have the power to influence your destiny Ava. Choose wisely and be that mother to your unborn children."

With that May kissed Ava goodbye.

"We will always be the closest of friends Ava. Our paths and futures are indeterminably linked. We will meet again," she confirmed with all sincerity.

In the next moment Ava was back in the Papandreou Research Laboratories in London.

---------------------------------------------------------------------------

## Chapter 26

By the time Ava returned to Yuri's apartment, she had formulated a plan and knew exactly what she had to do now. Yuri greeted her with genuine joy, immediately taking her in a close embrace. That embrace felt natural to both of them.

"Oh Yuri, you have no idea just how much I needed that," Ava enthused, savouring the moment.

"You've been gone so long. I've been worried sick about you."

Ava could see from the sincerity mirrored in Yuri's eyes that his statement was genuine. He frowned as he stroked Ava's face with the palm of his hand. The frown turned to wonderment.

"Oh my God Ava, your face is perfect!" Yuri was astounded.

"Well thank you, kind Sir," she teased. "I do try my best."

"No I mean, well yes you are beautiful, but I meant your face, it's healed. How?" he asked, puzzled at how that could possibly be.

"Dear Yuri, you are such a treasure. What would I do without you?" she kissed him on the cheek. "It's a long story, one that I will tell you another day."

It was the truth. Yuri was dear to her now. He meant everything to her. Yuri was her one constant in life and she needed to let him down gently, before the cuddle progressed into something more intimate.

"I have to go away again Yuri. There is something that I have to do and I don't know if I will be coming back."

Yuri looked crest-fallen.

"What could be so important?" he looked at Ava pleadingly in the hope that she would reconsider her decision. "I've only just found you again."

"I can't tell you darling Yuri, but this task is something that must be done; something that can only be done by me. I cannot rest until I have at least tried, whatever the outcome turns out to be."

The look in Ava's eyes told Yuri that, whatever the task was, the final outcome could turn out badly; very badly.

"If I were to travel with you, then I could protect you. Looking after you Ava has been my sole purpose in life for these last two years. I can't give you up so easily."

Yuri could not hide or stop his cheeks from blushing. He was forced to look away, feeling foolish for opening his heart up to Ava.

"You could try praying for me," Ava smiled thinly recognising the perverse futility of that statement. "Knowing that I have you to come back to will help me endure this assignment; really it will Yuri. But right now, I need to pack."

"At least tell me where you are going," he implored, fatalistically.

"Moscow Yuri. I am going to Moscow."

-----------------------------------------------------------------------

Chapter 27

Ava's long flight to Moscow passed without any distractions, giving Ava the opportunity to plan the details of her mission. The first part of her plan involved gaining access to the old ornate mirror in the Papandreou Research Laboratories there. She had to assume that her pass had either been revoked or had time-expired. Her first obstacle would involve getting past the heavily armed front security gate. Fortunately, Ava's perfect retention served her well, remembering the guard numbers, patrol routes to and from the gate, and changeover times. For her plan to work, it would be essential that Demitri wasn't there. She had already established that he was in Greece, but with the Hydra found dead at the London laboratories, there would be massive concerns and security would have been tightened. In fact, Demitri could now be anywhere in the world, she had to concede. It was almost certain that he would be intent on finding her to avenge the Hydra. Ava was painfully aware that if Demitri was to find her, she was not ready to confront him. Not yet!

It was late afternoon when Ava's British Airways flight landed at Moscow Domodedovo Airport. She wanted a good night's rest to ensure that she arrived fresh at the research laboratories, at five-thirty the next morning. That would be thirty minutes before the night shift handed over to the day guards, a time when they would be tired and at their least alert. If all went well, it would give her thirty minutes to get into the 5D sector and through the mirror. That would leave Ava a safety margin of ten minutes before the new guards did their 5D security walk-down.

Ava booked herself in to the Metropol Hotel, opposite the Bolshoi Theatre, as was customary. She reserved an early dinner, resisting the temptation to go over the road, for old time's sake, and visit the Bolshoi. Anyway, it would be far too dangerous, she reasoned.

Ava dined in the impressive Art Nouveau restaurant. She had decided to dress up for dinner and look her best. After all, if this assignment went wrong, it could easily turn out to be her last supper, triggering fond thoughts of Leonardo da Vinci. Ava idly wondered if he would have been proud of her, for what she had done and what she now hoped to achieve. Ava looked stunning in a simple black dress, with her red hair up, and matching red lipstick. She remembered all too painfully that it was this look that Callum had always favoured and raised a glass to the empty chair in front of her.

"To absent friends," Ava spoke the words and sipped from the glass. "I'm doing this for you Callum, and every other person who was dear to me."

The single tear that ran down her cheek betrayed Ava's attempt at bravery.

She went through the details of her planned journey one last time. There could be no room for errors. Ava needed to go back in time twenty-three years to her fifth birthday. That was when her mother Anastasia had taken her to the Moscow Zoo, staying afterwards at the Metropol Hotel. Ava needed to book a room close by during the morning of the 15th June 1993, prepare herself and be at the bar in the Bolshoi at one o'clock. Ideally, Ava would have liked to have stayed at the Metropol, but the risk of meeting herself there as a little girl, or Demitri meeting her mother prematurely, was too great. The first of those risks would have resulted in her immediate demise and the death of her younger self. Further, the meeting of Demitri and her mother too soon would almost certainly risk total failure of the mission.

Ava knew absolutely the date and the year that she needed to return to, because it was the anniversary of her fifth birthday; but what she was not so sure about, was the exact time. Her abiding childhood memory was of her mother leaving the Metropol to meet Demitri across the road at the Bolshoi during the mid-afternoon. Ava's complex plan involved her getting to the Bolshoi by one o'clock and Demitri arriving earlier than her mother. If she was able to accomplish this, then she might have time to seduce him. That way, they could leave for Ava's hotel before her mother arrived, preventing their ever meeting and her mother's subsequent death.

"It's a shit plan," Ava declared to nobody but herself. Too much depended on luck. What if Mum's early and he is late? She wondered. For a while Ava pondered the conundrum, coming up with a more accurate summation of her strategy.

"No, it's not a *shit plan* at all. It's a really shit plan," she added.

The last time she had tried to seduce Demitri at the bar of the Bolshoi, he rejected her and she had an hour to work on him then, not just minutes!

Ava's spirits were dampened as she contemplated the slim chance of a successful outcome, which led her to the first of a string of Dirty Martinis...

"You are far too attractive to look so sad young lady and certainly too beautiful to dine alone. May I?"

Ava was dull-witted and slow to respond. Before the word *no* could leave her lips, the man sat himself in front of her.

"So, what brings such a lovely girl like you to Moscow?"

The man was balding, in his forties, with a cheesy smile and too many teeth crammed into a small mouth. Ava had never met a man who looked so self-assured; a real lounge lizard. She was about to reply, but apparently had missed her opportunity. He continued regardless.

"I love it here. Always stay whenever I visit. This place is so close to the Bolshoi don't you know? Do you like ballet?" again the cheesy smirk.

"Well actually I dance..."

Apparently Ava once again was too slow responding, the man taking the slightest pause as an excuse to continue.

"I just love the ballet, you should try watching sometime. I have tickets as it happens."

Ava averted her eyes. One more cheesy grin would be enough to give her the excuse that she was looking for to punch this self-important oaf's lights out. She stopped listening while he babbled on.

"I take it that's a yes then?" he cupped her hand with his.

Ava looked up. Another vacuous, cheesy smile, and one too many for her to tolerate.

Leaning slightly forward Ava made eye contact before hissing "Piss off!"

She punched the air angrily in front of his face to reinforce the rejection. To her astonishment, the man tumbled out of his chair cartwheeling backwards into the wall behind. He stayed there mildly concussed whilst all conversation in the dining room fell silent. All eyes were turned upon Ava.

"I didn't touch him, I swear."

Ava picked up her bag, leaving the dining room hastily.

Twenty minutes later Ava was in bed contemplating what had happened. She had not physically touched the man. All she wanted was him out of her face. Somehow, she had unleashed some telekinetic force from within. Ava remembered May saying that all that she needed to release her latent powers was, *purpose, clarity of vision and imagination*, and that she had left some kind of key in her mind that she would find to unlock them.

"Imagination, that's it. That's the key; my imagination!" she called out aloud in realisation.

It was a moment of clarity for Ava. Suddenly everything clicked into place. That was why her powers had only manifested themselves in the past during intense moments of black rage; it was focussed hatred. Ava realised that she was too young to have knowledge or control over that emotion as a child, at a time when she needed to protect her mother, and had been too drugged to have any clarity of thought to help Katarina. The big difference now, was that Ava knew that the emotions were not purely limited to hate or rage. Whatever emotion, she simply needed to imagine what she wanted to happen, but with purpose, together with clarity of vision, and it would immediately manifest itself.

The mountain that Ava needed to climb tomorrow didn't seem so steep now, or quite so daunting. For the first time, Ava actually believed that she had the ability to achieve the impossible, create an alternative possibility. Ava drifted into a deep and contented sleep. Not even her demons dared haunt her that night.

-------------------------------------------------------------------------------

The taxi dropped Ava outside the gates of the Papandreou Research Laboratories at a little after five fifteen the next morning. She was a little early and extremely nervous. Ava walked to the bottom of the road and back in order to kill time and settle her nerves. It was now five twenty-nine. Ava composed herself as she walked more confidently than she felt towards the security gate.

"This is all in the name of justice," she confirmed out loud to bolster her courage.

Despite the chill of the Moscow morning air, Ava had her coat open allowing her cleavage to clearly show, having chosen to wear the low-cut dress that she normally wore only for Demitri. Ava had always found it amazing that a simple thing like showing her bust could distract a man and stop him thinking. She recognised the two guards stood in readiness at the gate, with their AK-47 assault rifles held in the port arms position.

"Good morning brave soldiers," she flirted. "Did you know that a woman finds a man armed and dangerous extremely sexy?"

Both guards recognised Ava instantly and relaxed. One even managed to take his eyes of her breasts for a brief moment in order to smile at her. Ava presented her pass to the man in the gate house, whom she also recognised, but there was another guard sat behind him, whom she did not. His appearance suggested that he was more superior, immediately giving Ava cause for concern.

"Pass please Miss," the guard at the counter asked, without even glancing at her cleavage.

Ava stood on tiptoes and leant into the cabin window with her breasts strategically pressed up against the sill, accentuating them. She smiled expansively as she handed over her pass, but the guard still paid no attention to her attempted distraction. They must be broken, she mused.

"I'm sorry Miss, but this pass has expired," he advised and handed it back to her.

"No, you are mistaken." Ava returned the pass to the guard. "It is valid up until the end of 2016, don't you see?"

Ava had used auto suggestion, simple mind control. The guard saw just what Ava wanted him to see.

"I'm so sorry Miss, end of shift. I must be getting tired." He turned to the two armed guards at the barrier. "Let Miss Thompson through."

One of the guards raised the barrier. The other simply looked dejected and disappointed as Ava closed her coat, the breasts that he had been so carefully observing, walked out through the barrier, disappearing into the distance. That was the biggest hurdle over. Ava walked purposely towards the 5D section.

"Did I just hear you say the name *Thompson*?" the senior guard who had his back to the proceedings asked. "That's the Kaplinski girl's other name, isn't it?"

Realising his oversight, the guard bellowed out of the cabin window.

"Stop her!"

Ava broke into a run, as the two armed guards unslung their assault rifles. They aimed at the road either side of her and the

Tarmac exploded around Ava's feet. She stopped instinctively, raised her arms and turned reticently to face her captors. They advanced menacingly, with their rifles trained on her.

What the fuck am I doing? Ava asked herself, furious about her premature capitulation. She quickly gathered her wits and shouted back at the guards defiantly.

"Fuck you!"

Ava concentrated in the way that May had told her, with purpose, clarity of vision and imagination. She imagined that their weapons were red hot. Her intense thoughts caused the molecules within the metal of their AK-47s to vibrate and rub together, creating heat through friction. The science associated was very much the same as that used in microwave ovens. Moments later the guards screamed out in agony, dropping their weapons. The bullets inside the magazines began to explode under the extreme heat, sending the guards running to cover in panic. Ava took advantage of the moment, turned and fled towards the laboratory.

"Get after her you fools! Use your pistols and shoot to kill!" the senior guard screamed out from the cabin.

A bullet fizzed past Ava's ear, stopping her in her tracks. She spun on her heels to face them, the look on her face was menacing. The low early morning sunlight caught Ava's shock of red hair in a way that made it look as if ablaze, accentuating her malevolence. Ava thrust her arms out, summoning the same telekinetic force that she had used on the lounge lizard at the hotel, imagining the guards cartwheeling backwards. The two guards suddenly felt the impact of Ava's mind, like a horse kicking them in the chest, the shockwave spinning them backwards into the side of a parked truck. After that, neither guard stirred; both had broken their necks on impact.

Seconds later, the air was split by the wailing of a siren. Ava's acute hearing picked up the sound of multiple boots slapping the road in the distance and immediately took to her heels. Ava had a good head start, but needed to negotiate the retinal scanner to gain access to the lab. She had factored into her plan that the scanner wouldn't recognise her, and that she would need to ask a guard to let her in. As she had already passed security at the gate house, that would normally not have been a problem. Now with guards in pursuit, it was.

Ava tried to channel the clarity of thought she needed to trigger her powers, but it was difficult to concentrate, when she was being chased down by God knows how many guards; and shot at besides. Ava was forming a plan despite her current predicament. She recalled how she had destroyed all the electrical appliances in the laboratory before, through the static charge of her rage. Ava decided she would simply create that same scenario and fry the wiring in the sliding door. Her fear was that it might default to locked, in that scenario.

Ava flew down the white corridors with their shiny steel, flush fitting doors, sliding perilously on the polished floors in her high heels, costing her valuable seconds. Breathlessly, she arrived at the 5D sector. There was no sound of her pursuers. Ava was still ahead of the game. She concentrated on generating that static charge which grew inside her until her mane of red hair stood up on end. Ava reached out for the sliding door, releasing a fat spark that cracked across the air-space between her hand and the steel. The lights immediately went out in the corridor, and the dimmer back up emergency lighting came on. It was gloomy but the light was more than enough to see by. Ava tried to slide the door open, but it had fused in the locked position, just as she had feared.

"Shit!" Ava cursed.

Think damn you woman, think! *Infinite possibilities*, May had said. Use your imagination exactly as you were instructed to do. Choose another possibility! Ava reprimanded herself for her slow-witted actions.

Ava could hear the pounding of heavy boots echoing up the corridor, getting ever closer. She closed her eyes, putting everything out of her mind. Instead of standing outside the laboratory, Ava imagined herself stood in front of the old ornate mirror, a different possibility. She built up a detailed image of the scenario in her mind; the layout of the room, the ornate scrolling on the mirror's guilt frame, everything. When Ava opened her eyes, she was gazing at her own reflection in that very mirror; the alternative possibility created.

"Infinite possibilities," she murmured in amazement.

Ava was suddenly brought back to reality by the heavy banging on the door. The guards were outside. She quickly gathered her thoughts, despite the sound of automatic gunfire as the guards tried to release the door. Ava spoke to her reflection.

"Right Ava, concentrate. The time and date is eleven o'clock in the morning of 15th June 1993, and the place is the ladies room in the Savoy Hotel, in Meshchansky, Moscow."

Ava could picture the ladies room in the minutest of detail, a combined result of numerous visits there in the past and her photographic memory. She had a genuine fear of getting lost in time and space though, hoping that the tiniest details might make a difference. Ava put her hand on the mirror and it vibrated reassuringly.

"Thank God," Ava murmured with relief, before taking a deep breath and stepping into the unknown.

---------------------------------------------------------------------------

"Jesus Christ, you almost scared the life out of me!" the middle-aged woman scalded. "Don't creep up on people like that. You could give them a heart attack."

Ava apologised profusely, and then used the chance encounter to gain some information.

"This may seem a silly question but what is the date today?"

"June 15th, my daughter's twentieth birthday as it happens."

The lady looked happy about the unintended reminder.

"Oh how lovely. She was born in 1973 then?" Ava deduced, hopefully.

"Yes, she was."

A puzzled expression crossed the lady's face as to why Ava might have said that, but let it pass.

"That's excellent!" Ava smiled, reflecting at the success of her journey. "I hope she has a lovely day, truly."

Ava smiled cordially and left the cloakroom.

"Strange girl," the lady muttered dismissively as she dried her hands.

Ava checked in at the front desk, thankful that they had a room available. It was the one thing that she had not been able to pre-plan. A good omen, she decided, but had to use a little mind control to convince the receptionist that she would pay later.

Perhaps just for once in my miserable life, I'm going to be lucky, Ava thought, heading up to her room to prepare for her planned rendezvous at the Bolshoi.

-------------------------------------------------------------------------

The Moscow Savoy was only a five-minute walk from the Bolshoi. Ava used those valuable minutes to compose herself and to prepare for her seduction of Demitri Papandreou. On the plus-side, their relationship in the future and the knowledge that she had gained from it gave her a distinct advantage. She knew exactly how Demitri liked to treat his women and felt safe that he couldn't possibly recognise her. Also he was a philanderer and didn't love her mother. It was natural that Demitri would cheat on her, given the chance.

Demitri preferred challenge over subservience, so she would use that to her advantage. Ava had no idea how long she would have for this seduction. It could be as much as a few hours, or only minutes if he arrived late. The worst case scenario would be that her mother caught Ava in the act of killing her adversary. In that eventuality, Ava would have no other option but to kill him in front of her. That could potentially result in a fight to the death with her mother. Ava knew that her abilities were not strong enough to compete and the thought of harming the woman who had brought her into this world was repugnant. If anyone was to die it would be Ava. She didn't want to even contemplate the possibility of that scenario, hoping that her luck held out and the seduction went to plan.

Walking in through the grand entrance of the Bolshoi was like stepping back in time to her childhood, which of course it was. Everything was exactly as it had been when she enrolled as a five-year old under the sponsorship of some unknown benefactor. Ava shuddered at the thought of Demitri's cold-blooded plot to father her and, then isolate her to use as a weapon against the Angels in the future. Only a cruel emotionless bastard like Demitri could have contrived such a morally barren, despicable plan. Ava's hatred of the man for what he had done to everyone around him was the driving force that propelled her forward to complete her mission.

It was one o'clock precisely when Ava sat at the barstool in the Bolshoi and ordered a Dirty Martini. As she stirred the drink placed in front of her, it prompted her to remember the night when she first saw Demitri sat at the barstool opposite, almost a lifetime ago now. So much had happened since then. She remembered how physically attracted she had been to him, but the thought of that sickened her now. Even that meeting had been part of his game plan of entrapment. The fact that he could so easily murder her mother and have sex with his daughter, was gut wrenchingly sick. Knowing all of this gave her strength and, when the time came, she would take his life every bit as easily as she had Bortnik's. These thoughts shamed her however, thoughts of losing so much of her humanity and innocence. Ava took solace in the fact that she was an unwilling participant in all of this. Demitri was the thief who had stolen everything from her.

Ava needed her thoughts to be clear and so she stirred her Martini rather than sipped it. Demitri was one of the most powerful and deadly of all Shadows. Ava knew that she would need to have her wits about her to succeed in her mission.

At two-thirty, things we're looking bleak. There was still a thirty minute window of opportunity though, which Ava could reasonably depend on, but the whole plan relied too heavily on luck. Ava was beginning to lose her nerve.

Noticing the familiar line of photographs behind the bar Ava remarked that in another life, hers also would adorn the wall. They were past and present prima ballerinas. Furthest to the right was that of the Bolshoi's latest incumbent. The photograph was the same one that Ava had kept on her dressing table for the last twenty three years. There was a signature in the bottom right hand corner which read:

'*Anastasia Kaplinski*' and it was dated *1993*. Recent, Ava mused.

She looked up and immediately froze. Demitri was there. All of her confidence suddenly evaporated under the magnitude of his presence. Clarity of vision and purpose, Ava reminded herself, recalling May's advice. The Matriarch's words served to focus her mind and somehow Ava seemed to feel the strength of Maelströminha's presence, it was uncannily familiar, as if she was there beside her. Ava wondered whether that could actually be the case, in this new world of mirrors and infinite possibility that she now lived in.

Ava turned her head slightly, widening her eyes momentarily towards Demitri for just long enough to feign interest, before casually looking away, ignoring him. Painful and precious minutes passed by as she wove her seductress' web. Ava was just beginning to regret her aloofness, when she heard Demitri's familiar voice.

"Can I get you another of those?"

As Ava turned to face Demitri, his smile made her catch her breath, suppressing a gasp that threatened to strangle her. His looks and charisma still had an effect on her, despite everything that she knew he had done, and would do, if he was allowed to survive. Demitri looked just the same as he did in her reality, despite the twenty-three year time difference. But then he was not human. Ava rescued herself by looking back at her mother's photograph, picturing him with his hands around her throat murdering her. She quickly regained her composure and objectivity.

"I don't usually accept drinks from strangers," Ava demurred.

"And I don't usually offer," Demitri smiled at her charmingly. "So honours even then, wouldn't you say?"

"Right, I'm sure." Ava fixed him knowingly. "So this isn't a pick-up then?"

"Do I look like that kind of a man?"

Ava thought that Demitri's attempt at innocence not only looked forced, but somewhat pathetic.

"You look like a man who enjoys his conquests to me," Ava countered, "and yes, you do look that kind of man. But I will share another Martini with you if you are of a mind to waste your money."

Demitri's smile was wolfish. He had already decided there would be much more, and the money far from wasted. Women never refused him sex.

"Very well, as you like. But I would have preferred to share a bottle of Champagne with you somewhere else other than here, more private perhaps?"

Demitri brashly escalated his offer and used that dangerous smile of his to its best advantage.

"And why not here?" Ava challenged. "Are you expecting someone; another woman perhaps?"

Ava had the hindsight of history on her side. It amused her as Demitri squirmed uncomfortably at the truth.

"A business meeting actually and one that I would prefer to miss." Demitri had recovered his composure and sounded convincing.

"Ah, of course *a business meeting,*" Ava mocked him. "And where might we share this bottle of Champagne?"

"Where are you staying?" Demitri asked directly.

"Oh, you are confident Mr?" Ava paused in the interrogative.

"My name is Demitri and your name is?" he returned.

He was now confident in the inevitability of Ava's sweet surrender. It showed in his easy body language.

"Ava," she replied simply. "And my hotel is the Savoy, just down the road."

As Ava stood picking up her purse she gave him a look that was a mixture challenge and mockery.

"You had better be good."

"Oh, I am Ava. I am," he confirmed, with unashamed arrogance, escorting her out of the Bolshoi.

-------------------------------------------------------------------------

Anastasia Kaplinski entered the lounge at the Bolshoi charged with expectancy. She was addicted to her man. Despite his philandering and violent tendencies, he was singularly the most handsome, dangerous and exciting man she had ever encountered. Everyone had warned her off him, including Maelströminha herself. Anastasia knew that he was almost certainly criminally flawed, but she couldn't help herself. She craved him with every fibre of her body. Demitri was her addiction.

Anastasia stood in the middle of the crowded room searching for Demitri, oblivious to the admiring looks of all the men and women there. As prima ballerina, she was quite the celebrity and, could have chosen from almost all of the eligible men there. None interested her. Anastasia was slim, elegant and looked stunning in the whisper of a dress that she wore. She had chosen it specifically for Demitri. It was black and hung to the knee, tailored to the waist both back and front, the kind of dress that invited a wardrobe malfunction and needed to be worn with consideration; possibly a little too outrageous to be worn other than in the evening. But Anastasia was only out to impress one man, her man. She walked over to the bar. Sofia, a close friend, was on duty and so she called her over. Sofia appeared guarded.

"Hello Sophia." Anastasia's smile was genuine and affectionate. "Has Demitri been in today?"

There was a moment's hesitation before she answered. By then, Anastasia had already sensed, and then *read,* that there was something wrong.

"Yes, but he left about twenty minutes ago. He wasn't in for long." Sofia didn't want to elaborate on the subject. "Can I get you a drink?"

"Please Sofia, the usual."

Sofia poured a glass of Prosecco and handed it to her friend.

"Thank you. Who did he leave with?" Anastasia wasn't going to let her friend off the hook that easily. She knew Demitri would not have been alone.

"A woman as usual," Sophia conceded and cupped Anastasia's hand supportively.

"Who?" Anastasia asked, glumly.

"Well, at first I thought that it was you, except for her red hair. Honestly, she could have been your twin sister; same features, figure, age and she even had the deportment of a ballerina. It was uncanny. Actually, I *really* thought it was you and that you had dyed your hair."

"At least she's not younger than me this time," Anastasia sighed ironically.

She was trying to put a brave face on the situation, but already tears of anger and disappointment flowed down her face. Her friend's weakness angered Sophia, such that she couldn't hold her tongue.

"He's such a bastard. Why do you put up with it?"

"Because I love him," Anastasia replied hopelessly.

"Love is something you should earn Anastasia. This man is killing you. Get out while you still can. One day that might not be an option," Sofia scalded before turning to serve another customer.

It was good advice.

--------------------------------------------------------------------------------

Leaving the Bolshoi was a huge relief for Ava. In fact, her plan could not have been going better. It would have been unimaginably difficult, maybe impossible to have dealt with the situation, if her mother had arrived before they had left. Her luck was still holding out. Ava's greatest reservation was whether she would fall under Demitri's spell and fail to finish her mission. He was being so charming and, there was no doubting that he still had a powerful hold over her emotions. Ava knew that she was not yet completely free of the radical indoctrination that she had received at the madrassa, and still had alarming lapses of rationality.

"Clarity of vision and purpose," Ava muttered to herself once again. "Focus woman!"

Ava found the short walk to the hotel to be a revelation. Demitri used so many of the lines that he had used to charm her back in the future, only serving to underline what a despicable

437

philanderer he was. Demitri was rapidly making it easier for Ava to hate him. She wondered how many women over the centuries of his existence had fallen prey to his charm.

When they reached the hotel, Demitri went directly to the bar and ordered the Champagne.

"Take it to room number?" Demitri looked over to Ava for confirmation.

"316." Ava feigned embarrassment and then whispered to him. "You are not too worried about my reputation are you Mr Papandreou?"

He bristled at the mention of his surname.

"I didn't say that my name was Papandreou. How do you know that?" Demitri was immediately on his guard. "Are you stalking me young lady?"

Ava has made her first mistake; a grave one. She had to think quickly.

"Don't be ridiculous. I just recognised you the moment that I saw you. I work in the pharmaceutical industry you see, and your picture was in one of the journals. It was an article about the Papandreou Research Laboratories and their achievements." Ava hoped that this explanation sounded convincing.

"Yes of course," Demitri conceded. "Excuse my reaction, except I get a lot of unwanted attention from women interested in me only with regard to my money."

Ava's relief was immense, but now she was flustered and completely out of focus.

"Shall we go on up?" she urged by way of distraction, leading the way.

Demitri followed warily, wondering what her game was. The woman was a liar, of that he was certain. His plans to develop the research laboratories were only in their infancy and stretched over the next decade. There had never been a release to the press, nor any achievements. He could instinctively tell that Ava wasn't human, but she wasn't Shadow either. That could only mean she was Angel and that spelled danger.

Shame not to fuck her before I kill her though, he thought, watching her backside sway as she walked to her room in front of him. Gift-horse and mouth comes to mind.

The waiter followed them up with the tray. He placed it on the bedside table, and waited patiently for his tip before leaving discretely. They removed their coats, almost formally. Demitri poured the Champagne, handing Ava a glass. He appraised her closely, now seeing the deceit in her eyes. There was treachery in them. Two women would die today he decided, noticing for the first time that they looked alike. A vengeful sister that he had never known of, he assumed, one who couldn't stand how he treated Anastasia. That would explain everything.

"To us and infinite possibility," he toasted.

Along with his glass, Demitri raised a suggestive brow. His look was suddenly predatory. It unnerved Ava. She panicked, scared that he had read her. Infinite possibility was what Maelströminha had talked of.

"You take a lot for granted sir," Ava countered nervously, getting cold feet.

"I have?" Demitri challenged with a leer.

The sudden change in Demitri's demeanour, coupled with her stupid mistake of blurting out his last name, had totally derailed Ava. She lost her objectivity and confidence in the moment, shrinking in the sheer might of Demitri's presence; her mixed emotions, confused by her indoctrination. Now, Ava felt inferior and plagued by doubt. Months of conditioning in the madrassa suddenly came crashing in on her, confusing her still further, triggering the guilt and duty that had been so rigorously instilled into her. The force of Demitri's backhanded blow across the side of her face delivered the final building block of Ava's submission and renewed subservience.

"What are you here for, you traitorous bitch?" Demitri's eyes were murderous.

He took Ava by the wrists, driving her backwards until she collapsed on the sofa. It happened so quickly. Ava's long legs were spread wide open before she realised what was happening to her, Demitri already knelt between them, his trousers pulled down and his readiness for the act he was about to perform, more than apparent.

"Not this way," Ava pleaded helplessly.

They were the same pathetic words she had used before, when Demitri had raped her at the Metropol in her past future. The brutal act also took Ava back to when she was fourteen years old, when one of her aunt's tacky boyfriends had raped her in the same manner. She had pleaded with the man then, but to no avail. History seemed to be repeating itself again and again, proof absolute in Ava's mind that she was evil and deserved what was happening to her.

Demitri pulled Ava's flimsy black dress open, exposing her black lace panties. He slipped his fingers inside the gusset and ripped them away with ease. Ava immediately went into a state of shock. In her delirium, the man about to rape her no longer looked like Demitri; instead it was that vile man from her childhood. The man now violently dragging her pelvis towards his was aged in his sixties, stinking of stale booze and cigarettes. The memory made her gag. He leered back at her through horn-rimmed spectacles, as he prepared himself to violate her.

"No don't, don't. Please!" Ava begged.

Again, they were the same futile words that she had used all those years ago, having as much effect now as they did then; none. Ava felt the pain of the man's brutal penetration, causing the bile from her stomach to surge upwards, burning her throat.

"Shut up you conniving bitch!" Demitri yelled, slapping Ava across the face again.

Ava capitulated, just as she always had done; her slim body painfully absorbing every brutal thrust and her mind regressing into that dark place, where only her devils could find her. Ava had taken solace in that remoteness, her mind now out of her body. The pain was only physical; her spirit was in some other place where even Demitri couldn't harm her.

Minutes, or even hours passed, Ava couldn't tell. She had no perception of time in the place to where her mind had escaped to. She suddenly became aware of a presence, another spirit without form; all Ava could sense was an air of immense disappointment.

"Fight Ava! Fight for Anastasia! Are you going to capitulate and let her die again? How many of those that you love will you let him kill? Show some self-respect woman! Did you not listen to a word I said, there on the mountain?" the voice in her head was that of Maelströminha.

Ava's eyes suddenly flew open. The man raping her was no longer her childhood molester. It was her disgusting father, Demitri, and she was no longer afraid of him, no longer his victim.

"You bastard!" she yelled defiantly. "I will kill you for all that you have done!"

Demitri took Ava by the throat, just as he planned to do later that day to her mother, Anastasia. His powerful hands closed around Ava's windpipe, suffocating her, the look in his eyes was demonic, that of pure malevolence.

"Die in the knowledge that your bitch sister will suffer the same fate later today!" Demitri's face showed neither compassion nor remorse.

Demitri's intent to kill her mother and Maelströminha's divine intervention, were just the catalysts Ava needed to break free from the chains of capitulation and lethargy that until then we're binding her. The golden flecks in her vivid blue eyes darkened,

441

merging into the darkest brown as her rage mounted. Ava reached up and clasped her hands together behind Demitri's neck, pulling his face harder into hers with a strength that exceeded anything that the rapist could have expected.

Clarity of vision and purpose, Ava repeated in her mind, to reinforce her resolve. She focussed on the memory of Demitri choking her mother as she pressed her lips against his. Her eyes, now black with rage.

"Fuck me you bastard, fuck me!" Ava demanded.

Ava's foul words together with his act of violence heightened Demitri's sexual tension immeasurably. He increased the tempo of his rape and the pressure on Ava's throat, squeezing the life out of her, but Ava held on doggedly to that last breath. Demitri was so engrossed in the disgusting act that he was performing and his mounting urge that he never felt Ava slip into his mind, taking control of him. By the time that he did, it was too late. She had total control of his mind and with it, his body. The rape stopped in the instant and he released his grip on her throat.

"Now you have *really* pissed me off Daddy, yes, Daddy!"

The look on Ava's face showed all the pain and anger of a lifetime of abuse. She released sufficient of his mind to enable him to talk and understand.

"Before I kill you, I want you to know who I am, what you have done to your daughter and why you are about to die."

"My daughter, but that's not possible?" Demitri protested.

"You targeted and impregnated my mother, diluting her near pure Angel genes to create a monster. That monster is me and I have come back from the future for revenge!"

Ava's hatred was both palpable and terrifying to Demitri. He struggled to comprehend the enormity of what he was hearing. Ava continued clinically, dispassionately; her control absolute.

"Later today, on the night of my fifth birthday, Daddy," Ava emphasised the word *Daddy*, "you strangle my mother at the Metropol Hotel in front of my eyes and leave her hanging from the chandelier. Tonight, is my fifth birthday *Daddy*. Aren't you going to wish me happy birthday? Or was that a birthday fuck?"

Only then did Demitri fully understand. His face now twisted in horror. Fear coiled like a snake in his stomach. He knew at that moment he was a dead man in waiting. There was always the risk that his bastard child would discover her powers before he found the opportunity to kill her.

"You are from the future then?" Demitri confirmed, trying to pull away from Ava, but it was futile; she had control over all of his motor neuron responses. He was effectively paralysed. "So you must have discovered the power of the mirrors," he realised, spitting his words out contemptuously.

"Yes, I am from the future, and I have come to take away yours." Ava's eyes blazed with hatred and disdain. "But first I want you to look into my mind and see the damage that you have done to me, the misery that you have caused."

Ava cupped Demitri's temples in the palms of her hands and gazed through his eyes, down into the depths of his psyche. Demitri felt the irresistible strength of Ava's ability as she drew him into her mind, her thoughts and memories.

In only minutes, Demitri lived through all of the pain and anguish that Ava had suffered at his hands and through his actions. He saw her mother's murder through a child's eyes and the years of desperate grief that followed, then her consequential rape at the hands of her aunt's low-life boyfriend, while she was being looked after in foster care. Demitri witnessed Ava's loneliness through two decades at the Bolshoi, as she devoted herself to dancing by day and to pleasing him as her patron, by night. He re-lived the horror of Ava and Katarina's torment, carried out by Bortnik and his thugs, followed by the rape he inflicted on his daughter. Demitri felt Ava's total desolation after hearing the news of the depraved murders of Katarina and her aunt, along with the total isolation that followed. He endured with her the horror of the madrassa and, felt every lash of the whip that the Mullah had ordered, slicing into her back. Finally, and possibly the cruellest of all, he experienced every emotion that she had experienced and suffered in the taking of Callum's life, the only man that Ava had ever truly loved.

Demitri had never experienced true emotion before; it wasn't in his genetic make-up. Emotion was something that his race had always regarded as a weakness. Now he was caught up in Ava's emotions and moved to tears by them. The experience was only transitory though, an experience that would pass, but in that brief moment Demitri was exposed to it and desolated. This time it was Ava who showed no compassion.

"Tonight, you were going to kill my mother Demitri. I couldn't let you do that."

Ava's eyes searched Demitri's face for some sign of humanity or true regret, something she could use to forgive him and spare him; but there was nothing. No emotion or regret whatsoever. That moment of compassion had passed and Demitri had returned to nature, reverted to character.

"I loved you in another life Demitri but you used my love to destroy me and everyone round me that I cared for. How could you do such a thing? How could you rape your own daughter and then later make her your lover?"

Her eyes were still searching Demitri's for some reason not to kill him. Again she found none.

"You have no soul Demitri and there is no hope of redemption for you. You don't deserve to live."

Ava released more control to allow Demitri to freely speak his mind, perhaps repent for all of his actions. Instead arrogantly, he squandered the chance, venting off his rage.

"I know not of this future that you accuse me of, you abomination of nature! All I do know is that the Hydra will hunt you down for this, kill you and all those who were ever dear to you," his malice was almost tangible.

"Then you should know that in the year 2016, at your laboratories in London, I cut the bitch's throat and she bled to death like a pig. If she crops up again in some alternate future, I will do it again; gladly!"

Demitri's nostrils flared with anger at the mention of the Hydra's death by Ava's hand. He was just about to rant on and curse her to Hell, when he inexplicably felt himself rising to the ceiling. It was another of Ava's newly found, in-born abilities, levitation. She imagined him floating there, and in the next moment he simply was.

"You give me no choice Demitri. No matter what point in time or space, if it comes to a choice between my mother and you, you lose."

Ava's tone was without emotion; even the look she gave him was only cursory. She imagined Demitri spread-eagled on a rack, his limbs being impossibly stretched from his body. Demitri's frantic screams for mercy went unheard. Ava was only focussed on revenge. She threw her arms wide open, ripping him apart. Demitri was still conscious though and able to scream out in agony.

"This was the birthday present that I have longed for since you had me kill Callum. Know this as justice!"

With that, Ava threw her arms at the window, sending all parts of Demitri crashing through it, down to the street three floors below. At once, Ava collapsed on the bedroom floor in tears that were a mixture of relief and grief. She had somehow managed to add patricide to her long list of sins. Ava despaired for the salvation of her soul.

Minutes passed like hours, until it finally dawned on Ava that the police would be arriving soon, asking difficult questions. She could already hear the commotion in the street below and the sirens of the emergency services. Ava quickly gathered her things together and left the room.

As she stepped out of the lift into the foyer, the waiter pointed at her. He was just about to call out, "That's her!" when Ava held up her hand stopping the comment before it had a chance to be spoken. She had exercised control over his mind causing him to fall silent. Ava walked calmly to the hotel entrance, out into the street, leaving all of the carnage behind. Glancing to the side, she saw Demitri's torso impaled on the railings, with his limbs scattered around him. His head was slanted in her direction, leering at her even in death.

Ava had one last thing to do before returning to her own place in time, she needed to meet her mother and explain everything.

-------------------------------------------------------------------------

# Chapter 28

When Ava walked into the Bolshoi, she recognised her mother immediately, her heart leaping in anticipation. Anastasia was sat at the bar looking sullen, with an empty wine glass in front of her. She pushed it across to the barmaid who seemed to be admonishing her.

"You've had three already Anastasia. He's not coming. Get used to it! Why don't you just go home and enjoy your daughter's birthday?" Sophia was clearly annoyed.

"Just fill it Sophia and stop giving me grief. I want a drink not a lecture."

Anastasia was feeling too sorry for herself to be sensitive to her friend's own feelings, nor those of her daughter waiting at home.

"Can you make that two please?" Ava asked smiling sympathetically.

Sophia duly left to pour two more glasses of Prosecco, but not before delivering yet another barb towards Anastasia.

"At least you aren't drinking on your own now," she jibed.

Ava continued quickly before her mother could voice an objection.

"I couldn't help but notice how much alike we looked. I had to come over and meet you," Ava smiled warmly, even though her heart felt as if it was breaking.

"Oh, my God, aren't we just! We could be sisters," Anastasia looked totally astonished.

Ava was unsure quite how to play this encounter. How do you tell someone that you have just killed the one that they thought they loved? Let alone say that she was her daughter from the future. Equally Ava couldn't leave her mother alone to face the news of Demitri's death and say nothing. Sophia placed the drinks in front of them. Anastasia proposed a toast.

"To honorary sisters then." They chinked glasses.

"Or to mother and daughter," Ava added ironically.

"Do I really look that old? I'm just having a bad day," Anastasia quipped, laughing at the nonsense of the comment.

Ava had given herself an opening, but had no idea how to take the conversation forwards. She sincerely hoped that she would find the right words at the right time.

"No of course you don't. You look even more beautiful than I imagined you would be."

Anastasia almost choked as she sipped the wine.

"*Than you imagined I would be*? Who on Earth are you?"

The alarm bells were ringing. Anastasia now knew that this wasn't a chance meeting. Despite her inebriation, Anastasia's acute Angel senses kicked into gear, allowing her to make a rapid assessment of the woman sat next to her. Instantly Anastasia could tell that she was not human in origin, nor was she Angel. Anastasia shared Ava's ability to see people's auras. The woman in front of her had an aura that was bright pink and light. She immediately felt more at ease, as this type of aura was normally associated with a loving, tender and sensual person. There was an element of danger about the woman though and, quite strangely, her scent was familiar, but one that Anastasia could not quite place.

Ava couldn't reply to her mother's direct question, she simply wouldn't have been ready for the answer. She needed to proceed gently, guiding her mother towards the answers that would explain everything.

"We share a mutual friend Anastasia," Ava began, but her mother cut her off.

"You even know my name? Now you really are beginning to unsettle me," Anastasia shifted uneasily on her barstool. "So, who is this mutual friend?"

"Maelströminha," Ava answered tentatively.

Anastasia's eyes immediately scanned the room, searching for anyone who might have overheard Ava's comment or potentially looked suspicious.

"Shh! That's not a name you say in public. It could get you killed!" Anastasia picked up her bag. "Drink up; we're leaving. It's not safe here."

They walked in silence for several minutes. It was a comfortable silence though, as each could sense the other's good nature. However, both women knew that there was more information that needed to be exchanged. All Ava really wanted to do was to throw her arms around her mother and hold her for the first time in over two decades. For now though, she had to content herself with their closeness. Even that one thing felt amazing. Finally, Anastasia broke the silence.

"How do you know Maelströminha and what is your name?"

She smiled openly and honestly; after all they were both acquainted to the perfect entity.

"My name is Ava. Maelströminha came to me when I was about to take my own life," Ava returned Anastasia's smile sheepishly.

"How strange, she first came to me when I was pregnant and about to do the same thing. That was more than five years ago." Anastasia raised her eyes to the heavens in remembrance. "I was young and in love with the wrong man. It was a forbidden relationship, something that never should have happened. I felt isolated, guilty and he treated me badly. Death seemed the only way out. Anyway, Maelströminha found me and, now I have a beautiful five-year old daughter and the boyfriend from Hell. I guess there is some balance in there somewhere. What's your story Ava?"

"Not so different really, except for the baby. We both share the same boyfriend from Hell though." Ironically the pun had not been intended. "My boyfriend killed my mother, my aunt and my best friend, before going on to make a murderess of me."

"A murderess?" Anastasia gasped.

Ava's confession stunned Anastasia. She looked with pity upon the desolate expression on Ava's face and could see that what she was being told was the truth.

Anastasia maternally took Ava into her arms and Ava immediately burst into tears, sobbing her heart out. Anastasia shushed her, both being oblivious to the curious stares of the strangers passing by. Ava felt safe in that embrace and didn't want it to end, ever. She had missed her mother's love so much. Anastasia waited until Ava's crying lessened.

"Where is this man now Ava?" she asked stroking Ava's soft red hair. "Are you safe?"

"He's here in Moscow and we are safe now, because I have just killed him. I'm sorry but I had to. He was going to kill you tonight." Ava's eyes sought forgiveness, understanding.

"Your boyfriend was going to kill me?" Anastasia was both bewildered and shocked. "You don't really mean that of course?"

"I swear it Mum. On my life I swear it," Ava implored. "It would have happened tonight at the Metropol in front of your daughter who is five years old today and who you took to the zoo."

"I am not your mother Ava. I already have a daughter by that name." Anastasia began to feel threatened, confused. "Have you been following me, stalking me?"

Anastasia looked angry.

"What do you know of my daughter?" she insisted.

"No, you don't understand. For me this happened over twenty years ago. Look at me Mum. Don't you see me? Don't you recognise your own daughter?"

"This is not funny Ava, if that's your real name. You're scaring me. Stop it now!"

Ava could see the panic rising in her mother but the story had to be told.

"This evening you would have put me to bed at the Metropol early, because I played up. I was jealous you see, but that's no matter. Later, your boyfriend Demitri Papandreou strangles you and fakes your suicide. Afterwards nobody believed me Mum, nobody!"

The tears were now streaming down Ava's face, her eyeliner leaving dark streaks on her cheeks.

"I have carried this burden in my heart for twenty-three painful years, and the guilt that I never tried to save you."

With her inborn Angel perception and ability to reach into people's minds, Anastasia was beginning to find Ava's outrageous story plausible at the very least. She needed to test her further.

"If what you say is true, then why would you feel guilty?"

"Because even then I had the same powers within me that you possess," Ava howled as if someone had ripped her heart out.

"I truly believed that your death was a direct result of me not loving you enough to summon my abilities to save you. God forgive me but it's true. I'm so sorry Mum. How can you ever forgive me? This has been my cross to bear every single day of my life since that moment and I can't cope with the guilt anymore."

Ava folded at her knees in despair but Anastasia took her weight with ease.

"We need a coffee Ava," Anastasia suggested, steering her into the café next to them.

They sat at the back of the crowded café, where at least they had some semblance of privacy. Anastasia held Ava for some time, her own senses telling her that everything that she had been told was the truth. Everyone has their own unique chemical composition. Finally Anastasia began to recognise the familiar smell beside her. Ava *was* family. There was much yet to unfold, Anastasia concluded, already open to the possibility that Ava could be her daughter from the future.

The shop offered counter service only, but eventually a young barista recognised their dilemma and took their order. Ten minutes later, he duly delivered two strong coffees. Both Ava and Anastasia drank them in silence and relished the closeness of each other. Words were unimportant to assist the bond that was quickly forming between them. Anastasia stealthily looked into Ava's mind but couldn't discern all of the facts. Ava had learned to hide her thoughts, just as she had; it was part of their shared gift. However, Anastasia could see the truth. She knew for certain that what Ava was telling her, was most definitely truthful. Well at least the truth as far as Ava believed it to be, Anastasia acknowledged. She was wise enough to know that the truth and a person's perception of it are not necessarily one and the same. However she conceded that it was a positive start.

In those quiet and personal moments, Anastasia reflected on all that Ava had said and, perhaps more importantly, what she had not. The girl clearly had a striking resemblance to herself and she could imagine her daughter growing up looking the same. Anastasia also noted that Ava had the posture and deportment of a ballerina, so there was at least some form of tenuous connection there. The girl knew Demitri by his full name and that they were staying at the Metropol. She even knew that they had spent the day at the zoo and that it was her daughter's fifth birthday. The girl in her arms was either an incredibly informed imposter or her daughter, but not from this period in time. As an Angel, Anastasia knew much of the mysteries of the mirrors, so this situation was far from impossible. It was Anastasia who broke the silence at last.

"If all that you say is true Ava, then no five-year old should carry guilt for all the atrocities and failings of their parents. The guilt lays with them, not the child. Despite your heartfelt feelings and belief you are absolved of any of this. I absolve you!" Anastasia stroked Ava's hair tenderly as she spoke. "Where are you from Ava? I sense that you are of me but not mine. Help me to better understand, please."

There was a comfortable silence as Ava considered the best way to tell her story. She wanted to enjoy her mother's cuddle for as long as she reasonably could, knowing that she would soon receive her wrath when the full story was revealed.

"I will tell you all there is to know, but with one condition," Ava eased herself up from her mother's shoulder until she could see her face. "You must promise me that no matter what I tell you that you will remember me as I am now, at this moment, in this embrace forever. Only then judge me as you will."

"I promise you Ava, as we are now. Whatever is revealed."

Anastasia's smile was honest and boundless. Ava felt that smile alone was sufficient to carry her into eternity; less than she wanted but more than she deserved.

"I ask you to believe me to be your daughter, transported back from the future, and know that you already understand that concept as a possibility. I was orphaned at the age of five when I lost my mother, lost you."

Ava had to break eye contact with her mother. She was confused and embarrassed by a mixture of so many emotions and was barely able to maintain her composure. The slightest loss of control right now would turn her into a babbling mess.

"You were murdered on the night of my fifth birthday by a man whose face I could never recall. I only remember witnessing the dreadful event. Following your death, I was adopted by your sister Alisa who later fell upon bad times and bad men, one of whom I killed for what he did to me when I was only fourteen."

Anastasia was shocked and horrified by that sickening statement. Ava went on quickly, much too ashamed to be questioned about exactly what had happened.

"I was given a scholarship by an anonymous benefactor who enrolled me at the Bolshoi," Ava suddenly preened. "I'm a prima ballerina just like you." She laughed nervously and continued equally so.

"Anyway, my sponsor, a man who I had never seen, had his own agenda. He forced me to educate myself to his impossibly high standards. I know now that he was grooming me, but didn't at the time. I devoted ten hours a day to his demands and my studies. That was from the age of five until only last year." Ava risked glancing at her mother. "I'm clever Mum," she said proudly, with a weak smile.

Anastasia gripped Ava's hand. She no longer doubted the girl sat next to her and kissed her on the cheek to reassure her, giving her the strength she needed to continue with her story.

"I thought then that my life was at least in order, and loved my dancing. I had good friends including one special girlfriend, Katarina, whom I loved." Ava was heart-broken at the mention of Katarina's name and Anastasia's heart went out to her. "I let her down though and lost her on the orders of that same vile man that I later found out was my sponsor. We were both drugged and abducted. Katarina was murdered, and my sponsor raped me, although I never knew it was him at the time."

Once again, Ava couldn't face her mother. The self-perceived shame of the experience and, not wanting her mother to dwell on an image of her daughter being raped, caused her to hurry on around the matter.

"The other constant in my life was your sister, Aunt Alisa. She meant everything to me after you died, but my sponsor had her killed too. That was the final part of his plan to isolate me, removing anyone who meant anything to me."

Anastasia was stricken by the news that not only would she herself fall victim to the murderer, but also her beloved sister; even though her death hadn't happened yet.

"Go on," she encouraged, squeezing Ava's hand supportively.

"My sponsor sent me to a madrassa in Pakistan where I was systematically beaten and radicalised. After six months, a man came to my rescue and liberated me. His name was Demitri Papandreou."

Just the mention of his name took Anastasia's breath away.

"Demitri freed me from my torment. I thought that he was my saviour and I fell in love with him."

This time Ava found the courage to lift her eyes in order to look at her mother. The words had to be spoken, regardless of the pain that they would cause.

"Forgive me but we became lovers. Eventually, I realised that I meant nothing to him. Everything was calculated to manipulate me. I was just another pawn that he was ready to use, then sacrifice."

The wrath that Ava expected from her mother never came. She neither looked angry nor surprised. Relieved, Ava continued relating her story.

"Demitri never loved me at all, in fact I see now that he hated me. It was just another part of his insidious control, along with my isolation and radicalisation. Demitri convinced me that the Angels were our enemies and, that the Shadows were fighting a holy war against them. His plan was for me to take up the fight as one of the Hydra's jihadists, get close to the Angel generals and kill them."

Ava paused to collect herself. Her overriding feeling was guilt for everything that she had done, which made telling the story all the more difficult.

"Demitri ordered me to get close to a man called Callum Knight and seduce him. God forgive me but I did. He was the most amazing man. I found it hard to believe that, although he was a military man, that he was capable of any malicious harm. This caused me to question my beliefs. When I told Demitri, he flew into a black rage and punished me severely."

Images of Demitri combined with the dreadful and degrading encounter in the hotel, came flooding back. Ava had to dig deep to sweep the memories aside in order to continue.

"I fell deeply in love with Callum and he fell in love with me." Ava suddenly felt foolish. "God, you must think that I give my heart at the drop of a hat, but that's not me. I couldn't grasp the severity of the situation that I had become embroiled in, if truth be known. Callum was so gentle, so very special. When I killed him, it felt like I had killed myself. I wanted to die alongside him and would have willingly done so, but for a dear man called Yuri and, of course, Maelströminha."

Admitting her sins to her mother like this was cathartic. Ava buried her face in her mother's shoulder and once again broke down. Other customers in the café were starting to point in their direction, looking at them. Ava was completely unaware of the unwarranted attention and Anastasia impervious to it. She just waited for Ava to finish her sobbing. It gave her time to reflect on her own feelings.

Anastasia no longer had the slightest doubt that what Ava was telling her was the absolute and unquestionable truth. It was the strangest sensation holding her own daughter from a future time period, and it gave her a feeling of eternity and permanence. Ava was living proof that all moments in time exist concurrently and that nothing truly passes. The magnitude of meeting her daughter and hearing about the miserable tormented life that she had led, purely because of her own failings to deal with Demitri, was an epiphany.

Anastasia had already read between the lines and knew what direction Ava was going with her story. She had deduced that the boyfriend from Hell that Ava said that they both shared was not meant arbitrarily. She meant it specifically. Ava was referring to her sponsor Demitri and that they were safe, because she had already killed him.

Somehow, Anastasia felt no remorse for the man, quite the contrary. Ava had removed a burden from her that she had been unable to do herself. It was like a cancer had been cut out of her body. Instead of feeling grief for her own loss, she felt anger for what he had done, both to her and to Ava. Anastasia sensed Ava was ready to listen and now it was Anastasia's turn to talk. Again she stroked the hair at Ava's temple, remembering how much she had loved that as a child.

"I know you are worried about how I'm feeling right now, but you don't need to be. Knowing what that monster has done to you, changes everything. Treating me as he did was one thing, but to do what he has done to you, his daughter, is sick and heartless beyond belief. It is the other way around Ava, I should be asking your forgiveness, and I am."

Anastasia's comment had relieved Ava of her biggest fear and now she felt at peace and loved in her mother's arms. Ava had waited so long for this moment, a moment that she believed could never happen. She had a question to ask; something that just didn't make sense.

"Mum, why would you have let Demitri kill you? I know you have the powers inside you to protect yourself, even to kill him if you wanted to. So why then?"

"Oh, Ava you still have much to learn about women, particularly weak women like me. Did you ever hear the expression, a woman who allows herself to be beaten by her man either likes it or deserves it? Well I don't hold with that expression, but perhaps a part of me did. Deep down, I knew our affair was wrong. Maelströminha even told me herself that I did not need to suffer the abuse, but I ignored her good advice."

Anastasia had a distant look in her eye, one of deep regret and shame. She continued her lament.

"I knew that he was an evil person Ava, but couldn't help myself. I was in love you see. It is as inexplicably simple as that," Anastasia admitted. "At some point during the relationship I must have capitulated, I guess, given up on myself, my dreams and aspirations. Men can consume you, if you let them Ava, and I let him. It is hard to believe that you came back from the future to save me, when it was me who failed you so miserably in the past. I don't deserve your love and devotion."

It was Anastasia's turn to cry, but her tears were a mixture of sorrow and joy, mostly joy. Simply knowing that her daughter had survived to adulthood, despite all that fate had thrown at her, filled Anastasia with pride and deep gratitude. Further, the knowledge made her happier than she could ever have imagined.

"We must look a right pair," Anastasia pointed out, wiping her nose. "Let's get out of here before they start selling tickets."

They walked aimlessly, arm in arm, through the streets of Moscow, chatting very much like any normal mother and daughter would. Ava hadn't realised until that point, that they were approaching the Savoy Hotel.

"Not this way Mum," Ava directed, just a little too urgently. Anastasia immediately picked up on her daughter's anxiety.

"That's where it happened isn't it?" she questioned, indicating the hotel.

"Yes, it is. I'm sorry." Ava looked at the floor, ashamed of her atrocity.

"Don't apologise Ava, please. I want to see. It will give me closure and maybe you too."

They walked on towards the hotel, comfortable in each other's company. Ava was hoping that someone had the presence of mind and decency to cover Demitri's corpse, hiding the macabre details of his death from view. A small crowd had gathered at the scene and the area was cordoned off, but unfortunately for Ava, Demitri's corpse remained in pieces and uncovered. Three police cars and an ambulance were in attendance. Anastasia looked up to the shattered window on the third floor then down to the grotesque sight of a man's body impaled on the railings below. Even from a distance, it was clear that it was Demitri and that he had been mutilated. Anastasia shuddered, but did not pass judgement.

Demitri's limbs lay randomly where they fell. Glass and other debris from the window frame were strewn around. They both stared morbidly at the stain on the pavement where Demitri's life blood had soaked into the concrete. Strangely neither woman shed a tear; instead both experienced a feeling of release. Words were no longer necessary between mother and daughter. Their evolved minds had linked. They now shared their emotions on a far higher level than mere mortals. After time to reflect, Ava turned the subject around to the practicality of their unique situation.

"I don't know how this all ends Mum. I know that I can't stay here because May told me that I cannot coexist in another time. It's too dangerous for both me and," Ava struggled to find the words, smiling at her clumsiness, "and little me, I suppose. I must return to my time, but I will go back a happy woman at last. Well I think I will be happy," she added.

"You think?" Anastasia couldn't hide her surprise at Ava's after thought.

"Well, yes. Coming here will have changed the order of so many things. Little or nothing will have remained the same in my future. When I return, I will still be me, but I won't have had the same life experiences that little Ava will have experienced. We will be different."

This was uncharted territory and Anastasia nodded, accepting her daughter's explanation.

"In truth Mum, I don't even know if I will have changed things for the better. Maybe you didn't survive despite me killing Demitri. Perhaps fate deemed that you have an accident or something. Or even little Ava, then I will not even exist in order to come back and change events. The possible outcomes are too horrible to think about."

Ava began to panic as the unknown possibilities crowded in on her mind.

"And my friend Katarina and Aunt Alisa; what of them? Will they still be there? And Callum, will he ever know me? Without Demitri will he still be alive? Everyone could be dead. Up until today, everybody I have ever loved has died. Everybody!" Ava was lost in her own fears and despair.

"Ava!" Anastasia's voice was firm. "What did May tell you about your future?"

Anastasia knew Maelströminha well enough to know that she would have given Ava at least some indication of her future, some hope, before she embarked upon her quest. All at once Ava was filled with a feeling so warm that it spread throughout her body. It was that of hope!

"She said that the mirrors often showed her the birth of two children, a girl and then a boy."

"So, there is hope for you then Ava. However, the biggest question must be who the father is?" Anastasia's expression was at the very least conspiratorial.

"Mother!" Ava feigned shock. "What sort of a girl do you think I am?"

They laughed gaily and it seemed so right for the women.

"I have missed you so much Mum. You can't imagine. Will you recognise me when I come back in twenty-three years' time? It's bizarre but that will only be tomorrow for me."

"I will be waiting and looking forward to that reunion Ava, and I won't look so very different, we Angels age well! Thanks to your love and devotion, I will have had the opportunity to watch you grow and develop over the years, sharing your troubles and triumphs together. I already owe you my life and I will reward you dearly for that when you return."

Ava wasn't used to having her mother around, nor how a mother is never easily distracted from probing into their children's private affairs.

"So, who is the father going to be?" Anastasia fixed her inquisitively with a raised eyebrow.

"Callum I hope." Ava blushed outrageously. "But then it could equally be Yuri. Only future events will help me to decide."

"Would either of these men have a choice?" Anastasia teased.

"Of course not Mum. That choice is mine. I just have to find out how my actions here have shaped their futures."

Ava ruefully pondered the uncertainty of her future. She had no idea of how the world would have changed, for better or worse, or even if she would ever find them. However, a little voice inside her head was telling her that everything would work out just fine. Maelströminha didn't look like a woman who left much to the hand of fate!

They came to a crossroads. One direction led to the Papandreou Research Laboratories and the old ornate mirror. In the other, was the Metropol Hotel, where Anastasia's five year old daughter and her sister Alisa were waiting for her. It was a natural place to part. Both knew that their time together in this world was short. Ava needed to return to her own time, her own future. Accepting this, mother and daughter embraced. Ava was reflective.

"I remember my fifth birthday so clearly Mum, when you took me to the zoo. Strangely that day is today. It started as the happiest day of my life, only to end with death and grief. Now, after so much misery, this particular day is a happy one once more.

Meeting you has simply wiped away all of that misery Mum. I feel almost reborn, and the future holds so many positive alternatives. Everything will be fine from now on. I just know."

It was hard to let go. At last, after long lingering goodbyes, they went their separate ways. Ava was elated; the burdens that had plagued her for so many years were gone. Everything she had wanted to achieve was done and done beyond her wildest expectations. Ava had felt certain that her mother would hate her for the actions she had taken, but instead Anastasia had at last seen Demitri in his true colours. Rather than hate her daughter, Ava's actions had helped remove her mother's abusive partner from her life. Her mother loved her, which was all that Ava had ever wanted.

*'Heaven has no rage like love to hatred turned, nor Hell a fury like a woman scorned.'*

Never had an adage spoken a greater truth.

---

Chapter 29

It was a twenty minute walk to the laboratories from the crossroads where they had parted, and the mirror that would take Ava back to her own time. She had not thought about how to gain access, but was now confident enough in her abilities that it no longer mattered.

For a moment, Ava thought she had lost her way daydreaming; things didn't look right. She checked the sign for the road name and it was correct. Even the nineteenth century buildings were exactly as she had remembered them. Instead of where the research laboratories should have been, there stood a disused railway yard. Ava had a moment of realisation. When Demitri had cross-examined her after accidentally using his last name, she had referred to the Papandreou Research Laboratories and their achievements. Clearly there were none. The place had not been built yet. Demitri's vision was still in the planning stage. He must have immediately smelt a rat. Ava cursed her stupidity, but now she had a greater problem to deal with. No lab, no mirror and no way home.

Ava was close to panic, wondering exactly what she should do next, when she caught sight of a slim elegant woman, carrying a baby on her hip. The woman's long, lustrous black hair was combed to one side, lying over her shoulder. She looked familiar. Both mother and child seemed to be smiling and looking in Ava's direction.

"May?" Ava whispered in disbelief.

She walked at first, and then ran to meet her.

"Oh, my God am I pleased to see you!"

Ava's enthusiasm was more than apparent. They embraced.

"Did you think that I would leave you here with no way home?" May mocked, still in that embrace.

"Well I don't know what I thought really. Actually, I think I was about to panic."

Niquita made her demands clear by reaching out open-armed to Ava, breaking their hold.

"Aw, she wants me," Ava took the child and Niquita immediately settled.

Ava was about to tell May all about the events that had happened, but stopped as she was unsure where to begin.

"It's all right Ava; you don't need to explain anything. I already know *everything* and am so amazed and proud of you."

Ava could see by May's genuine expression that what she was telling her was true. Besides, Ava now realised that May had been with her every step of the way, even appearing in her mind when she needed her most.

"You followed your mission right to the very end Ava, well almost to the end." May had a mischievous look in her eye.

"Almost?" Ava questioned.

"Well, there is the little matter of your unborn children to tend to, isn't there?"

"What are you saying May?" Ava was playing coy, but knew very well what she was alluding to. They giggled.

"You can't leave these things to chance Ava, I didn't," May confirmed in a sisterly fashion. "So, who is it going to be, Callum or Yuri?"

"What! How do you know?" Ava was completely derailed by May's knowledge of her private life.

"Ava. With a life that spans millennia, a mind that can read all, and, mirrors that show me every possibility in time and space, what then is left to chance?" May looked a little guilty. "I try to limit my given powers to guidance, but at the end of the day I am just a woman with a woman's curiosity."

"You have been peeking, haven't you?" Ava laughed at May's predicament.

She had been caught red-handed and blushed outrageously.

"So, what happens to me now? What do the mirrors say?" Ava pressed.

"It is not for me to say, nothing is for absolute certain. You must complete your own personal journey Ava, as we all must. The mirrors predict many things depending on your personal decisions and external influences. You cannot control that part, but be consistent with your choices. Just follow your heart Ava and the future will end well for you."

Ava was still considering the advice when May pressed her question.

"You still haven't answered my question Ava. Who is the father going to be?" Ava flushed with embarrassment.

"God, I just got the same grilling from my mother. Callum perhaps, but I don't know. There was something very special about Yuri too, something that I almost missed." Ava agonised over her predicament. "To be honest I don't know and, maybe the choice ultimately does not matter. I just hope that I'm lucky enough that one of them sees something in me that appeals to them. I will be a stranger when, or if I meet them on my return, and that will feel so strange."

Yes, perhaps you might be a stranger, but they will know of you. It's not a case of you never existing; it's just that you may have yet to cross paths." May could sense Ava's despair. "Ava. You are young, beautiful and intelligent. How hard can it be to attract your soul mate?"

They burst out laughing, which was just what Ava needed. May had one last thing to say to her before they parted.

"You have fulfilled your destiny Ava, which was to prevent the fifth dimension from falling into the hands of the Shadows and all the destruction that would have followed. By going back to the past and killing Demitri, the world owes you a debt of gratitude, but you have changed everything that is to follow. You were never with me on that mountain and, therefore you did not kill the Hydra. In fact, you won't have killed anyone, except for Demitri Papandreou here. Most likely she will be there in your own time when you return and she might seek you out."

There was a look in May's eyes and Ava wondered what else she had seen in the mirrors. A cold shiver of premonition ran down Ava's spine and May sensed it.

"I am only asking you to be careful Ava."

Ava nodded in acknowledgement. It was time to part.

"Can you take me home to my own time now please May? I need to know what I have done and how I fit in to this new time frame." Ava was visibly anxious.

"I will soon, but first you must prepare yourself for certain things." Ava sensed impending doom and shuddered.

"When you return to your own time, more than twenty years will have passed. In those twenty years, many things will have happened, some better and some worse. There will have been births, marriages and even deaths. What I am saying Ava, is that you can't take for granted that all of the people who you have loved will be available or even exist."

"Infinite possibilities then May," Ava confirmed with a wry grin on her face.

"Yes Ava, but in the balance of all probabilities I see happiness for you. You must believe in that."

"I think that I do now May. This journey cannot end in misery; it just cannot. I won't let it." Ava looked imploringly at May. "Take me home please."

May held Ava's gaze and placed her hand behind her neck, tipping her forehead to touch hers.

"Let me have your mind please Ava."

Ava submitted herself to May's consciousness and felt her warmth entering her spirit.

"That feels amazing," she murmured.

Ava closed her eyes to enjoy the moment. It felt like all her senses were heightened and being stimulated simultaneously.

"Don't stop," Ava whispered.

She opened her eyes but May was already gone. Ava stood alone at the side of the road exactly where she had been before, but the railway yard was now gone. In its place stood an industrial park with aluminium clad warehouses and retail outlets. She was back in her own time. Clearly the Papandreou Research Laboratories had never been built, confirming the success of her mission.

Ava was still buoyed from her brief meeting with Maelströminha, clear in her mind about what she wanted to do next, which was to go back to the Bolshoi, where the dramas of her adolescent life had all begun. Ava wondered whether any of the events in her life as she knew them, ever actually happened in this reality. One person in particular was on her mind, someone who she had both grieved and carried guilt for ever since the day she had let her down; Katarina.

It was early evening when Ava walked into the Bolshoi, charged with expectation. She noted from the billboard outside, that there were no performances that night and wondered whether Katarina had even followed a career in the ballet. The bar and surroundings looked nothing like it had done when she danced there in her alternative life, perhaps indicating that the place was under different ownership. She noted though, that the familiar photographs of past prima ballerinas were still lined up behind the bar. Ava's mouth dropped as she looked at the ballerinas over the last twenty years. Her mother's was still there, *Anastasia Kaplinski* dated *1993*, but her own name never appeared.

"I didn't make the grade," Ava lamented. Her eyes moved to the last incumbent. "Oh, my God it's Katarina!"

The photograph was of *Katarina Romanov* dated *2012*.

You made it Kat. You fulfilled your dream! So at least one of us did. Ava was thrilled for her, but couldn't help her own disappointment and wondered as to what had become of her. I was of the troupe perhaps? She mused.

Ava took a chair at the bar, called the young barman over and ordered a Dirty Martini. He looked fresh out of school, she thought as he served her. That's the first sign of getting old, Ava mused, stirring her drink.

Thoughts of Yuri idly meandered through her mind and Ava wondered what might have become of him. She hadn't expected to see him working at the bar though, as he was only doing that to watch over her in another life. Ava decided to use the Internet in the foyer later and search for him there, along with Callum and her mother. She called the barman back over.

"Will the dancers be coming to the bar tonight as it's their night off?"

In Ava's day, the girls would normally meet here in the bar on those nights, before going to the clubs.

"They should be here anytime now, Miss. I heard them talking about it last night." He smiled and moved on to serve another customer.

My luck is still holding out. Ava thought.

An hour and three Martinis later, Ava was abruptly brought back from her thoughts by the sound of a raucous group of young women. They had clearly made themselves up whilst consuming more than a couple of bottles of wine. A petite brunette was in the

468

centre of the melee, shorter than the others such that Ava couldn't quite see her. The group split to go to the bar and Ava's heart leapt. It was Katarina!

For what seemed like an eternity, the room felt devoid of air. Ava had to force herself to breathe. She watched Katarina walk to the bar as if in slow motion. This was the girl Ava had shared her life and love with, but who would now only see her as a complete stranger. All at once Ava's new found confidence dried up. All she could do was stare at Katarina and sip nervously at her Martini.

Ava watched the affectations of the girls as they posed and pouted, enjoying the men's eyes on them. They chatted conspiratorially, whispering their exchanges and giggling gaily as they glanced coyly at the subjects of their conversations. Ava remembered fondly how she used to be at the centre of that buzz and it saddened her that she was now on the outside. Katarina had caught Ava watching her several times, but on each occasion Ava had lost her nerve and looked away. She glanced and got caught again. Ava looked away hurriedly in embarrassment, busying herself with the cocktail stick, stirring her drink.

"Do I know you?"

The familiar voice was a shock to Ava's senses and she knocked her drink over in surprise.

"Katarina, you made me jump!" Ava righted her glass and pushed the spilled liquid away from her with a drinks mat.

"Oh, I'm so sorry. Let me buy you another."

Katarina placed her hand on Ava's arm by way of an apology. The sensation of her touch sent a tingling shiver through Ava's body. It was as if her friend and lover had been resurrected.

"That's OK. It was clumsy of me. I have probably had enough to drink anyway." Ava smiled easily and naturally. "But I would like to buy us one more and talk with you if I may?"

"I would like that. Same as you as it happens, a Dirty Martini." Katarina had a mischievous look on her face. "Then perhaps you can tell me why you were staring at me and how you know my name?"

Ava signalled to the barman for two more drinks.

"I recognised you from your picture on the billboard outside and noticed that you look like someone that I used to dance with." Ava conceded that her explanation was in part the truth.

"Good try, but my picture isn't on the board outside." Katarina fixed her with a curious look. "So, you are a dancer too. What style? And, if you don't mind me asking, what's your name?"

"Ballet, like you, and I'm Ava, Ava Kaplinski. Perhaps you have heard of me?" Ava hoped her question didn't sound too desperate.

"No, I'm sorry Ava. You do look strangely familiar though, as if I know you from a long time ago." Ava could see that Katarina was at odds with herself as she continued. "For some inexplicable reason, I felt compelled to come over to you. It was almost a compulsion, weird really." Katarina looked a little embarrassed about her admission.

Could there be links between alternative times and possibilities? Ava wondered. Or did I coerce her to come to me? She hoped not, but the possibility was a real one. Ava wasn't sure, but the joy she felt in her heart was immeasurable. Katarina sensed it too.

"Look I have to go back to my friends Ava, but I feel we should meet again. Would you come and watch me dance tomorrow night? We could maybe have a drink at the bar afterwards," Katarina looked a little uncomfortable for being so forward.

"I would love that Kat. What are you dancing?"

"Swan Lake; I'm dancing the double-role of Odette-Odile. As a fellow ballerina, you can critique my thirty-two *fouettés en tournant*, or the curse of Pierina Legnani, as more accurately describes it. God the legacy that woman gave us!"

Katarina got up to leave.

"Sorry, but I must go." She pecked Ava on the cheek and added whimsically. "Don't know why I did that. Strange that you called me Kat, but it felt right. I liked it, and I will look out for you in the audience. Don't let me down, please."

With that Katarina left and re-joined her friends. Moments later, they trooped out of the bar to let their hair down in venues less formal.

Ava looked at her reflection in the mirror behind the bar. She recalled the last time she had done so, after her fracas there with Bortnik. She was reminded that she had dealt with his depravity in perfunctory manner. Ava was full of rage at the time and had scowled, causing the mirror to shatter. Now she saw something entirely different, a woman with a dream and the resolve and conviction to achieve it. She let the memories of the past twenty years run through her mind, particularly the very last one, and wondered how she had ever endured. Ava decided that it had largely been because of the devoted love she had received in abundance from Katarina.

"What doesn't kill you makes you stronger," she mumbled fatalistically and downed her Martini.

Ava felt a positivity in her that was almost tangible. She now knew that she had control of her life, although she didn't quite know her *raison d'être*. At that precise moment Bortnik walked into the Bolshoi and Ava gasped, openly shocked.

"But you're dead?" she uttered, almost inaudibly.

At first Ava couldn't believe her eyes, but then the logic of the situation came to her. Although she had killed him, the Hydra and Demitri, the only one that was going to stay dead was Demitri. From the moment she had killed him and from that moment onwards, history had changed. Nothing after that event

471

would happen in the same order, or even at all. Ava was never an orphan or Demitri's ward. She never danced at the Bolshoi, was never radicalised and would never have met the Hydra, let alone have killed her. The fact that Katarina had never met her, or knew of her as a dancer, was proof of this.

True to his colours, Bortnik headed for the two young women sat in the corner of the lounge. Ava judged that they were not yet out of their teens, both slim and dressed stylishly to suit the venue, contrasting only in that one was blonde and the other brunette. Bortnik flopped his mass into the chair next to them.

"Champagne for the beauties at this table!" he called out across the lounge to no one in particular.

All the waiters there would have already been alerted as to his arrival and come running, lest they suffered his abuse. Bortnik mopped his brow with a damp handkerchief, grinning at his quarry.

"Consider yourselves rescued from the dullness of this place. Tell me where you have always wanted to go in Moscow and I will take you there tonight. Casinos, clubs, restaurants, just name it and Sergio will fulfil your dreams. It will be my pleasure."

Unusually he appeared to mean every word of what he said, particularly the bit about it being *his pleasure*. The girls were young and inexperienced and didn't want to appear rude. Their Champagne arrived with a dish of marinated olives and a mixture of salted nuts. The nervous young waiter poured three glasses of Bollinger, which the girls felt obliged to accept and Bortnik devoured a fistful of nuts.

"We don't usually drink alcohol and I'm driving, so perhaps just this one?"

"Of course no pressure, what do you take me for anyway? I just like to give a girl a good time and the opportunity to experience the finer things of life. I have daughters and know how hard it is for them to afford Moscow prices."

Bortnik stretched his arms out expansively in false ambivalence. Besides he had the Rohypnol to fall back on, should all else fail.

"Can we take a rain check on that? Only we have an early start in the morning. Perhaps we can do it another time?" the blonde demurred, smiling at him as sweetly as she could.

This was unacceptable to Bortnik. He immediately became surly.

"You accept a bottle of the finest Champagne from a man, and then deny him of your company? Think again young ladies. What do you take me for, a fool?"

The girls exchanged glances and gave way to the pressure, testament to their lack of experience.

"Very well but not too late," the brunette capitulated on their behalf.

Bortnik clashed his glass heavy-handedly into the girls' in a toast and then picked up an olive, tossing it into his cavernous mouth.

Ava's acute hearing enabled her to understand every word exchanged. More so, she could read the fear and confusion in the young girls' minds and the depraved intent in Bortnik's. It was also all she needed to endorse her decision, made only minutes ago, about her new-found purpose in life. Her *raison d'être* was even more clear to her now, which was to rid the world of disgusting creatures like Bortnik. She would once again be an assassin, but this time as defender of the truth.

She watched as the olive left Bortnik's pudgy hand and looped into his open mouth. At that moment, Ava's hatred for this man rose to impossible and unsupportable heights. Her eyes blackened, like thunderheads, the storm brewing inside her. She imagined her hands around his throat, choking the life out of him.

The olive caught in Bortnik's throat. He stood in panic, clasping his neck, gagging as his body tried to rid itself of the foreign object. Ava willed his fingers to tighten, preventing that reflex.

Bortnik's expression turned from panic to terror. The girls left their seats, horrified, then took their chance and made their way swiftly to the exit. Ava could hear the clatter of their high heels on the pavement fading as they ran desperately for safety.

Bortnik quickly turned purple, his eyes bulging from their sockets. Ava wanted him to know why he was dying and forced him to face her across the lounge. In those last few seconds of his life she left him in no doubt. Bortnik fell to the floor like a bull elephant, stopped in its tracks by the hunter's rifle; his eyes stared sightlessly back at her, as his final breath left him like a rush of wind.

"Stay dead this time, you fat bastard!" she cursed.

Ava left the bar for the Internet connection in the Bolshoi foyer, without so much as backward glance. She had endured enough at the hands of the Shadows to have any remorse.

I will be good at this assassin job, she mused.

---------------------------------------------------------------------------

Ava logged onto her laptop, selected 'Google' and began her searches. The first, and most important, was to find out if her mother was still alive and where she was now. The search only took moments. Anastasia Kaplinski was still very much alive and a legend in Russia, now working as a Public Relations figurehead, promoting the various dance academies in Russia. Ava's heart soared with a mixture of relief, pride and euphoria. Another quick search showed that her mother still lived in their family home at Pokrovsky Hills, a prestigious complex on the northwest side of Moscow. Ava couldn't wait to finally go home after more than twenty years in the wilderness.

It just gets better and better, she thought.

Ava quickly tempered her elation. There was still much to investigate and not everything would be good news, as May had alluded to.

What about me, she wondered, what became of me?"

Ava entered her name, selected Wikipedia and skimmed over the text. There was no mention of dancing, not even semi-professionally. She immediately reflected on her conversation with Katarina where she had proclaimed to be a dancer too.

'Perhaps you have heard of me?' She had said.

Ava cringed at what Katarina must have thought about her wild and unsupportable claim. She must have at least known, and even been friends with, most of the professional dancers in the Moscow elite.

Undaunted, Ava read on. She had graduated at the Lomonosov Moscow State University in 2009, studying politics. Then in 2012, after some work experience through governmental departments, she had been selected to work for the Russian Prime Minister, Dmitry Medvedev. The new President of Russia, Vladimir Putin, had himself only just been elected, and Medvedev was his appointment, bought and paid for. Apparently, Ava had held that position until the winter of 2014, when she moved to London.

"No way!" Ava almost shouted out the words.

Ava was stunned by what she was reading; even more so by the picture that accompanied her profile. After leaving her employment with the Russian government Ava had taken the roll of Advisor for Foreign Affairs in Britain's Security Service, better known as MI5. The photograph was of the Prime Minister at a meeting of the United Nations Security Council in 2015, shaking hands with the President. In the background were four delegates supporting the Prime Minister. From left to right they were Kayla Lovell, Callum Knight, herself and Yuri Alexandrov. Ava gasped as the room seemed to close in on her and spin. She struggled to breathe, thinking she was going to faint.

"Are you alright Miss? Miss, are you alright?" the concerned voice was a man's and unfamiliar to her.

"I don't know. I'm pregnant can't you see?"

Ava pointed in shock at the photograph. Her heavy baby bump was clear for anyone to see.

"Congratulations Miss. Can I get you a glass of water?"

"Please," Ava answered robotically, still not truly aware of his presence.

Ava's hands fell naturally to her flat stomach, a benign smile beginning to light her face. She held herself and rocked gently on her chair, no longer pregnant so that must mean that she was already a mother.

"Oh, my God!" Ava gasped putting her hand to her mouth as the magnitude of her situation dawned upon her.

Ava ran her fingers over the image of herself on the screen, touching her bump. May had said that the mirrors, more often than not, had hinted at the probability of two children; a girl and then a boy.

So, you must be a little girl then, Ava mused, or are you my second and a little boy?

Ava clapped her hands in glee then flicked from the image of Callum to Yuri and back for several minutes. When at last she had accustomed herself to the enormity of her situation, she questioned the images.

"Who's the Daddy then?"

--------------------------------------------------------------------------

### THE END

(Ava Kaplinski's struggles continue in book 2 'Scorned' also available on Amazon in eBook format and Paperback)

--------------------------------------------------------------------------

### AUTHOR's NOTE

*If you enjoyed this book, please leave a review on Amazon as they are vital for me to succeed as an author in this competitive market place.*

*I hope you enjoyed 'Forsaken' as much as I did writing it for you. Other books in the series, available on Amazon as eBooks and Paperbacks, are: 'Scorned', 'The Assassin', 'Retribution' (available spring/summer 2021) and 'Angels & Shadows', the prequel.*

Printed in Great Britain
by Amazon